PENGUIN BOOKS

DUBLINERS
Text, Criticism, and Notes

Robert Scholes, Professor of English at Brown University, has also taught at the University of Virginia. He is the author of *The Cornell Joyce Collection: A Catalogue* and *The Fabulators*, a study of recent experimental fiction; co-editor with Richard Kain of *The Workshop of Daedalus*; and co-author with Robert Kellogg of *The Nature of Narrative*.

A. Walton Litz, who has taught at Columbia and Princeton, is the author of two books on Joyce: *The Art of James Joyce* and *James Joyce*. Among his other publications are *Jane Austen: A Study of Her Artistic Development* and *Modern American Fiction: Essays in Criticism*.

THE VIKING CRITICAL LIBRARY

Malcolm Cowley, *General Editor*

Winesburg, Ohio
by Sherwood Anderson
Edited by John H. Ferres

Death of a Salesman
by Arthur Miller
Edited by Gerald Weales

*A Portrait of the Artist
as a Young Man*
by James Joyce
Edited by Chester G. Anderson

Sons and Lovers
by D.H. Lawrence
Edited by Julian Moynahan

Dubliners
by James Joyce
Edited by Robert Scholes
and A. Walton Litz

The Power and the Glory
by Graham Greene
Edited by R.W.B. Lewis
and Peter J. Conn

The Crucible
by Arthur Miller
Edited by Gerald Weales

The Grapes of Wrath
by John Steinbeck
Edited by Peter Lisca

*One Flew Over the
Cuckoo's Nest*
by Ken Kesey
Edited by John C. Pratt

Herzog
by Saul Bellow
Edited by Irving Howe

THE VIKING CRITICAL LIBRARY

JAMES JOYCE

Dubliners

TEXT, CRITICISM, AND NOTES

EDITED BY ROBERT SCHOLES

BROWN UNIVERSITY

AND A. WALTON LITZ

PRINCETON UNIVERSITY

PENGUIN BOOKS

Penguin Books Ltd, Harmondsworth, Middlesex, England
Penguin Books, 625 Madison Avenue, New York, New York 10022, U.S.A.
Penguin Books Australia Ltd, Ringwood, Victoria, Australia
Penguin Books Canada Ltd, 2801 John Street, Markham, Ontario, Canada L3R 1B4
Penguin Books (N.Z.) Ltd, 182–190 Wairau Road, Auckland 10, New Zealand

Dubliners first published in the United States of America by B. W. Huebsch 1916
Text of *Dubliners* corrected by Robert Scholes in consultation with
Richard Ellmann and first published in the United States of America by
The Viking Press 1968
The Viking Critical Library *Dubliners*, incorporating further corrections by
Robert Scholes, based on suggestions by Jack P. Dalton, first published in
the United States of America by The Viking Press 1969
Reprinted 1971 (twice), 1972, 1973, 1974 (twice), 1975
Published in Penguin Books 1976

Reprinted 1977

LIBRARY OF CONGRESS CATALOGING IN PUBLICATION DATA
Joyce, James, 1882–1941.
Dubliners: text, criticism, and notes.
Reprint of the 1969 ed. published by The Viking Press, New York,
which was issued as no. 5 of The Viking Critical Library.
Bibliography: p.
I. Scholes, Robert E.   II. Litz, A. Walton.   III. Title.
[PZ3.J853Du16]   [PR6019.09]   823'.9'12   76-49451
ISBN 0 14 015.505 8

Printed in the United States of America by
The Murray Printing Company, Forge Village, Massachusetts
Set in Electra

CONTENTS

Editors' Preface   1

I. *DUBLINERS*: The Text   5

The Sisters   9
An Encounter   19
Araby   29
Eveline   36
After the Race   42
Two Gallants   49
The Boarding House   61
A Little Cloud   70
Counterparts   86
Clay   99
A Painful Case   107
Ivy Day in the Committee Room   118
A Mother   136
Grace   150
The Dead   175
A Note on the Text   225

II. *DUBLINERS*: Background   227

Chronology   229
Facsimiles from "A Painful Case"   234
The Composition and Revision of the Stories   236
Epiphanies and Epicleti   253
The Evidence of the Letters   257

v

III. *DUBLINERS*: Criticism 295

Editors' Introduction 297
Frank O'Connor, "Work in Progress" 304
Brewster Ghiselin, "The Unity of Joyce's
   Dubliners" 316
Edward Brandabur, "The Sisters" 333
Harry Stone, " 'Araby' and the Writings of
   James Joyce" 344
A. Walton Litz, "Two Gallants" 368
Robert Scholes, "Counterparts" 379
Richard Ellmann, "The Backgrounds of
   'The Dead' " 388
Allen Tate, "The Dead" 404
Kenneth Burke, " 'Stages' in 'The Dead' " 410
C. C. Loomis, "Structure and Sympathy in
   'The Dead' " 417
Florence L. Walzl, "Gabriel and Michael: The
   Conclusion of 'The Dead' " 423

Topics for Discussion and Papers 445
Selected Bibliography 453
Notes to the Stories 462

Editors' Preface

Dubliners was the first work in which James Joyce became wholly himself. Although he was always as much poet as novelist, Joyce's early poems are mainly derivative and of secondary intensity, filled with echoes of Elizabethan songs and the "mood" poems of the 1890s; it is in the prose of *Dubliners* that we first hear the authentic rhythms of Joyce the poet. Joyce was aware of this paradox, and as *Dubliners* developed he became more and more dissatisfied with the shadowy poems of *Chamber Music*: by 1906 he could tell his brother Stanislaus that "a page of *A Little Cloud* gives me more pleasure than all my verses." Similarly, the long autobiographical fragment called *Stephen Hero*, which was written at the same time as *Dubliners* and later transformed into *A Portrait of the Artist as a Young Man*, seems awkward and old-fashioned in contrast to the polished stories. Although *Stephen Hero* is deeply personal and revealing in its subject-matter, its form is curiously anonymous, and we may guess that Joyce grew dissatisfied with it because it lacked the intensity and allusiveness he had already achieved in the stories of *Dubliners*.

So *Dubliners* is, in a very real sense, the foundation of Joyce's art. In shaping its stories he developed that mastery of naturalistic detail and symbolic design which is the hallmark of his mature fiction. In its subject-matter, its form, and its language, *Dubliners* leads naturally and inevitably into the world of the later books, just as its characters often wander through their streets. The stories are carefully structured so as to guide the reader from the perspectives of childhood and adolescence to those of public life, and in this pattern the collection anticipates the design of *A Portrait of the Artist*. But the real hero of the stories is not an individual but the city itself, a city whose geography and history and inhabitants are all part of a coherent vision; and in this aspect *Dubliners* anticipates the anatomy of the modern city made by Joyce in *Ulysses*. Even *Finnegans Wake*, with its fabric of rumor and "popular" culture, may be seen as a grotesque extension of the world of *Dubliners*.

The first aim of this volume is to provide an authoritative text of the stories. The text is that prepared for the Viking Compass edition by Robert Scholes, in consultation with Richard Ellmann, and it is based on a careful collation of all available sources (see "A Note on the Text," p. 225).

The second aim of this volume is to provide a variety of perspectives for the reader of *Dubliners*. Since Joyce's lengthy correspondence with publisher and friends concerning the attempts to "censor" *Dubliners* reveals a great deal about his aesthetic aims and the particular plan of the stories, we have reprinted all the significant parts of that correspondence. In addition, we have provided an early draft of one story, which shows the distance Joyce traveled in the years from 1904 to 1907. This early draft should give the reader a graphic sense of Joyce's direction as he reworked both the texture of his stories and the larger plan of the collection. When an early story such as "After the Race" is compared with "The Dead," or the first draft of "The Sisters" with the final version, it becomes obvious that the making of *Dubliners* was also the making of a style.

In the course of half a century Joyce's colloquialisms and local references have become increasingly more obscure, demanding more annotation than we had at first believed necessary. In the notes to the stories we have tried to explain all the local allusions, slang terms, and Irishisms that are likely to trouble the general reader; we have also provided lengthier notes on the religious and political issues which underlie many of the stories. The notes to each story open with a headnote summarizing useful background information not given elsewhere in the volume, and placing the story in the process of composition; for a wider view of the place of *Dubliners* in Joyce's career the reader should turn to the "Chronology." Since the stories of *Dubliners* are embedded in a literal landscape which often takes on symbolic overtones, we have provided maps that locate the principal landmarks and lines of action.

The section on the Epiphanies attempts to clarify one of the most puzzling problems in any study of Joyce's early aesthetic. But the question of the Epiphanies is only one of many relevant critical questions, and in the "Criticism" section we have reprinted essays which reflect the entire range of current critical opinion. Beginning with general essays on the design of *Dubliners*, this section moves through essays on individual stories and culminates in a series of essays which offer various approaches to Joyce's masterpiece, "The Dead." In "Topics for Discussion and Papers" we have suggested ways in which the reader can build upon these critical essays, and in the "Selected Bibliography" we have provided guides for further study and research.

During their years of writing on Joyce the editors have accumulated more debts than can be formally acknowledged. However, we would like to give specific thanks to those involved in the making of this volume, especially Malcolm Cowley and Charles Noyes of The Viking Press. Their advice has made it a better book. The explanatory notes owe obvious debts to previous commentators on *Dubliners*, especially Marvin Magalaner and Don Gifford. We would also like to thank William Stowe and the Reverend Austin MacCurtain, S.J., for their help with some of the difficult annotations.

—R.S.

A.W.L.

I

✿✿✿✿✿✿✿✿✿✿✿✿✿✿✿✿✿✿✿✿✿✿✿✿✿✿✿✿✿✿✿✿✿✿✿✿

Dubliners:

The Text

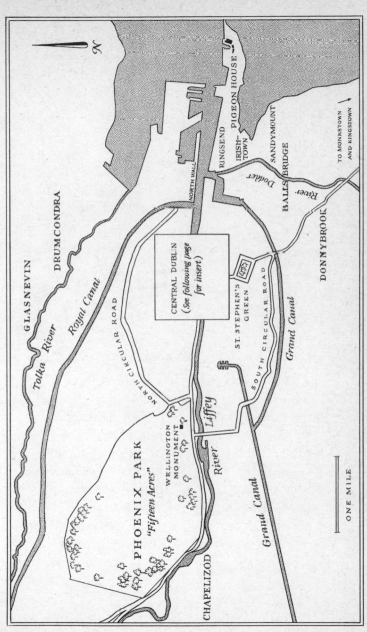

DUBLIN AND ENVIRONS

N

GLASNEVIN

DRUMCONDRA

Tolka River

Royal Canal

NORTH CIRCULAR ROAD

PHOENIX PARK
"Fifteen Acres"

WELLINGTON MONUMENT

CHAPELIZOD

River Liffey

Grand Canal

CENTRAL DUBLIN
(See following page for insert)

NORTH WALL

RINGSEND

IRISH-TOWN

PIGEON HOUSE

SANDYMOUNT

BALLSBRIDGE

River Dodder

DONNYBROOK

TO MONKSTOWN AND KINGSTOWN

ST. STEPHEN'S GREEN

SOUTH CIRCULAR ROAD

Grand Canal

ONE MILE

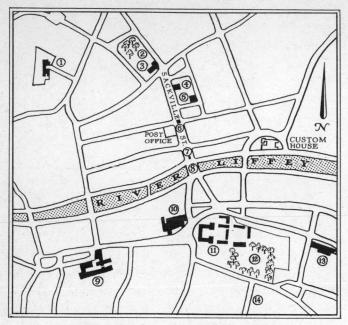

CENTRAL DUBLIN

1. KING'S INNS
2. RUTLAND SQUARE
3. THE ROTUNDA
4. GRESHAM HOTEL
5. THE CATHOLIC
   PRO-CATHEDRAL
6. NELSON'S PILLAR
7. STATUE OF O'CONNELL

8. O'CONNELL BRIDGE
9. THE CASTLE
10. BANK OF IRELAND
11. TRINITY COLLEGE
    (DUBLIN UNIVERSITY)
12. COLLEGE PARK
13. WESTLAND ROW STATION
14. KILDARE STREET

THE SISTERS

THERE was no hope for him this time: it was the third stroke. Night after night I had passed the house (it was vacation time) and studied the lighted square of window: and night after night I had found it lighted in the same way, faintly and evenly. If he was dead, I thought, I would see the reflection of candles on the darkened blind for I knew that two candles must be set at the head of a corpse. He had often said to me: *I am not long for this world,* and I had thought his words idle. Now I knew they were true. Every night as I gazed up at the window I said softly to myself the word *paralysis.* It had always sounded strangely in my ears, like the word *gnomon* in the Euclid and the word *simony* in the Catechism. But now it sounded to me like the name of some maleficent and sinful being. It filled me with fear, and yet I longed to be nearer to it and to look upon its deadly work.

Old Cotter was sitting at the fire, smoking, when I came downstairs to supper. While my aunt was ladling out my stirabout he said, as if returning to some former remark of his:

—No, I wouldn't say he was exactly . . . but there was

9

something queer . . . there was something uncanny about him. I'll tell you my opinion. . . .

He began to puff at his pipe, no doubt arranging his opinion in his mind. Tiresome old fool! When we knew him first he used to be rather interesting, talking of faints and worms; but I soon grew tired of him and his endless stories about the distillery.

—I have my own theory about it, he said. I think it was one of those . . . peculiar cases. . . . But it's hard to say. . . .

He began to puff again at his pipe without giving us his theory. My uncle saw me staring and said to me:

—Well, so your old friend is gone, you'll be sorry to hear.

—Who? said I.

—Father Flynn.

—Is he dead?

—Mr Cotter here has just told us. He was passing by the house.

I knew that I was under observation so I continued eating as if the news had not interested me. My uncle explained to old Cotter.

—The youngster and he were great friends. The old chap taught him a great deal, mind you; and they say he had a great wish for him.

—God have mercy on his soul, said my aunt piously.

Old Cotter looked at me for a while. I felt that his little beady black eyes were examining me but I would not satisfy him by looking up from my plate. He returned to his pipe and finally spat rudely into the grate.

—I wouldn't like children of mine, he said, to have too much to say to a man like that.

—How do you mean, Mr Cotter? asked my aunt.

—What I mean is, said old Cotter, it's bad for children. My idea is: let a young lad run about and play with young lads of his own age and not be . . . Am I right, Jack?

—That's my principle, too, said my uncle. Let him learn to box his corner. That's what I'm always saying to that Rosicrucian there: take exercise. Why, when I was a nipper every morning of my life I had a cold bath, winter and summer. And that's what stands to me now. Education is all very fine and large. . . . Mr Cotter might take a pick of that leg of mutton, he added to my aunt.

—No, no, not for me, said old Cotter.

My aunt brought the dish from the safe and laid it on the table.

—But why do you think it's not good for children, Mr Cotter? she asked.

—It's bad for children, said old Cotter, because their minds are so impressionable. When children see things like that, you know, it has an effect. . . .

I crammed my mouth with stirabout for fear I might give utterance to my anger. Tiresome old red-nosed imbecile!

It was late when I fell asleep. Though I was angry with old Cotter for alluding to me as a child I puzzled my head to extract meaning from his unfinished sentences. In the dark of my room I imagined that I saw again the heavy grey face of the paralytic. I drew the blankets over my head and tried to think of Christmas. But the grey face still followed me. It murmured; and I understood that it desired to confess something. I felt my soul receding into some pleasant and vicious region; and there again I found it waiting for me. It began to confess to me in a murmuring voice and I wondered why it smiled continually and why the lips were so moist with spittle. But then I remembered that it had died of paralysis and I felt that I too was smiling feebly as if to absolve the simoniac of his sin.

The next morning after breakfast I went down to look at the little house in Great Britain Street. It was an unassuming shop, registered under the vague name of *Drapery*. The drapery consisted mainly of children's bootees and umbrellas; and on ordinary days a notice used to hang in the window, saying: *Umbrellas Re-covered*. No notice was visible now for the shutters were up. A crape bouquet was tied to the door-knocker with ribbon. Two poor women and a telegram boy were reading the card pinned on the crape. I also approached and read:

July 1st, 1895
The Rev. James Flynn (formerly of S. Catherine's Church, Meath Street), aged sixty-five years.
R.I.P.

The reading of the card persuaded me that he was dead and I was disturbed to find myself at check. Had he not been dead I would have gone into the little dark room behind the shop to find him sitting in his arm-chair by the fire, nearly smothered in his great-coat. Perhaps my aunt would have given me a packet of High Toast for him and this present would have roused him from his stupefied doze. It was always I who emptied the packet into his black snuff-box for his hands trembled too much to allow him to do this without spilling half the snuff about the floor. Even as he raised his large trembling hand to his nose little clouds of smoke dribbled through his fingers over the front of his coat. It may have been these constant showers of snuff which gave his ancient priestly garments their green faded look for the red handkerchief, blackened, as it always was, with the snuff-stains of a week, with which he tried to brush away the fallen grains, was quite inefficacious.

I wished to go in and look at him but I had not the courage to knock. I walked away slowly along the sunny side of the street, reading all the theatrical advertisements in the shop-windows as I went. I found it strange that neither I nor the day seemed in a mourning mood and I felt even annoyed at discovering in myself a sensation of freedom as if I had been freed from something by his death. I wondered at this for, as my uncle had said the night before, he had taught me a great deal. He had studied in the Irish college in Rome and he had taught me to pronounce Latin properly. He had told me stories about the catacombs and about Napoleon Bonaparte, and he had explained to me the meaning of the different ceremonies of the Mass and of the different vestments worn by the priest. Sometimes he had amused himself by putting difficult questions to me, asking me what one should do in certain circumstances or whether such and such sins were mortal or venial or only imperfections. His questions showed me how complex and mysterious were certain institutions of the Church which I had always regarded as the simplest acts. The duties of the priest towards the Eucharist and towards the secrecy of the confessional seemed so grave to me that I wondered how anybody had ever found in himself the courage to undertake them; and I was not surprised when he told me that the fathers of the Church had written books as thick as the *Post Office Directory* and as closely printed as the law notices in the newspaper, elucidating all these intricate questions. Often when I thought of this I could make no answer or only a very foolish and halting one upon which he used to smile and nod his head twice or thrice. Sometimes he used to put me through the responses of the Mass which he had made me learn by heart; and, as I pattered, he used to smile pensively and nod his head, now and then pushing huge pinches of snuff up each nostril alternately. When he smiled he used to uncover his big discoloured teeth and let his tongue lie upon his lower lip—a habit which had made me feel uneasy in the beginning of our acquaintance before I knew him well.

As I walked along in the sun I remembered old Cotter's words and tried to remember what had happened afterwards in the dream. I remembered that I had noticed long velvet curtains and a swinging lamp of antique fashion. I felt that I had been very far away, in some land where the customs were strange—in Persia, I thought. . . . But I could not remember the end of the dream.

In the evening my aunt took me with her to visit the house of mourning. It was after sunset; but the window-panes of the houses that looked to the west reflected the tawny gold of a great bank of clouds. Nannie received us in the hall; and, as it would have been unseemly to have shouted at her, my aunt shook hands with her for all. The old woman pointed upwards interrogatively and, on my aunt's nodding, proceeded to toil up the narrow staircase before us, her bowed head being scarcely above the level of the banister-rail. At the first land-ing she stopped and beckoned us forward encouragingly to-wards the open door of the dead-room. My aunt went in and the old woman, seeing that I hesitated to enter, began to beckon to me again repeatedly with her hand.

I went in on tiptoe. The room through the lace end of the blind was suffused with dusky golden light amid which the candles looked like pale thin flames. He had been coffined. Nannie gave the lead and we three knelt down at the foot of the bed. I pretended to pray but I could not gather my thoughts because the old woman's mutterings distracted me. I noticed how clumsily her skirt was hooked at the back and how the heels of her cloth boots were trodden down all to one side. The fancy came to me that the old priest was smiling as he lay there in his coffin.

But no. When we rose and went up to the head of the bed I saw that he was not smiling. There he lay, solemn and copious, vested as for the altar, his large hands loosely retaining a chal-ice. His face was very truculent, grey and massive, with black cavernous nostrils and circled by a scanty white fur. There was a heavy odour in the room—the flowers.

We blessed ourselves and came away. In the little room downstairs we found Eliza seated in his arm-chair in state. I groped my way towards my usual chair in the corner while

Nannie went to the sideboard and brought out a decanter of sherry and some wine-glasses. She set these on the table and invited us to take a little glass of wine. Then, at her sister's bidding, she poured out the sherry into the glasses and passed them to us. She pressed me to take some cream crackers also but I declined because I thought I would make too much noise eating them. She seemed to be somewhat disappointed at my refusal and went over quietly to the sofa where she sat down behind her sister. No one spoke: we all gazed at the empty fireplace.

My aunt waited until Eliza sighed and then said:

—Ah, well, he's gone to a better world.

Eliza sighed again and bowed her head in assent. My aunt fingered the stem of her wine-glass before sipping a little.

—Did he . . . peacefully? she asked.

—O, quite peacefully, ma'am, said Eliza. You couldn't tell when the breath went out of him. He had a beautiful death, God be praised.

—And everything . . . ?

—Father O'Rourke was in with him a Tuesday and anointed him and prepared him and all.

—He knew then?

—He was quite resigned.

—He looks quite resigned, said my aunt.

—That's what the woman we had in to wash him said. She said he just looked as if he was asleep, he looked that peaceful and resigned. No one would think he'd make such a beautiful corpse.

—Yes, indeed, said my aunt.

She sipped a little more from her glass and said:

—Well, Miss Flynn, at any rate it must be a great comfort for you to know that you did all you could for him. You were both very kind to him, I must say.

Eliza smoothed her dress over her knees.

—Ah, poor James! she said. God knows we done all we could, as poor as we are—we wouldn't see him want anything while he was in it.

Nannie had leaned her head against the sofa-pillow and seemed about to fall asleep.

—There's poor Nannie, said Eliza, looking at her, she's wore out. All the work we had, she and me, getting in the woman to wash him and then laying him out and then the coffin and then arranging about the Mass in the chapel. Only for Father O'Rourke I don't know what we'd have done at all. It was him brought us all them flowers and them two candlesticks out of the chapel and wrote out the notice for the *Freeman's General* and took charge of all the papers for the cemetery and poor James's insurance.

—Wasn't that good of him? said my aunt.

Eliza closed her eyes and shook her head slowly.

—Ah, there's no friends like the old friends, she said, when all is said and done, no friends that a body can trust.

—Indeed, that's true, said my aunt. And I'm sure now that he's gone to his eternal reward he won't forget you and all your kindness to him.

—Ah, poor James! said Eliza. He was no great trouble to us. You wouldn't hear him in the house any more than now. Still, I know he's gone and all to that. . . .

—It's when it's all over that you'll miss him, said my aunt.

—I know that, said Eliza. I won't be bringing him in his cup of beef-tea any more, nor you, ma'am, sending him his snuff. Ah, poor James!

She stopped, as if she were communing with the past and then said shrewdly:

—Mind you, I noticed there was something queer coming over him latterly. Whenever I'd bring in his soup to him there I'd find him with his breviary fallen to the floor, lying back in the chair and his mouth open.

She laid a finger against her nose and frowned: then she continued:

—But still and all he kept on saying that before the summer was over he'd go out for a drive one fine day just to see the old house again where we were all born down in Irishtown and take me and Nannie with him. If we could only get one of them new-fangled carriages that makes no noise that Father O'Rourke told him about—them with the rheumatic wheels —for the day cheap, he said, at Johnny Rush's over the way there and drive out the three of us together of a Sunday evening. He had his mind set on that. . . . Poor James!

—The Lord have mercy on his soul! said my aunt.

Eliza took out her handkerchief and wiped her eyes with it. Then she put it back again in her pocket and gazed into the empty grate for some time without speaking.

—He was too scrupulous always, she said. The duties of the priesthood was too much for him. And then his life was, you might say, crossed.

—Yes, said my aunt. He was a disappointed man. You could see that.

A silence took possession of the little room and, under cover of it, I approached the table and tasted my sherry and then returned quietly to my chair in the corner. Eliza seemed to have fallen into a deep revery. We waited respectfully for her to break the silence: and after a long pause she said slowly:

—It was that chalice he broke. . . . That was the beginning of it. Of course, they say it was all right, that it contained nothing, I mean. But still. . . . They say it was the boy's fault. But poor James was so nervous, God be merciful to him!

—And was that it? said my aunt. I heard something. . . .

Eliza nodded.

—That affected his mind, she said. After that he began to mope by himself, talking to no one and wandering about by himself. So one night he was wanted for to go on a call and they couldn't find him anywhere. They looked high up and low down; and still they couldn't see a sight of him anywhere. So then the clerk suggested to try the chapel. So then they got the keys and opened the chapel and the clerk and Father O'Rourke and another priest that was there brought in a light for to look for him. . . . And what do you think but there he was, sitting up by himself in the dark in his confession-box, wide-awake and laughing-like softly to himself?

She stopped suddenly as if to listen. I too listened; but there was no sound in the house: and I knew that the old priest was lying still in his coffin as we had seen him, solemn and truculent in death, an idle chalice on his breast.

Eliza resumed:

—Wide-awake and laughing-like to himself. . . . So then, of course, when they saw that, that made them think that there was something gone wrong with him. . . .

AN ENCOUNTER

I⟊ was Joe Dillon who introduced the Wild West to us. He had a little library made up of old numbers of *The Union Jack*, *Pluck* and *The Halfpenny Marvel*. Every evening after school we met in his back garden and arranged Indian battles. He and his fat young brother Leo the idler held the loft of the stable while we tried to carry it by storm; or we fought a pitched battle on the grass. But, however well we fought, we never won siege or battle and all our bouts ended with Joe Dillon's war dance of victory. His parents went to eight-o'clock mass every morning in Gardiner Street and the peaceful odour of Mrs Dillon was prevalent in the hall of the house. But he played too fiercely for us who were younger and more timid. He looked like some kind of an Indian when he capered round the garden, an old tea-cosy on his head, beating a tin with his fist and yelling:

—Ya! yaka, yaka, yaka!

Everyone was incredulous when it was reported that he had a vocation for the priesthood. Nevertheless it was true.

A spirit of unruliness diffused itself among us and, under its influence, differences of culture and constitution were waived. We banded ourselves together, some boldly, some in jest and some almost in fear: and of the number of these latter, the reluctant Indians who were afraid to seem studious or lacking in robustness, I was one. The adventures related in the literature of the Wild West were remote from my nature but, at least, they opened doors of escape. I liked better some American detective stories which were traversed from time to time by unkempt fierce and beautiful girls. Though there was nothing wrong in these stories and though their intention was sometimes literary they were circulated secretly at school. One day when Father Butler was hearing the four pages of Roman History clumsy Leo Dillon was discovered with a copy of *The Halfpenny Marvel.*

—This page or this page? This page? Now, Dillon, up! *Hardly had the day* . . . Go on! What day? *Hardly had the day dawned* . . . Have you studied it? What have you there in your pocket?

Everyone's heart palpitated as Leo Dillon handed up the paper and everyone assumed an innocent face. Father Butler turned over the pages, frowning.

—What is this rubbish? he said. *The Apache Chief!* Is this what you read instead of studying your Roman History? Let me not find any more of this wretched stuff in this college. The man who wrote it, I suppose, was some wretched scribbler that writes these things for a drink. I'm surprised at boys like you, educated, reading such stuff. I could understand it if you were . . . National School boys. Now, Dillon, I advise you strongly, get at your work or . . .

This rebuke during the sober hours of school paled much of the glory of the Wild West for me and the confused puffy face of Leo Dillon awakened one of my consciences. But when the restraining influence of the school was at a distance I began to hunger again for wild sensations, for the escape which those chronicles of disorder alone seemed to offer me. The mimic warfare of the evening became at last as wearisome to me as the routine of school in the morning because I wanted real adventures to happen to myself. But real adventures, I reflected, do not happen to people who remain at home: they must be sought abroad.

The summer holidays were near at hand when I made up my mind to break out of the weariness of school-life for one day at least. With Leo Dillon and a boy named Mahony I planned a day's miching. Each of us saved up sixpence. We were to meet at ten in the morning on the Canal Bridge. Mahony's big sister was to write an excuse for him and Leo Dillon was to tell his brother to say he was sick. We arranged to go along the Wharf Road until we came to the ships, then to cross in the ferryboat and walk out to see the Pigeon House. Leo Dillon was afraid we might meet Father Butler or someone out of the college; but Mahony asked, very sensibly, what would Father Butler be doing out at the Pigeon House. We were reassured: and I brought the first stage of the plot to an end by collecting sixpence from the other two, at the same time showing them my own sixpence. When we were making the last arrangements on the eve we were all vaguely excited. We shook hands, laughing, and Mahony said:

—Till to-morrow, mates.

That night I slept badly. In the morning I was firstcomer to the bridge as I lived nearest. I hid my books in the long grass near the ashpit at the end of the garden where nobody ever came and hurried along the canal bank. It was a mild sunny morning in the first week of June. I sat up on the coping of the bridge admiring my frail canvas shoes which I had diligently pipeclayed overnight and watching the docile horses pulling a tramload of business people up the hill. All the branches of the tall trees which lined the mall were gay with little light green leaves and the sunlight slanted through them on to the water. The granite stone of the bridge was beginning to be warm and I began to pat it with my hands in time to an air in my head. I was very happy.

When I had been sitting there for five or ten minutes I saw Mahony's grey suit approaching. He came up the hill, smiling, and clambered up beside me on the bridge. While we were waiting he brought out the catapult which bulged from his inner pocket and explained some improvements which he had made in it. I asked him why he had brought it and he told me he had brought it to have some gas with the birds. Mahony used slang freely, and spoke of Father Butler as Bunsen Burner. We waited on for a quarter of an hour more but still there was no sign of Leo Dillon. Mahony, at last, jumped down and said:

—Come along. I knew Fatty'd funk it.

—And his sixpence . . . ? I said.

—That's forfeit, said Mahony. And so much the better for us—a bob and a tanner instead of a bob.

We walked along the North Strand Road till we came to the Vitriol Works and then turned to the right along the Wharf Road. Mahony began to play the Indian as soon as we were out of public sight. He chased a crowd of ragged girls, brandishing his unloaded catapult and, when two ragged boys began, out of chivalry, to fling stones at us, he proposed that we should charge them. I objected that the boys were too small, and so we walked on, the ragged troop screaming after us: *Swaddlers! Swaddlers!* thinking that we were Protestants because Mahony, who was dark-complexioned, wore the silver badge of a cricket club in his cap. When we came to the Smoothing Iron we arranged a siege; but it was a failure because you must have at least three. We revenged ourselves on Leo Dillon by saying what a funk he was and guessing how many he would get at three o'clock from Mr Ryan.

We came then near the river. We spent a long time walking

about the noisy streets flanked by high stone walls, watching the working of cranes and engines and often being shouted at for our immobility by the drivers of groaning carts. It was noon when we reached the quays and, as all the labourers seemed to be eating their lunches, we bought two big currant buns and sat down to eat them on some metal piping beside the river. We pleased ourselves with the spectacle of Dublin's commerce—the barges signalled from far away by their curls of woolly smoke, the brown fishing fleet beyond Ringsend, the big white sailing-vessel which was being discharged on the opposite quay. Mahony said it would be right skit to run away to sea on one of those big ships and even I, looking at the high masts, saw, or imagined, the geography which had been scantily dosed to me at school gradually taking substance under my eyes. School and home seemed to recede from us and their influences upon us seemed to wane.

We crossed the Liffey in the ferryboat, paying our toll to be transported in the company of two labourers and a little Jew with a bag. We were serious to the point of solemnity, but once during the short voyage our eyes met and we laughed. When we landed we watched the discharging of the graceful three-master which we had observed from the other quay. Some bystander said that she was a Norwegian vessel. I went to the stern and tried to decipher the legend upon it but, failing to do so, I came back and examined the foreign sailors to see had any of them green eyes for I had some confused notion. . . . The sailors' eyes were blue and grey and even black. The only sailor whose eyes could have been called green was a tall man who amused the crowd on the quay by calling out cheerfully every time the planks fell:

—All right! All right!

When we were tired of this sight we wandered slowly into Ringsend. The day had grown sultry, and in the windows of the grocers' shops musty biscuits lay bleaching. We bought some biscuits and chocolate which we ate sedulously as we wandered through the squalid streets where the families of the fishermen live. We could find no dairy and so we went into a huckster's shop and bought a bottle of raspberry lemonade each. Refreshed by this, Mahony chased a cat down a lane, but the cat escaped into a wide field. We both felt rather tired and when we reached the field we made at once for a sloping bank over the ridge of which we could see the Dodder.

It was too late and we were too tired to carry out our project of visiting the Pigeon House. We had to be home before four o'clock lest our adventure should be discovered. Mahony looked regretfully at his catapult and I had to suggest going home by train before he regained any cheerfulness. The sun went in behind some clouds and left us to our jaded thoughts and the crumbs of our provisions.

There was nobody but ourselves in the field. When we had lain on the bank for some time without speaking I saw a man approaching from the far end of the field. I watched him lazily as I chewed one of those green stems on which girls tell fortunes. He came along by the bank slowly. He walked with one hand upon his hip and in the other hand he held a stick with which he tapped the turf lightly. He was shabbily dressed in a suit of greenish-black and wore what we used to call a jerry hat with a high crown. He seemed to be fairly old for his moustache was ashen-grey. When he passed at our feet he glanced up at us quickly and then continued his way. We followed him with our eyes and saw that when he had gone on for perhaps fifty paces he turned about and began to retrace his steps. He walked towards us very slowly, always tapping the ground with his stick, so slowly that I thought he was looking for something in the grass.

He stopped when he came level with us and bade us goodday. We answered him and he sat down beside us on the slope slowly and with great care. He began to talk of the weather, saying that it would be a very hot summer and adding that the seasons had changed greatly since he was a boy—a long time ago. He said that the happiest time of one's life was undoubtedly one's schoolboy days and that he would give anything to be young again. While he expressed these sentiments which bored us a little we kept silent. Then he began to talk of school and of books. He asked us whether we had read the poetry of Thomas Moore or the works of Sir Walter Scott and Lord Lytton. I pretended that I had read every book he mentioned so that in the end he said:

—Ah, I can see you are a bookworm like myself. Now, he added, pointing to Mahony who was regarding us with open eyes, he is different; he goes in for games.

He said he had all Sir Walter Scott's works and all Lord Lytton's works at home and never tired of reading them. Of course, he said, there were some of Lord Lytton's works which boys couldn't read. Mahony asked why couldn't boys read them —a question which agitated and pained me because I was afraid the man would think I was as stupid as Mahony. The man, however, only smiled. I saw that he had great gaps in his mouth between his yellow teeth. Then he asked us which of us had the most sweethearts. Mahony mentioned lightly that he had three totties. The man asked me how many had I. I answered that I had none. He did not believe me and said he was sure I must have one. I was silent.

—Tell us, said Mahony pertly to the man, how many have you yourself?

The man smiled as before and said that when he was our age he had lots of sweethearts.

—Every boy, he said, has a little sweetheart.

His attitude on this point struck me as strangely liberal in a man of his age. In my heart I thought that what he said about boys and sweethearts was reasonable. But I disliked the words in his mouth and I wondered why he shivered once or twice as if he feared something or felt a sudden chill. As he proceeded I noticed that his accent was good. He began to speak to us about girls, saying what nice soft hair they had and how soft their hands were and how all girls were not so good as they seemed to be if one only knew. There was nothing he liked, he said, so much as looking at a nice young girl, at her nice white hands and her beautiful soft hair. He gave me the impression that he was repeating something which he had learned by heart or that, magnetised by some words of his own speech, his mind was slowly circling round and round in the same orbit. At times he spoke as if he were simply alluding to some fact that everybody knew, and at times he lowered his voice and spoke mysteriously as if he were telling us something secret which he did not wish others to overhear. He repeated his phrases over and over again, varying them and surrounding them with his monotonous voice. I continued to gaze towards the foot of the slope, listening to him.

After a long while his monologue paused. He stood up slowly, saying that he had to leave us for a minute or so, a few minutes, and, without changing the direction of my gaze, I saw him walking slowly away from us towards the near end of the field. We remained silent when he had gone. After a silence of a few minutes I heard Mahony exclaim:

—I say! Look what he's doing!

As I neither answered nor raised my eyes Mahony exclaimed again:

—I say . . . He's a queer old josser!

—In case he asks us for our names, I said, let you be Murphy and I'll be Smith.

We said nothing further to each other. I was still considering whether I would go away or not when the man came back and sat down beside us again. Hardly had he sat down when Mahony, catching sight of the cat which had escaped him, sprang up and pursued her across the field. The man and I watched the chase. The cat escaped once more and Mahony began to throw stones at the wall she had escaladed. Desisting from this, he began to wander about the far end of the field, aimlessly.

After an interval the man spoke to me. He said that my friend was a very rough boy and asked did he get whipped often at school. I was going to reply indignantly that we were not National School boys to be *whipped*, as he called it; but I remained silent. He began to speak on the subject of chastising boys. His mind, as if magnetised again by his speech, seemed to circle slowly round and round its new centre. He said that when boys were that kind they ought to be whipped and well whipped. When a boy was rough and unruly there was nothing would do him any good but a good sound whipping. A slap on the hand or a box on the ear was no good: what he wanted was to get a nice warm whipping. I was surprised at this sentiment and involuntarily glanced up at his face. As I did so I met the gaze of a pair of bottle-green eyes peering at me from under a twitching forehead. I turned my eyes away again.

The man continued his monologue. He seemed to have forgotten his recent liberalism. He said that if ever he found a boy talking to girls or having a girl for a sweetheart he would whip him and whip him; and that would teach him not to be talking to girls. And if a boy had a girl for a sweetheart and told lies about it then he would give him such a whipping as no boy ever got in this world. He said that there was nothing in this world he would like so well as that. He described to me how he would whip such a boy as if he were unfolding some elaborate mystery. He would love that, he said, better than anything in this world; and his voice, as he led me monotonously through the mystery, grew almost affectionate and seemed to plead with me that I should understand him.

I waited till his monologue paused again. Then I stood up abruptly. Lest I should betray my agitation I delayed a few moments pretending to fix my shoe properly and then, saying that I was obliged to go, I bade him good-day. I went up the slope calmly but my heart was beating quickly with fear that he would seize me by the ankles. When I reached the top of the slope I turned round and, without looking at him, called loudly across the field:

—Murphy!

My voice had an accent of forced bravery in it and I was ashamed of my paltry stratagem. I had to call the name again before Mahony saw me and hallooed in answer. How my heart beat as he came running across the field to me! He ran as if to bring me aid. And I was penitent; for in my heart I had always despised him a little.

ARABY

NORTH RICHMOND STREET, being blind, was a quiet street except at the hour when the Christian Brothers' School set the boys free. An uninhabited house of two storeys stood at the blind end, detached from its neighbours in a square ground. The other houses of the street, conscious of decent lives within them, gazed at one another with brown imperturbable faces.

The former tenant of our house, a priest, had died in the back drawing-room. Air, musty from having been long enclosed, hung in all the rooms, and the waste room behind the kitchen was littered with old useless papers. Among these I found a few paper-covered books, the pages of which were curled and damp: *The Abbot*, by Walter Scott, *The Devout Communicant* and *The Memoirs of Vidocq*. I liked the last best because its leaves were yellow. The wild garden behind the house contained a central apple-tree and a few straggling bushes under one of which I found the late tenant's rusty bicycle-pump. He had been a very charitable priest; in his will he had left all his money to institutions and the furniture of his house to his sister.

When the short days of winter came dusk fell before we had well eaten our dinners. When we met in the street the houses had grown sombre. The space of sky above us was the colour of ever-changing violet and towards it the lamps of the street lifted their feeble lanterns. The cold air stung us and we played till our bodies glowed. Our shouts echoed in the silent street. The career of our play brought us through the dark muddy lanes behind the houses where we ran the gantlet of the rough tribes from the cottages, to the back doors of the dark dripping gardens where odours arose from the ashpits, to the dark odorous stables where a coachman smoothed and combed the horse or shook music from the buckled harness. When we returned to the street light from the kitchen windows had filled the areas. If my uncle was seen turning the corner we hid in the shadow until we had seen him safely housed. Or if Mangan's sister came out on the doorstep to call her brother in to his tea we watched her from our shadow peer up and down the street. We waited to see whether she would remain or go in and, if she remained, we left our shadow and walked up to Mangan's steps resignedly. She was waiting for us, her figure defined by the light from the half-opened door. Her brother always teased her before he obeyed and I stood by the railings looking at her. Her dress swung as she moved her body and the soft rope of her hair tossed from side to side.

Every morning I lay on the floor in the front parlour watching her door. The blind was pulled down to within an inch of the sash so that I could not be seen. When she came out on the doorstep my heart leaped. I ran to the hall, seized my books and followed her. I kept her brown figure always in my eye and, when we came near the point at which our ways diverged, I quickened my pace and passed her. This happened morning after morning. I had never spoken to her, except for a few casual words, and yet her name was like a summons to all my foolish blood.

Her image accompanied me even in places the most hostile to romance. On Saturday evenings when my aunt went marketing I had to go to carry some of the parcels. We walked through the flaring streets, jostled by drunken men and bargaining women, amid the curses of labourers, the shrill litanies of shop-boys who stood on guard by the barrels of pigs' cheeks, the nasal chanting of street-singers, who sang a *come-all-you* about O'Donovan Rossa, or a ballad about the troubles in our native land. These noises converged in a single sensation of life for me: I imagined that I bore my chalice safely through a throng of foes. Her name sprang to my lips at moments in strange prayers and praises which I myself did not understand. My eyes were often full of tears (I could not tell why) and at times a flood from my heart seemed to pour itself out into my bosom. I thought little of the future. I did not know whether I would ever speak to her or not or, if I spoke to her, how I could tell her of my confused adoration. But my body was like a harp and her words and gestures were like fingers running upon the wires.

One evening I went into the back drawing-room in which the priest had died. It was a dark rainy evening and there was no sound in the house. Through one of the broken panes I heard the rain impinge upon the earth, the fine incessant needles of water playing in the sodden beds. Some distant lamp or lighted window gleamed below me. I was thankful that I could see so little. All my senses seemed to desire to veil themselves and, feeling that I was about to slip from them, I pressed the palms of my hands together until they trembled, murmuring: *O love! O love!* many times.

At last she spoke to me. When she addressed the first words to me I was so confused that I did not know what to answer. She asked me was I going to *Araby*. I forget whether I answered yes or no. It would be a splendid bazaar, she said; she would love to go.

—And why can't you? I asked.

While she spoke she turned a silver bracelet round and round her wrist. She could not go, she said, because there would be a retreat that week in her convent. Her brother and two other boys were fighting for their caps and I was alone at the railings. She held one of the spikes, bowing her head towards me. The light from the lamp opposite our door caught the white curve of her neck, lit up her hair that rested there and, falling, lit up the hand upon the railing. It fell over one side of her dress and caught the white border of a petticoat, just visible as she stood at ease.

—It's well for you, she said.

—If I go, I said, I will bring you something.

What innumerable follies laid waste my waking and sleeping thoughts after that evening! I wished to annihilate the tedious intervening days. I chafed against the work of school. At night in my bedroom and by day in the classroom her image came between me and the page I strove to read. The syllables of the word *Araby* were called to me through the silence in which my soul luxuriated and cast an Eastern enchantment over me. I asked for leave to go to the bazaar on Saturday night. My aunt was surprised and hoped it was not some Freemason affair. I answered few questions in class. I watched my master's face pass from amiability to sternness; he hoped I was not beginning to idle. I could not call my wandering thoughts together. I had hardly any patience with the serious work of life which, now that it stood between me and my desire, seemed to me child's play, ugly monotonous child's play.

On Saturday morning I reminded my uncle that I wished to go to the bazaar in the evening. He was fussing at the hall-stand, looking for the hat-brush, and answered me curtly:

—Yes, boy, I know.

As he was in the hall I could not go into the front parlour and lie at the window. I left the house in bad humour and walked slowly towards the school. The air was pitilessly raw and already my heart misgave me.

When I came home to dinner my uncle had not yet been home. Still it was early. I sat staring at the clock for some time and, when its ticking began to irritate me, I left the room. I mounted the staircase and gained the upper part of the house. The high cold empty gloomy rooms liberated me and I went from room to room singing. From the front window I saw my companions playing below in the street. Their cries reached me weakened and indistinct and, leaning my forehead against the cool glass, I looked over at the dark house where she lived. I may have stood there for an hour, seeing nothing but the brown-clad figure cast by my imagination, touched discreetly by the lamplight at the curved neck, at the hand upon the railings and at the border below the dress.

When I came downstairs again I found Mrs Mercer sitting at the fire. She was an old garrulous woman, a pawnbroker's widow, who collected used stamps for some pious purpose. I had to endure the gossip of the tea-table. The meal was prolonged beyond an hour and still my uncle did not come. Mrs Mercer stood up to go: she was sorry she couldn't wait any longer, but it was after eight o'clock and she did not like to be out late, as the night air was bad for her. When she had gone I began to walk up and down the room, clenching my fists. My aunt said:

—I'm afraid you may put off your bazaar for this night of Our Lord.

At nine o'clock I heard my uncle's latchkey in the halldoor. I heard him talking to himself and heard the hallstand rocking when it had received the weight of his overcoat. I could interpret these signs. When he was midway through his dinner I asked him to give me the money to go to the bazaar. He had forgotten.

—The people are in bed and after their first sleep now, he said.

I did not smile. My aunt said to him energetically:

—Can't you give him the money and let him go? You've kept him late enough as it is.

My uncle said he was very sorry he had forgotten. He said he believed in the old saying: *All work and no play makes Jack a dull boy*. He asked me where I was going and, when I had told him a second time he asked me did I know *The Arab's Farewell to his Steed*. When I left the kitchen he was about to recite the opening lines of the piece to my aunt.

I held a florin tightly in my hand as I strode down Buckingham Street towards the station. The sight of the streets thronged with buyers and glaring with gas recalled to me the purpose of my journey. I took my seat in a third-class carriage of a deserted train. After an intolerable delay the train moved out of the station slowly. It crept onward among ruinous houses and over the twinkling river. At Westland Row Station a crowd of people pressed to the carriage doors; but the porters moved them back, saying that it was a special train for the bazaar. I remained alone in the bare carriage. In a few minutes the train drew up beside an improvised wooden platform. I passed out on to the road and saw by the lighted dial of a clock that it was ten minutes to ten. In front of me was a large building which displayed the magical name.

I could not find any sixpenny entrance and, fearing that the bazaar would be closed, I passed in quickly through a turnstile, handing a shilling to a weary-looking man. I found myself in a big hall girdled at half its height by a gallery. Nearly all the stalls were closed and the greater part of the hall was in darkness. I recognised a silence like that which pervades a church after a service. I walked into the centre of the bazaar timidly. A few people were gathered about the stalls which were still open. Before a curtain, over which the words *Café Chantant* were written in coloured lamps, two men were counting money on a salver. I listened to the fall of the coins.

Remembering with difficulty why I had come I went over to one of the stalls and examined porcelain vases and flowered tea-sets. At the door of the stall a young lady was talking and laughing with two young gentlemen. I remarked their English accents and listened vaguely to their conversation.

—O, I never said such a thing!

—O, but you did!

—O, but I didn't!

—Didn't she say that?

—Yes. I heard her.

—O, there's a . . . fib!

Observing me the young lady came over and asked me did I wish to buy anything. The tone of her voice was not encouraging; she seemed to have spoken to me out of a sense of duty. I looked humbly at the great jars that stood like eastern guards at either side of the dark entrance to the stall and murmured:

—No, thank you.

The young lady changed the position of one of the vases and went back to the two young men. They began to talk of the same subject. Once or twice the young lady glanced at me over her shoulder.

I lingered before her stall, though I knew my stay was useless, to make my interest in her wares seem the more real. Then I turned away slowly and walked down the middle of the bazaar. I allowed the two pennies to fall against the sixpence in my pocket. I heard a voice call from one end of the gallery that the light was out. The upper part of the hall was now completely dark.

Gazing up into the darkness I saw myself as a creature driven and derided by vanity; and my eyes burned with anguish and anger.

EVELINE

She sat at the window watching the evening invade the avenue. Her head was leaned against the window curtains and in her nostrils was the odour of dusty cretonne. She was tired.

Few people passed. The man out of the last house passed on his way home; she heard his footsteps clacking along the concrete pavement and afterwards crunching on the cinder path before the new red houses. One time there used to be a field there in which they used to play every evening with other people's children. Then a man from Belfast bought the field and built houses in it—not like their little brown houses but bright brick houses with shining roofs. The children of the avenue used to play together in that field—the Devines, the Waters, the Dunns, little Keogh the cripple, she and her brothers and sisters. Ernest, however, never played: he was too grown up. Her father used often to hunt them in out of the field with his blackthorn stick; but usually little Keogh used to keep *nix* and call out when he saw her father coming. Still they seemed to have been rather happy then. Her father was not so bad then; and besides, her mother was alive. That was a long time ago; she and her brothers and sisters were all grown up; her mother was dead. Tizzie Dunn was dead, too, and the Waters had gone back to England. Everything changes. Now she was going to go away like the others, to leave her home.

Home! She looked round the room, reviewing all its familiar objects which she had dusted once a week for so many years, wondering where on earth all the dust came from. Perhaps she would never see again those familiar objects from which she had never dreamed of being divided. And yet during all those years she had never found out the name of the priest whose yellowing photograph hung on the wall above the broken harmonium beside the coloured print of the promises made to Blessed Margaret Mary Alacoque. He had been a school friend of her father. Whenever he showed the photograph to a visitor her father used to pass it with a casual word:

—He is in Melbourne now.

She had consented to go away, to leave her home. Was that wise? She tried to weigh each side of the question. In her home anyway she had shelter and food; she had those whom she had known all her life about her. Of course she had to work hard both in the house and at business. What would they say of her in the Stores when they found out that she had run away with a fellow? Say she was a fool, perhaps; and her place would be filled up by advertisement. Miss Gavan would be glad. She had always had an edge on her, especially whenever there were people listening.

—Miss Hill, don't you see these ladies are waiting?

—Look lively, Miss Hill, please.

She would not cry many tears at leaving the Stores.

But in her new home, in a distant unknown country, it would not be like that. Then she would be married—she, Eveline. People would treat her with respect then. She would not be treated as her mother had been. Even now, though she was over nineteen, she sometimes felt herself in danger of her father's violence. She knew it was that that had given her the palpitations. When they were growing up he had never gone for her, like he used to go for Harry and Ernest, because she was a girl; but latterly he had begun to threaten her and say what he would do to her only for her dead mother's sake. And now she had nobody to protect her. Ernest was dead and Harry, who was in the church decorating business, was nearly always down somewhere in the country. Besides, the invariable squabble for money on Saturday nights had begun to weary her unspeakably. She always gave her entire wages—seven shillings—and Harry always sent up what he could but the trouble was to get any money from her father. He said she used to squander the money, that she had no head, that he wasn't going to give her his hard-earned money to throw about the streets, and much more, for he was usually fairly bad of a Saturday night. In the end he would give her the money and ask her had she any intention of buying Sunday's dinner. Then she had to rush out as quickly as she could and do her marketing, holding her black leather purse tightly in her hand as she elbowed her way through the crowds and returning home late under her load of provisions. She had hard work to keep the house together and to see that the two young children who had been left to her charge went to school regularly and got their meals regularly. It was hard work—a hard life—but now that she was about to leave it she did not find it a wholly undesirable life.

She was about to explore another life with Frank. Frank was very kind, manly, open-hearted. She was to go away with him by the night-boat to be his wife and to live with him in Buenos Ayres where he had a home waiting for her. How well she remembered the first time she had seen him; he was lodging in a house on the main road where she used to visit. It seemed a few weeks ago. He was standing at the gate, his peaked cap pushed back on his head and his hair tumbled forward over a face of bronze. Then they had come to know each other. He used to meet her outside the Stores every evening and see her home. He took her to see *The Bohemian Girl* and she felt elated as she sat in an unaccustomed part of the theatre with him. He was awfully fond of music and sang a little. People knew that they were courting and, when he sang about the lass that loves a sailor, she always felt pleasantly confused. He used to call her Poppens out of fun. First of all it had been an excitement for her to have a fellow and then she had begun to like him. He had tales of distant countries. He had started as a deck boy at a pound a month on a ship of the Allan Line going out to Canada. He told her the names of the ships he had been on and the names of the different services. He had sailed through the Straits of Magellan and he told her stories of the terrible Patagonians. He had fallen on his feet in Buenos Ayres, he said, and had come over to the old country just for a holiday. Of course, her father had found out the affair and had forbidden her to have anything to say to him.

—I know these sailor chaps, he said.

One day he had quarrelled with Frank and after that she had to meet her lover secretly.

The evening deepened in the avenue. The white of two letters in her lap grew indistinct. One was to Harry; the other was to her father. Ernest had been her favourite but she liked Harry too. Her father was becoming old lately, she noticed; he would miss her. Sometimes he could be very nice. Not long before, when she had been laid up for a day, he had read her out a ghost story and made toast for her at the fire. Another day, when their mother was alive, they had all gone for a picnic to the Hill of Howth. She remembered her father putting on her mother's bonnet to make the children laugh.

Her time was running out but she continued to sit by the window, leaning her head against the window curtain, inhaling the odour of dusty cretonne. Down far in the avenue she could hear a street organ playing. She knew the air. Strange that it should come that very night to remind her of the promise to her mother, her promise to keep the home together as long as she could. She remembered the last night of her mother's illness; she was again in the close dark room at the other side of the hall and outside she heard a melancholy air of Italy. The organ-player had been ordered to go away and given sixpence. She remembered her father strutting back into the sickroom saying:

—Damned Italians! coming over here!

As she mused the pitiful vision of her mother's life laid its spell on the very quick of her being—that life of commonplace sacrifices closing in final craziness. She trembled as she heard again her mother's voice saying constantly with foolish insistence:

—Derevaun Seraun! Derevaun Seraun!

She stood up in a sudden impulse of terror. Escape! She must escape! Frank would save her. He would give her life, perhaps love, too. But she wanted to live. Why should she be unhappy? She had a right to happiness. Frank would take her in his arms, fold her in his arms. He would save her.

· · · · · · · · ·

She stood among the swaying crowd in the station at the North Wall. He held her hand and she knew that he was speaking to her, saying something about the passage over and over again. The station was full of soldiers with brown baggages. Through the wide doors of the sheds she caught a glimpse of the black mass of the boat, lying in beside the quay wall, with illumined portholes. She answered nothing. She felt her cheek pale and cold and, out of a maze of distress, she prayed to God to direct her, to show her what was her duty. The boat blew a long mournful whistle into the mist. If she went, to-morrow she would be on the sea with Frank, steaming towards Buenos Ayres. Their passage had been booked.

Could she still draw back after all he had done for her? Her distress awoke a nausea in her body and she kept moving her lips in silent fervent prayer.

A bell clanged upon her heart. She felt him seize her hand:

—Come!

All the seas of the world tumbled about her heart. He was drawing her into them: he would drown her. She gripped with both hands at the iron railing.

—Come!

No! No! No! It was impossible. Her hands clutched the iron in frenzy. Amid the seas she sent a cry of anguish!

—Eveline! Evvy!

He rushed beyond the barrier and called to her to follow. He was shouted at to go on but he still called to her. She set her white face to him, passive, like a helpless animal. Her eyes gave him no sign of love or farewell or recognition.

AFTER THE RACE

THE cars came scudding in towards Dublin, running evenly like pellets in the groove of the Naas Road. At the crest of the hill at Inchicore sightseers had gathered in clumps to watch the cars careering homeward and through this channel of poverty and inaction the Continent sped its wealth and industry. Now and again the clumps of people raised the cheer of the gratefully oppressed. Their sympathy, however, was for the blue cars—the cars of their friends, the French.

The French, moreover, were virtual victors. Their team had finished solidly; they had been placed second and third and the driver of the winning German car was reported a Belgian. Each blue car, therefore, received a double round of welcome as it topped the crest of the hill and each cheer of welcome was acknowledged with smiles and nods by those in the car. In one of these trimly built cars was a party of four young men whose spirits seemed to be at present well above the level of successful Gallicism: in fact, these four young men were almost hilarious. They were Charles Ségouin, the owner of the car; André Rivière, a young electrician of Canadian birth; a huge Hungarian named Villona and a neatly groomed young man named Doyle. Ségouin was in good humour because he had unexpectedly received some orders in advance (he was about to start a motor establishment in Paris) and Rivière was in good humour because he was to be appointed manager of the establishment; these two young men (who were cousins) were also in good humour because of the success of the French cars. Villona was in good humour because he had had a very satisfactory luncheon; and besides he was an optimist by nature. The fourth member of the party, however, was too excited to be genuinely happy.

He was about twenty-six years of age, with a soft, light brown moustache and rather innocent-looking grey eyes. His father, who had begun life as an advanced Nationalist, had modified his views early. He had made his money as a butcher in Kingstown and by opening shops in Dublin and in the suburbs he had made his money many times over. He had also been fortunate enough to secure some of the police contracts and in the end he had become rich enough to be alluded to in the Dublin newspapers as a merchant prince. He had sent his son to England to be educated in a big Catholic college and had afterwards sent him to Dublin University to study law. Jimmy did not study very earnestly and took to bad courses for a while. He had money and he was popular; and he divided his time curiously between musical and motoring circles. Then he had been sent for a term to Cambridge to see a little life. His father, remonstrative, but covertly proud of the excess, had paid his bills and brought him home. It was at Cambridge that he had met Ségouin. They were not much more than acquaintances as yet but Jimmy found great pleasure in the society of one who had seen so much of the world and was reputed to own some of the biggest hotels in France. Such a person (as his father agreed) was well worth knowing, even if he had not been the charming companion he was. Villona was entertaining also—a brilliant pianist—but, unfortunately, very poor.

The car ran on merrily with its cargo of hilarious youth. The two cousins sat on the front seat; Jimmy and his Hungarian friend sat behind. Decidedly Villona was in excellent spirits; he kept up a deep bass hum of melody for miles of the road. The Frenchmen flung their laughter and light words over their shoulders and often Jimmy had to strain forward to catch the quick phrase. This was not altogether pleasant for him, as he had nearly always to make a deft guess at the meaning and shout back a suitable answer in the teeth of a high wind. Besides Villona's humming would confuse anybody; the noise of the car, too.

Rapid motion through space elates one; so does notoriety; so does the possession of money. These were three good reasons for Jimmy's excitement. He had been seen by many of his friends that day in the company of these Continentals. At the control Ségouin had presented him to one of the French competitors and, in answer to his confused murmur of compliment, the swarthy face of the driver had disclosed a line of shining white teeth. It was pleasant after that honour to return to the profane world of spectators amid nudges and significant looks. Then as to money—he really had a great sum under his control. Ségouin, perhaps, would not think it a great sum but Jimmy who, in spite of temporary errors, was at heart the inheritor of solid instincts knew well with what difficulty it had been got together. This knowledge had previously kept his bills within the limits of reasonable recklessness and, if he had been so conscious of the labour latent in money when there had been question merely of some freak of the higher intelligence, how much more so now when he was about to stake the greater part of his substance! It was a serious thing for him.

Of course, the investment was a good one and Ségouin had

managed to give the impression that it was by a favour of friendship the mite of Irish money was to be included in the capital of the concern. Jimmy had a respect for his father's shrewdness in business matters and in this case it had been his father who had first suggested the investment; money to be made in the motor business, pots of money. Moreover Ségouin had the unmistakable air of wealth. Jimmy set out to translate into days' work that lordly car in which he sat. How smoothly it ran. In what style they had come careering along the country roads! The journey laid a magical finger on the genuine pulse of life and gallantly the machinery of human nerves strove to answer the bounding courses of the swift blue animal.

They drove down Dame Street. The street was busy with unusual traffic, loud with the horns of motorists and the gongs of impatient tram-drivers. Near the Bank Ségouin drew up and Jimmy and his friend alighted. A little knot of people collected on the footpath to pay homage to the snorting motor. The party was to dine together that evening in Ségouin's hotel and, meanwhile, Jimmy and his friend, who was staying with him, were to go home to dress. The car steered out slowly for Grafton Street while the two young men pushed their way through the knot of gazers. They walked northward with a curious feeling of disappointment in the exercise, while the city hung its pale globes of light above them in a haze of summer evening.

In Jimmy's house this dinner had been pronounced an occasion. A certain pride mingled with his parents' trepidation, a certain eagerness, also, to play fast and loose for the names of great foreign cities have at least this virtue. Jimmy, too, looked very well when he was dressed and, as he stood in the hall giving a last equation to the bows of his dress tie, his father may have felt even commercially satisfied at having secured for his son qualities often unpurchasable. His father, therefore, was unusually friendly with Villona and his manner expressed a real respect for foreign accomplishments; but this subtlety of his host was probably lost upon the Hungarian, who was beginning to have a sharp desire for his dinner.

The dinner was excellent, exquisite. Ségouin, Jimmy decided, had a very refined taste. The party was increased by a young Englishman named Routh whom Jimmy had seen with Ségouin at Cambridge. The young men supped in a snug room lit by electric candle-lamps. They talked volubly and with little reserve. Jimmy, whose imagination was kindling, conceived the lively youth of the Frenchmen twined elegantly upon the firm framework of the Englishman's manner. A graceful image of his, he thought, and a just one. He admired the dexterity with which their host directed the conversation. The five young men had various tastes and their tongues had been loosened. Villona, with immense respect, began to discover to the mildly surprised Englishman the beauties of the English madrigal, deploring the loss of old instruments. Rivière, not wholly ingenuously, undertook to explain to Jimmy the triumph of the French mechanicians. The resonant voice of the Hungarian was about to prevail in ridicule of the spurious lutes of the romantic painters when Ségouin shepherded his party into politics. Here was congenial ground for all. Jimmy, under generous influences, felt the buried zeal of his father wake to life within him: he aroused the torpid Routh at last. The room grew doubly hot and Ségouin's task grew harder each moment: there was even danger of personal spite. The alert host at an opportunity lifted his glass to Humanity and, when the toast had been drunk, he threw open a window significantly.

That night the city wore the mask of a capital. The five young men strolled along Stephen's Green in a faint cloud of aromatic smoke. They talked loudly and gaily and their cloaks dangled from their shoulders. The people made way for them. At the corner of Grafton Street a short fat man was putting two handsome ladies on a car in charge of another fat man.

The car drove off and the short fat man caught sight of the party.

—André.

—It's Farley!

A torrent of talk followed. Farley was an American. No one knew very well what the talk was about. Villona and Rivière were the noisiest, but all the men were excited. They got up on a car, squeezing themselves together amid much laughter. They drove by the crowd, blended now into soft colours, to a music of merry bells. They took the train at Westland Row and in a few seconds, as it seemed to Jimmy, they were walking out of Kingstown Station. The ticket-collector saluted Jimmy; he was an old man:

—Fine night, sir!

It was a serene summer night; the harbour lay like a darkened mirror at their feet. They proceeded towards it with linked arms, singing *Cadet Roussel* in chorus, stamping their feet at every:

—*Ho! Ho! Hohé, vraiment!*

They got into a rowboat at the slip and made out for the American's yacht. There was to be supper, music, cards. Villona said with conviction:

—It is beautiful!

There was a yacht piano in the cabin. Villona played a waltz for Farley and Rivière, Farley acting as cavalier and Rivière as lady. Then an impromptu square dance, the men devising original figures. What merriment! Jimmy took his part with a will; this was seeing life, at least. Then Farley got out of breath and cried *Stop!* A man brought in a light supper, and the young men sat down to it for form' sake. They drank, however: it was Bohemian. They drank Ireland, England, France, Hungary, the United States of America. Jimmy made a speech, a long speech, Villona saying *Hear! hear!* whenever there was a pause. There was a great clapping of hands when he sat down. It must have been a good speech. Farley clapped him on the back and laughed loudly. What jovial fellows! What good company they were!

Cards! cards! The table was cleared. Villona returned quietly to his piano and played voluntaries for them. The other men played game after game, flinging themselves boldly into the adventure. They drank the health of the Queen of Hearts and of the Queen of Diamonds. Jimmy felt obscurely the lack of an audience: the wit was flashing. Play ran very high and paper began to pass. Jimmy did not know exactly who was winning but he knew that he was losing. But it was his own fault for he frequently mistook his cards and the other men had to calculate his I.O.U.'s for him. They were devils of fellows but he wished they would stop: it was getting late. Someone gave the toast of the yacht *The Belle of Newport* and then someone proposed one great game for a finish.

The piano had stopped; Villona must have gone up on deck. It was a terrible game. They stopped just before the end of it to drink for luck. Jimmy understood that the game lay between Routh and Ségouin. What excitement! Jimmy was excited too; he would lose, of course. How much had he written away? The men rose to their feet to play the last tricks, talking and gesticulating. Routh won. The cabin shook with the young men's cheering and the cards were bundled together. They began then to gather in what they had won. Farley and Jimmy were the heaviest losers.

He knew that he would regret in the morning but at present he was glad of the rest, glad of the dark stupor that would cover up his folly. He leaned his elbows on the table and rested his head between his hands, counting the beats of his temples. The cabin door opened and he saw the Hungarian standing in a shaft of grey light:

—Daybreak, gentlemen!

TWO GALLANTS

THE grey warm evening of August had descended upon the city and a mild warm air, a memory of summer, circulated in the streets. The streets, shuttered for the repose of Sunday, swarmed with a gaily coloured crowd. Like illumined pearls the lamps shone from the summits of their tall poles upon the living texture below which, changing shape and hue unceasingly, sent up into the warm grey evening air an unchanging unceasing murmur.

Two young men came down the hill of Rutland Square. One of them was just bringing a long monologue to a close. The other, who walked on the verge of the path and was at times obliged to step on to the road, owing to his companion's rudeness, wore an amused listening face. He was squat and ruddy. A yachting cap was shoved far back from his forehead and the narrative to which he listened made constant waves of expression break forth over his face from the corners of his nose and eyes and mouth. Little jets of wheezing laughter followed one another out of his convulsed body. His eyes, twinkling with cunning enjoyment, glanced at every moment towards his companion's face. Once or twice he rearranged the light waterproof which he had slung over one shoulder in toreador fashion. His breeches, his white rubber shoes and his jauntily slung waterproof expressed youth. But his figure fell into rotundity at the waist, his hair was scant and grey and his face, when the waves of expression had passed over it, had a ravaged look.

When he was quite sure that the narrative had ended he laughed noiselessly for fully half a minute. Then he said:

—Well! . . . That takes the biscuit!

His voice seemed winnowed of vigour; and to enforce his words he added with humour:

—That takes the solitary, unique, and, if I may so call it, *recherché* biscuit!

He became serious and silent when he had said this. His tongue was tired for he had been talking all the afternoon in a public-house in Dorset Street. Most people considered Lenehan a leech but, in spite of this reputation, his adroitness and eloquence had always prevented his friends from forming any general policy against him. He had a brave manner of coming up to a party of them in a bar and of holding himself nimbly at the borders of the company until he was included in a round. He was a sporting vagrant armed with a vast stock of stories, limericks and riddles. He was insensitive to all kinds of discourtesy. No one knew how he achieved the stern task of living, but his name was vaguely associated with racing tissues.

—And where did you pick her up, Corley? he asked.

Corley ran his tongue swiftly along his upper lip.

—One night, man, he said, I was going along Dame Street and I spotted a fine tart under Waterhouse's clock and said good-night, you know. So we went for a walk round by the canal and she told me she was a slavey in a house in Baggot Street. I put my arm round her and squeezed her a bit that night. Then next Sunday, man, I met her by appointment. We went out to Donnybrook and I brought her into a field there. She told me she used to go with a dairyman. . . . It was fine, man. Cigarettes every night she'd bring me and paying the tram out and back. And one night she brought me two bloody fine cigars—O, the real cheese, you know, that the old fellow used to smoke. . . . I was afraid, man, she'd get in the family way. But she's up to the dodge.

—Maybe she thinks you'll marry her, said Lenehan.

—I told her I was out of a job, said Corley. I told her I was in Pim's. She doesn't know my name. I was too hairy to tell her that. But she thinks I'm a bit of class, you know.

Lenehan laughed again, noiselessly.

—Of all the good ones ever I heard, he said, that emphatically takes the biscuit.

Corley's stride acknowledged the compliment. The swing of his burly body made his friend execute a few light skips from the path to the roadway and back again. Corley was the son of an inspector of police and he had inherited his father's frame and gait. He walked with his hands by his sides, holding himself erect and swaying his head from side to side. His head was large, globular and oily; it sweated in all weathers; and his large round hat, set upon it sideways, looked like a bulb which had grown out of another. He always stared straight before him as if he were on parade and, when he wished to gaze after someone in the street, it was necessary for him to move his body from the hips. At present he was about town. Whenever any job was vacant a friend was always ready to give him the hard word. He was often to be seen walking with policemen in plain clothes, talking earnestly. He knew the inner side of all affairs and was fond of delivering final judgments. He spoke without listening to the speech of his companions. His conversation was mainly about himself: what he had said to such a person and what such a person had said to him and what he had said to settle the matter. When he reported these dialogues he aspirated the first letter of his name after the manner of Florentines.

Lenehan offered his friend a cigarette. As the two young men walked on through the crowd Corley occasionally turned to smile at some of the passing girls but Lenehan's gaze was fixed on the large faint moon circled with a double halo. He watched earnestly the passing of the grey web of twilight across its face. At length he said:

—Well . . . tell me, Corley, I suppose you'll be able to pull it off all right, eh?

Corley closed one eye expressively as an answer.

—Is she game for that? asked Lenehan dubiously. You can never know women.

—She's all right, said Corley. I know the way to get around her, man. She's a bit gone on me.

—You're what I call a gay Lothario, said Lenehan. And the proper kind of a Lothario, too!

A shade of mockery relieved the servility of his manner. To save himself he had the habit of leaving his flattery open to the interpretation of raillery. But Corley had not a subtle mind.

—There's nothing to touch a good slavey, he affirmed. Take my tip for it.

—By one who has tried them all, said Lenehan.

—First I used to go with girls, you know, said Corley, unbosoming; girls off the South Circular. I used to take them out, man, on the tram somewhere and pay the tram or take them to a band or a play at the theatre or buy them chocolate and sweets or something that way. I used to spend money on them right enough, he added, in a convincing tone, as if he were conscious of being disbelieved.

But Lenehan could well believe it; he nodded gravely.

—I know that game, he said, and it's a mug's game.

—And damn the thing I ever got out of it, said Corley.

—Ditto here, said Lenehan.

—Only off of one of them, said Corley.

He moistened his upper lip by running his tongue along it. The recollection brightened his eyes. He too gazed at the pale disc of the moon, now nearly veiled, and seemed to meditate.

—She was . . . a bit of all right, he said regretfully.

He was silent again. Then he added:

—She's on the turf now. I saw her driving down Earl Street one night with two fellows with her on a car.

—I suppose that's your doing, said Lenehan.

—There was others at her before me, said Corley philosophically.

This time Lenehan was inclined to disbelieve. He shook his head to and fro and smiled.

—You know you can't kid me, Corley, he said.

—Honest to God! said Corley. Didn't she tell me herself?

Lenehan made a tragic gesture.

—Base betrayer! he said.

As they passed along the railings of Trinity College, Lenehan skipped out into the road and peered up at the clock.

—Twenty after, he said.

—Time enough, said Corley. She'll be there all right. I always let her wait a bit.

Lenehan laughed quietly.

—Ecod! Corley, you know how to take them, he said.

—I'm up to all their little tricks, Corley confessed.

—But tell me, said Lenehan again, are you sure you can bring it off all right? You know it's a ticklish job. They're damn close on that point. Eh? . . . What?

His bright, small eyes searched his companion's face for reassurance. Corley swung his head to and fro as if to toss aside an insistent insect, and his brows gathered.

—I'll pull it off, he said. Leave it to me, can't you?

Lenehan said no more. He did not wish to ruffle his friend's temper, to be sent to the devil and told that his advice was not wanted. A little tact was necessary. But Corley's brow was soon smooth again. His thoughts were running another way.

—She's a fine decent tart, he said, with appreciation; that's what she is.

They walked along Nassau Street and then turned into Kildare Street. Not far from the porch of the club a harpist stood in the roadway, playing to a little ring of listeners. He plucked at the wires heedlessly, glancing quickly from time to time at the face of each new-comer and from time to time, wearily also, at the sky. His harp too, heedless that her coverings had fallen about her knees, seemed weary alike of the eyes of strangers and of her master's hands. One hand played in the bass the melody of *Silent, O Moyle*, while the other hand careered in the treble after each group of notes. The notes of the air throbbed deep and full.

The two young men walked up the street without speaking, the mournful music following them. When they reached Stephen's Green they crossed the road. Here the noise of trams, the lights and the crowd released them from their silence.

—There she is! said Corley.

At the corner of Hume Street a young woman was standing. She wore a blue dress and a white sailor hat. She stood on the curbstone, swinging a sunshade in one hand. Lenehan grew lively.

—Let's have a squint at her, Corley, he said.

Corley glanced sideways at his friend and an unpleasant grin appeared on his face.

—Are you trying to get inside me? he asked.

—Damn it! said Lenehan boldly, I don't want an introduction. All I want is to have a look at her. I'm not going to eat her.

—O . . . A look at her? said Corley, more amiably. Well

. . . I'll tell you what. I'll go over and talk to her and you can pass by.

—Right! said Lenehan.

Corley had already thrown one leg over the chains when Lenehan called out:

—And after? Where will we meet?

—Half ten, answered Corley, bringing over his other leg.

—Where?

—Corner of Merrion Street. We'll be coming back.

—Work it all right now, said Lenehan in farewell.

Corley did not answer. He sauntered across the road swaying his head from side to side. His bulk, his easy pace and the solid sound of his boots had something of the conqueror in them. He approached the young woman and, without saluting, began at once to converse with her. She swung her sunshade more quickly and executed half turns on her heels. Once or twice when he spoke to her at close quarters she laughed and bent her head.

Lenehan observed them for a few minutes. Then he walked rapidly along beside the chains to some distance and crossed the road obliquely. As he approached Hume Street corner he found the air heavily scented and his eyes made a swift anxious scrutiny of the young woman's appearance. She had her Sunday finery on. Her blue serge skirt was held at the waist by a belt of black leather. The great silver buckle of her belt seemed to depress the centre of her body, catching the light stuff of her white blouse like a clip. She wore a short black jacket with mother-of-pearl buttons and a ragged black boa. The ends of her tulle collarette had been carefully disordered and a big bunch of red flowers was pinned in her bosom, stems upwards. Lenehan's eyes noted approvingly her stout short muscular body. Frank rude health glowed in her face, on her fat red cheeks and in her unabashed blue eyes.

Her features were blunt. She had broad nostrils, a straggling mouth which lay open in a contented leer, and two projecting front teeth. As he passed Lenehan took off his cap and, after about ten seconds, Corley returned a salute to the air. This he did by raising his hand vaguely and pensively changing the angle of position of his hat.

Lenehan walked as far as the Shelbourne Hotel where he halted and waited. After waiting for a little time he saw them coming towards him and, when they turned to the right, he followed them, stepping lightly in his white shoes, down one side of Merrion Square. As he walked on slowly, timing his pace to theirs, he watched Corley's head which turned at every moment towards the young woman's face like a big ball revolving on a pivot. He kept the pair in view until he had seen them climbing the stairs of the Donnybrook tram; then he turned about and went back the way he had come.

Now that he was alone his face looked older. His gaiety seemed to forsake him and, as he came by the railings of the Duke's Lawn, he allowed his hand to run along them. The air which the harpist had played began to control his movements. His softly padded feet played the melody while his fingers swept a scale of variations idly along the railings after each group of notes.

He walked listlessly round Stephen's Green and then down Grafton Street. Though his eyes took note of many elements of the crowd through which he passed they did so morosely. He found trivial all that was meant to charm him and did not answer the glances which invited him to be bold. He knew that he would have to speak a great deal, to invent and to amuse, and his brain and throat were too dry for such a task. The problem of how he could pass the hours till he met Corley again troubled him a little. He could think of no way of passing them but to keep on walking. He turned to the left when he came to the corner of Rutland Square and felt more at ease in the dark quiet street, the sombre look of which suited his mood. He paused at last before the window of a poor-looking shop over which the words *Refreshment Bar* were printed in white letters. On the glass of the window were two flying inscriptions: *Ginger Beer* and *Ginger Ale*. A cut ham was exposed on a great blue dish while near it on a plate lay a segment of very light plum-pudding. He eyed this food earnestly for some time and then, after glancing warily up and down the street, went into the shop quickly.

He was hungry for, except some biscuits which he had asked two grudging curates to bring him, he had eaten nothing since breakfast-time. He sat down at an uncovered wooden table opposite two work-girls and a mechanic. A slatternly girl waited on him.

—How much is a plate of peas? he asked.

—Three halfpence, sir, said the girl.

—Bring me a plate of peas, he said, and a bottle of ginger beer.

He spoke roughly in order to belie his air of gentility for his entry had been followed by a pause of talk. His face was heated. To appear natural he pushed his cap back on his head and planted his elbows on the table. The mechanic and the two work-girls examined him point by point before resuming their conversation in a subdued voice. The girl brought him a plate of hot grocer's peas, seasoned with pepper and vinegar, a fork and his ginger beer. He ate his food greedily and found it so good that he made a note of the shop mentally. When he had eaten all the peas he sipped his ginger beer and sat for some time thinking of Corley's adventure. In his imagination he beheld the pair of lovers walking along some dark road; he heard Corley's voice in deep energetic gallantries and saw again the leer of the young woman's mouth. This vision made him feel keenly his own poverty of purse and spirit. He was tired of knocking about, of pulling the devil by the tail, of shifts and intrigues. He would be thirty-one in November. Would he never get a good job? Would he never have a home of his own? He thought how pleasant it would be to have a warm fire to sit by and a good dinner to sit down to. He had walked the streets long enough with friends and with girls. He knew what those friends were worth: he knew the girls too. Experience had embittered his heart against the world. But all hope had not left him. He felt better after having eaten than he had felt before, less weary of his life, less vanquished in spirit. He might yet be able to settle down in some snug corner and live happily if he could only come across some good simple-minded girl with a little of the ready.

He paid twopence halfpenny to the slatternly girl and went out of the shop to begin his wandering again. He went into Capel Street and walked along towards the City Hall. Then he turned into Dame Street. At the corner of George's Street he met two friends of his and stopped to converse with them. He was glad that he could rest from all his walking. His friends asked him had he seen Corley and what was the latest. He replied that he had spent the day with Corley. His friends talked very little. They looked vacantly after some figures in the crowd and sometimes made a critical remark. One said that he had seen Mac an hour before in Westmoreland Street. At this Lenehan said that he had been with Mac the night before in Egan's. The young man who had seen Mac in Westmoreland Street asked was it true that Mac had won a bit over a billiard match. Lenehan did not know: he said that Holohan had stood them drinks in Egan's.

He left his friends at a quarter to ten and went up George's Street. He turned to the left at the City Markets and walked on into Grafton Street. The crowd of girls and young men had thinned and on his way up the street he heard many groups and couples bidding one another good-night. He went as far as the clock of the College of Surgeons: it was on the stroke of ten. He set off briskly along the northern side of the Green, hurrying for fear Corley should return too soon. When he reached the corner of Merrion Street he took his stand in the shadow of a lamp and brought out one of the cigarettes which he had reserved and lit it. He leaned against the lamp-post and kept his gaze fixed on the part from which he expected to see Corley and the young woman return.

His mind became active again. He wondered had Corley managed it successfully. He wondered if he had asked her yet or if he would leave it to the last. He suffered all the pangs and thrills of his friend's situation as well as those of his own. But the memory of Corley's slowly revolving head calmed him somewhat: he was sure Corley would pull it off all right. All at once the idea struck him that perhaps Corley had seen her home by another way and given him the slip. His eyes searched the street: there was no sign of them. Yet it was surely half-an-hour since he had seen the clock of the College of Surgeons. Would Corley do a thing like that? He lit his last cigarette and began to smoke it nervously. He strained his eyes as each tram stopped at the far corner of the square. They must have gone home by another way. The paper of his cigarette broke and he flung it into the road with a curse.

Suddenly he saw them coming towards him. He started with delight and, keeping close to his lamp-post, tried to read the result in their walk. They were walking quickly, the young woman taking quick short steps, while Corley kept beside her with his long stride. They did not seem to be speaking. An intimation of the result pricked him like the point of a sharp instrument. He knew Corley would fail; he knew it was no go.

They turned down Baggot Street and he followed them at once, taking the other footpath. When they stopped he stopped too. They talked for a few moments and then the young woman went down the steps into the area of a house. Corley remained standing at the edge of the path, a little distance from the front steps. Some minutes passed. Then the hall-door was opened slowly and cautiously. A woman came running down the front steps and coughed. Corley turned and went towards her. His broad figure hid hers from view for a few seconds and then she reappeared running up the steps. The door closed on her and Corley began to walk swiftly towards Stephen's Green.

Lenehan hurried on in the same direction. Some drops of light rain fell. He took them as a warning and, glancing back towards the house which the young woman had entered to see that he was not observed, he ran eagerly across the road. Anxiety and his swift run made him pant. He called out:

—Hallo, Corley!

Corley turned his head to see who had called him, and then continued walking as before. Lenehan ran after him, settling the waterproof on his shoulders with one hand.

—Hallo, Corley! he cried again.

He came level with his friend and looked keenly in his face. He could see nothing there.

—Well? he said. Did it come off?

They had reached the corner of Ely Place. Still without answering Corley swerved to the left and went up the side street. His features were composed in stern calm. Lenehan kept up with his friend, breathing uneasily. He was baffled and a note of menace pierced through his voice.

—Can't you tell us? he said. Did you try her?

Corley halted at the first lamp and stared grimly before him. Then with a grave gesture he extended a hand towards the light and, smiling, opened it slowly to the gaze of his disciple. A small gold coin shone in the palm.

THE BOARDING

HOUSE

Mrs Mooney was a butcher's daughter. She was a woman who was quite able to keep things to herself: a determined woman. She had married her father's foreman and opened a butcher's shop near Spring Gardens. But as soon as his father-in-law was dead Mr Mooney began to go to the devil. He drank, plundered the till, ran headlong into debt. It was no use making him take the pledge: he was sure to break out again a few days after. By fighting his wife in the presence of customers and by buying bad meat he ruined his business. One night he went for his wife with the cleaver and she had to sleep in a neighbour's house.

After that they lived apart. She went to the priest and got a separation from him with care of the children. She would give him neither money nor food nor house-room; and so he was obliged to enlist himself as a sheriff's man. He was a shabby stooped little drunkard with a white face and a white moustache and white eyebrows, pencilled above his little eyes, which were pink-veined and raw; and all day long he sat in the bailiff's room, waiting to be put on a job. Mrs Mooney, who had taken what remained of her money out of the butcher business and set up a boarding house in Hardwicke Street, was a big imposing woman. Her house had a floating population made up of tourists from Liverpool and the Isle of Man and, occasionally, *artistes* from the music halls. Its resident population was made up of clerks from the city. She governed her house cunningly and firmly, knew when to give credit, when to be stern and when to let things pass. All the resident young men spoke of her as *The Madam*.

Mrs Mooney's young men paid fifteen shillings a week for board and lodgings (beer or stout at dinner excluded). They shared in common tastes and occupations and for this reason they were very chummy with one another. They discussed with one another the chances of favourites and outsiders. Jack Mooney, the Madam's son, who was clerk to a commission agent in Fleet Street, had the reputation of being a hard case. He was fond of using soldiers' obscenities: usually he came home in the small hours. When he met his friends he had always a good one to tell them and he was always sure to be on to a good thing—that is to say, a likely horse or a likely *artiste*. He was also handy with the mits and sang comic songs. On Sunday nights there would often be a reunion in Mrs Mooney's front drawing-room. The music-hall *artistes* would oblige; and Sheridan played waltzes and polkas and vamped accompaniments. Polly Mooney, the Madam's daughter, would also sing. She sang:

> *I'm a . . . naughty girl.*
> *You needn't sham:*
> *You know I am.*

Polly was a slim girl of nineteen; she had light soft hair and a small full mouth. Her eyes, which were grey with a shade of green through them, had a habit of glancing upwards when she spoke with anyone, which made her look like a little perverse madonna. Mrs Mooney had first sent her daughter to be a typist in a corn-factor's office but, as a disreputable sheriff's man used to come every other day to the office, asking to be allowed to say a word to his daughter, she had taken her daughter home again and set her to do housework. As Polly was very lively the intention was to give her the run of the young men. Besides, young men like to feel that there is a young woman not very far away. Polly, of course, flirted with the young men but Mrs Mooney, who was a shrewd judge, knew that the young men were only passing the time away: none of them meant business. Things went on so for a long time and Mrs Mooney began to think of sending Polly back to typewriting when she noticed that something was going on between Polly and one of the young men. She watched the pair and kept her own counsel.

Polly knew that she was being watched, but still her mother's persistent silence could not be misunderstood. There had been no open complicity between mother and daughter, no open understanding but, though people in the house began to talk of the affair, still Mrs Mooney did not intervene. Polly began to grow a little strange in her manner and the young man was evidently perturbed. At last, when she judged it to be the right moment, Mrs Mooney intervened. She dealt with moral problems as a cleaver deals with meat: and in this case she had made up her mind.

It was a bright Sunday morning of early summer, promising heat, but with a fresh breeze blowing. All the windows of the boarding house were open and the lace curtains ballooned gently towards the street beneath the raised sashes. The belfry of George's Church sent out constant peals and worshippers, singly or in groups, traversed the little circus before the church, revealing their purpose by their self-contained demeanour no less than by the little volumes in their gloved hands. Breakfast was over in the boarding house and the table of the breakfast-room was covered with plates on which lay yellow streaks of eggs with morsels of bacon-fat and bacon-rind. Mrs Mooney sat in the straw arm-chair and watched the servant Mary remove the breakfast things. She made Mary collect the crusts and pieces of broken bread to help to make Tuesday's bread-pudding. When the table was cleared, the broken bread collected, the sugar and butter safe under lock and key, she began to reconstruct the interview which she had had the night before with Polly. Things were as she had suspected: she had been frank in her questions and Polly had been frank in her answers. Both had been somewhat awkward, of course. She had been made awkward by her not wishing to receive the news in too cavalier a fashion or to seem to have connived and Polly had been made awkward not merely because allusions of that kind always made her awkward but also because she did not wish it to be thought that in her wise innocence she had divined the intention behind her mother's tolerance.

Mrs Mooney glanced instinctively at the little gilt clock on the mantelpiece as soon as she had become aware through her revery that the bells of George's Church had stopped ringing. It was seventeen minutes past eleven: she would have lots of time to have the matter out with Mr Doran and then catch short twelve at Marlborough Street. She was sure she would win. To begin with she had all the weight of social opinion on her side: she was an outraged mother. She had allowed him to live beneath her roof, assuming that he was a man of honour, and he had simply abused her hospitality. He was thirty-four or thirty-five years of age, so that youth could not be pleaded as his excuse; nor could ignorance be his excuse since he was a man who had seen something of the world. He had simply taken advantage of Polly's youth and inexperience: that was evident. The question was: What reparation would he make?

There must be reparation made in such cases. It is all very well for the man: he can go his ways as if nothing had happened, having had his moment of pleasure, but the girl has to bear the brunt. Some mothers would be content to patch up such an affair for a sum of money; she had known cases of it. But she would not do so. For her only one reparation could make up for the loss of her daughter's honour: marriage.

She counted all her cards again before sending Mary up to Mr Doran's room to say that she wished to speak with him. She felt sure she would win. He was a serious young man, not rakish or loud-voiced like the others. If it had been Mr Sheridan or Mr Meade or Bantam Lyons her task would have been much harder. She did not think he would face publicity. All the lodgers in the house knew something of the affair; details had been invented by some. Besides, he had been employed for thirteen years in a great Catholic wine-merchant's office and publicity would mean for him, perhaps, the loss of his sit. Whereas if he agreed all might be well. She knew he had a good screw for one thing and she suspected he had a bit of stuff put by.

Nearly the half-hour! She stood up and surveyed herself in the pier-glass. The decisive expression of her great florid face satisfied her and she thought of some mothers she knew who could not get their daughters off their hands.

Mr Doran was very anxious indeed this Sunday morning. He had made two attempts to shave but his hand had been so unsteady that he had been obliged to desist. Three days' reddish beard fringed his jaws and every two or three minutes a mist gathered on his glasses so that he had to take them off and polish them with his pocket-handkerchief. The recollection of his confession of the night before was a cause of acute pain to him; the priest had drawn out every ridiculous detail of the affair and in the end had so magnified his sin that he was almost thankful at being afforded a loophole of reparation. The harm was done. What could he do now but marry her or run away? He could not brazen it out. The affair would be sure to be talked of and his employer would be certain to hear of it. Dublin is such a small city: everyone knows everyone else's business. He felt his heart leap warmly in his throat as he heard in his excited imagination old Mr Leonard calling out in his rasping voice: *Send Mr Doran here, please.*

All his long years of service gone for nothing! All his industry and diligence thrown away! As a young man he had sown his wild oats, of course; he had boasted of his free-thinking and denied the existence of God to his companions in publichouses. But that was all passed and done with . . . nearly. He still bought a copy of *Reynolds's Newspaper* every week but he attended to his religious duties and for nine-tenths of the year lived a regular life. He had money enough to settle down on; it was not that. But the family would look down on her. First of all there was her disreputable father and then her mother's boarding house was beginning to get a certain fame. He had a notion that he was being had. He could imagine his friends talking of the affair and laughing. She *was* a little vulgar; sometimes she said *I seen* and *If I had've known.* But what would grammar matter if he really loved her? He could not make up his mind whether to like her or despise her for what she had done. Of course, he had done it too. His instinct urged him to remain free, not to marry. Once you are married you are done for, it said.

While he was sitting helplessly on the side of the bed in shirt and trousers she tapped lightly at his door and entered. She told him all, that she had made a clean breast of it to her mother and that her mother would speak with him that morning. She cried and threw her arms round his neck, saying:

—O, Bob! Bob! What am I to do? What am I to do at all? She would put an end to herself, she said.

He comforted her feebly, telling her not to cry, that it would be all right, never fear. He felt against his shirt the agitation of her bosom.

It was not altogether his fault that it had happened. He remembered well, with the curious patient memory of the celibate, the first casual caresses her dress, her breath, her fingers had given him. Then late one night as he was undressing for bed she had tapped at his door, timidly. She wanted to relight her candle at his for hers had been blown out by a gust. It was her bath night. She wore a loose open combing-jacket of printed flannel. Her white instep shone in the opening of her furry slippers and the blood glowed warmly behind her perfumed skin. From her hands and wrists too as she lit and steadied her candle a faint perfume arose.

On nights when he came in very late it was she who warmed up his dinner. He scarcely knew what he was eating, feeling her beside him alone, at night, in the sleeping house. And her thoughtfulness! If the night was anyway cold or wet or windy there was sure to be a little tumbler of punch ready for him. Perhaps they could be happy together. . . .

They used to go upstairs together on tiptoe, each with a candle, and on the third landing exchange reluctant goodnights. They used to kiss. He remembered well her eyes, the touch of her hand and his delirium. . . .

But delirium passes. He echoed her phrase, applying it to himself: *What am I to do?* The instinct of the celibate warned him to hold back. But the sin was there; even his sense of honour told him that reparation must be made for such a sin.

While he was sitting with her on the side of the bed Mary came to the door and said that the missus wanted to see him in the parlour. He stood up to put on his coat and waistcoat, more helpless than ever. When he was dressed he went over to her to comfort her. It would be all right, never fear. He left her crying on the bed and moaning softly: *O my God!*

Going down the stairs his glasses became so dimmed with moisture that he had to take them off and polish them. He longed to ascend through the roof and fly away to another country where he would never hear again of his trouble, and yet a force pushed him downstairs step by step. The implacable faces of his employer and of the Madam stared upon his discomfiture. On the last flight of stairs he passed Jack Mooney who was coming up from the pantry nursing two bottles of *Bass*. They saluted coldly; and the lover's eyes rested for a second or two on a thick bulldog face and a pair of thick short arms. When he reached the foot of the staircase he glanced up and saw Jack regarding him from the door of the return-room.

Suddenly he remembered the night when one of the music-hall *artistes*, a little blond Londoner, had made a rather free allusion to Polly. The reunion had been almost broken up on account of Jack's violence. Everyone tried to quiet him. The music-hall *artiste*, a little paler than usual, kept smiling and saying that there was no harm meant: but Jack kept shouting at him that if any fellow tried that sort of a game on with *his* sister he'd bloody well put his teeth down his throat, so he would.

.   .   .   .

Polly sat for a little time on the side of the bed, crying. Then she dried her eyes and went over to the looking-glass. She dipped the end of the towel in the water-jug and refreshed her eyes with the cool water. She looked at herself in profile and readjusted a hairpin above her ear. Then she went back to the bed again and sat at the foot. She regarded the pillows for a long time and the sight of them awakened in her mind secret amiable memories. She rested the nape of her neck against the cool iron bed-rail and fell into a revery. There was no longer any perturbation visible on her face.

She waited on patiently, almost cheerfully, without alarm, her memories gradually giving place to hopes and visions of the future. Her hopes and visions were so intricate that she no longer saw the white pillows on which her gaze was fixed or remembered that she was waiting for anything.

At last she heard her mother calling. She started to her feet and ran to the banisters.

—Polly! Polly!

—Yes, mamma?

—Come down, dear. Mr Doran wants to speak to you.

Then she remembered what she had been waiting for.

A LITTLE CLOUD

Eɪɢʜᴛ years before he had seen his friend off at the North Wall and wished him godspeed. Gallaher had got on. You could tell that at once by his travelled air, his well-cut tweed suit and fearless accent. Few fellows had talents like his and fewer still could remain unspoiled by such success. Gallaher's heart was in the right place and he had deserved to win. It was something to have a friend like that.

Little Chandler's thoughts ever since lunch-time had been of his meeting with Gallaher, of Gallaher's invitation and of the great city London where Gallaher lived. He was called Little Chandler because, though he was but slightly under the average stature, he gave one the idea of being a little man. His hands were white and small, his frame was fragile, his voice was quiet and his manners were refined. He took the greatest care of his fair silken hair and moustache and used perfume discreetly on his handkerchief. The half-moons of his nails were perfect and when he smiled you caught a glimpse of a row of childish white teeth.

As he sat at his desk in the King's Inns he thought what changes those eight years had brought. The friend whom he had known under a shabby and necessitous guise had become a brilliant figure on the London Press. He turned often from his tiresome writing to gaze out of the office window. The glow of a late autumn sunset covered the grass plots and walks. It cast a shower of kindly golden dust on the untidy nurses and decrepit old men who drowsed on the benches; it flickered upon all the moving figures—on the children who ran screaming along the gravel paths and on everyone who passed through the gardens. He watched the scene and thought of life; and (as always happened when he thought of life) he became sad. A gentle melancholy took possession of him. He felt how useless it was to struggle against fortune, this being the burden of wisdom which the ages had bequeathed to him.

He remembered the books of poetry upon his shelves at home. He had bought them in his bachelor days and many an evening, as he sat in the little room off the hall, he had been tempted to take one down from the bookshelf and read out something to his wife. But shyness had always held him back; and so the books had remained on their shelves. At times he repeated lines to himself and this consoled him.

When his hour had struck he stood up and took leave of his desk and of his fellow-clerks punctiliously. He emerged from under the feudal arch of the King's Inns, a neat modest figure, and walked swiftly down Henrietta Street. The golden sunset was waning and the air had grown sharp. A horde of grimy children populated the street. They stood or ran in the roadway or crawled up the steps before the gaping doors or squatted like mice upon the thresholds. Little Chandler gave them no thought. He picked his way deftly through all that minute vermin-like life and under the shadow of the gaunt spectral mansions in which the old nobility of Dublin had roistered. No memory of the past touched him, for his mind was full of a present joy.

He had never been in Corless's but he knew the value of the name. He knew that people went there after the theatre to eat oysters and drink liqueurs; and he had heard that the waiters there spoke French and German. Walking swiftly by at night he had seen cabs drawn up before the door and richly dressed ladies, escorted by cavaliers, alight and enter quickly. They wore noisy dresses and many wraps. Their faces were powdered and they caught up their dresses, when they touched earth, like alarmed Atalantas. He had always passed without turning his head to look. It was his habit to walk swiftly in the street even by day and whenever he found himself in the city late at night he hurried on his way apprehensively and excitedly. Sometimes, however, he courted the causes of his fear. He chose the darkest and narrowest streets and, as he walked boldly forward, the silence that was spread about his footsteps troubled him, the wandering silent figures troubled him; and at times a sound of low fugitive laughter made him tremble like a leaf.

He turned to the right towards Capel Street. Ignatius Gallaher on the London Press! Who would have thought it possible eight years before? Still, now that he reviewed the past, Little Chandler could remember many signs of future greatness in his friend. People used to say that Ignatius Gallaher was wild. Of course, he did mix with a rakish set of fellows at that time, drank freely and borrowed money on all sides. In the end he had got mixed up in some shady affair, some money transaction: at least, that was one version of his flight. But nobody denied him talent. There was always a certain . . . something in Ignatius Gallaher that impressed you in spite of yourself. Even when he was out at elbows and at his wits' end for money he kept up a bold face. Little Chandler remembered (and the remembrance brought a slight flush of pride to his cheek) one of Ignatius Gallaher's sayings when he was in a tight corner:

—Half time, now, boys, he used to say light-heartedly. Where's my considering cap?

That was Ignatius Gallaher all out; and, damn it, you couldn't but admire him for it.

Little Chandler quickened his pace. For the first time in his life he felt himself superior to the people he passed. For the first time his soul revolted against the dull inelegance of Capel Street. There was no doubt about it: if you wanted to succeed you had to go away. You could do nothing in Dublin. As he crossed Grattan Bridge he looked down the river towards the lower quays and pitied the poor stunted houses. They seemed to him a band of tramps, huddled together along the river-banks, their old coats covered with dust and soot, stupefied by the panorama of sunset and waiting for the first chill of night to bid them arise, shake themselves and begone. He wondered whether he could write a poem to express his idea. Perhaps Gallaher might be able to get it into some London paper for him. Could he write something original? He was not sure what idea he wished to express but the thought that a poetic moment had touched him took life within him like an infant hope. He stepped onward bravely.

Every step brought him nearer to London, farther from his own sober inartistic life. A light began to tremble on the horizon of his mind. He was not so old—thirty-two. His temperament might be said to be just at the point of maturity. There were so many different moods and impressions that he wished to express in verse. He felt them within him. He tried to weigh his soul to see if it was a poet's soul. Melancholy was the dominant note of his temperament, he thought, but it was a melancholy tempered by recurrences of faith and resignation and simple joy. If he could give expression to it in a book of poems perhaps men would listen. He would never be popular: he saw that. He could not sway the crowd but he might appeal to a little circle of kindred minds. The English critics, perhaps, would recognise him as one of the Celtic school by reason of the melancholy tone of his poems; besides that, he would put in allusions. He began to invent sentences and phrases from the notices which his book would get. *Mr Chandler has the gift of easy and graceful verse. . . . A wistful sadness pervades these poems. . . . The Celtic note.* It was a pity his name was not more Irish-looking. Perhaps it would be better to insert his mother's name before the surname: Thomas Malone Chandler, or better still: T. Malone Chandler. He would speak to Gallaher about it.

He pursued his revery so ardently that he passed his street and had to turn back. As he came near Corless's his former agitation began to overmaster him and he halted before the door in indecision. Finally he opened the door and entered.

The light and noise of the bar held him at the doorway for a few moments. He looked about him, but his sight was confused by the shining of many red and green wine-glasses. The bar seemed to him to be full of people and he felt that the people were observing him curiously. He glanced quickly to right and left (frowning slightly to make his errand appear serious), but when his sight cleared a little he saw that nobody had turned to look at him: and there, sure enough, was Ignatius Gallaher leaning with his back against the counter and his feet planted far apart.

—Hallo, Tommy, old hero, here you are! What is it to be? What will you have? I'm taking whisky: better stuff than we get across the water. Soda? Lithia? No mineral? I'm the same. Spoils the flavour. . . . Here, *garçon*, bring us two halves of malt whisky, like a good fellow. . . . Well, and how have you been pulling along since I saw you last? Dear God, how old we're getting! Do you see any signs of aging in me—eh, what? A little grey and thin on the top—what?

Ignatius Gallaher took off his hat and displayed a large closely cropped head. His face was heavy, pale and clean-shaven. His eyes, which were of bluish slate-colour, relieved his unhealthy pallor and shone out plainly above the vivid orange tie he wore. Between these rival features the lips appeared very long and shapeless and colourless. He bent his head and felt with two sympathetic fingers the thin hair at the crown. Little Chandler shook his head as a denial. Ignatius Gallaher put on his hat again.

—It pulls you down, he said, Press life. Always hurry and scurry, looking for copy and sometimes not finding it: and then, always to have something new in your stuff. Damn proofs and printers, I say, for a few days. I'm deuced glad, I can tell you, to get back to the old country. Does a fellow good, a bit of a holiday. I feel a ton better since I landed again in dear dirty Dublin. . . . Here you are, Tommy. Water? Say when.

Little Chandler allowed his whisky to be very much diluted.

—You don't know what's good for you, my boy, said Ignatius Gallaher. I drink mine neat.

—I drink very little as a rule, said Little Chandler modestly. An odd half-one or so when I meet any of the old crowd: that's all.

—Ah, well, said Ignatius Gallaher, cheerfully, here's to us and to old times and old acquaintance.

They clinked glasses and drank the toast.

—I met some of the old gang to-day, said Ignatius Gallaher. O'Hara seems to be in a bad way. What's he doing?

—Nothing, said Little Chandler. He's gone to the dogs.

—But Hogan has a good sit, hasn't he?

—Yes; he's in the Land Commission.

—I met him one night in London and he seemed to be very flush. . . . Poor O'Hara! Boose, I suppose?

—Other things, too, said Little Chandler shortly.

Ignatius Gallaher laughed.

—Tommy, he said, I see you haven't changed an atom. You're the very same serious person that used to lecture me on Sunday mornings when I had a sore head and a fur on my tongue. You'd want to knock about a bit in the world. Have you never been anywhere, even for a trip?

—I've been to the Isle of Man, said Little Chandler.

Ignatius Gallaher laughed.

—The Isle of Man! he said. Go to London or Paris: Paris, for choice. That'd do you good.

—Have you seen Paris?

—I should think I have! I've knocked about there a little.

—And is it really so beautiful as they say? asked Little Chandler.

He sipped a little of his drink while Ignatius Gallaher finished his boldly.

—Beautiful? said Ignatius Gallaher, pausing on the word and on the flavour of his drink. It's not so beautiful, you know. Of course, it is beautiful. . . . But it's the life of Paris; that's the thing. Ah, there's no city like Paris for gaiety, movement, excitement. . . .

Little Chandler finished his whisky and, after some trouble, succeeded in catching the barman's eye. He ordered the same again.

—I've been to the Moulin Rouge, Ignatius Gallaher continued when the barman had removed their glasses, and I've been to all the Bohemian cafés. Hot stuff! Not for a pious chap like you, Tommy.

Little Chandler said nothing until the barman returned with the two glasses: then he touched his friend's glass lightly and reciprocated the former toast. He was beginning to feel somewhat disillusioned. Gallaher's accent and way of expressing himself did not please him. There was something vulgar in his friend which he had not observed before. But perhaps it was only the result of living in London amid the bustle and competition of the Press. The old personal charm was still there under this new gaudy manner. And, after all, Gallaher had lived, he had seen the world. Little Chandler looked at his friend enviously.

—Everything in Paris is gay, said Ignatius Gallaher. They believe in enjoying life—and don't you think they're right? If you want to enjoy yourself properly you must go to Paris. And, mind you, they've a great feeling for the Irish there. When they heard I was from Ireland they were ready to eat me, man.

Little Chandler took four or five sips from his glass.

—Tell me, he said, is it true that Paris is so . . . immoral as they say?

Ignatius Gallaher made a catholic gesture with his right arm.

—Every place is immoral, he said. Of course you do find spicy bits in Paris. Go to one of the students' balls, for instance. That's lively, if you like, when the *cocottes* begin to let themselves loose. You know what they are, I suppose?

—I've heard of them, said Little Chandler.

Ignatius Gallaher drank off his whisky and shook his head.

—Ah, he said, you may say what you like. There's no woman like the Parisienne—for style, for go.

—Then it is an immoral city, said Little Chandler, with timid insistence—I mean, compared with London or Dublin?

—London! said Ignatius Gallaher. It's six of one and half-a-dozen of the other. You ask Hogan, my boy. I showed him a bit about London when he was over there. He'd open your eye. . . . I say, Tommy, don't make punch of that whisky: liquor up.

—No, really. . . .

—O, come on, another one won't do you any harm. What is it? The same again, I suppose?

—Well . . . all right.

—*François*, the same again. . . . Will you smoke, Tommy?

Ignatius Gallaher produced his cigar-case. The two friends lit their cigars and puffed at them in silence until their drinks were served.

—I'll tell you my opinion, said Ignatius Gallaher, emerging after some time from the clouds of smoke in which he had taken refuge, it's a rum world. Talk of immorality! I've heard of cases—what am I saying?—I've known them: cases of . . . immorality. . . .

Ignatius Gallaher puffed thoughtfully at his cigar and then, in a calm historian's tone, he proceeded to sketch for his friend some pictures of the corruption which was rife abroad. He summarised the vices of many capitals and seemed inclined to award the palm to Berlin. Some things he could not vouch for (his friends had told him), but of others he had had personal experience. He spared neither rank nor caste. He revealed many of the secrets of religious houses on the Continent and described some of the practices which were fashionable in high society and ended by telling, with details, a story about an English duchess—a story which he knew to be true. Little Chandler was astonished.

—Ah, well, said Ignatius Gallaher, here we are in old jog-along Dublin where nothing is known of such things.

—How dull you must find it, said Little Chandler, after all the other places you've seen!

—Well, said Ignatius Gallaher, it's a relaxation to come over here, you know. And, after all, it's the old country, as they say, isn't it? You can't help having a certain feeling for it. That's human nature. . . . But tell me something about yourself. Hogan told me you had . . . tasted the joys of connubial bliss. Two years ago, wasn't it?

Little Chandler blushed and smiled.

—Yes, he said. I was married last May twelve months.

—I hope it's not too late in the day to offer my best wishes, said Ignatius Gallaher. I didn't know your address or I'd have done so at the time.

He extended his hand, which Little Chandler took.

—Well, Tommy, he said, I wish you and yours every joy in life, old chap, and tons of money, and may you never die till I shoot you. And that's the wish of a sincere friend, an old friend. You know that?

—I know that, said Little Chandler.

—Any youngsters? said Ignatius Gallaher.

Little Chandler blushed again.

—We have one child, he said.

—Son or daughter?

—A little boy.

Ignatius Gallaher slapped his friend sonorously on the back.

—Bravo, he said, I wouldn't doubt you, Tommy.

Little Chandler smiled, looked confusedly at his glass and bit his lower lip with three childishly white front teeth.

—I hope you'll spend an evening with us, he said, before you go back. My wife will be delighted to meet you. We can have a little music and—

—Thanks awfully, old chap, said Ignatius Gallaher, I'm sorry we didn't meet earlier. But I must leave to-morrow night.

—To-night, perhaps . . . ?

—I'm awfully sorry, old man. You see I'm over here with another fellow, clever young chap he is too, and we arranged to go to a little card-party. Only for that . . .

—O, in that case. . . .

—But who knows? said Ignatius Gallaher considerately. Next year I may take a little skip over here now that I've broken the ice. It's only a pleasure deferred.

—Very well, said Little Chandler, the next time you come

we must have an evening together. That's agreed now, isn't it?

—Yes, that's agreed, said Ignatius Gallaher. Next year if I come, *parole d'honneur*.

—And to clinch the bargain, said Little Chandler, we'll just have one more now.

Ignatius Gallaher took out a large gold watch and looked at it.

—Is it to be the last? he said. Because you know, I have an a.p.

—O, yes, positively, said Little Chandler.

—Very well, then, said Ignatius Gallaher, let us have another one as a *deoc an doruis*—that's good vernacular for a small whisky, I believe.

Little Chandler ordered the drinks. The blush which had risen to his face a few moments before was establishing itself. A trifle made him blush at any time: and now he felt warm and excited. Three small whiskies had gone to his head and Gallaher's strong cigar had confused his mind, for he was a delicate and abstinent person. The adventure of meeting Gallaher after eight years, of finding himself with Gallaher in Corless's surrounded by lights and noise, of listening to Gallaher's stories and of sharing for a brief space Gallaher's vagrant and triumphant life, upset the equipoise of his sensitive nature. He felt acutely the contrast between his own life and his friend's, and it seemed to him unjust. Gallaher was his inferior in birth and education. He was sure that he could do something better than his friend had ever done, or could ever do, something higher than mere tawdry journalism if he only got the chance. What was it that stood in his way? His unfortunate timidity! He wished to vindicate himself in some way, to assert his manhood. He saw behind Gallaher's refusal of his invitation. Gallaher was only patronising him by his friendliness just as he was patronising Ireland by his visit.

The barman brought their drinks. Little Chandler pushed one glass towards his friend and took up the other boldly.

—Who knows? he said, as they lifted their glasses. When you come next year I may have the pleasure of wishing long life and happiness to Mr and Mrs Ignatius Gallaher.

Ignatius Gallaher in the act of drinking closed one eye expressively over the rim of his glass. When he had drunk he smacked his lips decisively, set down his glass and said:

—No blooming fear of that, my boy. I'm going to have my fling first and see a bit of life and the world before I put my head in the sack—if I ever do.

—Some day you will, said Little Chandler calmly.

Ignatius Gallaher turned his orange tie and slate-blue eyes full upon his friend.

—You think so? he said.

—You'll put your head in the sack, repeated Little Chandler stoutly, like everyone else if you can find the girl.

He had slightly emphasised his tone and he was aware that he had betrayed himself; but, though the colour had heightened in his cheek, he did not flinch from his friend's gaze. Ignatius Gallaher watched him for a few moments and then said:

—If ever it occurs, you may bet your bottom dollar there'll be no mooning and spooning about it. I mean to marry money. She'll have a good fat account at the bank or she won't do for me.

Little Chandler shook his head.

—Why, man alive, said Ignatius Gallaher, vehemently, do you know what it is? I've only to say the word and to-morrow I can have the woman and the cash. You don't believe it? Well, I know it. There are hundreds—what am I saying?— thousands of rich Germans and Jews, rotten with money, that'd only be too glad. . . . You wait a while, my boy. See if I don't play my cards properly. When I go about a thing I mean business, I tell you. You just wait.

He tossed his glass to his mouth, finished his drink and

laughed loudly. Then he looked thoughtfully before him and said in a calmer tone:

—But I'm in no hurry. They can wait. I don't fancy tying myself up to one woman, you know.

He imitated with his mouth the act of tasting and made a wry face.

—Must get a bit stale, I should think, he said.

. . . .

Little Chandler sat in the room off the hall, holding a child in his arms. To save money they kept no servant but Annie's young sister Monica came for an hour or so in the morning and an hour or so in the evening to help. But Monica had gone home long ago. It was a quarter to nine. Little Chandler had come home late for tea and, moreover, he had forgotten to bring Annie home the parcel of coffee from Bewley's. Of course she was in a bad humour and gave him short answers. She said she would do without any tea but when it came near the time at which the shop at the corner closed she decided to go out herself for a quarter of a pound of tea and two pounds of sugar. She put the sleeping child deftly in his arms and said:

—Here. Don't waken him.

A little lamp with a white china shade stood upon the table and its light fell over a photograph which was enclosed in a frame of crumpled horn. It was Annie's photograph. Little Chandler looked at it, pausing at the thin tight lips. She wore the pale blue summer blouse which he had brought her home as a present one Saturday. It had cost him ten and elevenpence; but what an agony of nervousness it had cost him! How he had suffered that day, waiting at the shop door until the shop was empty, standing at the counter and trying to appear at his ease while the girl piled ladies' blouses before him, paying at the desk and forgetting to take up the odd penny of his change, being called back by the cashier, and, finally, striving to hide his blushes as he left the shop by examining the parcel to see if it was securely tied. When he brought the blouse home Annie kissed him and said it was very pretty and stylish; but when she heard the price she threw the blouse on the table and said it was a regular swindle to charge ten and elevenpence for that. At first she wanted to take it back but when she tried it on she was delighted with it, especially with the make of the sleeves, and kissed him and said he was very good to think of her.

Hm! . . .

He looked coldly into the eyes of the photograph and they answered coldly. Certainly they were pretty and the face itself was pretty. But he found something mean in it. Why was it so unconscious and lady-like? The composure of the eyes irritated him. They repelled him and defied him: there was no passion in them, no rapture. He thought of what Gallaher had said about rich Jewesses. Those dark Oriental eyes, he thought, how full they are of passion, of voluptuous longing! . . . Why had he married the eyes in the photograph?

He caught himself up at the question and glanced nervously round the room. He found something mean in the pretty furniture which he had bought for his house on the hire system. Annie had chosen it herself and it reminded him of her. It too was prim and pretty. A dull resentment against his life awoke within him. Could he not escape from his little house? Was it too late for him to try to live bravely like Gallaher? Could he go to London? There was the furniture still to be paid for. If he could only write a book and get it published, that might open the way for him.

A volume of Byron's poems lay before him on the table. He opened it cautiously with his left hand lest he should waken the child and began to read the first poem in the book:

> Hushed are the winds and still the evening gloom,
> Not e'en a Zephyr wanders through the grove,
> Whilst I return to view my Margaret's tomb
> And scatter flowers on the dust I love.

He paused. He felt the rhythm of the verse about him in the room. How melancholy it was! Could he, too, write like that, express the melancholy of his soul in verse? There were so many things he wanted to describe: his sensation of a few hours before on Grattan Bridge, for example. If he could get back again into that mood. . . .

The child awoke and began to cry. He turned from the page and tried to hush it: but it would not be hushed. He began to rock it to and fro in his arms but its wailing cry grew keener. He rocked it faster while his eyes began to read the second stanza:

> *Within this narrow cell reclines her clay,*
> *That clay where once . . .*

It was useless. He couldn't read. He couldn't do anything. The wailing of the child pierced the drum of his ear. It was useless, useless! He was a prisoner for life. His arms trembled with anger and suddenly bending to the child's face he shouted:

—Stop!

The child stopped for an instant, had a spasm of fright and began to scream. He jumped up from his chair and walked hastily up and down the room with the child in his arms. It began to sob piteously, losing its breath for four or five seconds, and then bursting out anew. The thin walls of the room echoed the sound. He tried to soothe it but it sobbed more convulsively. He looked at the contracted and quivering face of the child and began to be alarmed. He counted seven sobs without a break between them and caught the child to his breast in fright. If it died! . . .

The door was burst open and a young woman ran in, panting.

—What is it? What is it? she cried.

The child, hearing its mother's voice, broke out into a paroxysm of sobbing.

—It's nothing, Annie . . . it's nothing. . . . He began to cry . . .

She flung her parcels on the floor and snatched the child from him.

—What have you done to him? she cried, glaring into his face.

Little Chandler sustained for one moment the gaze of her eyes and his heart closed together as he met the hatred in them. He began to stammer:

—It's nothing. . . . He . . . he began to cry. . . . I couldn't . . . I didn't do anything. . . . What?

Giving no heed to him she began to walk up and down the room, clasping the child tightly in her arms and murmuring:

—My little man! My little mannie! Was 'ou frightened, love? . . . There now, love! There now! . . . Lambabaun! Mamma's little lamb of the world! . . . There now!

Little Chandler felt his cheeks suffused with shame and he stood back out of the lamplight. He listened while the paroxysm of the child's sobbing grew less and less; and tears of remorse started to his eyes.

COUNTERPARTS

THE bell rang furiously and, when Miss Parker went to the tube, a furious voice called out in a piercing North of Ireland accent:

—Send Farrington here!

Miss Parker returned to her machine, saying to a man who was writing at a desk:

—Mr Alleyne wants you upstairs.

The man muttered *Blast him!* under his breath and pushed back his chair to stand up. When he stood up he was tall and of great bulk. He had a hanging face, dark wine-coloured, with fair eyebrows and moustache: his eyes bulged forward slightly and the whites of them were dirty. He lifted up the counter and, passing by the clients, went out of the office with a heavy step.

He went heavily upstairs until he came to the second landing, where a door bore a brass plate with the inscription *Mr Alleyne*. Here he halted, puffing with labour and vexation, and knocked. The shrill voice cried:

—Come in!

The man entered Mr Alleyne's room. Simultaneously Mr Alleyne, a little man wearing gold-rimmed glasses on a clean-shaven face, shot his head up over a pile of documents. The head itself was so pink and hairless that it seemed like a large egg reposing on the papers. Mr Alleyne did not lose a moment:

—Farrington? What is the meaning of this? Why have I always to complain of you? May I ask you why you haven't made a copy of that contract between Bodley and Kirwan? I told you it must be ready by four o'clock.

—But Mr Shelley said, sir—

—*Mr Shelley said, sir.* . . . Kindly attend to what I say and not to what *Mr Shelley says, sir.* You have always some excuse or another for shirking work. Let me tell you that if the contract is not copied before this evening I'll lay the matter before Mr Crosbie. . . . Do you hear me now?

—Yes, sir.

—Do you hear me now? . . . Ay and another little matter! I might as well be talking to the wall as talking to you. Understand once for all that you get a half an hour for your lunch and not an hour and a half. How many courses do you want, I'd like to know. . . . Do you mind me, now?

—Yes, sir.

Mr Alleyne bent his head again upon his pile of papers. The man stared fixedly at the polished skull which directed the affairs of Crosbie & Alleyne, gauging its fragility. A spasm of rage gripped his throat for a few moments and then passed, leaving after it a sharp sensation of thirst. The man recognised the sensation and felt that he must have a good night's drinking. The middle of the month was passed and, if he could get the copy done in time, Mr Alleyne might give him an order on the cashier. He stood still, gazing fixedly at the head upon the pile of papers. Suddenly Mr Alleyne began to upset all the papers, searching for something. Then, as if he had been unaware of the man's presence till that moment, he shot up his head again, saying:

—Eh? Are you going to stand there all day? Upon my word, Farrington, you take things easy!

—I was waiting to see . . .

—Very good, you needn't wait to see. Go downstairs and do your work.

The man walked heavily towards the door and, as he went out of the room, he heard Mr Alleyne cry after him that if the contract was not copied by evening Mr Crosbie would hear of the matter.

He returned to his desk in the lower office and counted the sheets which remained to be copied. He took up his pen and dipped it in the ink but he continued to stare stupidly at the last words he had written: *In no case shall the said Bernard Bodley be* . . . The evening was falling and in a few minutes they would be lighting the gas: then he could write. He felt that he must slake the thirst in his throat. He stood up from his desk and, lifting the counter as before, passed out of the office. As he was passing out the chief clerk looked at him inquiringly.

—It's all right, Mr Shelley, said the man, pointing with his finger to indicate the objective of his journey.

The chief clerk glanced at the hat-rack but, seeing the row complete, offered no remark. As soon as he was on the landing the man pulled a shepherd's plaid cap out of his pocket, put it on his head and ran quickly down the rickety stairs. From the street door he walked on furtively on the inner side of the path towards the corner and all at once dived into a doorway. He was now safe in the dark snug of O'Neill's shop, and, filling up the little window that looked into the bar with his inflamed face, the colour of dark wine or dark meat, he called out:

—Here, Pat, give us a g.p., like a good fellow.

The curate brought him a glass of plain porter. The man drank it at a gulp and asked for a caraway seed. He put his penny on the counter and, leaving the curate to grope for it in the gloom, retreated out of the snug as furtively as he had entered it.

Darkness, accompanied by a thick fog, was gaining upon the dusk of February and the lamps in Eustace Street had been lit. The man went up by the houses until he reached the door of the office, wondering whether he could finish his copy in time. On the stairs a moist pungent odour of perfumes saluted his nose: evidently Miss Delacour had come while he was out in O'Neill's. He crammed his cap back again into his pocket and re-entered the office, assuming an air of absent-mindedness.

—Mr Alleyne has been calling for you, said the chief clerk severely. Where were you?

The man glanced at the two clients who were standing at the counter as if to intimate that their presence prevented him from answering. As the clients were both male the chief clerk allowed himself a laugh.

—I know that game, he said. Five times in one day is a little bit. . . . Well, you better look sharp and get a copy of our correspondence in the Delacour case for Mr Alleyne.

This address in the presence of the public, his run upstairs and the porter he had gulped down so hastily confused the man and, as he sat down at his desk to get what was required, he realised how hopeless was the task of finishing his copy of the contract before half past five. The dark damp night was coming and he longed to spend it in the bars, drinking with his friends amid the glare of gas and the clatter of glasses. He got out the Delacour correspondence and passed out of the office. He hoped Mr Alleyne would not discover that the last two letters were missing.

The moist pungent perfume lay all the way up to Mr Alleyne's room. Miss Delacour was a middle-aged woman of Jewish appearance. Mr Alleyne was said to be sweet on her or on her money. She came to the office often and stayed a long time when she came. She was sitting beside his desk now in an aroma of perfumes, smoothing the handle of her umbrella and nodding the great black feather in her hat. Mr Alleyne had swivelled his chair round to face her and thrown his right foot jauntily upon his left knee. The man put the correspondence on the desk and bowed respectfully but neither Mr Alleyne nor Miss Delacour took any notice of his bow. Mr Alleyne tapped a finger on the correspondence and then flicked it towards him as if to say: *That's all right: you can go.*

The man returned to the lower office and sat down again at his desk. He stared intently at the incomplete phrase: *In no case shall the said Bernard Bodley be . . .* and thought how strange it was that the last three words began with the same letter. The chief clerk began to hurry Miss Parker, saying she would never have the letters typed in time for post. The man listened to the clicking of the machine for a few minutes and then set to work to finish his copy. But his head was not clear and his mind wandered away to the glare and rattle of the public-house. It was a night for hot punches. He struggled on with his copy, but when the clock struck five he had still fourteen pages to write. Blast it! He couldn't finish it in time. He longed to execrate aloud, to bring his fist down on something violently. He was so enraged that he wrote *Bernard Bernard* instead of *Bernard Bodley* and had to begin again on a clean sheet.

He felt strong enough to clear out the whole office single-handed. His body ached to do something, to rush out and revel in violence. All the indignities of his life enraged him. . . . Could he ask the cashier privately for an advance? No, the cashier was no good, no damn good: he wouldn't give an advance. . . . He knew where he would meet the boys: Leonard and O'Halloran and Nosey Flynn. The barometer of his emotional nature was set for a spell of riot.

His imagination had so abstracted him that his name was called twice before he answered. Mr Alleyne and Miss Delacour were standing outside the counter and all the clerks had turned round in anticipation of something. The man got up from his desk. Mr Alleyne began a tirade of abuse, saying that two letters were missing. The man answered that he knew nothing about them, that he had made a faithful copy. The tirade continued: it was so bitter and violent that the man could hardly restrain his fist from descending upon the head of the manikin before him.

—I know nothing about any other two letters, he said stupidly.

—*You—know—nothing.* Of course you know nothing, said Mr Alleyne. Tell me, he added, glancing first for approval to the lady beside him, do you take me for a fool? Do you think me an utter fool?

The man glanced from the lady's face to the little egg-shaped head and back again; and, almost before he was aware of it, his tongue had found a felicitous moment:

—I don't think, sir, he said, that that's a fair question to put to me.

There was a pause in the very breathing of the clerks. Everyone was astounded (the author of the witticism no less than his neighbours) and Miss Delacour, who was a stout amiable person, began to smile broadly. Mr Alleyne flushed to the hue of a wild rose and his mouth twitched with a dwarf's passion. He shook his fist in the man's face till it seemed to vibrate like the knob of some electric machine:

—You impertinent ruffian! You impertinent ruffian! I'll make short work of you! Wait till you see! You'll apologise to me

for your impertinence or you'll quit the office instanter! You'll
quit this, I'm telling you, or you'll apologise to me!

.   .   .   .

He stood in a doorway opposite the office watching to see
if the cashier would come out alone. All the clerks passed
out and finally the cashier came out with the chief clerk. It
was no use trying to say a word to him when he was with the
chief clerk. The man felt that his position was bad enough.
He had been obliged to offer an abject apology to Mr Alleyne
for his impertinence but he knew what a hornet's nest the office would be for him. He could remember the way in
which Mr Alleyne had hounded little Peake out of the office in
order to make room for his own nephew. He felt savage and
thirsty and revengeful, annoyed with himself and with everyone else. Mr Alleyne would never give him an hour's rest; his
life would be a hell to him. He had made a proper fool of himself this time. Could he not keep his tongue in his cheek? But
they had never pulled together from the first, he and Mr Alleyne, ever since the day Mr Alleyne had overheard him mim-
icking his North of Ireland accent to amuse Higgins and Miss
Parker: that had been the beginning of it. He might have tried
Higgins for the money, but sure Higgins never had anything
for himself. A man with two establishments to keep up, of
course he couldn't. . . .

He felt his great body again aching for the comfort of the
public-house. The fog had begun to chill him and he wondered could he touch Pat in O'Neill's. He could not touch him
for more than a bob—and a bob was no use. Yet he must get
money somewhere or other: he had spent his last penny for the
g.p. and soon it would be too late for getting money anywhere. Suddenly, as he was fingering his watch-chain, he
thought of Terry Kelly's pawn-office in Fleet Street. That was
the dart! Why didn't he think of it sooner?

He went through the narrow alley of Temple Bar quickly,

muttering to himself that they could all go to hell because he was going to have a good night of it. The clerk in Terry Kelly's said *A crown!* but the consignor held out for six shillings; and in the end the six shillings was allowed him literally. He came out of the pawn-office joyfully, making a little cylinder of the coins between his thumb and fingers. In Westmoreland Street the footpaths were crowded with young men and women returning from business and ragged urchins ran here and there yelling out the names of the evening editions. The man passed through the crowd, looking on the spectacle generally with proud satisfaction and staring masterfully at the office-girls. His head was full of the noises of tram-gongs and swishing trolleys and his nose already sniffed the curling fumes of punch. As he walked on he preconsidered the terms in which he would narrate the incident to the boys:

—So, I just looked at him—coolly, you know, and looked at her. Then I looked back at him again—taking my time, you know. *I don't think that that's a fair question to put to me*, says I.

Nosey Flynn was sitting up in his usual corner of Davy Byrne's and, when he heard the story, he stood Farrington a half-one, saying it was as smart a thing as ever he heard. Farrington stood a drink in his turn. After a while O'Halloran and Paddy Leonard came in and the story was repeated to them. O'Halloran stood tailors of malt, hot, all round and told the story of the retort he had made to the chief clerk when he was in Callan's of Fownes's Street; but, as the retort was after the manner of the liberal shepherds in the eclogues, he had to admit that it was not so clever as Farrington's retort. At this Farrington told the boys to polish off that and have another.

Just as they were naming their poisons who should come in but Higgins! Of course he had to join in with the others. The men asked him to give his version of it, and he did so with great vivacity for the sight of five small hot whiskies was very exhilarating. Everyone roared laughing when he showed the way in which Mr Alleyne shook his fist in Farrington's face. Then he imitated Farrington, saying, *And here was my nabs, as cool as you please*, while Farrington looked at the company out of his heavy dirty eyes, smiling and at times drawing forth stray drops of liquor from his moustache with the aid of his lower lip.

When that round was over there was a pause. O'Halloran had money but neither of the other two seemed to have any; so the whole party left the shop somewhat regretfully. At the corner of Duke Street Higgins and Nosey Flynn bevelled off to the left while the other three turned back towards the city. Rain was drizzling down on the cold streets and, when they reached the Ballast Office, Farrington suggested the Scotch House. The bar was full of men and loud with the noise of tongues and glasses. The three men pushed past the whining match-sellers at the door and formed a little party at the corner of the counter. They began to exchange stories. Leonard introduced them to a young fellow named Weathers who was performing at the Tivoli as an acrobat and knockabout *artiste*. Farrington stood a drink all round. Weathers said he would take a small Irish and Apollinaris. Farrington, who had definite notions of what was what, asked the boys would they have an Apollinaris too; but the boys told Tim to make theirs hot. The talk became theatrical. O'Halloran stood a round and then Farrington stood another round, Weathers protesting that the hospitality was too Irish. He promised to get them in behind the scenes and introduce them to some nice girls. O'Halloran said that he and Leonard would go but that Farrington wouldn't go because he was a married man; and Farrington's heavy dirty eyes leered at the company in token that he understood he was being chaffed. Weathers made them all have just one little tincture at his expense and promised to meet them later on at Mulligan's in Poolbeg Street.

When the Scotch House closed they went round to Mulligan's. They went into the parlour at the back and O'Halloran ordered small hot specials all round. They were all beginning to feel mellow. Farrington was just standing another round when Weathers came back. Much to Farrington's relief he drank a glass of bitter this time. Funds were running low but they had enough to keep them going. Presently two young women with big hats and a young man in a check suit came in and sat at a table close by. Weathers saluted them and told the company that they were out of the Tivoli. Farrington's eyes wandered at every moment in the direction of one of the young women. There was something striking in her appearance. An immense scarf of peacock-blue muslin was wound round her hat and knotted in a great bow under her chin; and she wore bright yellow gloves, reaching to the elbow. Farrington gazed admiringly at the plump arm which she moved very often and with much grace; and when, after a little time, she answered his gaze he admired still more her large dark brown eyes. The oblique staring expression in them fascinated him. She glanced at him once or twice and, when the party was leaving the room, she brushed against his chair and said *O, pardon!* in a London accent. He watched her leave the room in the hope that she would look back at him, but he was disappointed. He cursed his want of money and cursed all the rounds he had stood, particularly all the whiskies and Apollinaris which he had stood to Weathers. If there was one thing that he hated it was a sponge. He was so angry that he lost count of the conversation of his friends.

When Paddy Leonard called him he found that they were talking about feats of strength. Weathers was showing his biceps muscle to the company and boasting so much that the other two had called on Farrington to uphold the national honour. Farrington pulled up his sleeve accordingly and showed his biceps muscle to the company. The two arms were examined and compared and finally it was agreed to have a trial of strength. The table was cleared and the two men rested their elbows on it, clasping hands. When Paddy Leonard said *Go!* each was to try to bring down the other's hand on to the table. Farrington looked very serious and determined.

The trial began. After about thirty seconds Weathers brought his opponent's hand slowly down on to the table. Farrington's dark wine-coloured face flushed darker still with anger and humiliation at having been defeated by such a stripling.

—You're not to put the weight of your body behind it. Play fair, he said.

—Who's not playing fair? said the other.

—Come on again. The two best out of three.

The trial began again. The veins stood out on Farrington's forehead, and the pallor of Weathers' complexion changed to peony. Their hands and arms trembled under the stress. After a long struggle Weathers again brought his opponent's hand slowly on to the table. There was a murmur of applause from the spectators. The curate, who was standing beside the table, nodded his red head towards the victor and said with loutish familiarity:

—Ah! that's the knack!

—What the hell do you know about it? said Farrington fiercely, turning on the man. What do you put in your gab for?

—Sh, sh! said O'Halloran, observing the violent expression of Farrington's face. Pony up, boys. We'll have just one little smahan more and then we'll be off.

A very sullen-faced man stood at the corner of O'Connell Bridge waiting for the little Sandymount tram to take him home. He was full of smouldering anger and revengefulness. He felt humiliated and discontented; he did not even feel drunk; and he had only twopence in his pocket. He cursed everything. He had done for himself in the office, pawned his watch, spent all his money; and he had not even got drunk. He began to feel thirsty again and he longed to be back again in the hot reeking public-house. He had lost his reputation as a strong man, having been defeated twice by a mere boy. His heart swelled with fury and, when he thought of the woman in the big hat who had brushed against him and said *Pardon!* his fury nearly choked him.

His tram let him down at Shelbourne Road and he steered his great body along in the shadow of the wall of the barracks. He loathed returning to his home. When he went in by the side-door he found the kitchen empty and the kitchen fire nearly out. He bawled upstairs:

—Ada! Ada!

His wife was a little sharp-faced woman who bullied her husband when he was sober and was bullied by him when he was drunk. They had five children. A little boy came running down the stairs.

—Who is that? said the man, peering through the darkness.

—Me, pa.

—Who are you? Charlie?

—No, pa. Tom.

—Where's your mother?

—She's out at the chapel.

—That's right. . . . Did she think of leaving any dinner for me?

—Yes, pa. I—

—Light the lamp. What do you mean by having the place in darkness? Are the other children in bed?

The man sat down heavily on one of the chairs while the little boy lit the lamp. He began to mimic his son's flat accent, saying half to himself: *At the chapel. At the chapel, if you please!* When the lamp was lit he banged his fist on the table and shouted:

—What's for my dinner?

—I'm going . . . to cook it, pa, said the little boy.

The man jumped up furiously and pointed to the fire.

—On that fire! You let the fire out! By God, I'll teach you to do that again!

He took a step to the door and seized the walking-stick which was standing behind it.

—I'll teach you to let the fire out! he said, rolling up his sleeve in order to give his arm free play.

The little boy cried *O, pa!* and ran whimpering round the table, but the man followed him and caught him by the coat. The little boy looked about him wildly but, seeing no way of escape, fell upon his knees.

—Now, you'll let the fire out the next time! said the man, striking at him viciously with the stick. Take that, you little whelp!

The boy uttered a squeal of pain as the stick cut his thigh. He clasped his hands together in the air and his voice shook with fright.

—O, pa! he cried. Don't beat me, pa! And I'll . . . I'll say a *Hail Mary* for you. . . . I'll say a *Hail Mary* for you, pa, if you don't beat me. . . . I'll say a *Hail Mary*. . . .

CLAY

THE matron had given her leave to go out as soon as the women's tea was over and Maria looked forward to her evening out. The kitchen was spick and span: the cook said you could see yourself in the big copper boilers. The fire was nice and bright and on one of the side-tables were four very big barmbracks. These barmbracks seemed uncut; but if you went closer you would see that they had been cut into long thick even slices and were ready to be handed round at tea. Maria had cut them herself.

Maria was a very, very small person indeed but she had a very long nose and a very long chin. She talked a little through her nose, always soothingly: *Yes, my dear*, and *No, my dear*. She was always sent for when the women quarrelled over their tubs and always succeeded in making peace. One day the matron had said to her:

—Maria, you are a veritable peace-maker!

And the sub-matron and two of the Board ladies had heard the compliment. And Ginger Mooney was always saying what she wouldn't do to the dummy who had charge of the irons if it wasn't for Maria. Everyone was so fond of Maria.

The women would have their tea at six o'clock and she would be able to get away before seven. From Ballsbridge to the Pillar, twenty minutes; from the Pillar to Drumcondra, twenty minutes; and twenty minutes to buy the things. She would be there before eight. She took out her purse with the silver clasps and read again the words *A Present from Belfast*. She was very fond of that purse because Joe had brought it to her five years before when he and Alphy had gone to Belfast on a Whit-Monday trip. In the purse were two half-crowns and some coppers. She would have five shillings clear after paying tram fare. What a nice evening they would have, all the children singing! Only she hoped that Joe wouldn't come in drunk. He was so different when he took any drink.

Often he had wanted her to go and live with them; but she would have felt herself in the way (though Joe's wife was ever so nice with her) and she had become accustomed to the life of the laundry. Joe was a good fellow. She had nursed him and Alphy too; and Joe used often say:

—Mamma is mamma but Maria is my proper mother.

After the break-up at home the boys had got her that position in the *Dublin by Lamplight* laundry, and she liked it. She used to have such a bad opinion of Protestants but now she thought they were very nice people, a little quiet and serious, but still very nice people to live with. Then she had her plants in the conservatory and she liked looking after them. She had lovely ferns and wax-plants and, whenever anyone came to visit her, she always gave the visitor one or two slips from her conservatory. There was one thing she didn't like and that was the tracts on the walls; but the matron was such a nice person to deal with, so genteel.

When the cook told her everything was ready she went into the women's room and began to pull the big bell. In a few minutes the women began to come in by twos and threes, wiping their steaming hands in their petticoats and pulling down the sleeves of their blouses over their red steaming arms. They settled down before their huge mugs which the cook and the dummy filled up with hot tea, already mixed with milk and sugar in huge tin cans. Maria superintended the distribution of the barmbrack and saw that every woman got her four slices. There was a great deal of laughing and joking during the meal. Lizzie Fleming said Maria was sure to get the ring and, though Fleming had said that for so many Hallow Eves, Maria had to laugh and say she didn't want any ring or man either; and when she laughed her grey-green eyes sparkled with disappointed shyness and the tip of her nose nearly met the tip of her chin. Then Ginger Mooney lifted up her mug of tea and proposed Maria's health while all the other women clattered with their mugs on the table, and said she was sorry she hadn't a sup of porter to drink it in. And Maria laughed again till the tip of her nose nearly met the tip of her chin and till her minute body nearly shook itself asunder because she knew that Mooney meant well though, of course, she had the notions of a common woman.

But wasn't Maria glad when the women had finished their tea and the cook and the dummy had begun to clear away the tea-things! She went into her little bedroom and, remembering that the next morning was a mass morning, changed the hand of the alarm from seven to six. Then she took off her working skirt and her house-boots and laid her best skirt out on the bed and her tiny dress-boots beside the foot of the bed. She changed her blouse too and, as she stood before the mirror, she thought of how she used to dress for mass on Sunday morning when she was a young girl; and she looked with quaint affection at the diminutive body which she had so often adorned. In spite of its years she found it a nice tidy little body.

When she got outside the streets were shining with rain and

she was glad of her old brown raincloak. The tram was full and she had to sit on the little stool at the end of the car, facing all the people, with her toes barely touching the floor. She arranged in her mind all she was going to do and thought how much better it was to be independent and to have your own money in your pocket. She hoped they would have a nice evening. She was sure they would but she could not help thinking what a pity it was Alphy and Joe were not speaking. They were always falling out now but when they were boys together they used to be the best of friends: but such was life.

She got out of her tram at the Pillar and ferreted her way quickly among the crowds. She went into Downes's cakeshop but the shop was so full of people that it was a long time before she could get herself attended to. She bought a dozen of mixed penny cakes, and at last came out of the shop laden with a big bag. Then she thought what else would she buy: she wanted to buy something really nice. They would be sure to have plenty of apples and nuts. It was hard to know what to buy and all she could think of was cake. She decided to buy some plumcake but Downes's plumcake had not enough almond icing on top of it so she went over to a shop in Henry Street. Here she was a long time in suiting herself and the stylish young lady behind the counter, who was evidently a little annoyed by her, asked her was it wedding-cake she wanted to buy. That made Maria blush and smile at the young lady; but the young lady took it all very seriously and finally cut a thick slice of plumcake, parcelled it up and said:

—Two-and-four, please.

She thought she would have to stand in the Drumcondra tram because none of the young men seemed to notice her but an elderly gentleman made room for her. He was a stout gentleman and he wore a brown hard hat; he had a square red face and a greyish moustache. Maria thought he was a colonel-looking gentleman and she reflected how much more polite he was than the young men who simply stared straight before them. The gentleman began to chat with her about Hallow Eve and the rainy weather. He supposed the bag was full of good things for the little ones and said it was only right that the youngsters should enjoy themselves while they were young. Maria agreed with him and favoured him with demure nods and hems. He was very nice with her, and when she was getting out at the Canal Bridge she thanked him and bowed, and he bowed to her and raised his hat and smiled agreeably; and while she was going up along the terrace, bending her tiny head under the rain, she thought how easy it was to know a gentleman even when he has a drop taken.

Everybody said: *O, here's Maria!* when she came to Joe's house. Joe was there, having come home from business, and all the children had their Sunday dresses on. There were two big girls in from next door and games were going on. Maria gave the bag of cakes to the eldest boy, Alphy, to divide and Mrs Donnelly said it was too good of her to bring such a big bag of cakes and made all the children say:

—Thanks, Maria.

But Maria said she had brought something special for papa and mamma, something they would be sure to like, and she began to look for her plumcake. She tried in Downes's bag and then in the pockets of her raincloak and then on the hall-stand but nowhere could she find it. Then she asked all the children had any of them eaten it—by mistake, of course—but the children all said no and looked as if they did not like to eat cakes if they were to be accused of stealing. Everybody had a solution for the mystery and Mrs Donnelly said it was plain that Maria had left it behind her in the tram. Maria, remembering how confused the gentleman with the greyish moustache had made her, coloured with shame and vexation and disappointment. At the thought of the failure of her little surprise and of the two and fourpence she had thrown away for nothing she nearly cried outright.

But Joe said it didn't matter and made her sit down by the fire. He was very nice with her. He told her all that went on in his office, repeating for her a smart answer which he had made to the manager. Maria did not understand why Joe laughed so much over the answer he had made but she said that the manager must have been a very overbearing person to deal with. Joe said he wasn't so bad when you knew how to take him, that he was a decent sort so long as you didn't rub him the wrong way. Mrs Donnelly played the piano for the children and they danced and sang. Then the two next-door girls handed round the nuts. Nobody could find the nutcrackers and Joe was nearly getting cross over it and asked how did they expect Maria to crack nuts without a nutcracker. But Maria said she didn't like nuts and that they weren't to bother about her. Then Joe asked would she take a bottle of stout and Mrs Donnelly said there was port wine too in the house if she would prefer that. Maria said she would rather they didn't ask her to take anything: but Joe insisted.

So Maria let him have his way and they sat by the fire talking over old times and Maria thought she would put in a good word for Alphy. But Joe cried that God might strike him stone dead if ever he spoke a word to his brother again and Maria said she was sorry she had mentioned the matter. Mrs Donnelly told her husband it was a great shame for him to speak that way of his own flesh and blood but Joe said that Alphy was no brother of his and there was nearly being a row on the head of it. But Joe said he would not lose his temper on account of the night it was and asked his wife to open some more stout. The two next-door girls had arranged some Hallow Eve games and soon everything was merry again. Maria was delighted to see the children so merry and Joe and his wife in such good spirits. The next-door girls put some saucers on the table and then led the children up to the table, blindfold. One got the prayer-book and the other three got the water; and when one of the next-door girls got the ring Mrs Donnelly shook her finger at the blushing girl as much as to say: *O, I know all about it!* They insisted then on blindfolding Maria and leading her up to the table to see what she would get; and, while they were putting on the bandage, Maria laughed and laughed again till the tip of her nose nearly met the tip of her chin.

They led her up to the table amid laughing and joking and she put her hand out in the air as she was told to do. She moved her hand about here and there in the air and descended on one of the saucers. She felt a soft wet substance with her fingers and was surprised that nobody spoke or took off her bandage. There was a pause for a few seconds; and then a great deal of scuffling and whispering. Somebody said something about the garden, and at last Mrs Donnelly said something very cross to one of the next-door girls and told her to throw it out at once: that was no play. Maria understood that it was wrong that time and so she had to do it over again: and this time she got the prayer-book.

After that Mrs Donnelly played Miss McCloud's Reel for the children and Joe made Maria take a glass of wine. Soon they were all quite merry again and Mrs Donnelly said Maria would enter a convent before the year was out because she had got the prayer-book. Maria had never seen Joe so nice to her as he was that night, so full of pleasant talk and reminiscences. She said they were all very good to her.

At last the children grew tired and sleepy and Joe asked Maria would she not sing some little song before she went, one of the old songs. Mrs Donnelly said *Do, please, Maria!* and so Maria had to get up and stand beside the piano. Mrs Donnelly bade the children be quiet and listen to Maria's song. Then she played the prelude and said *Now, Maria!* and Maria, blushing very much, began to sing in a tiny quavering voice. She sang *I Dreamt that I Dwelt*, and when she came to the second verse she sang again:

> *I dreamt that I dwelt in marble halls*
> *With vassals and serfs at my side*
> *And of all who assembled within those walls*
> *That I was the hope and the pride.*
> *I had riches too great to count, could boast*
> *Of a high ancestral name,*
> *But I also dreamt, which pleased me most,*
> *That you loved me still the same.*

But no one tried to show her her mistake; and when she had ended her song Joe was very much moved. He said that there was no time like the long ago and no music for him like poor old Balfe, whatever other people might say; and his eyes filled up so much with tears that he could not find what he was looking for and in the end he had to ask his wife to tell him where the corkscrew was.

A PAINFUL CASE

Mr James Duffy lived in Chapelizod because he wished to live as far as possible from the city of which he was a citizen and because he found all the other suburbs of Dublin mean, modern and pretentious. He lived in an old sombre house and from his windows he could look into the disused distillery or upwards along the shallow river on which Dublin is built. The lofty walls of his uncarpeted room were free from pictures. He had himself bought every article of furniture in the room: a black iron bedstead, an iron washstand, four cane chairs, a clothes-rack, a coal-scuttle, a fender and irons and a square table on which lay a double desk. A bookcase had been made in an alcove by means of shelves of white wood. The bed was clothed with white bed-clothes and a black and scarlet rug covered the foot. A little hand-mirror hung above the washstand and during the day a white-shaded lamp stood as the sole ornament of the mantelpiece. The books on the white wooden shelves were arranged from below upwards according to bulk. A complete Wordsworth stood at one end of the lowest shelf and a copy of the *Maynooth Catechism*, sewn into the cloth cover of a notebook, stood at one end of the top shelf. Writing materials were always on the desk. In the desk lay a manuscript translation of Hauptmann's *Michael Kramer*, the stage directions of which were written in purple ink, and a little sheaf of papers held together by a brass pin. In these sheets a sentence was inscribed from time to time and, in an ironical moment, the headline of an advertisement for *Bile Beans* had been pasted on to the first sheet. On lifting the lid of the desk a faint fragrance escaped—the fragrance of new cedarwood pencils or of a bottle of gum or of an over-ripe apple which might have been left there and forgotten.

Mr Duffy abhorred anything which betokened physical or mental disorder. A mediæval doctor would have called him saturnine. His face, which carried the entire tale of his years, was of the brown tint of Dublin streets. On his long and rather large head grew dry black hair and a tawny moustache did not quite cover an unamiable mouth. His cheekbones also gave his face a harsh character; but there was no harshness in the eyes which, looking at the world from under their tawny eyebrows, gave the impression of a man ever alert to greet a redeeming instinct in others but often disappointed. He lived at a little distance from his body, regarding his own acts with doubtful side-glances. He had an odd autobiograpical habit which led him to compose in his mind from time to time a short sentence about himself containing a subject in the third person and a predicate in the past tense. He never gave alms to beggars and walked firmly, carrying a stout hazel.

He had been for many years cashier of a private bank in Baggot Street. Every morning he came in from Chapelizod by tram. At midday he went to Dan Burke's and took his lunch —a bottle of lager beer and a small trayful of arrowroot biscuits. At four o'clock he was set free. He dined in an eating-house in George's Street where he felt himself safe from the society of Dublin's gilded youth and where there was a certain plain honesty in the bill of fare. His evenings were spent either before his landlady's piano or roaming about the outskirts of the city. His liking for Mozart's music brought him sometimes to an opera or a concert: these were the only dissipations of his life.

He had neither companions nor friends, church nor creed. He lived his spiritual life without any communion with others, visiting his relatives at Christmas and escorting them to the cemetery when they died. He performed these two social duties for old dignity' sake but conceded nothing further to the conventions which regulate the civic life. He allowed himself to think that in certain circumstances he would rob his bank but, as these circumstances never arose, his life rolled out evenly—an adventureless tale.

One evening he found himself sitting beside two ladies in the Rotunda. The house, thinly peopled and silent, gave distressing prophecy of failure. The lady who sat next him looked round at the deserted house once or twice and then said:

—What a pity there is such a poor house to-night! It's so hard on people to have to sing to empty benches.

He took the remark as an invitation to talk. He was surprised that she seemed so little awkward. While they talked he tried to fix her permanently in his memory. When he learned that the young girl beside her was her daughter he judged her to be a year or so younger than himself. Her face, which must have been handsome, had remained intelligent. It was an oval face with strongly marked features. The eyes were very dark blue and steady. Their gaze began with a defiant note but was confused by what seemed a deliberate swoon of the pupil into the iris, revealing for an instant a temperament of great sensibility. The pupil reasserted itself quickly, this half-disclosed nature fell again under the reign of prudence, and her astrakhan jacket, moulding a bosom of a certain fulness, struck the note of defiance more definitely.

He met her again a few weeks afterwards at a concert in Earlsfort Terrace and seized the moments when her daughter's attention was diverted to become intimate. She alluded once or twice to her husband but her tone was not such as to make the allusion a warning. Her name was Mrs Sinico. Her husband's great-great-grandfather had come from Leghorn. Her husband was captain of a mercantile boat plying between Dublin and Holland; and they had one child.

Meeting her a third time by accident he found courage to make an appointment. She came. This was the first of many meetings; they met always in the evening and chose the most quiet quarters for their walks together. Mr Duffy, however, had a distaste for underhand ways and, finding that they were compelled to meet stealthily, he forced her to ask him to her house. Captain Sinico encouraged his visits, thinking that his daughter's hand was in question. He had dismissed his wife so sincerely from his gallery of pleasures that he did not suspect that anyone else would take an interest in her. As the husband was often away and the daughter out giving music lessons Mr Duffy had many opportunities of enjoying the lady's society. Neither he nor she had had any such adventure before and neither was conscious of any incongruity. Little by little he entangled his thoughts with hers. He lent her books, provided her with ideas, shared his intellectual life with her. She listened to all.

Sometimes in return for his theories she gave out some fact of her own life. With almost maternal solicitude she urged him to let his nature open to the full; she became his confessor. He told her that for some time he had assisted at the meetings of an Irish Socialist Party where he had felt himself a unique figure amidst a score of sober workmen in a garret lit by an inefficient oil-lamp. When the party had divided into three sections, each under its own leader and in its own garret, he had discontinued his attendances. The workmen's discussions, he said, were too timorous; the interest they took in the question of wages was inordinate. He felt that they were hard-featured realists and that they resented an exactitude which was the product of a leisure not within their reach. No social revolution, he told her, would be likely to strike Dublin for some centuries.

She asked him why did he not write out his thoughts. For what, he asked her, with careful scorn. To compete with phrasemongers, incapable of thinking consecutively for sixty seconds? To submit himself to the criticisms of an obtuse middle class which entrusted its morality to policemen and its fine arts to impresarios?

He went often to her little cottage outside Dublin; often they spent their evenings alone. Little by little, as their thoughts entangled, they spoke of subjects less remote. Her companionship was like a warm soil about an exotic. Many times she allowed the dark to fall upon them, refraining from lighting the lamp. The dark discreet room, their isolation, the music that still vibrated in their ears united them. This union exalted him, wore away the rough edges of his character, emotionalised his mental life. Sometimes he caught himself listening to the sound of his own voice. He thought that in her eyes he would ascend to an angelical stature; and, as he attached the fervent nature of his companion more and more closely to him, he heard the strange impersonal voice which he recognised as his own, insisting on the soul's incurable loneliness. We cannot give ourselves, it said: we are our own. The end of these discourses was that one night during which she had shown every sign of unusual excitement, Mrs Sinico caught up his hand passionately and pressed it to her cheek.

Mr Duffy was very much surprised. Her interpretation of his words disillusioned him. He did not visit her for a week;

then he wrote to her asking her to meet him. As he did not wish their last interview to be troubled by the influence of their ruined confessional they met in a little cakeshop near the Parkgate. It was cold autumn weather but in spite of the cold they wandered up and down the roads of the Park for nearly three hours. They agreed to break off their intercourse: every bond, he said, is a bond to sorrow. When they came out of the Park they walked in silence towards the tram; but here she began to tremble so violently that, fearing another collapse on her part, he bade her good-bye quickly and left her. A few days later he received a parcel containing his books and music.

Four years passed. Mr Duffy returned to his even way of life. His room still bore witness of the orderliness of his mind. Some new pieces of music encumbered the music-stand in the lower room and on his shelves stood two volumes by Nietzsche: *Thus Spake Zarathustra* and *The Gay Science*. He wrote seldom in the sheaf of papers which lay in his desk. One of his sentences, written two months after his last interview with Mrs Sinico, read: Love between man and man is impossible because there must not be sexual intercourse and friendship between man and woman is impossible because there must be sexual intercourse. He kept away from concerts lest he should meet her. His father died; the junior partner of the bank retired. And still every morning he went into the city by tram and every evening walked home from the city after having dined moderately in George's Street and read the evening paper for dessert.

One evening as he was about to put a morsel of corned beef and cabbage into his mouth his hand stopped. His eyes fixed themselves on a paragraph in the evening paper which he had propped against the water-carafe. He replaced the morsel of food on his plate and read the paragraph attentively. Then he drank a glass of water, pushed his plate to one side, doubled the paper down before him between his elbows and read the paragraph over and over again. The cabbage began to deposit a cold white grease on his plate. The girl came over to him to ask was his dinner not properly cooked. He said it was very good and ate a few mouthfuls of it with difficulty. Then he paid his bill and went out.

He walked along quickly through the November twilight, his stout hazel stick striking the ground regularly, the fringe of the buff *Mail* peeping out of a side-pocket of his tight reefer over-coat. On the lonely road which leads from the Parkgate to Chapelizod he slackened his pace. His stick struck the ground less emphatically and his breath, issuing irregularly, almost with a sighing sound, condensed in the wintry air. When he reached his house he went up at once to his bedroom and, taking the paper from his pocket, read the paragraph again by the failing light of the window. He read it not aloud, but moving his lips as a priest does when he reads the prayers *Secreto*. This was the paragraph:

DEATH OF A LADY AT SYDNEY PARADE

A PAINFUL CASE

To-day at the City of Dublin Hospital the Deputy Coroner (in the absence of Mr Leverett) held an inquest on the body of Mrs Emily Sinico, aged forty-three years, who was killed at Sydney Parade Station yesterday evening. The evidence showed that the deceased lady, while attempting to cross the line, was knocked down by the engine of the ten o'clock slow train from Kingstown, thereby sustaining injuries of the head and right side which led to her death.

James Lennon, driver of the engine, stated that he had been in the employment of the railway company for fifteen years. On hearing the guard's whistle he set the train in motion and a second or two afterwards brought it to rest in response to loud cries. The train was going slowly.

P. Dunne, railway porter, stated that as the train was about to start he observed a woman attempting to cross the lines. He ran towards her and shouted but, before he could reach her, she was caught by the buffer of the engine and fell to the ground.

A juror—You saw the lady fall?

Witness—Yes.

Police Sergeant Croly deposed that when he arrived he found the deceased lying on the platform apparently dead. He had the body taken to the waiting-room pending the arrival of the ambulance.

Constable 57E corroborated.

Dr Halpin, assistant house surgeon of the City of Dublin Hospital, stated that the deceased had two lower ribs fractured and had sustained severe contusions of the right shoulder. The right side of the head had been injured in the fall. The injuries were not sufficient to have caused death in a normal person. Death, in his opinion, had been probably due to shock and sudden failure of the heart's action.

Mr H. B. Patterson Finlay, on behalf of the railway company, expressed his deep regret at the accident. The company had always taken every precaution to prevent people crossing the lines except by the bridges, both by placing notices in every station and by the use of patent spring gates at level crossings. The deceased had been in the habit of crossing the lines late at night from platform to platform and, in view of certain other circumstances of the case, he did not think the railway officials were to blame.

Captain Sinico, of Leoville, Sydney Parade, husband of the deceased, also gave evidence. He stated that the deceased was his wife. He was not in Dublin at the time of the accident as he had arrived only that morning from Rotterdam. They had been married for twenty-two years and had lived happily until about two years ago when his wife began to be rather intemperate in her habits.

Miss Mary Sinico said that of late her mother had been in the habit of going out at night to buy spirits. She, witness, had often tried to reason with her mother and had induced her to join a league. She was not at home until an hour after the accident.

The jury returned a verdict in accordance with the medical evidence and exonerated Lennon from all blame.

The Deputy Coroner said it was a most painful case, and expressed great sympathy with Captain Sinico and his daughter. He urged on the railway company to take strong measures to prevent the possibility of similar accidents in the future. No blame attached to anyone.

Mr Duffy raised his eyes from the paper and gazed out of his window on the cheerless evening landscape. The river lay quiet beside the empty distillery and from time to time a light appeared in some house on the Lucan road. What an end! The whole narrative of her death revolted him and it revolted him to think that he had ever spoken to her of what he held sacred. The threadbare phrases, the inane expressions of sympathy, the cautious words of a reporter won over to conceal the details of a commonplace vulgar death attacked his stomach. Not merely had she degraded herself; she had degraded him. He saw the squalid tract of her vice, miserable and malodorous. His soul's companion! He thought of the hobbling wretches whom he had seen carrying cans and bottles to be filled by the barman. Just God, what an end! Evidently she had been unfit to live, without any strength of purpose, an easy prey to habits, one of the wrecks on which civilisation has been reared. But that she could have sunk so low! Was it possible he had deceived himself so utterly about her? He remembered her outburst of that night and interpreted it in a harsher sense than he had ever done. He had no difficulty now in approving of the course he had taken.

As the light failed and his memory began to wander he thought her hand touched his. The shock which had first attacked his stomach was now attacking his nerves. He put on his overcoat and hat quickly and went out. The cold air met him on the threshold; it crept into the sleeves of his coat. When he came to the public-house at Chapelizod Bridge he went in and ordered a hot punch.

The proprietor served him obsequiously but did not venture to talk. There were five or six working-men in the shop discussing the value of a gentleman's estate in County Kildare. They drank at intervals from their huge pint tumblers and smoked, spitting often on the floor and sometimes dragging the sawdust over their spits with their heavy boots. Mr Duffy sat on his stool and gazed at them, without seeing or hearing them. After a while they went out and he called for another punch. He sat a long time over it. The shop was very quiet. The proprietor sprawled on the counter reading the *Herald* and yawning. Now and again a tram was heard swishing along the lonely road outside.

As he sat there, living over his life with her and evoking alternately the two images in which he now conceived her, he realised that she was dead, that she had ceased to exist, that she had become a memory. He began to feel ill at ease. He asked himself what else could he have done. He could not have carried on a comedy of deception with her; he could not have lived with her openly. He had done what seemed to him best. How was he to blame? Now that she was gone he understood how lonely her life must have been, sitting night after night alone in that room. His life would be lonely too until he, too, died, ceased to exist, became a memory—if anyone remembered him.

It was after nine o'clock when he left the shop. The night

was cold and gloomy. He entered the Park by the first gate and walked along under the gaunt trees. He walked through the bleak alleys where they had walked four years before. She seemed to be near him in the darkness. At moments he seemed to feel her voice touch his ear, her hand touch his. He stood still to listen. Why had he withheld life from her? Why had he sentenced her to death? He felt his moral nature falling to pieces.

When he gained the crest of the Magazine Hill he halted and looked along the river towards Dublin, the lights of which burned redly and hospitably in the cold night. He looked down the slope and, at the base, in the shadow of the wall of the Park, he saw some human figures lying. Those venal and furtive loves filled him with despair. He gnawed the rectitude of his life; he felt that he had been outcast from life's feast. One human being had seemed to love him and he had denied her life and happiness: he had sentenced her to ignominy, a death of shame. He knew that the prostrate creatures down by the wall were watching him and wished him gone. No one wanted him; he was outcast from life's feast. He turned his eyes to the grey gleaming river, winding along towards Dublin. Beyond the river he saw a goods train winding out of Kingsbridge Station, like a worm with a fiery head winding through the darkness, obstinately and laboriously. It passed slowly out of sight; but still he heard in his ears the laborious drone of the engine reiterating the syllables of her name.

He turned back the way he had come, the rhythm of the engine pounding in his ears. He began to doubt the reality of what memory told him. He halted under a tree and allowed the rhythm to die away. He could not feel her near him in the darkness nor her voice touch his ear. He waited for some minutes listening. He could hear nothing: the night was perfectly silent. He listened again: perfectly silent. He felt that he was alone.

IVY DAY IN THE COMMITTEE ROOM

O<small>LD</small> J<small>ACK</small> raked the cinders together with a piece of cardboard and spread them judiciously over the whitening dome of coals. When the dome was thinly covered his face lapsed into darkness but, as he set himself to fan the fire again, his crouching shadow ascended the opposite wall and his face slowly re-emerged into light. It was an old man's face, very bony and hairy. The moist blue eyes blinked at the fire and the moist mouth fell open at times, munching once or twice mechanically when it closed. When the cinders had caught he laid the piece of cardboard against the wall, sighed and said:

—That's better now, Mr O'Connor.

Mr O'Connor, a grey-haired young man, whose face was disfigured by many blotches and pimples, had just brought the tobacco for a cigarette into a shapely cylinder but when spoken to he undid his handiwork meditatively. Then he began to roll the tobacco again meditatively and after a moment's thought decided to lick the paper.

—Did Mr Tierney say when he'd be back? he asked in a husky falsetto.

—He didn't say.

Mr O'Connor put his cigarette into his mouth and began to search his pockets. He took out a pack of thin pasteboard cards.

—I'll get you a match, said the old man.

—Never mind, this'll do, said Mr O'Connor.

He selected one of the cards and read what was printed on it:

MUNICIPAL ELECTIONS
ROYAL EXCHANGE WARD

Mr Richard J. Tierney, P.L.G., respectfully solicits the favour of your vote and influence at the coming election in the Royal Exchange Ward

Mr O'Connor had been engaged by Mr Tierney's agent to canvass one part of the ward but, as the weather was inclement and his boots let in the wet, he spent a great part of the day sitting by the fire in the Committee Room in Wicklow Street with Jack, the old caretaker. They had been sitting thus since the short day had grown dark. It was the sixth of October, dismal and cold out of doors.

Mr O'Connor tore a strip off the card and, lighting it, lit his cigarette. As he did so the flame lit up a leaf of dark glossy ivy in the lapel of his coat. The old man watched him attentively and then, taking up the piece of cardboard again, began to fan the fire slowly while his companion smoked.

—Ah, yes, he said, continuing, it's hard to know what way to bring up children. Now who'd think he'd turn out like that! I sent him to the Christian Brothers and I done what I could for him, and there he goes boosing about. I tried to make him someway decent.

He replaced the cardboard wearily.

—Only I'm an old man now I'd change his tune for him. I'd take the stick to his back and beat him while I could stand over him—as I done many a time before. The mother, you know, she cocks him up with this and that. . . .

—That's what ruins children, said Mr O'Connor.

—To be sure it is, said the old man. And little thanks you get for it, only impudence. He takes th'upper hand of me whenever he sees I've a sup taken. What's the world coming to when sons speaks that way to their father?

—What age is he? said Mr O'Connor.

—Nineteen, said the old man.

—Why don't you put him to something?

—Sure, amn't I never done at the drunken bowsy ever since he left school? *I won't keep you*, I says. *You must get a job for yourself*. But, sure, it's worse whenever he gets a job; he drinks it all.

Mr O'Connor shook his head in sympathy, and the old man fell silent, gazing into the fire. Someone opened the door of the room and called out:

—Hello! Is this a Freemasons' meeting?

—Who's that? said the old man.

—What are you doing in the dark? asked a voice.

—Is that you, Hynes? asked Mr O'Connor.

—Yes. What are you doing in the dark? said Mr Hynes, advancing into the light of the fire.

He was a tall slender young man with a light brown moustache. Imminent little drops of rain hung at the brim of his hat and the collar of his jacket-coat was turned up.

—Well, Mat, he said to Mr O'Connor, how goes it?

Mr O'Connor shook his head. The old man left the hearth and, after stumbling about the room returned with two candlesticks which he thrust one after the other into the fire and carried to the table. A denuded room came into view and the fire lost all its cheerful colour. The walls of the room were bare except for a copy of an election address. In the middle of the room was a small table on which papers were heaped.

Mr Hynes leaned against the mantelpiece and asked:

—Has he paid you yet?

—Not yet, said Mr O'Connor. I hope to God he'll not leave us in the lurch to-night.

Mr Hynes laughed.

—O, he'll pay you. Never fear, he said.

—I hope he'll look smart about it if he means business, said Mr O'Connor.

—What do you think, Jack? said Mr Hynes satirically to the old man.

The old man returned to his seat by the fire, saying:

—It isn't but he has it, anyway. Not like the other tinker.

—What other tinker? said Mr Hynes.

—Colgan, said the old man scornfully.

—Is it because Colgan's a working-man you say that? What's the difference between a good honest bricklayer and a publican—eh? Hasn't the working-man as good a right to be in the Corporation as anyone else—ay, and a better right than those shoneens that are always hat in hand before any fellow with a handle to his name? Isn't that so, Mat? said Mr Hynes, addressing Mr O'Connor.

—I think you're right, said Mr O'Connor.

—One man is a plain honest man with no hunker-sliding about him. He goes in to represent the labour classes. This fellow you're working for only wants to get some job or other.

—Of course, the working-classes should be represented, said the old man.

—The working-man, said Mr Hynes, gets all kicks and no halfpence. But it's labour produces everything. The working-man is not looking for fat jobs for his sons and nephews and cousins. The working-man is not going to drag the honour of Dublin in the mud to please a German monarch.

—How's that? said the old man.

—Don't you know they want to present an address of welcome to Edward Rex if he comes here next year? What do we want kowtowing to a foreign king?

—Our man won't vote for the address, said Mr O'Connor. He goes in on the Nationalist ticket.

—Won't he? said Mr Hynes. Wait till you see whether he will or not. I know him. Is it Tricky Dicky Tierney?

—By God! perhaps you're right, Joe, said Mr O'Connor. Anyway, I wish he'd turn up with the spondulics.

The three men fell silent. The old man began to rake more cinders together. Mr Hynes took off his hat, shook it and then turned down the collar of his coat, displaying, as he did so, an ivy leaf in the lapel.

—If this man was alive, he said, pointing to the leaf, we'd have no talk of an address of welcome.

—That's true, said Mr O'Connor.

—Musha, God be with them times! said the old man. There was some life in it then.

The room was silent again. Then a bustling little man with a snuffling nose and very cold ears pushed in the door. He walked over quickly to the fire, rubbing his hands as if he intended to produce a spark from them.

—No money, boys, he said.

—Sit down here, Mr Henchy, said the old man, offering him his chair.

—O, don't stir, Jack, don't stir, said Mr Henchy.

He nodded curtly to Mr Hynes and sat down on the chair which the old man vacated.

—Did you serve Aungier Street? he asked Mr O'Connor.

—Yes, said Mr O'Connor, beginning to search his pockets for memoranda.

—Did you call on Grimes?

—I did.

—Well? How does he stand?

—He wouldn't promise. He said: *I won't tell anyone what way I'm going to vote*. But I think he'll be all right.

—Why so?

—He asked me who the nominators were; and I told him. I mentioned Father Burke's name. I think it'll be all right.

Mr Henchy began to snuffle and to rub his hands over the fire at a terrific speed. Then he said:

—For the love of God, Jack, bring us a bit of coal. There must be some left.

The old man went out of the room.

—It's no go, said Mr Henchy, shaking his head. I asked the little shoeboy, but he said: *O, now, Mr Henchy, when I see the work going on properly I won't forget you, you may be sure*. Mean little tinker! 'Usha, how could he be anything else?

—What did I tell you, Mat? said Mr Hynes. Tricky Dicky Tierney.

—O, he's as tricky as they make 'em, said Mr Henchy. He hasn't got those little pigs' eyes for nothing. Blast his soul! Couldn't he pay up like a man instead of: *O, now, Mr Henchy, I must speak to Mr Fanning. . . . I've spent a lot of money?* Mean little shoeboy of hell! I suppose he forgets the time his little old father kept the hand-me-down shop in Mary's Lane.

—But is that a fact? asked Mr O'Connor.

—God, yes, said Mr Henchy. Did you never hear that? And the men used to go in on Sunday morning before the houses were open to buy a waistcoat or a trousers—moya! But Tricky Dicky's little old father always had a tricky little black bottle up in a corner. Do you mind now? That's that. That's where he first saw the light.

The old man returned with a few lumps of coal which he placed here and there on the fire.

—That's a nice how-do-you-do, said Mr O'Connor. How does he expect us to work for him if he won't stump up?

—I can't help it, said Mr Henchy. I expect to find the bailiffs in the hall when I go home.

Mr Hynes laughed and, shoving himself away from the mantelpiece with the aid of his shoulders, made ready to leave.

—It'll be all right when King Eddie comes, he said. Well, boys, I'm off for the present. See you later. 'Bye, 'bye.

He went out of the room slowly. Neither Mr Henchy nor the old man said anything but, just as the door was closing, Mr O'Connor, who had been staring moodily into the fire, called out suddenly:

—'Bye, Joe.

Mr Henchy waited a few moments and then nodded in the direction of the door.

—Tell me, he said across the fire, what brings our friend in here? What does he want?

—'Usha, poor Joe! said Mr O'Connor, throwing the end of his cigarette into the fire, he's hard up like the rest of us.

Mr Henchy snuffled vigorously and spat so copiously that he nearly put out the fire which uttered a hissing protest.

—To tell you my private and candid opinion, he said, I think he's a man from the other camp. He's a spy of Colgan's if you ask me. *Just go round and try and find out how they're getting on. They won't suspect you.* Do you twig?

—Ah, poor Joe is a decent skin, said Mr O'Connor.

—His father was a decent respectable man, Mr Henchy admitted. Poor old Larry Hynes! Many a good turn he did in his day! But I'm greatly afraid our friend is not nineteen carat. Damn it, I can understand a fellow being hard up but what I can't understand is a fellow sponging. Couldn't he have some spark of manhood about him?

—He doesn't get a warm welcome from me when he comes, said the old man. Let him work for his own side and not come spying around here.

—I don't know, said Mr O'Connor dubiously, as he took out cigarette-papers and tobacco. I think Joe Hynes is a straight man. He's a clever chap, too, with the pen. Do you remember that thing he wrote . . . ?

—Some of these hillsiders and fenians are a bit too clever if you ask me, said Mr Henchy. Do you know what my private and candid opinion is about some of those little jokers? I believe half of them are in the pay of the Castle.

—There's no knowing, said the old man.

—O, but I know it for a fact, said Mr Henchy. They're Castle hacks. . . . I don't say Hynes. . . . No, damn it, I think he's a stroke above that. . . . But there's a certain little nobleman with a cock-eye—you know the patriot I'm alluding to?

Mr O'Connor nodded.

—There's a lineal descendant of Major Sirr for you if you like! O, the heart's blood of a patriot! That's a fellow now that'd sell his country for fourpence—ay—and go down on his bended knees and thank the Almighty Christ he had a country to sell.

There was a knock at the door.

—Come in! said Mr Henchy.

A person resembling a poor clergyman or a poor actor appeared in the doorway. His black clothes were tightly buttoned on his short body and it was impossible to say whether he wore a clergyman's collar or a layman's because the collar of his shabby frock-coat, the uncovered buttons of which reflected the candlelight, was turned up about his neck. He wore a round hat of hard black felt. His face, shining with raindrops, had the appearance of damp yellow cheese save where two rosy spots indicated the cheekbones. He opened his very long mouth suddenly to express disappointment and at the same time opened wide his very bright blue eyes to express pleasure and surprise.

—O, Father Keon! said Mr Henchy, jumping up from his chair. Is that you? Come in!

—O, no, no, no! said Father Keon quickly, pursing his lips as if he were addressing a child.

—Won't you come in and sit down?

—No, no, no! said Father Keon, speaking in a discreet indulgent velvety voice. Don't let me disturb you now! I'm just looking for Mr Fanning. . . .

—He's round at the *Black Eagle*, said Mr Henchy. But won't you come in and sit down a minute?

—No, no, thank you. It was just a little business matter, said Father Keon. Thank you, indeed.

He retreated from the doorway and Mr. Henchy, seizing one of the candlesticks, went to the door to light him downstairs.

—O, don't trouble, I beg!

—No, but the stairs is so dark.

—No, no, I can see. . . . Thank you, indeed.

—Are you right now?

—All right, thanks. . . . Thanks.

Mr Henchy returned with the candlestick and put it on the table. He sat down again at the fire. There was silence for a few moments.

—Tell me, John, said Mr O'Connor, lighting his cigarette with another pasteboard card.

—Hm?

—What is he exactly?

—Ask me an easier one, said Mr Henchy.

—Fanning and himself seem to me very thick. They're often in Kavanagh's together. Is he a priest at all?

—'Mmmyes, I believe so. . . . I think he's what you call a black sheep. We haven't many of them, thank God! but we have a few. . . . He's an unfortunate man of some kind. . . .

—And how does he knock it out? asked Mr O'Connor.

—That's another mystery.

—Is he attached to any chapel or church or institution or—

—No, said Mr Henchy. I think he's travelling on his own account. . . . God forgive me, he added, I thought he was the dozen of stout.

—Is there any chance of a drink itself? asked Mr O'Connor.

—I'm dry too, said the old man.

—I asked that little shoeboy three times, said Mr Henchy, would he send up a dozen of stout. I asked him again now but he was leaning on the counter in his shirt-sleeves having a deep goster with Alderman Cowley.

—Why didn't you remind him? said Mr O'Connor.

—Well, I couldn't go over while he was talking to Alderman Cowley. I just waited till I caught his eye, and said: *About that little matter I was speaking to you about. . . . That'll be all right, Mr H.*, he said. Yerra, sure the little hop-o'-my-thumb has forgotten all about it.

—There's some deal on in that quarter, said Mr O'Connor thoughtfully. I saw the three of them hard at it yesterday at Suffolk Street corner.

—I think I know the little game they're at, said Mr Henchy. You must owe the City Fathers money nowadays if you want to be made Lord Mayor. Then they'll make you Lord Mayor. By God! I'm thinking seriously of becoming a City Father myself. What do you think? Would I do for the job?

Mr O'Connor laughed.

—So far as owing money goes. . . .

—Driving out of the Mansion House, said Mr Henchy, in all my vermin, with Jack here standing up behind me in a powdered wig—eh?

—And make me your private secretary, John.

—Yes. And I'll make Father Keon my private chaplain. We'll have a family party.

—Faith, Mr Henchy, said the old man, you'd keep up better

style than some of them. I was talking one day to old Keegan, the porter. *And how do you like your new master, Pat?* says I to him. *You haven't much entertaining now,* says I. *Entertaining!* says he. *He'd live on the smell of an oil-rag.* And do you know what he told me? Now, I declare to God, I didn't believe him.

—What? said Mr Henchy and Mr O'Connor.

—He told me: *What do you think of a Lord Mayor of Dublin sending out for a pound of chops for his dinner? How's that for high living?* says he. *Wisha! wisha,* says I. *A pound of chops,* says he, *coming into the Mansion House. Wisha!* says I, *what kind of people is going at all now?*

At this point there was a knock at the door, and a boy put in his head.

—What is it? said the old man.

—From the *Black Eagle*, said the boy, walking in sideways and depositing a basket on the floor with a noise of shaken bottles.

The old man helped the boy to transfer the bottles from the basket to the table and counted the full tally. After the transfer the boy put his basket on his arm and asked:

—Any bottles?

—What bottles? said the old man.

—Won't you let us drink them first? said Mr Henchy.

—I was told to ask for bottles.

—Come back to-morrow, said the old man.

—Here, boy! said Mr Henchy, will you run over to O'Farrell's and ask him to lend us a corkscrew—for Mr Henchy, say. Tell him we won't keep it a minute. Leave the basket there.

The boy went out and Mr Henchy began to rub his hands cheerfully, saying:

—Ah, well, he's not so bad after all. He's as good as his word, anyhow.

—There's no tumblers, said the old man.

—O, don't let that trouble you, Jack, said Mr Henchy. Many's the good man before now drank out of the bottle.

—Anyway, it's better than nothing, said Mr O'Connor.

—He's not a bad sort, said Mr Henchy, only Fanning has such a loan of him. He means well, you know, in his own tinpot way.

The boy came back with the corkscrew. The old man opened three bottles and was handing back the corkscrew when Mr Henchy said to the boy:

—Would you like a drink, boy?

—If you please, sir, said the boy.

The old man opened another bottle grudgingly, and handed it to the boy.

—What age are you? he asked.

—Seventeen, said the boy.

As the old man said nothing further the boy took the bottle, said: *Here's my best respects, sir* to Mr Henchy, drank the contents, put the bottle back on the table and wiped his mouth with his sleeve. Then he took up the corkscrew and went out of the door sideways, muttering some form of salutation.

—That's the way it begins, said the old man.

—The thin end of the wedge, said Mr Henchy.

The old man distributed the three bottles which he had opened and the men drank from them simultaneously. After having drunk each placed his bottle on the mantelpiece within hand's reach and drew in a long breath of satisfaction.

—Well, I did a good day's work to-day, said Mr Henchy, after a pause.

—That so, John?

—Yes. I got him one or two sure things in Dawson Street, Crofton and myself. Between ourselves, you know, Crofton (he's a decent chap, of course), but he's not worth a damn as a canvasser. He hasn't a word to throw to a dog. He stands and looks at the people while I do the talking.

Here two men entered the room. One of them was a very fat man, whose blue serge clothes seemed to be in danger of falling from his sloping figure. He had a big face which resembled a young ox's face in expression, staring blue eyes and a grizzled moustache. The other man, who was much younger and frailer, had a thin clean-shaven face. He wore a very high double collar and a wide-brimmed bowler hat.

—Hello, Crofton! said Mr Henchy to the fat man. Talk of the devil. . . .

—Where did the boose come from? asked the young man. Did the cow calve?

—O, of course, Lyons spots the drink first thing! said Mr O'Connor, laughing.

—Is that the way you chaps canvass, said Mr Lyons, and Crofton and I out in the cold and rain looking for votes?

—Why, blast your soul, said Mr Henchy, I'd get more votes in five minutes than you two'd get in a week.

—Open two bottles of stout, Jack, said Mr O'Connor.

—How can I? said the old man, when there's no corkscrew?

—Wait now, wait now! said Mr Henchy, getting up quickly. Did you ever see this little trick?

He took two bottles from the table and, carrying them to the fire, put them on the hob. Then he sat down again by the fire and took another drink from his bottle. Mr Lyons sat on the edge of the table, pushed his hat towards the nape of his neck and began to swing his legs.

—Which is my bottle? he asked.

—This lad, said Mr Henchy.

Mr Crofton sat down on a box and looked fixedly at the other bottle on the hob. He was silent for two reasons. The first reason, sufficient in itself, was that he had nothing to say; the second reason was that he considered his companions beneath him. He had been a canvasser for Wilkins, the Conservative, but when the Conservatives had withdrawn their man and, choosing the lesser of two evils, given their support to the Nationalist candidate, he had been engaged to work for Mr Tierney.

In a few minutes an apologetic *Pok!* was heard as the cork flew out of Mr Lyons' bottle. Mr Lyons jumped off the table, went to the fire, took his bottle and carried it back to the table.

—I was just telling them, Crofton, said Mr Henchy, that we got a good few votes to-day.

—Who did you get? asked Mr Lyons.

—Well, I got Parkes for one, and I got Atkinson for two, and I got Ward of Dawson Street. Fine old chap he is, too—regular old toff, old Conservative! *But isn't your candidate a Nationalist?* said he. *He's a respectable man*, said I. *He's in favour of whatever will benefit this country. He's a big ratepayer*, I said. *He has extensive house property in the city and three places of business and isn't it to his own advantage to keep down the rates? He's a prominent and respected citizen*, said I, *and a Poor Law Guardian, and he doesn't belong to any party, good, bad, or indifferent*. That's the way to talk to 'em.

—And what about the address to the King? said Mr Lyons, after drinking and smacking his lips.

—Listen to me, said Mr Henchy. What we want in this country, as I said to old Ward, is capital. The King's coming here will mean an influx of money into this country. The citizens of Dublin will benefit by it. Look at all the factories down by the quays there, idle! Look at all the money there is in the country if we only worked the old industries, the mills, the shipbuilding yards and factories. It's capital we want.

—But look here, John, said Mr O'Connor. Why should we welcome the King of England? Didn't Parnell himself . . .

—Parnell, said Mr Henchy, is dead. Now, here's the way I look at it. Here's this chap come to the throne after his old mother keeping him out of it till the man was grey. He's a man of the world, and he means well by us. He's a jolly fine decent fellow, if you ask me, and no damn nonsense about him. He just says to himself: *The old one never went to see these wild Irish. By Christ, I'll go myself and see what they're like.* And are we going to insult the man when he comes over here on a friendly visit? Eh? Isn't that right, Crofton?

Mr Crofton nodded his head.

—But after all now, said Mr Lyons argumentatively, King Edward's life, you know, is not the very . . .

—Let bygones be bygones, said Mr Henchy. I admire the man personally. He's just an ordinary knockabout like you and me. He's fond of his glass of grog and he's a bit of a rake, perhaps, and he's a good sportsman. Damn it, can't we Irish play fair?

—That's all very fine, said Mr Lyons. But look at the case of Parnell now.

—In the name of God, said Mr Henchy, where's the analogy between the two cases?

—What I mean, said Mr Lyons, is we have our ideals. Why, now, would we welcome a man like that? Do you think now after what he did Parnell was a fit man to lead us? And why, then, would we do it for Edward the Seventh?

—This is Parnell's anniversary, said Mr O'Connor, and don't let us stir up any bad blood. We all respect him now that he's dead and gone—even the Conservatives, he added, turning to Mr Crofton.

Pok! The tardy cork flew out of Mr Crofton's bottle. Mr Crofton got up from his box and went to the fire. As he returned with his capture he said in a deep voice:

—Our side of the house respects him because he was a gentleman.

—Right you are, Crofton! said Mr Henchy fiercely. He was the only man that could keep that bag of cats in order. *Down, ye dogs! Lie down, ye curs!* That's the way he treated them. Come in, Joe! Come in! he called out, catching sight of Mr Hynes in the doorway.

Mr Hynes came in slowly.

—Open another bottle of stout, Jack, said Mr Henchy. O, I forgot there's no corkscrew! Here, show me one here and I'll put it at the fire.

The old man handed him another bottle and he placed it on the hob.

—Sit down, Joe, said Mr O'Connor, we're just talking about the Chief.

—Ay, ay! said Mr Henchy.

Mr Hynes sat on the side of the table near Mr Lyons but said nothing.

—There's one of them, anyhow, said Mr Henchy, that didn't renege him. By God, I'll say for you, Joe! No, by God, you stuck to him like a man!

—O, Joe, said Mr O'Connor suddenly. Give us that thing you wrote—do you remember? Have you got it on you?

—O, ay! said Mr Henchy. Give us that. Did you ever hear that, Crofton? Listen to this now: splendid thing.

—Go on, said Mr O'Connor. Fire away, Joe.

Mr Hynes did not seem to remember at once the piece to which they were alluding but, after reflecting a while, he said:

—O, that thing is it. . . . Sure, that's old now.

—Out with it, man! said Mr O'Connor.

—'Sh, 'sh, said Mr Henchy. Now, Joe!

Mr Hynes hesitated a little longer. Then amid the silence he took off his hat, laid it on the table and stood up. He seemed to be rehearsing the piece in his mind. After a rather long pause he announced:

THE DEATH OF PARNELL

6th October 1891

He cleared his throat once or twice and then began to recite:

> He is dead. Our Uncrowned King is dead.
>   O, Erin, mourn with grief and woe
> For he lies dead whom the fell gang
>   Of modern hypocrites laid low.
>
> He lies slain by the coward hounds
>   He raised to glory from the mire;
> And Erin's hopes and Erin's dreams
>   Perish upon her monarch's pyre.
>
> In palace, cabin or in cot
>   The Irish heart where'er it be
> Is bowed with woe—for he is gone
>   Who would have wrought her destiny.
>
> He would have had his Erin famed,
>   The green flag gloriously unfurled,
> Her statesmen, bards and warriors raised
>   Before the nations of the World.
>
> He dreamed (alas, 'twas but a dream!)
>   Of Liberty: but as he strove
> To clutch that idol, treachery
>   Sundered him from the thing he loved.
>
> Shame on the coward caitiff hands
>   That smote their Lord or with a kiss
> Betrayed him to the rabble-rout
>   Of fawning priests—no friends of his.

May everlasting shame consume
The memory of those who tried
To befoul and smear th' exalted name
Of one who spurned them in his pride.

He fell as fall the mighty ones,
Nobly undaunted to the last,
And death has now united him
With Erin's heroes of the past.

No sound of strife disturb his sleep!
Calmly he rests: no human pain
Or high ambition spurs him now
The peaks of glory to attain.

They had their way: they laid him low.
But Erin, list, his spirit may
Rise, like the Phœnix from the flames,
When breaks the dawning of the day,

The day that brings us Freedom's reign.
And on that day may Erin well
Pledge in the cup she lifts to Joy
One grief—the memory of Parnell.

Mr Hynes sat down again on the table. When he had finished his recitation there was a silence and then a burst of clapping: even Mr Lyons clapped. The applause continued for a little time. When it had ceased all the auditors drank from their bottles in silence.

Pok! The cork flew out of Mr Hynes' bottle, but Mr Hynes remained sitting, flushed and bareheaded on the table. He did not seem to have heard the invitation.

—Good man, Joe! said Mr O'Connor, taking out his cigarette papers and pouch the better to hide his emotion.

—What do you think of that, Crofton? cried Mr Henchy. Isn't that fine? What?

Mr Crofton said that it was a very fine piece of writing.

A MOTHER

Mr Holohan, assistant secretary of the *Eire Abu* Society, had been walking up and down Dublin for nearly a month, with his hands and pockets full of dirty pieces of paper, arranging about the series of concerts. He had a game leg and for this his friends called him Hoppy Holohan. He walked up and down constantly, stood by the hour at street corners arguing the point and made notes; but in the end it was Mrs Kearney who arranged everything.

Miss Devlin had become Mrs Kearney out of spite. She had been educated in a high-class convent where she had learned French and music. As she was naturally pale and unbending in manner she made few friends at school. When she came to the age of marriage she was sent out to many houses where her playing and ivory manners were much admired. She sat amid the chilly circle of her accomplishments, waiting for some suitor to brave it and offer her a brilliant life. But the young men whom she met were ordinary and she gave them no encouragement, trying to console her romantic desires by eating a great deal of Turkish Delight in secret. However, when she drew near the limit and her friends began to loosen their tongues about her she silenced them by marrying Mr Kearney, who was a bootmaker on Ormond Quay.

He was much older than she. His conversation, which was serious, took place at intervals in his great brown beard. After the first year of married life Mrs Kearney perceived that such a man would wear better than a romantic person but she never put her own romantic ideas away. He was sober, thrifty and pious; he went to the altar every first Friday, sometimes with her, oftener by himself. But she never weakened in her religion and was a good wife to him. At some party in a strange house when she lifted her eyebrow ever so slightly he stood up to take his leave and, when his cough troubled him, she put the eider-down quilt over his feet and made a strong rum punch. For his part he was a model father. By paying a small sum every week into a society he ensured for both his daughters a dowry of one hundred pounds each when they came to the age of twenty-four. He sent the elder daughter, Kathleen, to a good convent, where she learned French and music and afterwards paid her fees at the Academy. Every year in the month of July Mrs Kearney found occasion to say to some friend:

—My good man is packing us off to Skerries for a few weeks.

If it was not Skerries it was Howth or Greystones.

When the Irish Revival began to be appreciable Mrs Kearney determined to take advantage of her daughter's name and brought an Irish teacher to the house. Kathleen and her sister sent Irish picture postcards to their friends and these friends sent back other Irish picture postcards. On special Sundays when Mr Kearney went with his family to the pro-cathedral a little crowd of people would assemble after mass at the corner of Cathedral Street. They were all friends of the Kearneys—musical friends or Nationalist friends; and, when they had played every little counter of gossip, they shook hands with one another all together, laughing at the crossing of so many hands and said good-bye to one another in Irish. Soon the name of Miss Kathleen Kearney began to be heard often on people's lips. People said that she was very clever at music and a very nice girl and, moreover, that she was a believer in the language movement. Mrs Kearney was well content at this. Therefore she was not surprised when one day Mr Holohan came to her and proposed that her daughter should be the accompanist at a series of four grand concerts which his Society was going to give in the Antient Concert Rooms. She brought him into the drawing-room, made him sit down and brought out the decanter and the silver biscuit-barrel. She entered heart and soul into the details of the enterprise, advised and dissuaded; and finally a contract was drawn up by which Kathleen was to receive eight guineas for her services as accompanist at the four grand concerts.

As Mr Holohan was a novice in such delicate matters as the wording of bills and the disposing of items for a programme Mrs Kearney helped him. She had tact. She knew what *artistes* should go into capitals and what *artistes* should go into small type. She knew that the first tenor would not like to come on after Mr Meade's comic turn. To keep the audience continually diverted she slipped the doubtful items in between the old favourites. Mr Holohan called to see her every day to have her advice on some point. She was invariably friendly and advising—homely, in fact. She pushed the decanter towards him, saying:

—Now, help yourself, Mr Holohan!

And while he was helping himself she said:

—Don't be afraid! Don't be afraid of it!

Everything went on smoothly. Mrs Kearney bought some lovely blush-pink charmeuse in Brown Thomas's to let into the front of Kathleen's dress. It cost a pretty penny; but there are occasions when a little expense is justifiable. She took a dozen of two-shilling tickets for the final concert and sent them to those friends who could not be trusted to come otherwise. She forgot nothing and, thanks to her, everything that was to be done was done.

The concerts were to be on Wednesday, Thursday, Friday and Saturday. When Mrs Kearney arrived with her daughter at the Antient Concert Rooms on Wednesday night she did not like the look of things. A few young men, wearing bright blue badges in their coats, stood idle in the vestibule; none of them wore evening dress. She passed by with her daughter and a quick glance through the open door of the hall showed her the cause of the stewards' idleness. At first she wondered had she mistaken the hour. No, it was twenty minutes to eight.

In the dressing-room behind the stage she was introduced to the secretary of the Society, Mr Fitzpatrick. She smiled and shook his hand. He was a little man with a white vacant face. She noticed that he wore his soft brown hat carelessly on the side of his head and that his accent was flat. He held a programme in his hand and, while he was talking to her, he chewed one end of it into a moist pulp. He seemed to bear disappointments lightly. Mr Holohan came into the dressing-room every few minutes with reports from the box-office. The *artistes* talked among themselves nervously, glanced from time to time at the mirror and rolled and unrolled their music. When it was nearly half-past eight the few people in the hall began to express their desire to be entertained. Mr Fitzpatrick came in, smiled vacantly at the room, and said:

—Well now, ladies and gentlemen, I suppose we'd better open the ball.

Mrs Kearney rewarded his very flat final syllable with a quick stare of contempt and then said to her daughter encouragingly:

—Are you ready, dear?

When she had an opportunity she called Mr Holohan aside

and asked him to tell her what it meant. Mr Holohan did not know what it meant. He said that the Committee had made a mistake in arranging for four concerts: four was too many.

—And the *artistes!* said Mrs Kearney. Of course they are doing their best, but really they are no good.

Mr Holohan admitted that the *artistes* were no good but the Committee, he said, had decided to let the first three concerts go as they pleased and reserve all the talent for Saturday night. Mrs Kearney said nothing but, as the mediocre items followed one another on the platform and the few people in the hall grew fewer and fewer, she began to regret that she had put herself to any expense for such a concert. There was something she didn't like in the look of things and Mr Fitzpatrick's vacant smile irritated her very much. However, she said nothing and waited to see how it would end. The concert expired shortly before ten and everyone went home quickly.

The concert on Thursday night was better attended but Mrs Kearney saw at once that the house was filled with paper. The audience behaved indecorously as if the concert were an informal dress rehearsal. Mr Fitzpatrick seemed to enjoy himself; he was quite unconscious that Mrs Kearney was taking angry note of his conduct. He stood at the edge of the screen, from time to time jutting out his head and exchanging a laugh with two friends in the corner of the balcony. In the course of the evening Mrs Kearney learned that the Friday concert was to be abandoned and that the Committee was going to move heaven and earth to secure a bumper house on Saturday night. When she heard this she sought out Mr Holohan. She buttonholed him as he was limping out quickly with a glass of lemonade for a young lady and asked him was it true. Yes, it was true.

—But, of course, that doesn't alter the contract, she said. The contract was for four concerts.

Mr Holohan seemed to be in a hurry; he advised her to speak to Mr Fitzpatrick. Mrs Kearney was now beginning to be alarmed. She called Mr Fitzpatrick away from his screen and told him that her daughter had signed for four concerts and that, of course, according to the terms of the contract, she should receive the sum originally stipulated for whether the society gave the four concerts or not. Mr Fitzpatrick, who did not catch the point at issue very quickly, seemed unable to resolve the difficulty and said that he would bring the matter before the Committee. Mrs Kearney's anger began to flutter in her cheek and she had all she could do to keep from asking:

—And who is the *Cometty*, pray?

But she knew that it would not be ladylike to do that: so she was silent.

Little boys were sent out into the principal streets of Dublin early on Friday morning with bundles of handbills. Special puffs appeared in all the evening papers reminding the music-loving public of the treat which was in store for it on the following evening. Mrs Kearney was somewhat reassured but she thought well to tell her husband part of her suspicions. He listened carefully and said that perhaps it would be better if he went with her on Saturday night. She agreed. She respected her husband in the same way as she respected the General Post Office, as something large, secure and fixed; and though she knew the small number of his talents she appreciated his abstract value as a male. She was glad that he had suggested coming with her. She thought her plans over.

The night of the grand concert came. Mrs Kearney, with her husband and daughter, arrived at the Antient Concert Rooms three-quarters of an hour before the time at which the concert was to begin. By ill luck it was a rainy evening. Mrs Kearney placed her daughter's clothes and music in charge of her husband and went all over the building looking for Mr Holohan or Mr Fitzpatrick. She could find neither. She asked the stewards was any member of the Committee in the hall and, after a great deal of trouble, a steward brought out a little woman named Miss Beirne to whom Mrs Kearney explained that she wanted to see one of the secretaries. Miss Beirne expected them any minute and asked could she do anything. Mrs Kearney looked searchingly at the oldish face which was screwed into an expression of trustfulness and enthusiasm and answered:

—No, thank you!

The little woman hoped they would have a good house. She looked out at the rain until the melancholy of the wet street effaced all the trustfulness and enthusiasm from her twisted features. Then she gave a little sigh and said:

—Ah, well! We did our best, the dear knows.

Mrs Kearney had to go back to the dressing-room.

The *artistes* were arriving. The bass and the second tenor had already come. The bass, Mr Duggan, was a slender young man with a scattered black moustache. He was the son of a hall porter in an office in the city and, as a boy, he had sung prolonged bass notes in the resounding hall. From this humble state he had raised himself until he had become a first-rate *artiste*. He had appeared in grand opera. One night, when an operatic *artiste* had fallen ill, he had undertaken the part of the king in the opera of *Maritana* at the Queen's Theatre. He sang his music with great feeling and volume and was warmly welcomed by the gallery; but, unfortunately, he marred the good impression by wiping his nose in his gloved hand once or twice out of thoughtlessness. He was unassuming and spoke little. He said *yous* so softly that it passed unnoticed and he never drank anything stronger than milk for his voice' sake. Mr Bell, the second tenor, was a fair-haired little man who competed every year for prizes at the Feis Ceoil. On his fourth trial he had been awarded a bronze medal. He was extremely nervous and extremely jealous of other tenors and he covered his nervous jealousy with an ebullient friendliness. It was his humour to have people know what an ordeal a concert was to him. Therefore when he saw Mr Duggan he went over to him and asked:

—Are you in it too?

—Yes, said Mr Duggan.

Mr Bell laughed at his fellow-sufferer, held out his hand and said:

—Shake!

Mrs Kearney passed by these two young men and went to the edge of the screen to view the house. The seats were being filled up rapidly and a pleasant noise circulated in the auditorium. She came back and spoke to her husband privately. Their conversation was evidently about Kathleen for they both glanced at her often as she stood chatting to one of her Nationalist friends, Miss Healy, the contralto. An unknown solitary woman with a pale face walked through the room. The women followed with keen eyes the faded blue dress which was stretched upon a meagre body. Someone said that she was Madam Glynn, the soprano.

—I wonder where did they dig her up, said Kathleen to Miss Healy. I'm sure I never heard of her.

Miss Healy had to smile. Mr Holohan limped into the dressing-room at that moment and the two young ladies asked him who was the unknown woman. Mr Holohan said that she was Madam Glynn from London. Madam Glynn took her stand in a corner of the room, holding a roll of music stiffly before her and from time to time changing the direction of her startled gaze. The shadow took her faded dress into shelter but fell revengefully into the little cup behind her collar-bone. The noise of the hall became more audible. The first tenor and the baritone arrived together. They were both well dressed, stout and complacent and they brought a breath of opulence among the company.

Mrs Kearney brought her daughter over to them, and talked to them amiably. She wanted to be on good terms with them but, while she strove to be polite, her eyes followed Mr Holohan in his limping and devious courses. As soon as she could she excused herself and went out after him.

—Mr Holohan, I want to speak to you for a moment, she said.

They went down to a discreet part of the corridor. Mrs Kearney asked him when was her daughter going to be paid. Mr Holohan said that Mr Fitzpatrick had charge of that. Mrs Kearney said that she didn't know anything about Mr Fitzpatrick. Her daughter had signed a contract for eight guineas and she would have to be paid. Mr Holohan said that it wasn't his business.

—Why isn't it your business? asked Mrs Kearney. Didn't you yourself bring her the contract? Anyway, if it's not your business it's my business and I mean to see to it.

—You'd better speak to Mr Fitzpatrick, said Mr Holohan distantly.

—I don't know anything about Mr Fitzpatrick, repeated Mrs Kearney. I have my contract, and I intend to see that it is carried out.

When she came back to the dressing-room her cheeks were slightly suffused. The room was lively. Two men in outdoor dress had taken possession of the fireplace and were chatting familiarly with Miss Healy and the baritone. They were the *Freeman* man and Mr O'Madden Burke. The *Freeman* man had come in to say that he could not wait for the concert as he had to report the lecture which an American priest was giving in the Mansion House. He said they were to leave the report for him at the *Freeman* office and he would see that it went in. He was a grey-haired man, with a plausible voice and careful manners. He held an extinguished cigar in his hand and the aroma of cigar smoke floated near him. He had not intended to stay a moment because concerts and *artistes* bored him considerably but he remained leaning against the mantelpiece. Miss Healy stood in front of him, talking and laughing. He was old enough to suspect one reason for her politeness but young enough in spirit to turn the moment to account. The warmth, fragrance and colour of her body appealed to his senses. He was pleasantly conscious that the bosom which he saw rise and fall slowly beneath him rose and fell at that moment for him, that the laughter and fragrance and wilful glances were his tribute. When he could stay no longer he took leave of her regretfully.

—O'Madden Burke will write the notice, he explained to Mr Holohan, and I'll see it in.

—Thank you very much, Mr Hendrick, said Mr Holohan. You'll see it in, I know. Now, won't you have a little something before you go?

—I don't mind, said Mr Hendrick.

The two men went along some tortuous passages and up a dark staircase and came to a secluded room where one of the stewards was uncorking bottles for a few gentlemen. One of these gentlemen was Mr O'Madden Burke, who had found out the room by instinct. He was a suave elderly man who balanced his imposing body, when at rest, upon a large silk umbrella. His magniloquent western name was the moral umbrella upon which he balanced the fine problem of his finances. He was widely respected.

While Mr Holohan was entertaining the *Freeman* man Mrs Kearney was speaking so animatedly to her husband that he had to ask her to lower her voice. The conversation of the others in the dressing-room had become strained. Mr Bell, the first item, stood ready with his music but the accompanist made no sign. Evidently something was wrong. Mr Kearney looked straight before him, stroking his beard, while Mrs Kearney spoke into Kathleen's ear with subdued emphasis.

From the hall came sounds of encouragement, clapping and stamping of feet. The first tenor and the baritone and Miss Healy stood together, waiting tranquilly, but Mr Bell's nerves were greatly agitated because he was afraid the audience would think that he had come late.

Mr Holohan and Mr O'Madden Burke came into the room. In a moment Mr Holohan perceived the hush. He went over to Mrs Kearney and spoke with her earnestly. While they were speaking the noise in the hall grew louder. Mr Holohan became very red and excited. He spoke volubly, but Mrs Kearney said curtly at intervals:

—She won't go on. She must get her eight guineas.

Mr Holohan pointed desperately towards the hall where the audience was clapping and stamping. He appealed to Mr Kearney and to Kathleen. But Mr Kearney continued to stroke his beard and Kathleen looked down, moving the point of her new shoe: it was not her fault. Mrs Kearney repeated:

—She won't go on without her money.

After a swift struggle of tongues Mr Holohan hobbled out in haste. The room was silent. When the strain of the silence had become somewhat painful Miss Healy said to the baritone:

—Have you seen Mrs Pat Campbell this week?

The baritone had not seen her but he had been told that she was very fine. The conversation went no further. The first tenor bent his head and began to count the links of the gold chain which was extended across his waist, smiling and humming random notes to observe the effect on the frontal sinus. From time to time everyone glanced at Mrs Kearney.

The noise in the auditorium had risen to a clamour when Mr Fitzpatrick burst into the room, followed by Mr Holohan, who was panting. The clapping and stamping in the hall were punctuated by whistling. Mr Fitzpatrick held a few bank-notes in his hand. He counted out four into Mrs Kearney's hand and said she would get the other half at the interval. Mrs Kearney said:

—This is four shillings short.

But Kathleen gathered in her skirt and said: *Now, Mr Bell*, to the first item, who was shaking like an aspen. The singer and the accompanist went out together. The noise in the hall died away. There was a pause of a few seconds: and then the piano was heard.

The first part of the concert was very successful except for Madam Glynn's item. The poor lady sang *Killarney* in a bodiless gasping voice, with all the old-fashioned mannerisms of intonation and pronunciation which she believed lent elegance to her singing. She looked as if she had been resurrected from an old stage-wardrobe and the cheaper parts of the hall made fun of her high wailing notes. The first tenor and the contralto, however, brought down the house. Kathleen played a selection of Irish airs which was generously applauded. The first part closed with a stirring patriotic recitation delivered by a young lady who arranged amateur theatricals. It was deservedly applauded; and, when it was ended, the men went out for the interval, content.

All this time the dressing-room was a hive of excitement. In one corner were Mr Holohan, Mr Fitzpatrick, Miss Beirne, two of the stewards, the baritone, the bass, and Mr O'Madden Burke. Mr O'Madden Burke said it was the most scandalous exhibition he had ever witnessed. Miss Kathleen Kearney's musical career was ended in Dublin after that, he said. The baritone was asked what did he think of Mrs Kearney's conduct. He did not like to say anything. He had been paid his money and wished to be at peace with men. However, he said that Mrs Kearney might have taken the *artistes* into consideration. The stewards and the secretaries debated hotly as to what should be done when the interval came.

—I agree with Miss Beirne, said Mr O'Madden Burke. Pay her nothing.

In another corner of the room were Mrs Kearney and her husband, Mr Bell, Miss Healy and the young lady who had recited the patriotic piece. Mrs Kearney said that the Committee had treated her scandalously. She had spared neither trouble nor expense and this was how she was repaid.

They thought they had only a girl to deal with and that, therefore, they could ride roughshod over her. But she would show them their mistake. They wouldn't have dared to have treated her like that if she had been a man. But she would see that her daughter got her rights: she wouldn't be fooled. If they didn't pay her to the last farthing she would make Dublin ring. Of course she was sorry for the sake of the *artistes*. But what else could she do? She appealed to the second tenor who said he thought she had not been well treated. Then she appealed to Miss Healy. Miss Healy wanted to join the other group but she did not like to do so because she was a great friend of Kathleen's and the Kearneys had often invited her to their house.

As soon as the first part was ended Mr Fitzpatrick and Mr Holohan went over to Mrs Kearney and told her that the other four guineas would be paid after the Committee meeting on the following Tuesday and that, in case her daughter did not play for the second part, the Committee would consider the contract broken and would pay nothing.

—I haven't seen any Committee, said Mrs Kearney angrily. My daughter has her contract. She will get four pounds eight into her hand or a foot she won't put on that platform.

—I'm surprised at you, Mrs Kearney, said Mr Holohan. I never thought you would treat us this way.

—And what way did you treat me? asked Mrs Kearney.

Her face was inundated with an angry colour and she looked as if she would attack someone with her hands.

—I'm asking for my rights, she said.

—You might have some sense of decency, said Mr Holo-han.

—Might I, indeed? . . . And when I ask when my daughter is going to be paid I can't get a civil answer.

She tossed her head and assumed a haughty voice:

—You must speak to the secretary. It's not my business. I'm a great fellow fol-the-diddle-I-do.

—I thought you were a lady, said Mr Holohan, walking away from her abruptly.

After that Mrs Kearney's conduct was condemned on all hands: everyone approved of what the Committee had done. She stood at the door, haggard with rage, arguing with her husband and daughter, gesticulating with them. She waited until it was time for the second part to begin in the hope that the secretaries would approach her. But Miss Healy had kindly consented to play one or two accompaniments. Mrs Kearney had to stand aside to allow the baritone and his accompanist to pass up to the platform. She stood still for an instant like an angry stone image and, when the first notes of the song struck her ear, she caught up her daughter's cloak and said to her husband:

—Get a cab!

He went out at once. Mrs Kearney wrapped the cloak round her daughter and followed him. As she passed through the doorway she stopped and glared into Mr Holohan's face.

—I'm not done with you yet, she said.

—But I'm done with you, said Mr Holohan.

Kathleen followed her mother meekly. Mr Holohan began to pace up and down the room, in order to cool himself for he felt his skin on fire.

—That's a nice lady! he said. O, she's a nice lady!

—You did the proper thing, Holohan, said Mr O'Madden Burke, poised upon his umbrella in approval.

GRACE

Two gentlemen who were in the lavatory at the time tried to lift him up: but he was quite helpless. He lay curled up at the foot of the stairs down which he had fallen. They succeeded in turning him over. His hat had rolled a few yards away and his clothes were smeared with the filth and ooze of the floor on which he had lain, face downwards. His eyes were closed and he breathed with a grunting noise. A thin stream of blood trickled from the corner of his mouth.

These two gentlemen and one of the curates carried him up the stairs and laid him down again on the floor of the bar. In two minutes he was surrounded by a ring of men. The manager of the bar asked everyone who he was and who was with him. No one knew who he was but one of the curates said he had served the gentleman with a small rum.

—Was he by himself? asked the manager.

—No, sir. There was two gentlemen with him.

—And where are they?

No one knew; a voice said:

—Give him air. He's fainted.

The ring of onlookers distended and closed again elastically. A dark medal of blood had formed itself near the man's head on the tessellated floor. The manager, alarmed by the grey pallor of the man's face, sent for a policeman.

His collar was unfastened and his necktie undone. He opened his eyes for an instant, sighed and closed them again. One of the gentlemen who had carried him upstairs held a dinged silk hat in his hand. The manager asked repeatedly did no one know who the injured man was or where had his friends gone. The door of the bar opened and an immense constable entered. A crowd which had followed him down the laneway collected outside the door, struggling to look in through the glass panels.

The manager at once began to narrate what he knew. The constable, a young man with thick immobile features, listened. He moved his head slowly to right and left and from the manager to the person on the floor, as if he feared to be the victim of some delusion. Then he drew off his glove, produced a small book from his waist, licked the lead of his pencil and made ready to indite. He asked in a suspicious provincial accent:

—Who is the man? What's his name and address?

A young man in a cycling-suit cleared his way through the ring of bystanders. He knelt down promptly beside the injured man and called for water. The constable knelt down also to help. The young man washed the blood from the injured man's mouth and then called for some brandy. The constable repeated the order in an authoritative voice until a curate came running with the glass. The brandy was forced down the man's throat. In a few seconds he opened his eyes and looked about him. He looked at the circle of faces and then, understanding, strove to rise to his feet.

—You're all right now? asked the young man in the cycling-suit.

—Sha, 's nothing, said the injured man, trying to stand up.

He was helped to his feet. The manager said something about a hospital and some of the bystanders gave advice. The battered silk hat was placed on the man's head. The constable asked:

—Where do you live?

The man, without answering, began to twirl the ends of his moustache. He made light of his accident. It was nothing, he said: only a little accident. He spoke very thickly.

—Where do you live? repeated the constable.

The man said they were to get a cab for him. While the point was being debated a tall agile gentleman of fair complexion, wearing a long yellow ulster, came from the far end of the bar. Seeing the spectacle he called out:

—Hallo, Tom, old man! What's the trouble?

—Sha, 's nothing, said the man.

The new-comer surveyed the deplorable figure before him and then turned to the constable saying:

—It's all right, constable. I'll see him home.

The constable touched his helmet and answered:

—All right, Mr Power!

—Come now, Tom, said Mr Power, taking his friend by the arm. No bones broken. What? Can you walk?

The young man in the cycling-suit took the man by the other arm and the crowd divided.

—How did you get yourself into this mess? asked Mr Power.

—The gentleman fell down the stairs, said the young man.

—I' 'ery 'uch o'liged to you, sir, said the injured man.

—Not at all.

—'an't we have a little . . . ?

—Not now. Not now.

The three men left the bar and the crowd sifted through the doors into the laneway. The manager brought the constable to the stairs to inspect the scene of the accident. They agreed that the gentleman must have missed his footing. The customers returned to the counter and a curate set about removing the traces of blood from the floor.

When they came out into Grafton Street Mr Power whistled for an outsider. The injured man said again as well as he could:

—I' 'ery 'uch o'liged to you, sir. I hope we'll 'eet again. 'y na'e is Kernan.

The shock and the incipient pain had partly sobered him.

—Don't mention it, said the young man.

They shook hands. Mr Kernan was hoisted on to the car and, while Mr Power was giving directions to the carman, he expressed his gratitude to the young man and regretted that they could not have a little drink together.

—Another time, said the young man.

The car drove off towards Westmoreland Street. As it passed the Ballast Office the clock showed half-past nine. A keen east wind hit them blowing from the mouth of the river. Mr Kernan was huddled together with cold. His friend asked him to tell how the accident had happened.

—I 'an't, 'an, he answered, 'y 'ongue is hurt.

—Show.

The other leaned over the well of the car and peered into Mr Kernan's mouth but he could not see. He struck a match and, sheltering it in the shell of his hands, peered again into the mouth which Mr Kernan opened obediently. The swaying movement of the car brought the match to and from the opened mouth. The lower teeth and gums were covered with clotted blood and a minute piece of the tongue seemed to have been bitten off. The match was blown out.

—That's ugly, said Mr Power.

—Sha, 's nothing, said Mr Kernan, closing his mouth and pulling the collar of his filthy coat across his neck.

Mr Kernan was a commercial traveller of the old school

which believed in the dignity of its calling. He had never been seen in the city without a silk hat of some decency and a pair of gaiters. By grace of these two articles of clothing, he said, a man could always pass muster. He carried on the tradition of his Napoleon, the great Blackwhite, whose memory he evoked at times by legend and mimicry. Modern business methods had spared him only so far as to allow him a little office in Crowe Street on the window blind of which was written the name of his firm with the address—London, E.C. On the mantelpiece of this little office a little leaden battalion of canisters was drawn up and on the table before the window stood four or five china bowls which were usually half full of a black liquid. From these bowls Mr Kernan tasted tea. He took a mouthful, drew it up, saturated his palate with it and then spat it forth into the grate. Then he paused to judge.

Mr Power, a much younger man, was employed in the Royal Irish Constabulary Office in Dublin Castle. The arc of his social rise intersected the arc of his friend's decline but Mr Kernan's decline was mitigated by the fact that certain of those friends who had known him at his highest point of success still esteemed him as a character. Mr Power was one of these friends. His inexplicable debts were a byword in his circle; he was a debonair young man.

The car halted before a small house on the Glasnevin road and Mr Kernan was helped into the house. His wife put him to bed while Mr Power sat downstairs in the kitchen asking the children where they went to school and what book they were in. The children—two girls and a boy, conscious of their father's helplessness and of their mother's absence, began some horseplay with him. He was surprised at their manners and at their accents and his brow grew thoughtful. After a while Mrs Kernan entered the kitchen, exclaiming:

—Such a sight! O, he'll do for himself one day and that's the holy alls of it. He's been drinking since Friday.

Mr Power was careful to explain to her that he was not responsible, that he had come on the scene by the merest accident. Mrs Kernan, remembering Mr Power's good offices during domestic quarrels as well as many small, but opportune loans, said:

—O, you needn't tell me that, Mr Power. I know you're a friend of his not like some of those others he does be with. They're all right so long as he has money in his pocket to keep him out from his wife and family. Nice friends! Who was he with to-night, I'd like to know?

Mr Power shook his head but said nothing.

—I'm so sorry, she continued, that I've nothing in the house to offer you. But if you wait a minute I'll send round to Fogarty's at the corner.

Mr Power stood up.

—We were waiting for him to come home with the money. He never seems to think he has a home at all.

—O, now, Mrs Kernan, said Mr Power, we'll make him turn over a new leaf. I'll talk to Martin. He's the man. We'll come here one of these nights and talk it over.

She saw him to the door. The carman was stamping up and down the footpath and swinging his arms to warm himself.

—It's very kind of you to bring him home, she said.

—Not at all, said Mr Power.

He got up on the car. As it drove off he raised his hat to her gaily.

—We'll make a new man of him, he said. Good-night, Mrs Kernan.

.   .   .   .

Mrs Kernan's puzzled eyes watched the car till it was out of sight. Then she withdrew them, went into the house and emptied her husband's pockets.

She was an active, practical woman of middle age. Not long before she had celebrated her silver wedding and renewed her intimacy with her husband by waltzing with him to Mr Power's accompaniment. In her days of courtship Mr Kernan had seemed to her a not ungallant figure: and she still hurried to the chapel door whenever a wedding was reported and, seeing the bridal pair, recalled with vivid pleasure how she had passed out of the Star of the Sea Church in Sandymount, leaning on the arm of a jovial well-fed man who was dressed smartly in a frock-coat and lavender trousers and carried a silk hat gracefully balanced upon his other arm. After three weeks she had found a wife's life irksome and, later on, when she was beginning to find it unbearable, she had become a mother. The part of mother presented to her no insuperable difficulties and for twenty-five years she had kept house shrewdly for her husband. Her two eldest sons were launched. One was in a draper's shop in Glasgow and the other was clerk to a tea-merchant in Belfast. They were good sons, wrote regularly and sometimes sent home money. The other children were still at school.

Mr Kernan sent a letter to his office next day and remained in bed. She made beef-tea for him and scolded him roundly. She accepted his frequent intemperance as part of the climate, healed him dutifully whenever he was sick and always tried to make him eat a breakfast. There were worse husbands. He had never been violent since the boys had grown up and she knew that he would walk to the end of Thomas Street and back again to book even a small order.

Two nights after his friends came to see him. She brought them up to his bedroom, the air of which was impregnated with a personal odour, and gave them chairs at the fire. Mr Kernan's tongue, the occasional stinging pain of which had made him somewhat irritable during the day, became more polite. He sat propped up in the bed by pillows and the little colour in his puffy cheeks made them resemble warm cinders. He apologised to his guests for the disorder of the room but at the same time looked at them a little proudly, with a veteran's pride.

He was quite unconscious that he was the victim of a plot which his friends, Mr Cunningham, Mr M'Coy and Mr Power had disclosed to Mrs Kernan in the parlour. The idea had been Mr Power's but its development was entrusted to Mr Cunningham. Mr Kernan came of Protestant stock and, though he had been converted to the Catholic faith at the time of his marriage, he had not been in the pale of the Church for twenty years. He was fond, moreover, of giving side-thrusts at Catholicism.

Mr Cunningham was the very man for such a case. He was an elder colleague of Mr Power. His own domestic life was not very happy. People had great sympathy with him for it was known that he had married an unpresentable woman who was an incurable drunkard. He had set up house for her six times; and each time she had pawned the furniture on him.

Everyone had respect for poor Martin Cunningham. He was a thoroughly sensible man, influential and intelligent. His blade of human knowledge, natural astuteness particularised by long association with cases in the police courts, had been tempered by brief immersions in the waters of general philosophy. He was well informed. His friends bowed to his opinions and considered that his face was like Shakespeare's.

When the plot had been disclosed to her Mrs Kernan had said:

—I leave it all in your hands, Mr Cunningham.

After a quarter of a century of married life she had very few illusions left. Religion for her was a habit and she suspected that a man of her husband's age would not change greatly before death. She was tempted to see a curious appropriateness in his accident and, but that she did not wish to seem bloody-minded, she would have told the gentlemen that

Mr Kernan's tongue would not suffer by being shortened. However, Mr Cunningham was a capable man; and religion was religion. The scheme might do good and, at least, it could do no harm. Her beliefs were not extravagant. She believed steadily in the Sacred Heart as the most generally useful of all Catholic devotions and approved of the sacraments. Her faith was bounded by her kitchen but, if she was put to it, she could believe also in the banshee and in the Holy Ghost.

The gentlemen began to talk of the accident. Mr Cunningham said that he had once known a similar case. A man of seventy had bitten off a piece of his tongue during an epileptic fit and the tongue had filled in again so that no one could see a trace of the bite.

—Well, I'm not seventy, said the invalid.

—God forbid, said Mr Cunningham.

—It doesn't pain you now? asked Mr M'Coy.

Mr M'Coy had been at one time a tenor of some reputation. His wife, who had been a soprano, still taught young children to play the piano at low terms. His line of life had not been the shortest distance between two points and for short periods he had been driven to live by his wits. He had been a clerk in the Midland Railway, a canvasser for advertisements for *The Irish Times* and for *The Freeman's Journal*, a town traveller for a coal firm on commission, a private inquiry agent, a clerk in the office of the Sub-Sheriff and he had recently become secretary to the City Coroner. His new office made him professionally interested in Mr Kernan's case.

—Pain? Not much, answered Mr Kernan. But it's so sickening. I feel as if I wanted to retch off.

—That's the boose, said Mr Cunningham firmly.

—No, said Mr Kernan. I think I caught a cold on the car. There's something keeps coming into my throat, phlegm or—

—Mucus, said Mr M'Coy.

—It keeps coming like from down in my throat; sickening thing.

—Yes, yes, said Mr M'Coy, that's the thorax.

He looked at Mr Cunningham and Mr Power at the same time with an air of challenge. Mr Cunningham nodded his head rapidly and Mr Power said:

—Ah, well, all's well that ends well.

—I'm very much obliged to you, old man, said the invalid. Mr Power waved his hand.

—Those other two fellows I was with—

—Who were you with? asked Mr Cunningham.

—A chap. I don't know his name. Damn it now, what's his name? Little chap with sandy hair. . . .

—And who else?

—Harford.

—Hm, said Mr Cunningham.

When Mr Cunningham made that remark people were silent. It was known that the speaker had secret sources of information. In this case the monosyllable had a moral intention. Mr Harford sometimes formed one of a little detachment which left the city shortly after noon on Sunday with the purpose of arriving as soon as possible at some public-house on the outskirts of the city where its members duly qualified themselves as *bona-fide* travellers. But his fellow-travellers had never consented to overlook his origin. He had begun life as an obscure financier by lending small sums of money to workmen at usurious interest. Later on he had become the partner of a very fat short gentleman, Mr Goldberg, of the Liffey Loan Bank. Though he had never embraced more than the Jewish ethical code his fellow-Catholics, whenever they had smarted in person or by proxy under his exactions, spoke of him bitterly as an Irish Jew and an illiterate and saw divine disapproval of usury made manifest through the person of his idiot son. At other times they remembered his good points.

—I wonder where did he go to, said Mr Kernan.

He wished the details of the incident to remain vague. He wished his friends to think there had been some mistake, that Mr Harford and he had missed each other. His friends, who knew quite well Mr Harford's manners in drinking, were silent. Mr Power said again:

—All's well that ends well.

Mr Kernan changed the subject at once.

—That was a decent young chap, that medical fellow, he said. Only for him—

—O, only for him, said Mr Power, it might have been a case of seven days without the option of a fine.

—Yes, yes, said Mr Kernan, trying to remember. I remember now there was a policeman. Decent young fellow, he seemed. How did it happen at all?

—It happened that you were peloothered, Tom, said Mr Cunningham gravely.

—True bill, said Mr Kernan, equally gravely.

—I suppose you squared the constable, Jack, said Mr M'Coy.

Mr Power did not relish the use of his Christian name. He was not straight-laced but he could not forget that Mr M'Coy had recently made a crusade in search of valises and portmanteaus to enable Mrs M'Coy to fulfil imaginary engagements in the country. More than he resented the fact that he had been victimised he resented such low playing of the game. He answered the question, therefore, as if Mr Kernan had asked it.

The narrative made Mr Kernan indignant. He was keenly conscious of his citizenship, wished to live with his city on terms mutually honourable and resented any affront put upon him by those whom he called country bumpkins.

—Is this what we pay rates for? he asked. To feed and clothe these ignorant bostoons . . . and they're nothing else.

Mr Cunningham laughed. He was a Castle official only during office hours.

—How could they be anything else, Tom? he said.

He assumed a thick provincial accent and said in a tone of command:

—65, catch your cabbage!

Everyone laughed. Mr M'Coy, who wanted to enter the conversation by any door, pretended that he had never heard the story. Mr Cunningham said:

—It is supposed—they say, you know—to take place in the depot where they get these thundering big country fellows, omadhauns, you know, to drill. The sergeant makes them stand in a row against the wall and held up their plates.

He illustrated the story by grotesque gestures.

—At dinner, you know. Then he has a bloody big bowl of cabbage before him on the table and a bloody big spoon like a shovel. He takes up a wad of cabbage on the spoon and pegs it across the room and the poor devils have to try and catch it on their plates: *65, catch your cabbage*.

Everyone laughed again: but Mr Kernan was somewhat indignant still. He talked of writing a letter to the papers.

—These yahoos coming up here, he said, think they can boss the people. I needn't tell you, Martin, what kind of men they are.

Mr Cunningham gave a qualified assent.

—It's like everything else in this world, he said. You get some bad ones and you get some good ones.

—O yes, you get some good ones, I admit, said Mr Kernan, satisfied.

—It's better to have nothing to say to them, said Mr M'Coy. That's my opinion!

Mrs Kernan entered the room and, placing a tray on the table, said:

—Help yourselves, gentlemen.

Mr Power stood up to officiate, offering her his chair. She declined it, saying she was ironing downstairs, and, after having exchanged a nod with Mr Cunningham behind Mr Power's back, prepared to leave the room. Her husband called out to her:

—And have you nothing for me, duckie?

—O, you! The back of my hand to you! said Mrs Kernan tartly.

Her husband called after her:

—Nothing for poor little hubby!

He assumed such a comical face and voice that the distribution of the bottles of stout took place amid general merriment.

The gentlemen drank from their glasses, set the glasses again on the table and paused. Then Mr Cunningham turned towards Mr Power and said casually:

—On Thursday night, you said, Jack?

—Thursday, yes, said Mr Power.

—Righto! said Mr Cunningham promptly.

—We can meet in M'Auley's, said Mr M'Coy. That'll be the most convenient place.

—But we mustn't be late, said Mr Power earnestly, because it is sure to be crammed to the doors.

—We can meet at half-seven, said Mr M'Coy.

—Righto! said Mr Cunningham.

—Half-seven at M'Auley's be it!

There was a short silence. Mr Kernan waited to see whether he would be taken into his friends' confidence. Then he asked:

—What's in the wind?

—O, it's nothing, said Mr Cunningham. It's only a little matter that we're arranging about for Thursday.

—The opera, is it? said Mr Kernan.

—No, no, said Mr Cunningham in an evasive tone, it's just a little . . . spiritual matter.

—O, said Mr Kernan.

There was silence again. Then Mr Power said, point-blank:

—To tell you the truth, Tom, we're going to make a retreat.

—Yes, that's it, said Mr Cunningham, Jack and I and M'Coy here—we're all going to wash the pot.

He uttered the metaphor with a certain homely energy and, encouraged by his own voice, proceeded:

—You see, we may as well all admit we're a nice collection of scoundrels, one and all. I say, one and all, he added with gruff charity and turning to Mr Power. Own up now!

—I own up, said Mr Power.

—And I own up, said Mr M'Coy.

—So we're going to wash the pot together, said Mr Cunningham.

A thought seemed to strike him. He turned suddenly to the invalid and said:

—Do you know what, Tom, has just occurred to me? You might join in and we'd have a four-handed reel.

—Good idea, said Mr Power. The four of us together.

Mr Kernan was silent. The proposal conveyed very little meaning to his mind but, understanding that some spiritual agencies were about to concern themselves on his behalf, he thought he owed it to his dignity to show a stiff neck. He took no part in the conversation for a long while but listened, with an air of calm enmity, while his friends discussed the Jesuits.

—I haven't such a bad opinion of the Jesuits, he said, intervening at length. They're an educated order. I believe they mean well too.

—They're the grandest order in the Church, Tom, said Mr Cunningham, with enthusiasm. The General of the Jesuits stands next to the Pope.

—There's no mistake about it, said Mr M'Coy, if you want a thing well done and no flies about it you go to a Jesuit. They're the boyos have influence. I'll tell you a case in point. . . .

—The Jesuits are a fine body of men, said Mr Power.

—It's a curious thing, said Mr Cunningham, about the Jesuit Order. Every other order of the Church had to be reformed at some time or other but the Jesuit Order was never once reformed. It never fell away.

—Is that so? asked Mr M'Coy.

—That's a fact, said Mr Cunningham. That's history.

—Look at their church, too, said Mr Power. Look at the congregation they have.

—The Jesuits cater for the upper classes, said Mr M'Coy.

—Of course, said Mr Power.

—Yes, said Mr Kernan. That's why I have a feeling for them. It's some of those secular priests, ignorant, bumptious—

—They're all good men, said Mr Cunningham, each in his own way. The Irish priesthood is honoured all the world over.

—O yes, said Mr Power.

—Not like some of the other priesthoods on the continent, said Mr M'Coy, unworthy of the name.

—Perhaps you're right, said Mr Kernan, relenting.

—Of course I'm right, said Mr Cunningham. I haven't been in the world all this time and seen most sides of it without being a judge of character.

The gentlemen drank again, one following another's example. Mr Kernan seemed to be weighing something in his mind. He was impressed. He had a high opinion of Mr Cunningham as a judge of character and as a reader of faces. He asked for particulars.

—O, it's just a retreat, you know, said Mr Cunningham. Father Purdon is giving it. It's for business men, you know.

—He won't be too hard on us, Tom, said Mr Power persuasively.

—Father Purdon? Father Purdon? said the invalid.

—O, you must know him, Tom, said Mr Cunningham, stoutly. Fine jolly fellow! He's a man of the world like ourselves.

—Ah, . . . yes. I think I know him. Rather red face; tall.

—That's the man.

—And tell me, Martin. . . . Is he a good preacher?

—Mmmno. . . . It's not exactly a sermon, you know. It's just a kind of a friendly talk, you know, in a common-sense way.

Mr Kernan deliberated. Mr M'Coy said:

—Father Tom Burke, that was the boy!

—O, Father Tom Burke, said Mr Cunningham, that was a born orator. Did you ever hear him, Tom?

—Did I ever hear him! said the invalid, nettled. Rather! I heard him. . . .

—And yet they say he wasn't much of a theologian, said Mr Cunningham.

—Is that so? said Mr M'Coy.

—O, of course, nothing wrong, you know. Only sometimes, they say, he didn't preach what was quite orthodox.

—Ah! . . . he was a splendid man, said Mr M'Coy.

—I heard him once, Mr Kernan continued. I forget the subject of his discourse now. Crofton and I were in the back of the . . . pit, you know . . . the—

—The body, said Mr Cunningham.

—Yes, in the back near the door. I forget now what. . . . O yes, it was on the Pope, the late Pope. I remember it well. Upon my word it was magnificent, the style of the oratory. And his voice! God! hadn't he a voice! *The Prisoner of the Vatican*, he called him. I remember Crofton saying to me when we came out—

—But he's an Orangeman, Crofton, isn't he? said Mr Power.

—'Course he is, said Mr Kernan, and a damned decent Orangeman too. We went into Butler's in Moore Street—faith, I was genuinely moved, tell you the God's truth—and I remember well his very words. *Kernan*, he said, *we worship at different altars*, he said, *but our belief is the same*. Struck me as very well put.

—There's a good deal in that, said Mr Power. There used

always be crowds of Protestants in the chapel when Father Tom was preaching.

—There's not much difference between us, said Mr M'Coy. We both believe in—

He hesitated for a moment.

—. . . in the Redeemer. Only they don't believe in the Pope and in the mother of God.

—But, of course, said Mr Cunningham quietly and effectively, our religion is *the* religion, the old, original faith.

—Not a doubt of it, said Mr Kernan warmly.

Mrs Kernan came to the door of the bedroom and announced:

—Here's a visitor for you!

—Who is it?

—Mr Fogarty.

—O, come in! come in!

A pale oval face came forward into the light. The arch of its fair trailing moustache was repeated in the fair eyebrows looped above pleasantly astonished eyes. Mr Fogarty was a modest grocer. He had failed in business in a licensed house in the city because his financial condition had constrained him to tie himself to second-class distillers and brewers. He had opened a small shop on Glasnevin Road where, he flattered himself, his manners would ingratiate him with the housewives of the district. He bore himself with a certain grace, complimented little children and spoke with a neat enunciation. He was not without culture.

Mr Fogarty brought a gift with him, a half-pint of special whisky. He inquired politely for Mr Kernan, placed his gift on the table and sat down with the company on equal terms. Mr Kernan appreciated the gift all the more since he was aware that there was a small account for groceries unsettled between him and Mr Fogarty. He said:

—I wouldn't doubt you, old man. Open that, Jack, will you?

Mr Power again officiated. Glasses were rinsed and five small measures of whisky were poured out. This new influence enlivened the conversation. Mr Fogarty, sitting on a small area of the chair, was specially interested.

—Pope Leo XIII., said Mr Cunningham, was one of the lights of the age. His great idea, you know, was the union of the Latin and Greek Churches. That was the aim of his life.

—I often heard he was one of the most intellectual men in Europe, said Mr Power. I mean apart from his being Pope.

—So he was, said Mr Cunningham, if not *the* most so. His motto, you know, as Pope, was *Lux upon Lux—Light upon Light*.

—No, no, said Mr Fogarty eagerly. I think you're wrong there. It was *Lux in Tenebris*, I think—*Light in Darkness*.

—O, yes, said Mr M'Coy, *Tenebrae*.

—Allow me, said Mr Cunningham positively, it was *Lux upon Lux*. And Pius IX. his predecessor's motto was *Crux upon Crux*—that is, *Cross upon Cross*—to show the difference between their two pontificates.

The inference was allowed. Mr Cunningham continued.

—Pope Leo, you know, was a great scholar and a poet.

—He had a strong face, said Mr Kernan.

—Yes, said Mr Cunningham. He wrote Latin poetry.

—Is that so? said Mr Fogarty.

Mr M'Coy tasted his whisky contentedly and shook his head with a double intention, saying:

—That's no joke, I can tell you.

—We didn't learn that, Tom, said Mr Power, following Mr M'Coy's example, when we went to the penny-a-week school.

—There was many a good man went to the penny-a-week school with a sod of turf under his oxter, said Mr Kernan sententiously. The old system was the best: plain honest education. None of your modern trumpery. . . .

—Quite right, said Mr Power.

—No superfluities, said Mr Fogarty.

He enunciated the word and then drank gravely.

—I remember reading, said Mr Cunningham, that one of Pope Leo's poems was on the invention of the photograph—in Latin, of course.

—On the photograph! exclaimed Mr Kernan.

—Yes, said Mr Cunningham.

He also drank from his glass.

—Well, you know, said Mr M'Coy, isn't the photograph wonderful when you come to think of it?

—O, of course, said Mr Power, great minds can see things.

—As the poet says: *Great minds are very near to madness*, said Mr Fogarty.

Mr Kernan seemed to be troubled in mind. He made an effort to recall the Protestant theology on some thorny points and in the end addressed Mr Cunningham.

—Tell me, Martin, he said. Weren't some of the Popes—of course, not our present man, or his predecessor, but some of the old Popes—not exactly . . . you know . . . up to the knocker?

There was a silence. Mr Cunningham said:

—O, of course, there were some bad lots. . . . But the astonishing thing is this. Not one of them, not the biggest drunkard, not the most . . . out-and-out ruffian, not one of them ever preached *ex cathedra* a word of false doctrine. Now isn't that an astonishing thing?

—That is, said Mr Kernan.

—Yes, because when the Pope speaks *ex cathedra*, Mr Fogarty explained, he is infallible.

—Yes, said Mr Cunningham.

—O, I know about the infallibility of the Pope. I remember I was younger then. . . . Or was it that—?

Mr Fogarty interrupted. He took up the bottle and helped the others to a little more. Mr M'Coy, seeing that there was not enough to go round, pleaded that he had not finished his first measure. The others accepted under protest. The light music of whisky falling into glasses made an agreeable interlude.

—What's that you were saying, Tom? asked Mr M'Coy.

—Papal infallibility, said Mr Cunningham, that was the greatest scene in the whole history of the Church.

—How was that, Martin? asked Mr Power.

Mr Cunningham held up two thick fingers.

—In the sacred college, you know, of cardinals and archbishops and bishops there were two men who held out against it while the others were all for it. The whole conclave except these two was unanimous. No! They wouldn't have it!

—Ha! said Mr M'Coy.

—And they were a German cardinal by the name of Dolling . . . or Dowling . . . or—

—Dowling was no German, and that's a sure five, said Mr Power, laughing.

—Well, this great German cardinal, whatever his name was, was one; and the other was John MacHale.

—What? cried Mr Kernan. Is it John of Tuam?

—Are you sure of that now? asked Mr Fogarty dubiously. I thought it was some Italian or American.

—John of Tuam, repeated Mr Cunningham, was the man.

He drank and the other gentlemen followed his lead. Then he resumed:

—There they were at it, all the cardinals and bishops and archbishops from all the ends of the earth and these two fighting dog and devil until at last the Pope himself stood up and declared infallibility a dogma of the Church *ex cathedra*. On the very moment John MacHale, who had been arguing and arguing against it, stood up and shouted out with the voice of a lion: *Credo!*

—*I believe!* said Mr Fogarty.

—*Credo!* said Mr Cunningham. That showed the faith he had. He submitted the moment the Pope spoke.

—And what about Dowling? asked Mr M'Coy.

—The German cardinal wouldn't submit. He left the Church.

Mr Cunningham's words had built up the vast image of the Church in the minds of his hearers. His deep raucous voice had thrilled them as it uttered the word of belief and submission. When Mrs Kernan came into the room drying her hands she came into a solemn company. She did not disturb the silence, but leaned over the rail at the foot of the bed.

—I once saw John MacHale, said Mr Kernan, and I'll never forget it as long as I live.

He turned towards his wife to be confirmed.

—I often told you that?

Mrs Kernan nodded.

—It was at the unveiling of Sir John Gray's statue. Edmund Dwyer Gray was speaking, blathering away, and here was this old fellow, crabbed-looking old chap, looking at him from under his bushy eyebrows.

Mr Kernan knitted his brows and, lowering his head like an angry bull, glared at his wife.

—God! he exclaimed, resuming his natural face, I never saw such an eye in a man's head. It was as much as to say: *I have you properly taped, my lad.* He had an eye like a hawk.

—None of the Grays was any good, said Mr Power.

There was a pause again. Mr Power turned to Mrs Kernan and said with abrupt joviality:

—Well, Mrs Kernan, we're going to make your man here a good holy pious and God-fearing Roman Catholic.

He swept his arm round the company inclusively.

—We're all going to make a retreat together and confess our sins—and God knows we want it badly.

—I don't mind, said Mr Kernan, smiling a little nervously.

Mrs Kernan thought it would be wiser to conceal her satisfaction. So she said:

—I pity the poor priest that has to listen to your tale.

Mr Kernan's expression changed.

—If he doesn't like it, he said bluntly, he can . . . do the other thing. I'll just tell him my little tale of woe. I'm not such a bad fellow—

Mr Cunningham intervened promptly.

—We'll all renounce the devil, he said, together, not forgetting his works and pomps.

—Get behind me, Satan! said Mr Fogarty, laughing and looking at the others.

Mr Power said nothing. He felt completely outgeneralled. But a pleased expression flickered across his face.

—All we have to do, said Mr Cunningham, is to stand up with lighted candles in our hands and renew our baptismal vows.

—O, don't forget the candle, Tom, said Mr M'Coy, whatever you do.

—What? said Mr Kernan. Must I have a candle?

—O yes, said Mr Cunningham.

—No, damn it all, said Mr Kernan sensibly, I draw the line there. I'll do the job right enough. I'll do the retreat business and confession, and . . . all that business. But . . . no candles! No, damn it all, I bar the candles!

He shook his head with farcical gravity.

—Listen to that! said his wife.

—I bar the candles, said Mr Kernan, conscious of having created an effect on his audience and continuing to shake his head to and fro. I bar the magic-lantern business.

Everyone laughed heartily.

—There's a nice Catholic for you! said his wife.

—No candles! repeated Mr Kernan obdurately. That's off!

.   .   .   .

The transept of the Jesuit Church in Gardiner Street was almost full; and still at every moment gentlemen entered from the side-door and, directed by the lay-brother, walked on tip-toe along the aisles until they found seating accommodation. The gentlemen were all well dressed and orderly. The light of the lamps of the church fell upon an assembly of black clothes and white collars, relieved here and there by tweeds, on dark mottled pillars of green marble and on lugubrious canvasses. The gentlemen sat in the benches, having hitched their trousers slightly above their knees and laid their hats in security. They sat well back and gazed formally at the dis-tant speck of red light which was suspended before the high altar.

In one of the benches near the pulpit sat Mr Cunningham and Mr Kernan. In the bench behind sat Mr M'Coy alone: and in the bench behind him sat Mr Power and Mr Fogarty. Mr M'Coy had tried unsuccessfully to find a place in the bench with the others and, when the party had settled down in the form of a quincunx, he had tried unsuccessfully to make comic remarks. As these had not been well received he had desisted. Even he was sensible of the decorous atmosphere and even he began to respond to the religious stimulus. In a whisper Mr Cunningham drew Mr Kernan's attention to Mr Harford, the moneylender, who sat some distance off, and to Mr Fan-ning, the registration agent and mayor maker of the city, who was sitting immediately under the pulpit beside one of the newly elected councillors of the ward. To the right sat old Michael Grimes, the owner of three pawnbroker's shops, and Dan Hogan's nephew, who was up for the job in the Town Clerk's office. Farther in front sat Mr Hendrick, the chief reporter of *The Freeman's Journal*, and poor O'Carroll, an old friend of Mr Kernan's, who had been at one time a considerable commercial figure. Gradually, as he recognised familiar faces, Mr Kernan began to feel more at home. His hat, which had been rehabilitated by his wife, rested upon his knees. Once or twice he pulled down his cuffs with one hand while he held the brim of his hat lightly, but firmly, with the other hand.

A powerful-looking figure, the upper part of which was draped with a white surplice, was observed to be struggling up into the pulpit. Simultaneously the congregation unsettled, produced handkerchiefs and knelt upon them with care. Mr Kernan followed the general example. The priest's figure now stood upright in the pulpit, two-thirds of its bulk, crowned by a massive red face, appearing above the balustrade.

Father Purdon knelt down, turned towards the red speck of light and, covering his face with his hands, prayed. After an interval he uncovered his face and rose. The congregation rose also and settled again on its benches. Mr Kernan restored his hat to its original position on his knee and presented an attentive face to the preacher. The preacher turned back each wide sleeve of his surplice with an elaborate large gesture and slowly surveyed the array of faces. Then he said:

For the children of this world are wiser in their generation than the children of light. Wherefore make unto yourselves friends out of the mammon of iniquity so that when you die they may receive you into everlasting dwellings.

Father Purdon developed the text with resonant assurance. It was one of the most difficult texts in all the Scriptures, he said, to interpret properly. It was a text which might seem to the casual observer at variance with the lofty morality elsewhere preached by Jesus Christ. But, he told his hearers, the text had seemed to him specially adapted for the guidance of those whose lot it was to lead the life of the world and who yet wished to lead that life not in the manner of worldlings. It was a text for business men and professional men. Jesus Christ, with His divine understanding of every cranny of our human nature, understood that all men were not called to the religious life, that by far the vast majority were forced to live in the world and, to a certain extent, for the world: and in this sentence He designed to give them a word of counsel, setting before them as exemplars in the religious life those very worshippers of Mammon who were of all men the least solicitous in matters religious.

He told his hearers that he was there that evening for no terrifying, no extravagant purpose; but as a man of the world speaking to his fellow-men. He came to speak to business men and he would speak to them in a businesslike way. If he might use the metaphor, he said, he was their spiritual accountant; and he wished each and every one of his hearers to open his books, the books of his spiritual life, and see if they tallied accurately with conscience.

Jesus Christ was not a hard taskmaster. He understood our little failings, understood the weakness of our poor fallen nature, understood the temptations of this life. We might have had, we all had from time to time, our temptations: we might have, we all had, our failings. But one thing only, he said, he would ask of his hearers. And that was: to be straight and manly with God. If their accounts tallied in every point to say:

—Well, I have verified my accounts. I find all well.

But if, as might happen, there were some discrepancies, to admit the truth, to be frank and say like a man:

—Well, I have looked into my accounts. I find this wrong and this wrong. But, with God's grace, I will rectify this and this. I will set right my accounts.

THE DEAD

LILY, the caretaker's daughter, was literally run off her feet. Hardly had she brought one gentleman into the little pantry behind the office on the ground floor and helped him off with his overcoat than the wheezy hall-door bell clanged again and she had to scamper along the bare hallway to let in another guest. It was well for her she had not to attend to the ladies also. But Miss Kate and Miss Julia had thought of that and had converted the bathroom upstairs into a ladies' dressing-room. Miss Kate and Miss Julia were there, gossiping and laughing and fussing, walking after each other to the head of the stairs, peering down over the banisters and calling down to Lily to ask her who had come.

It was always a great affair, the Misses Morkan's annual dance. Everybody who knew them came to it, members of the family, old friends of the family, the members of Julia's choir, any of Kate's pupils that were grown up enough and even some of Mary Jane's pupils too. Never once had it fallen flat. For years and years it had gone off in splendid style as long as anyone could remember; ever since Kate and Julia, after the death of their brother Pat, had left the house in Stoney Batter and taken Mary Jane, their only niece, to live with them in the dark gaunt house on Usher's Island, the upper part of which they had rented from Mr Fulham, the corn-factor on the ground floor. That was a good thirty years ago if it was a day. Mary Jane, who was then a little girl in short clothes, was now the main prop of the household for she had the organ in Haddington Road. She had been through the Academy and gave a pupils' concert every year in the upper room of the Antient Concert Rooms. Many of her pupils belonged to better-class families on the Kingstown and Dalkey line. Old as they were, her aunts also did their share. Julia, though she was quite grey, was still the leading soprano in Adam and Eve's, and Kate, being too feeble to go about much, gave music lessons to beginners on the old square piano in the back room. Lily, the caretaker's daughter, did house-maid's work for them. Though their life was modest they believed in eating well; the best of everything: diamond-bone sirloins, three-shilling tea and the best bottled stout. But Lily seldom made a mistake in the orders so that she got on well with her three mistresses. They were fussy, that was all. But the only thing they would not stand was back answers.

Of course they had good reason to be fussy on such a night. And then it was long after ten o'clock and yet there was no sign of Gabriel and his wife. Besides they were dreadfully afraid that Freddy Malins might turn up screwed. They would not wish for worlds that any of Mary Jane's pupils should see him under the influence; and when he was like that it was sometimes very hard to manage him. Freddy Malins always came late but they wondered what could be keeping Gabriel: and that was what brought them every two minutes to the banisters to ask Lily had Gabriel or Freddy come.

—O, Mr Conroy, said Lily to Gabriel when she opened

the door for him, Miss Kate and Miss Julia thought you were never coming. Good-night, Mrs Conroy.

—I'll engage they did, said Gabriel, but they forget that my wife here takes three mortal hours to dress herself.

He stood on the mat, scraping the snow from his goloshes, while Lily led his wife to the foot of the stairs and called out:

—Miss Kate, here's Mrs Conroy.

Kate and Julia came toddling down the dark stairs at once. Both of them kissed Gabriel's wife, said she must be perished alive and asked was Gabriel with her.

—Here I am as right as the mail, Aunt Kate! Go on up. I'll follow, called out Gabriel from the dark.

He continued scraping his feet vigorously while the three women went upstairs, laughing, to the ladies' dressing-room. A light fringe of snow lay like a cape on the shoulders of his overcoat and like toecaps on the toes of his goloshes; and, as the buttons of his overcoat slipped with a squeaking noise through the snow-stiffened frieze, a cold fragrant air from out-of-doors escaped from crevices and folds.

—Is it snowing again, Mr Conroy? asked Lily.

She had preceded him into the pantry to help him off with his overcoat. Gabriel smiled at the three syllables she had given his surname and glanced at her. She was a slim, growing girl, pale in complexion and with hay-coloured hair. The gas in the pantry made her look still paler. Gabriel had known her when she was a child and used to sit on the lowest step nursing a rag doll.

—Yes, Lily, he answered, and I think we're in for a night of it.

He looked up at the pantry ceiling, which was shaking with the stamping and shuffling of feet on the floor above, listened for a moment to the piano and then glanced at the girl, who was folding his overcoat carefully at the end of a shelf.

—Tell me, Lily, he said in a friendly tone, do you still go to school?

—O no, sir, she answered. I'm done schooling this year and more.

—O, then, said Gabriel gaily, I suppose we'll be going to your wedding one of these fine days with your young man, eh?

The girl glanced back at him over her shoulder and said with great bitterness:

—The men that is now is only all palaver and what they can get out of you.

Gabriel coloured as if he felt he had made a mistake and, without looking at her, kicked off his goloshes and flicked actively with his muffler at his patent-leather shoes.

He was a stout tallish young man. The high colour of his cheeks pushed upwards even to his forehead where it scattered itself in a few formless patches of pale red; and on his hairless face there scintillated restlessly the polished lenses and the bright gilt rims of the glasses which screened his delicate and restless eyes. His glossy black hair was parted in the middle and brushed in a long curve behind his ears where it curled slightly beneath the groove left by his hat.

When he had flicked lustre into his shoes he stood up and pulled his waistcoat down more tightly on his plump body. Then he took a coin rapidly from his pocket.

—O Lily, he said, thrusting it into her hands, it's Christmas-time, isn't it? Just . . . here's a little. . . .

He walked rapidly towards the door.

—O no, sir! cried the girl, following him. Really, sir, I wouldn't take it.

—Christmas-time! Christmas-time! said Gabriel, almost trotting to the stairs and waving his hand to her in deprecation.

The girl, seeing that he had gained the stairs, called out after him:

—Well, thank you, sir.

He waited outside the drawing-room door until the waltz should finish, listening to the skirts that swept against it and to the shuffling of feet. He was still discomposed by the girl's bitter and sudden retort. It had cast a gloom over him which he tried to dispel by arranging his cuffs and the bows of his tie. Then he took from his waistcoat pocket a little paper and glanced at the headings he had made for his speech. He was undecided about the lines from Robert Browning for he feared they would be above the heads of his hearers. Some quotation that they could recognise from Shakespeare or from the Melodies would be better. The indelicate clacking of the men's heels and the shuffling of their soles reminded him that their grade of culture differed from his. He would only make himself ridiculous by quoting poetry to them which they could not understand. They would think that he was airing his superior education. He would fail with them just as he had failed with the girl in the pantry. He had taken up a wrong tone. His whole speech was a mistake from first to last, an utter failure.

Just then his aunts and his wife came out of the ladies' dressing-room. His aunts were two small plainly dressed old women. Aunt Julia was an inch or so the taller. Her hair, drawn low over the tops of her ears, was grey; and grey also, with darker shadows, was her large flaccid face. Though she was stout in build and stood erect her slow eyes and parted lips gave her the appearance of a woman who did not know where she was or where she was going. Aunt Kate was more vivacious. Her face, healthier than her sister's, was all puckers and creases, like a shrivelled red apple, and her hair, braided in the same old-fashioned way, had not lost its ripe nut colour.

They both kissed Gabriel frankly. He was their favourite nephew, the son of their dead elder sister, Ellen, who had married T. J. Conroy of the Port and Docks.

—Gretta tells me you're not going to take a cab back to Monkstown to-night, Gabriel, said Aunt Kate.

—No, said Gabriel, turning to his wife, we had quite enough of that last year, hadn't we? Don't you remember, Aunt Kate, what a cold Gretta got out of it? Cab windows rattling all the way, and the east wind blowing in after we passed Merrion. Very jolly it was. Gretta caught a dreadful cold.

Aunt Kate frowned severely and nodded her head at every word.

—Quite right, Gabriel, quite right, she said. You can't be too careful.

—But as for Gretta there, said Gabriel, she'd walk home in the snow if she were let.

Mrs Conroy laughed.

—Don't mind him, Aunt Kate, she said. He's really an awful bother, what with green shades for Tom's eyes at night and making him do the dumb-bells, and forcing Eva to eat the stirabout. The poor child! And she simply hates the sight of it! . . . O, but you'll never guess what he makes me wear now!

She broke out into a peal of laughter and glanced at her husband, whose admiring and happy eyes had been wandering from her dress to her face and hair. The two aunts laughed heartily too, for Gabriel's solicitude was a standing joke with them.

—Goloshes! said Mrs Conroy. That's the latest. Whenever it's wet underfoot I must put on my goloshes. To-night even he wanted me to put them on, but I wouldn't. The next thing he'll buy me will be a diving suit.

Gabriel laughed nervously and patted his tie reassuringly while Aunt Kate nearly doubled herself, so heartily did she enjoy the joke. The smile soon faded from Aunt Julia's face and her mirthless eyes were directed towards her nephew's face. After a pause she asked:

—And what are goloshes, Gabriel?

—Goloshes, Julia! exclaimed her sister. Goodness me, don't you know what goloshes are? You wear them over your . . . over your boots, Gretta, isn't it?

—Yes, said Mrs Conroy. Guttapercha things. We both have a pair now. Gabriel says everyone wears them on the continent.

—O, on the continent, murmured Aunt Julia, nodding her head slowly.

Gabriel knitted his brows and said, as if he were slightly angered:

—It's nothing very wonderful but Gretta thinks it very funny because she says the word reminds her of Christy Minstrels.

—But tell me, Gabriel, said Aunt Kate, with brisk tact. Of course, you've seen about the room. Gretta was saying . . .

—O, the room is all right, replied Gabriel. I've taken one in the Gresham.

—To be sure, said Aunt Kate, by far the best thing to do. And the children, Gretta, you're not anxious about them?

—O, for one night, said Mrs Conroy. Besides, Bessie will look after them.

—To be sure, said Aunt Kate again. What a comfort it is to have a girl like that, one you can depend on! There's that Lily, I'm sure I don't know what has come over her lately. She's not the girl she was at all.

Gabriel was about to ask his aunt some questions on this point but she broke off suddenly to gaze after her sister who had wandered down the stairs and was craning her neck over the banisters.

—Now, I ask you, she said, almost testily, where is Julia going? Julia! Julia! Where are you going?

Julia, who had gone halfway down one flight, came back and announced blandly:

—Here's Freddy.

At the same moment a clapping of hands and a final flourish of the pianist told that the waltz had ended. The drawing-room door was opened from within and some couples came out. Aunt Kate drew Gabriel aside hurriedly and whispered into his ear:

—Slip down, Gabriel, like a good fellow and see if he's all right, and don't let him up if he's screwed. I'm sure he's screwed. I'm sure he is.

Gabriel went to the stairs and listened over the banisters. He could hear two persons talking in the pantry. Then he recognised Freddy Malins' laugh. He went down the stairs noisily.

—It's such a relief, said Aunt Kate to Mrs Conroy, that Gabriel is here. I always feel easier in my mind when he's here. . . . Julia, there's Miss Daly and Miss Power will take some refreshment. Thanks for your beautiful waltz, Miss Daly. It made lovely time.

A tall wizen-faced man, with a stiff grizzled moustache and swarthy skin, who was passing out with his partner said:

—And may we have some refreshment, too, Miss Morkan?

—Julia, said Aunt Kate summarily, and here's Mr Browne and Miss Furlong. Take them in, Julia, with Miss Daly and Miss Power.

—I'm the man for the ladies, said Mr Browne, pursing his lips until his moustache bristled and smiling in all his wrinkles. You know, Miss Morkan, the reason they are so fond of me is—

He did not finish his sentence, but, seeing that Aunt Kate was out of earshot, at once led the three young ladies into the back room. The middle of the room was occupied by two square tables placed end to end, and on these Aunt Julia and the caretaker were straightening and smoothing a large cloth. On the sideboard were arrayed dishes and plates, and glasses and bundles of knives and forks and spoons. The top of the closed square piano served also as a sideboard for viands and sweets. At a smaller sideboard in one corner two young men were standing, drinking hop-bitters.

Mr Browne led his charges thither and invited them all, in jest, to some ladies' punch, hot, strong and sweet. As they said they never took anything strong he opened three bottles of lemonade for them. Then he asked one of the young men to move aside, and, taking hold of the decanter, filled out for himself a goodly measure of whisky. The young men eyed him respectfully while he took a trial sip.

—God help me, he said, smiling, it's the doctor's orders.

His wizened face broke into a broader smile, and the three young ladies laughed in musical echo to his pleasantry, swaying their bodies to and fro, with nervous jerks of their shoulders. The boldest said:

—O, now, Mr Browne, I'm sure the doctor never ordered anything of the kind.

Mr Browne took another sip of his whisky and said, with sidling mimicry:

—Well, you see, I'm like the famous Mrs Cassidy, who is reported to have said: *Now, Mary Grimes, if I don't take it, make me take it, for I feel I want it.*

His hot face had leaned forward a little too confidentially and he had assumed a very low Dublin accent so that the young ladies, with one instinct, received his speech in silence. Miss Furlong, who was one of Mary Jane's pupils, asked Miss Daly what was the name of the pretty waltz she had played; and Mr Browne, seeing that he was ignored, turned promptly to the two young men who were more appreciative.

A red-faced young woman, dressed in pansy, came into the room, excitedly clapping her hands and crying:

—Quadrilles! Quadrilles!

Close on her heels came Aunt Kate, crying:

—Two gentlemen and three ladies, Mary Jane!

—O, here's Mr Bergin and Mr Kerrigan, said Mary Jane.

Mr Kerrigan, will you take Miss Power? Miss Furlong, may I get you a partner, Mr Bergin. O, that'll just do now.

—Three ladies, Mary Jane, said Aunt Kate.

The two young gentlemen asked the ladies if they might have the pleasure, and Mary Jane turned to Miss Daly.

—O, Miss Daly, you're really awfully good, after playing for the last two dances, but really we're so short of ladies to-night.

—I don't mind in the least, Miss Morkan.

—But I've a nice partner for you, Mr Bartell D'Arcy, the tenor. I'll get him to sing later on. All Dublin is raving about him.

—Lovely voice, lovely voice! said Aunt Kate.

As the piano had twice begun the prelude to the first figure Mary Jane led her recruits quickly from the room. They had hardly gone when Aunt Julia wandered slowly into the room, looking behind her at something.

—What is the matter, Julia? asked Aunt Kate anxiously. Who is it?

Julia, who was carrying in a column of table-napkins, turned to her sister and said, simply, as if the question had surprised her:

—It's only Freddy, Kate, and Gabriel with him.

In fact right behind her Gabriel could be seen piloting Freddy Malins across the landing. The latter, a young man of about forty, was of Gabriel's size and build, with very round shoulders. His face was fleshy and pallid, touched with colour only at the thick hanging lobes of his ears and at the wide wings of his nose. He had coarse features, a blunt nose, a convex and receding brow, tumid and protruded lips. His heavy-lidded eyes and the disorder of his scanty hair made him look sleepy. He was laughing heartily in a high key at a story which he had been telling Gabriel on the stairs and at the same time rubbing the knuckles of his left fist backwards and forwards into his left eye.

—Good-evening, Freddy, said Aunt Julia.

Freddy Malins bade the Misses Morkan good-evening in what seemed an offhand fashion by reason of the habitual catch in his voice and then, seeing that Mr Browne was grinning at him from the sideboard, crossed the room on rather shaky legs and began to repeat in an undertone the story he had just told to Gabriel.

—He's not so bad, is he? said Aunt Kate to Gabriel.

Gabriel's brows were dark but he raised them quickly and answered:

—O no, hardly noticeable.

—Now, isn't he a terrible fellow! she said. And his poor mother made him take the pledge on New Year's Eve. But come on, Gabriel, into the drawing-room.

Before leaving the room with Gabriel she signalled to Mr Browne by frowning and shaking her forefinger in warning to and fro. Mr Browne nodded in answer and, when she had gone, said to Freddy Malins:

—Now, then, Teddy, I'm going to fill you out a good glass of lemonade just to buck you up.

Freddy Malins, who was nearing the climax of his story, waved the offer aside impatiently but Mr Browne, having first called Freddy Malins' attention to a disarray in his dress, filled out and handed him a full glass of lemonade. Freddy Malins' left hand accepted the glass mechanically, his right hand being engaged in the mechanical readjustment of his dress. Mr Browne, whose face was once more wrinkling with mirth, poured out for himself a glass of whisky while Freddy Malins exploded, before he had well reached the climax of his story, in a kink of high-pitched bronchitic laughter and, setting down his untasted and overflowing glass, began to rub the knuckles of his left fist backwards and forwards into his left eye, repeating words of his last phrase as well as his fit of laughter would allow him.

.   .   .   .

Gabriel could not listen while Mary Jane was playing her Academy piece, full of runs and difficult passages, to the hushed drawing-room. He liked music but the piece she was playing had no melody for him and he doubted whether it had any melody for the other listeners, though they had begged Mary Jane to play something. Four young men, who had come from the refreshment-room to stand in the doorway at the sound of the piano, had gone away quietly in couples after a few minutes. The only persons who seemed to follow the music were Mary Jane herself, her hands racing along the key-board or lifted from it at the pauses like those of a priestess in momentary imprecation, and Aunt Kate standing at her elbow to turn the page.

Gabriel's eyes, irritated by the floor, which glittered with beeswax under the heavy chandelier, wandered to the wall above the piano. A picture of the balcony scene in *Romeo and Juliet* hung there and beside it was a picture of the two murdered princes in the Tower which Aunt Julia had worked in red, blue and brown wools when she was a girl. Probably in the school they had gone to as girls that kind of work had been taught, for one year his mother had worked for him as a birthday present a waistcoat of purple tabinet, with little foxes' heads upon it, lined with brown satin and having round mulberry buttons. It was strange that his mother had had no musical talent though Aunt Kate used to call her the brains carrier of the Morkan family. Both she and Julia had always seemed a little proud of their serious and matronly sister. Her photograph stood before the pierglass. She held an open book on her knees and was pointing out something in it to Constantine who, dressed in a man-o'-war suit, lay at her feet. It was she who had chosen the names for her sons for she was very sensible of the dignity of family life. Thanks to her, Constantine was now senior curate in Balbriggan and, thanks to her, Gabriel himself had taken his degree in the Royal University. A shadow passed over his face as he remembered her sullen opposition to his marriage. Some slighting phrases she had used still rankled in his memory; she had once spoken of Gretta as being country cute and that was not true of Gretta at all. It was Gretta who had nursed her during all her last long illness in their house at Monkstown.

He knew that Mary Jane must be near the end of her piece. for she was playing again the opening melody with runs of scales after every bar and while he waited for the end the resentment died down in his heart. The piece ended with a trill of octaves in the treble and a final deep octave in the bass. Great applause greeted Mary Jane as, blushing and rolling up her music nervously, she escaped from the room. The most vigorous clapping came from the four young men in the doorway who had gone away to the refreshment-room at the beginning of the piece but had come back when the piano had stopped.

Lancers were arranged. Gabriel found himself partnered with Miss Ivors. She was a frank-mannered talkative young lady, with a freckled face and prominent brown eyes. She did not wear a low-cut bodice and the large brooch which was fixed in the front of her collar bore on it an Irish device.

When they had taken their places she said abruptly:

—I have a crow to pluck with you.

—With me? said Gabriel.

She nodded her head gravely.

—What is it? asked Gabriel, smiling at her solemn manner.

—Who is G. C.? answered Miss Ivors, turning her eyes upon him.

Gabriel coloured and was about to knit his brows, as if he did not understand, when she said bluntly:

—O, innocent Amy! I have found out that you write for *The Daily Express*. Now, aren't you ashamed of yourself?

—Why should I be ashamed of myself? asked Gabriel, blinking his eyes and trying to smile.

—Well, I'm ashamed of you, said Miss Ivors frankly. To say you'd write for a rag like that. I didn't think you were a West Briton.

A look of perplexity appeared on Gabriel's face. It was true that he wrote a literary column every Wednesday in *The Daily Express*, for which he was paid fifteen shillings. But that did not make him a West Briton surely. The books he received for review were almost more welcome than the paltry cheque. He loved to feel the covers and turn over the pages of newly printed books. Nearly every day when his teaching in the college was ended he used to wander down the quays to the second-hand booksellers, to Hickey's on Bachelor's Walk, to Webb's or Massey's on Aston's Quay, or to O'Clohissey's in the by-street. He did not know how to meet her charge. He wanted to say that literature was above politics. But they were friends of many years' standing and their careers had been parallel, first at the University and then as teachers: he could not risk a grandiose phrase with her. He continued blinking his eyes and trying to smile and murmured lamely that he saw nothing political in writing reviews of books.

When their turn to cross had come he was still perplexed and inattentive. Miss Ivors promptly took his hand in a warm grasp and said in a soft friendly tone:

—Of course, I was only joking. Come, we cross now.

When they were together again she spoke of the University question and Gabriel felt more at ease. A friend of hers had shown her his review of Browning's poems. That was how she had found out the secret: but she liked the review immensely. Then she said suddenly:

—O, Mr Conroy, will you come for an excursion to the Aran Isles this summer? We're going to stay there a whole month. It will be splendid out in the Atlantic. You ought to come. Mr Clancy is coming, and Mr Kilkelly and Kathleen Kearney. It would be splendid for Gretta too if she'd come. She's from Connacht, isn't she?

—Her people are, said Gabriel shortly.

—But you will come, won't you? said Miss Ivors, laying her warm hand eagerly on his arm.

—The fact is, said Gabriel, I have already arranged to go—

—Go where? asked Miss Ivors.

—Well, you know, every year I go for a cycling tour with some fellows and so—

—But where? asked Miss Ivors.

—Well, we usually go to France or Belgium or perhaps Germany, said Gabriel awkwardly.

—And why do you go to France and Belgium, said Miss Ivors, instead of visiting your own land?

—Well, said Gabriel, it's partly to keep in touch with the languages and partly for a change.

—And haven't you your own language to keep in touch with—Irish? asked Miss Ivors.

—Well, said Gabriel, if it comes to that, you know, Irish is not my language.

Their neighbours had turned to listen to the cross-examination. Gabriel glanced right and left nervously and tried to keep his good humour under the ordeal which was making a blush invade his forehead.

—And haven't you your own land to visit, continued Miss Ivors, that you know nothing of, your own people, and your own country?

—O, to tell you the truth, retorted Gabriel suddenly, I'm sick of my own country, sick of it!

—Why? asked Miss Ivors.

Gabriel did not answer for his retort had heated him.

—Why? repeated Miss Ivors.

They had to go visiting together and, as he had not answered her, Miss Ivors said warmly:

—Of course, you've no answer.

Gabriel tried to cover his agitation by taking part in the dance with great energy. He avoided her eyes for he had seen a sour expression on her face. But when they met in the long chain he was surprised to feel his hand firmly pressed. She looked at him from under her brows for a moment quizzically until he smiled. Then, just as the chain was about to start again, she stood on tiptoe and whispered into his ear:

—West Briton!

When the lancers were over Gabriel went away to a remote corner of the room where Freddy Malins' mother was sitting. She was a stout feeble old woman with white hair. Her voice had a catch in it like her son's and she stuttered slightly. She had been told that Freddy had come and that he was nearly all right. Gabriel asked her whether she had had a good crossing. She lived with her married daughter in Glasgow and came to Dublin on a visit once a year. She answered placidly that she had had a beautiful crossing and that the captain had been most attentive to her. She spoke also of the beautiful house her daughter kept in Glasgow, and of all the nice friends they had there. While her tongue rambled on Gabriel tried to banish from his mind all memory of the unpleasant incident with Miss Ivors. Of course the girl or woman, or whatever she was, was an enthusiast but there was a time for all things. Perhaps he ought not to have answered her like that. But she had no right to call him a West Briton before people, even in joke. She had tried to make him ridiculous before people, heckling him and staring at him with her rabbit's eyes.

He saw his wife making her way towards him through the waltzing couples. When she reached him she said into his ear:

—Gabriel, Aunt Kate wants to know won't you carve the

goose as usual. Miss Daly will carve the ham and I'll do the pudding.

—All right, said Gabriel.

—She's sending in the younger ones first as soon as this waltz is over so that we'll have the table to ourselves.

—Were you dancing? asked Gabriel.

—Of course I was. Didn't you see me? What words had you with Molly Ivors?

—No words. Why? Did she say so?

—Something like that. I'm trying to get that Mr D'Arcy to sing. He's full of conceit, I think.

—There were no words, said Gabriel moodily, only she wanted me to go for a trip to the west of Ireland and I said I wouldn't.

His wife clasped her hands excitedly and gave a little jump.

—O, do go, Gabriel, she cried. I'd love to see Galway again.

—You can go if you like, said Gabriel coldly.

She looked at him for a moment, then turned to Mrs Malins and said:

—There's a nice husband for you, Mrs Malins.

While she was threading her way back across the room Mrs Malins, without adverting to the interruption, went on to tell Gabriel what beautiful places there were in Scotland and beautiful scenery. Her son-in-law brought them every year to the lakes and they used to go fishing. Her son-in-law was a splendid fisher. One day he caught a fish, a beautiful big big fish, and the man in the hotel boiled it for their dinner.

Gabriel hardly heard what she said. Now that supper was coming near he began to think again about his speech and about the quotation. When he saw Freddy Malins coming across the room to visit his mother Gabriel left the chair free for him and retired into the embrasure of the window. The room had already cleared and from the back room came the clatter of plates and knives. Those who still remained in the drawing-room seemed tired of dancing and were conversing quietly in little groups. Gabriel's warm trembling fingers tapped the cold pane of the window. How cool it must be outside! How pleasant it would be to walk out alone, first along by the river and then through the park! The snow would be lying on the branches of the trees and forming a bright cap on the top of the Wellington Monument. How much more pleasant it would be there than at the supper-table!

He ran over the headings of his speech: Irish hospitality, sad memories, the Three Graces, Paris, the quotation from Browning. He repeated to himself a phrase he had written in his review: *One feels that one is listening to a thought-tormented music.* Miss Ivors had praised the review. Was she sincere? Had she really any life of her own behind all her propagandism? There had never been any ill-feeling between them until that night. It unnerved him to think that she would be at the supper-table, looking up at him while he spoke with her critical quizzing eyes. Perhaps she would not be sorry to see him fail in his speech. An idea came into his mind and gave him courage. He would say, alluding to Aunt Kate and Aunt Julia: *Ladies and Gentlemen, the generation which is now on the wane among us may have had its faults but for my part I think it had certain qualities of hospitality, of humour, of humanity, which the new and very serious and hypereducated generation that is growing up around us seems to me to lack.* Very good: that was one for Miss Ivors. What did he care that his aunts were only two ignorant old women?

A murmur in the room attracted his attention. Mr Browne was advancing from the door, gallantly escorting Aunt Julia, who leaned upon his arm, smiling and hanging her head. An irregular musketry of applause escorted her also as far as the piano and then, as Mary Jane seated herself on the stool, and Aunt Julia, no longer smiling, half turned so as to pitch her voice fairly into the room, gradually ceased. Gabriel rec-

ognised the prelude. It was that of an old song of Aunt Julia's
—*Arrayed for the Bridal*. Her voice, strong and clear in tone,
attacked with great spirit the runs which embellish the air
and though she sang very rapidly she did not miss even the
smallest of the grace notes. To follow the voice, without looking at the singer's face, was to feel and share the excitement
of swift and secure flight. Gabriel applauded loudly with all
the others at the close of the song and loud applause was borne
in from the invisible supper-table. It sounded so genuine that
a little colour struggled into Aunt Julia's face as she bent to
replace in the music-stand the old leather-bound song-book
that had her initials on the cover. Freddy Malins, who had
listened with his head perched sideways to hear her better,
was still applauding when everyone else had ceased and talking animatedly to his mother who nodded her head gravely
and slowly in acquiescence. At last, when he could clap no
more, he stood up suddenly and hurried across the room to
Aunt Julia whose hand he seized and held in both his hands,
shaking it when words failed him or the catch in his voice
proved too much for him.

—I was just telling my mother, he said, I never heard you
sing so well, never. No, I never heard your voice so good as it
is to-night. Now! Would you believe that now? That's the truth.
Upon my word and honour that's the truth. I never heard your
voice sound so fresh and so . . . so clear and fresh, never.

Aunt Julia smiled broadly and murmured something about
compliments as she released her hand from his grasp. Mr
Browne extended his open hand towards her and said to those
who were near him in the manner of a showman introducing
a prodigy to an audience:

—Miss Julia Morkan, my latest discovery!

He was laughing very heartily at this himself when Freddy
Malins turned to him and said:

—Well, Browne, if you're serious you might make a worse

discovery. All I can say is I never heard her sing half so well as long as I am coming here. And that's the honest truth.

—Neither did I, said Mr Browne. I think her voice has greatly improved.

Aunt Julia shrugged her shoulders and said with meek pride:

—Thirty years ago I hadn't a bad voice as voices go.

—I often told Julia, said Aunt Kate emphatically, that she was simply thrown away in that choir. But she never would be said by me.

She turned as if to appeal to the good sense of the others against a refractory child while Aunt Julia gazed in front of her, a vague smile of reminiscence playing on her face.

—No, continued Aunt Kate, she wouldn't be said or led by anyone, slaving there in that choir night and day, night and day. Six o'clock on Christmas morning! And all for what?

—Well, isn't it for the honour of God, Aunt Kate? asked Mary Jane, twisting round on the piano-stool and smiling.

Aunt Kate turned fiercely on her niece and said:

—I know all about the honour of God, Mary Jane, but I think it's not at all honourable for the pope to turn out the women out of the choirs that have slaved there all their lives and put little whipper-snappers of boys over their heads. I suppose it is for the good of the Church if the pope does it. But it's not just, Mary Jane, and it's not right.

She had worked herself into a passion and would have continued in defence of her sister for it was a sore subject with her but Mary Jane, seeing that all the dancers had come back, intervened pacifically:

—Now, Aunt Kate, you're giving scandal to Mr Browne who is of the other persuasion.

Aunt Kate turned to Mr Browne, who was grinning at this allusion to his religion, and said hastily:

—O, I don't question the pope's being right. I'm only a

stupid old woman and I wouldn't presume to do such a thing. But there's such a thing as common everyday politeness and gratitude. And if I were in Julia's place I'd tell that Father Healy straight up to his face . . .

—And besides, Aunt Kate, said Mary Jane, we really are all hungry and when we are hungry we are all very quarrelsome.

—And when we are thirsty we are also quarrelsome, added Mr Browne.

—So that we had better go to supper, said Mary Jane, and finish the discussion afterwards.

On the landing outside the drawing-room Gabriel found his wife and Mary Jane trying to persuade Miss Ivors to stay for supper. But Miss Ivors, who had put on her hat and was buttoning her cloak, would not stay. She did not feel in the least hungry and she had already overstayed her time.

—But only for ten minutes, Molly, said Mrs Conroy. That won't delay you.

—To take a pick itself, said Mary Jane, after all your dancing.

—I really couldn't, said Miss Ivors.

—I am afraid you didn't enjoy yourself at all, said Mary Jane hopelessly.

—Ever so much, I assure you, said Miss Ivors, but you really must let me run off now.

—But how can you get home? asked Mrs Conroy.

—O, it's only two steps up the quay.

Gabriel hesitated a moment and said:

—If you will allow me, Miss Ivors, I'll see you home if you really are obliged to go.

But Miss Ivors broke away from them.

—I won't hear of it, she cried. For goodness sake go in to your suppers and don't mind me. I'm quite well able to take care of myself.

—Well, you're the comical girl, Molly, said Mrs Conroy frankly.

—*Beannacht libh,* cried Miss Ivors, with a laugh, as she ran down the staircase.

Mary Jane gazed after her, a moody puzzled expression on her face, while Mrs Conroy leaned over the banisters to listen for the hall-door. Gabriel asked himself was he the cause of her abrupt departure. But she did not seem to be in ill humour: she had gone away laughing. He stared blankly down the staircase.

At that moment Aunt Kate came toddling out of the supper-room, almost wringing her hands in despair.

—Where is Gabriel? she cried. Where on earth is Gabriel? There's everyone waiting in there, stage to let, and nobody to carve the goose!

—Here I am, Aunt Kate! cried Gabriel, with sudden animation, ready to carve a flock of geese, if necessary.

A fat brown goose lay at one end of the table and at the other end, on a bed of creased paper strewn with sprigs of parsley, lay a great ham, stripped of its outer skin and peppered over with crust crumbs, a neat paper frill round its shin and beside this was a round of spiced beef. Between these rival ends ran parallel lines of side-dishes: two little minsters of jelly, red and yellow; a shallow dish full of blocks of blancmange and red jam, a large green leaf-shaped dish with a stalk-shaped handle, on which lay bunches of purple raisins and peeled almonds, a companion dish on which lay a solid rectangle of Smyrna figs, a dish of custard topped with grated nutmeg, a small bowl full of chocolates and sweets wrapped in gold and silver papers and a glass vase in which stood some tall celery stalks. In the centre of the table there stood, as sentries to a fruit-stand which upheld a pyramid of oranges and American apples, two squat old-fashioned decanters of cut glass, one containing port and the other dark sherry. On the closed square piano a pudding in a huge yellow dish lay in waiting and behind it were three squads of bottles of stout and ale and minerals, drawn up according to the colours of their uniforms, the first two black, with brown and red labels, the third and smallest squad white, with transverse green sashes.

Gabriel took his seat boldly at the head of the table and, having looked to the edge of the carver, plunged his fork firmly into the goose. He felt quite at ease now for he was an expert carver and liked nothing better than to find himself at the head of a well-laden table.

—Miss Furlong, what shall I send you? he asked. A wing or a slice of the breast?

—Just a small slice of the breast.

—Miss Higgins, what for you?

—O, anything at all, Mr Conroy.

While Gabriel and Miss Daly exchanged plates of goose and plates of ham and spiced beef Lily went from guest to guest with a dish of hot floury potatoes wrapped in a white napkin. This was Mary Jane's idea and she had also suggested apple sauce for the goose but Aunt Kate had said that plain roast goose without apple sauce had always been good enough for her and she hoped she might never eat worse. Mary Jane waited on her pupils and saw that they got the best slices and Aunt Kate and Aunt Julia opened and carried across from the piano bottles of stout and ale for the gentlemen and bottles of minerals for the ladies. There was a great deal of confusion and laughter and noise, the noise of orders and counter-orders, of knives and forks, of corks and glass-stoppers. Gabriel began to carve second helpings as soon as he had finished the first round without serving himself. Everyone protested loudly so that he compromised by taking a long draught of stout for he had found the carving hot work. Mary Jane settled down quietly to her supper but Aunt Kate and Aunt Julia were still toddling round the table, walking on each other's heels, getting in each other's way and giving each other unheeded orders. Mr

Browne begged of them to sit down and eat their suppers and so did Gabriel but they said there was time enough so that, at last, Freddy Malins stood up and, capturing Aunt Kate, plumped her down on her chair amid general laughter.

When everyone had been well served Gabriel said, smiling:

—Now, if anyone wants a little more of what vulgar people call stuffing let him or her speak.

A chorus of voices invited him to begin his own supper and Lily came forward with three potatoes which she had reserved for him.

—Very well, said Gabriel amiably, as he took another preparatory draught, kindly forget my existence, ladies and gentlemen, for a few minutes.

He set to his supper and took no part in the conversation with which the table covered Lily's removal of the plates. The subject of talk was the opera company which was then at the Theatre Royal. Mr Bartell D'Arcy, the tenor, a dark-complexioned young man with a smart moustache, praised very highly the leading contralto of the company but Miss Furlong thought she had a rather vulgar style of production. Freddy Malins said there was a negro chieftain singing in the second part of the Gaiety pantomime who had one of the finest tenor voices he had ever heard.

—Have you heard him? he asked Mr Bartell D'Arcy across the table.

—No, answered Mr Bartell D'Arcy carelessly.

—Because, Freddy Malins explained, now I'd be curious to hear your opinion of him. I think he has a grand voice.

—It takes Teddy to find out the really good things, said Mr Browne familiarly to the table.

—And why couldn't he have a voice too? asked Freddy Malins sharply. Is it because he's only a black?

Nobody answered this question and Mary Jane led the

table back to the legitimate opera. One of her pupils had given her a pass for *Mignon*. Of course it was very fine, she said, but it made her think of poor Georgina Burns. Mr Browne could go back farther still, to the old Italian companies that used to come to Dublin—Tietjens, Ilma de Murzka, Campanini, the great Trebelli, Giuglini, Ravelli, Aramburo. Those were the days, he said, when there was something like singing to be heard in Dublin. He told too of how the top gallery of the old Royal used to be packed night after night, of how one night an Italian tenor had sung five encores to *Let Me Like a Soldier Fall*, introducing a high C every time, and of how the gallery boys would sometimes in their enthusiasm unyoke the horses from the carriage of some great *prima donna* and pull her themselves through the streets to her hotel. Why did they never play the grand old operas now, he asked, *Dinorah*, *Lucrezia Borgia*? Because they could not get the voices to sing them: that was why.

—O, well, said Mr Bartell D'Arcy, I presume there are as good singers to-day as there were then.

—Where are they? asked Mr Browne defiantly.

—In London, Paris, Milan, said Mr Bartell D'Arcy warmly. I suppose Caruso, for example, is quite as good, if not better than any of the men you have mentioned.

—Maybe so, said Mr Browne. But I may tell you I doubt it strongly.

—O, I'd give anything to hear Caruso sing, said Mary Jane.

—For me, said Aunt Kate, who had been picking a bone, there was only one tenor. To please me, I mean. But I suppose none of you ever heard of him.

—Who was he, Miss Morkan? asked Mr Bartell D'Arcy politely.

—His name, said Aunt Kate, was Parkinson. I heard him when he was in his prime and I think he had then the purest tenor voice that was ever put into a man's throat.

—Strange, said Mr Bartell D'Arcy. I never even heard of him.

—Yes, yes, Miss Morkan is right, said Mr Browne. I remember hearing of old Parkinson but he's too far back for me.

—A beautiful pure sweet mellow English tenor, said Aunt Kate with enthusiasm.

Gabriel having finished, the huge pudding was transferred to the table. The clatter of forks and spoons began again. Gabriel's wife served out spoonfuls of the pudding and passed the plates down the table. Midway down they were held up by Mary Jane, who replenished them with raspberry or orange jelly or with blancmange and jam. The pudding was of Aunt Julia's making and she received praises for it from all quarters. She herself said that it was not quite brown enough.

—Well, I hope, Miss Morkan, said Mr Browne, that I'm brown enough for you because, you know, I'm all brown.

All the gentlemen, except Gabriel, ate some of the pudding out of compliment to Aunt Julia. As Gabriel never ate sweets the celery had been left for him. Freddy Malins also took a stalk of celery and ate it with his pudding. He had been told that celery was a capital thing for the blood and he was just then under doctor's care. Mrs Malins, who had been silent all through the supper, said that her son was going down to Mount Melleray in a week or so. The table then spoke of Mount Melleray, how bracing the air was down there, how hospitable the monks were and how they never asked for a penny-piece from their guests.

—And do you mean to say, asked Mr Browne incredulously, that a chap can go down there and put up there as if it were a hotel and live on the fat of the land and then come away without paying a farthing?

—O, most people give some donation to the monastery when they leave, said Mary Jane.

—I wish we had an institution like that in our Church, said Mr Browne candidly.

He was astonished to hear that the monks never spoke, got up at two in the morning and slept in their coffins. He asked what they did it for.

—That's the rule of the order, said Aunt Kate firmly.

—Yes, but why? asked Mr Browne.

Aunt Kate repeated that it was the rule, that was all. Mr Browne still seemed not to understand. Freddy Malins explained to him, as best he could, that the monks were trying to make up for the sins committed by all the sinners in the outside world. The explanation was not very clear for Mr Browne grinned and said:

—I like that idea very much but wouldn't a comfortable spring bed do them as well as a coffin?

—The coffin, said Mary Jane, is to remind them of their last end.

As the subject had grown lugubrious it was buried in a silence of the table during which Mrs Malins could be heard saying to her neighbour in an indistinct undertone:

—They are very good men, the monks, very pious men.

The raisins and almonds and figs and apples and oranges and chocolates and sweets were now passed about the table and Aunt Julia invited all the guests to have either port or sherry. At first Mr Bartell D'Arcy refused to take either but one of his neighbours nudged him and whispered something to him upon which he allowed his glass to be filled. Gradually as the last glasses were being filled the conversation ceased. A pause followed, broken only by the noise of the wine and by unsettlings of chairs. The Misses Morkan, all three, looked down at the tablecloth. Someone coughed once or twice and then a few gentlemen patted the table gently as a signal for silence. The silence came and Gabriel pushed back his chair and stood up.

The patting at once grew louder in encouragement and then ceased altogether. Gabriel leaned his ten trembling fingers on the tablecloth and smiled nervously at the company. Meeting a row of upturned faces he raised his eyes to the chandelier. The piano was playing a waltz tune and he could hear the skirts sweeping against the drawing-room door. People, perhaps, were standing in the snow on the quay outside, gazing up at the lighted windows and listening to the waltz music. The air was pure there. In the distance lay the park where the trees were weighted with snow. The Wellington Monument wore a gleaming cap of snow that flashed westward over the white field of Fifteen Acres.

He began:

—Ladies and Gentlemen.

—It has fallen to my lot this evening, as in years past, to perform a very pleasing task but a task for which I am afraid my poor powers as a speaker are all too inadequate.

—No, no! said Mr Browne.

—But, however that may be, I can only ask you to-night to take the will for the deed and to lend me your attention for a few moments while I endeavour to express to you in words what my feelings are on this occasion.

—Ladies and Gentlemen. It is not the first time that we have gathered together under this hospitable roof, around this hospitable board. It is not the first time that we have been the recipients—or perhaps, I had better say, the victims—of the hospitality of certain good ladies.

He made a circle in the air with his arm and paused. Everyone laughed or smiled at Aunt Kate and Aunt Julia and Mary Jane who all turned crimson with pleasure. Gabriel went on more boldly:

—I feel more strongly with every recurring year that our country has no tradition which does it so much honour and which it should guard so jealously as that of its hospitality.

It is a tradition that is unique as far as my experience goes (and I have visited not a few places abroad) among the modern nations. Some would say, perhaps, that with us it is rather a failing than anything to be boasted of. But granted even that, it is, to my mind, a princely failing, and one that I trust will long be cultivated among us. Of one thing, at least, I am sure. As long as this one roof shelters the good ladies aforesaid—and I wish from my heart it may do so for many and many a long year to come—the tradition of genuine warm-hearted courteous Irish hospitality, which our forefathers have handed down to us and which we in turn must hand down to our descendants, is still alive among us.

A hearty murmur of assent ran round the table. It shot through Gabriel's mind that Miss Ivors was not there and that she had gone away discourteously: and he said with confidence in himself:

—Ladies and Gentlemen.

—A new generation is growing up in our midst, a generation actuated by new ideas and new principles. It is serious and enthusiastic for these new ideas and its enthusiasm, even when it is misdirected, is, I believe, in the main sincere. But we are living in a sceptical and, if I may use the phrase, a thought-tormented age: and sometimes I fear that this new generation, educated or hypereducated as it is, will lack those qualities of humanity, of hospitality, of kindly humour which belonged to an older day. Listening to-night to the names of all those great singers of the past it seemed to me, I must confess, that we were living in a less spacious age. Those days might, without exaggeration, be called spacious days: and if they are gone beyond recall let us hope, at least, that in gatherings such as this we shall still speak of them with pride and affection, still cherish in our hearts the memory of those dead and gone great ones whose fame the world will not willingly let die.

—Hear, hear! said Mr Browne loudly.

—But yet, continued Gabriel, his voice falling into a softer inflection, there are always in gatherings such as this sadder thoughts that will recur to our minds: thoughts of the past, of youth, of changes, of absent faces that we miss here to-night. Our path through life is strewn with many such sad memories: and were we to brood upon them always we could not find the heart to go on bravely with our work among the living. We have all of us living duties and living affections which claim, and rightly claim, our strenuous endeavours.

—Therefore, I will not linger on the past. I will not let any gloomy moralising intrude upon us here to-night. Here we are gathered together for a brief moment from the bustle and rush of our everyday routine. We are met here as friends, in the spirit of good-fellowship, as colleagues, also to a certain extent, in the true spirit of *camaraderie*, and as the guests of —what shall I call them?—the Three Graces of the Dublin musical world.

The table burst into applause and laughter at this sally. Aunt Julia vainly asked each of her neighbours in turn to tell her what Gabriel had said.

—He says we are the Three Graces, Aunt Julia, said Mary Jane.

Aunt Julia did not understand but she looked up, smiling, at Gabriel, who continued in the same vein:

—Ladies and Gentlemen.

—I will not attempt to play to-night the part that Paris played on another occasion. I will not attempt to choose be-tween them. The task would be an invidious one and one beyond my poor powers. For when I view them in turn, whether it be our chief hostess herself, whose good heart, whose too good heart, has become a byword with all who know her, or her sister, who seems to be gifted with perennial youth and whose singing must have been a surprise and a revelation to us all to-night, or, last but not least, when I consider our youngest hostess, talented, cheerful, hard-working and the best of nieces, I confess, Ladies and Gentlemen, that I do not know to which of them I should award the prize.

Gabriel glanced down at his aunts and, seeing the large smile on Aunt Julia's face and the tears which had risen to Aunt Kate's eyes, hastened to his close. He raised his glass of port gallantly, while every member of the company fingered a glass expectantly, and said loudly:

—Let us toast them all three together. Let us drink to their health, wealth, long life, happiness and prosperity and may they long continue to hold the proud and self-won position which they hold in their profession and the position of honour and affection which they hold in our hearts.

All the guests stood up, glass in hand, and, turning towards the three seated ladies, sang in unison, with Mr Browne as leader:

> *For they are jolly gay fellows,*
> *For they are jolly gay fellows,*
> *For they are jolly gay fellows,*
> *Which nobody can deny.*

Aunt Kate was making frank use of her handkerchief and even Aunt Julia seemed moved. Freddy Malins beat time with his pudding-fork and the singers turned towards one another, as if in melodious conference, while they sang, with emphasis:

> *Unless he tells a lie,*
> *Unless he tells a lie.*

Then, turning once more towards their hostesses, they sang:

> *For they are jolly gay fellows,*
> *For they are jolly gay fellows,*
> *For they are jolly gay fellows,*
> *Which nobody can deny.*

The acclamation which followed was taken up beyond the door of the supper-room by many of the other guests and renewed time after time, Freddy Malins acting as officer with his fork on high.

.   .   .   .

The piercing morning air came into the hall where they were standing so that Aunt Kate said:

—Close the door, somebody. Mrs Malins will get her death of cold.

—Browne is out there, Aunt Kate, said Mary Jane.

—Browne is everywhere, said Aunt Kate, lowering her voice. Mary Jane laughed at her tone.

—Really, she said archly, he is very attentive.

—He has been laid on here like the gas, said Aunt Kate in the same tone, all during the Christmas.

She laughed herself this time good-humouredly and then added quickly:

—But tell him to come in, Mary Jane, and close the door. I hope to goodness he didn't hear me.

At that moment the hall-door was opened and Mr Browne came in from the doorstep, laughing as if his heart would break. He was dressed in a long green overcoat with mock astrakhan cuffs and collar and wore on his head an oval fur cap. He pointed down the snow-covered quay from where the sound of shrill prolonged whistling was borne in.

—Teddy will have all the cabs in Dublin out, he said.

Gabriel advanced from the little pantry behind the office, struggling into his overcoat and, looking round the hall, said:

—Gretta not down yet?

—She's getting on her things, Gabriel, said Aunt Kate.

—Who's playing up there? asked Gabriel.

—Nobody. They're all gone.

—O no, Aunt Kate, said Mary Jane. Bartell D'Arcy and Miss O'Callaghan aren't gone yet.

—Someone is strumming at the piano, anyhow, said Gabriel.

Mary Jane glanced at Gabriel and Mr Browne and said with a shiver:

—It makes me feel cold to look at you two gentlemen muffled up like that. I wouldn't like to face your journey home at this hour.

—I'd like nothing better this minute, said Mr Browne stoutly, than a rattling fine walk in the country or a fast drive with a good spanking goer between the shafts.

—We used to have a very good horse and trap at home, said Aunt Julia sadly.

—The never-to-be-forgotten Johnny, said Mary Jane, laughing.

Aunt Kate and Gabriel laughed too.

—Why, what was wonderful about Johnny? asked Mr Browne.

—The late lamented Patrick Morkan, our grandfather, that is, explained Gabriel, commonly known in his later years as the old gentleman, was a glue-boiler.

—O, now, Gabriel, said Aunt Kate, laughing, he had a starch mill.

—Well, glue or starch, said Gabriel, the old gentleman had a horse by the name of Johnny. And Johnny used to work in the old gentleman's mill, walking round and round in order to drive the mill. That was all very well; but now comes the tragic part about Johnny. One fine day the old gentleman thought he'd like to drive out with the quality to a military review in the park.

—The Lord have mercy on his soul, said Aunt Kate compassionately.

—Amen, said Gabriel. So the old gentleman, as I said, harnessed Johnny and put on his very best tall hat and his very best stock collar and drove out in grand style from his ancestral mansion somewhere near Back Lane, I think.

Everyone laughed, even Mrs Malins, at Gabriel's manner and Aunt Kate said:

—O now, Gabriel, he didn't live in Back Lane, really. Only the mill was there.

—Out from the mansion of his forefathers, continued Gabriel, he drove with Johnny. And everything went on beautifully until Johnny came in sight of King Billy's statue: and whether he fell in love with the horse King Billy sits on or whether he thought he was back again in the mill, anyhow he began to walk round the statue.

Gabriel paced in a circle round the hall in his goloshes amid the laughter of the others.

—Round and round he went, said Gabriel, and the old gentleman, who was a very pompous old gentleman, was highly indignant. *Go on, sir! What do you mean, sir? Johnny! Johnny! Most extraordinary conduct! Can't understand the horse!*

The peals of laughter which followed Gabriel's imitation of the incident were interrupted by a resounding knock at the hall-door. Mary Jane ran to open it and let in Freddy Malins. Freddy Malins, with his hat well back on his head and his shoulders humped with cold, was puffing and steaming after his exertions.

—I could only get one cab, he said.

—O, we'll find another along the quay, said Gabriel.

—Yes, said Aunt Kate. Better not keep Mrs Malins standing in the draught.

Mrs Malins was helped down the front steps by her son and Mr Browne and, after many manœuvres, hoisted into the cab. Freddy Malins clambered in after her and spent a long time settling her on the seat, Mr Browne helping him with advice. At last she was settled comfortably and Freddy Malins invited Mr Browne into the cab. There was a good deal of confused talk, and then Mr Browne got into the cab. The cabman settled his rug over his knees, and bent down for the address. The confusion grew greater and the cabman was directed differently by Freddy Malins and Mr Browne, each of whom had his head out through a window of the cab. The difficulty was to know where to drop Mr Browne along the route and Aunt Kate, Aunt Julia and Mary Jane helped the discussion from the doorstep with cross-directions and contradictions and abundance of laughter. As for Freddy Malins he was speechless with laughter. He popped his head in and out of the window every moment, to the great danger of his hat, and told his mother how the discussion was progressing till at last Mr Browne shouted to the bewildered cabman above the din of everybody's laughter:

—Do you know Trinity College?

—Yes, sir, said the cabman.

—Well, drive bang up against Trinity College gates, said Mr Browne, and then we'll tell you where to go. You understand now?

—Yes, sir, said the cabman.

—Make like a bird for Trinity College.

—Right, sir, cried the cabman.

The horse was whipped up and the cab rattled off along the quay amid a chorus of laughter and adieus.

Gabriel had not gone to the door with the others. He was in a dark part of the hall gazing up the staircase. A woman was standing near the top of the first flight, in the shadow also. He could not see her face but he could see the terracotta and salmonpink panels of her skirt which the shadow made appear black and white. It was his wife. She was leaning on the banisters, listening to something. Gabriel was surprised at her stillness and strained his ear to listen also. But he could hear little save the noise of laughter and dispute on the front steps, a few chords struck on the piano and a few notes of a man's voice singing.

He stood still in the gloom of the hall, trying to catch the air that the voice was singing and gazing up at his wife. There was grace and mystery in her attitude as if she were a symbol of something. He asked himself what is a woman standing on the stairs in the shadow, listening to distant music, a symbol of. If he were a painter he would paint her in that attitude. Her blue felt hat would show off the bronze of her hair against the darkness and the dark panels of her skirt would show off the light ones. *Distant Music* he would call the picture if he were a painter.

The hall-door was closed; and Aunt Kate, Aunt Julia and Mary Jane came down the hall, still laughing.

—Well, isn't Freddy terrible? said Mary Jane. He's really terrible.

Gabriel said nothing but pointed up the stairs towards where his wife was standing. Now that the hall-door was closed the voice and the piano could be heard more clearly. Gabriel held up his hand for them to be silent. The song seemed to be in the old Irish tonality and the singer seemed uncertain both of his words and of his voice. The voice, made plaintive by distance and by the singer's hoarseness, faintly illuminated the cadence of the air with words expressing grief:

> *O, the rain falls on my heavy locks*
> *And the dew wets my skin,*
> *My babe lies cold . . .*

—O, exclaimed Mary Jane. It's Bartell D'Arcy singing and he wouldn't sing all the night. O, I'll get him to sing a song before he goes.

—O do, Mary Jane, said Aunt Kate.

Mary Jane brushed past the others and ran to the staircase but before she reached it the singing stopped and the piano was closed abruptly.

—O, what a pity! she cried. Is he coming down, Gretta?

Gabriel heard his wife answer yes and saw her come down towards them. A few steps behind her were Mr Bartell D'Arcy and Miss O'Callaghan.

—O, Mr D'Arcy, cried Mary Jane, it's downright mean of you to break off like that when we were all in raptures listening to you.

—I have been at him all the evening, said Miss O'Callaghan, and Mrs Conroy too and he told us he had a dreadful cold and couldn't sing.

—O, Mr D'Arcy, said Aunt Kate, now that was a great fib to tell.

—Can't you see that I'm as hoarse as a crow? said Mr D'Arcy roughly.

He went into the pantry hastily and put on his overcoat. The others, taken aback by his rude speech, could find nothing to say. Aunt Kate wrinkled her brows and made signs to the others to drop the subject. Mr D'Arcy stood swathing his neck carefully and frowning.

—It's the weather, said Aunt Julia, after a pause.

—Yes, everybody has colds, said Aunt Kate readily, everybody.

—They say, said Mary Jane, we haven't had snow like it for thirty years; and I read this morning in the newspapers that the snow is general all over Ireland.

—I love the look of snow, said Aunt Julia sadly.

—So do I, said Miss O'Callaghan. I think Christmas is never really Christmas unless we have the snow on the ground.

—But poor Mr D'Arcy doesn't like the snow, said Aunt Kate, smiling.

Mr D'Arcy came from the pantry, fully swathed and buttoned, and in a repentant tone told them the history of his cold. Everyone gave him advice and said it was a great pity and urged him to be very careful of his throat in the night air. Gabriel watched his wife who did not join in the conversation. She was standing right under the dusty fanlight and the flame of the gas lit up the rich bronze of her hair which he had seen her drying at the fire a few days before. She was in the same attitude and seemed unaware of the talk about her. At last she turned towards them and Gabriel saw that there was colour on her cheeks and that her eyes were shining. A sudden tide of joy went leaping out of his heart.

—Mr D'Arcy, she said, what is the name of that song you were singing?

—It's called *The Lass of Aughrim*, said Mr D'Arcy, but I couldn't remember it properly. Why? Do you know it?

—*The Lass of Aughrim*, she repeated. I couldn't think of the name.

—It's a very nice air, said Mary Jane. I'm sorry you were not in voice to-night.

—Now, Mary Jane, said Aunt Kate, don't annoy Mr D'Arcy. I won't have him annoyed.

Seeing that all were ready to start she shepherded them to the door where good-night was said:

—Well, good-night, Aunt Kate, and thanks for the pleasant evening.

—Good-night, Gabriel. Good-night, Gretta!

—Good-night, Aunt Kate, and thanks ever so much. Good-night, Aunt Julia.

—O, good-night, Gretta, I didn't see you.

—Good-night, Mr D'Arcy. Good-night, Miss O'Callaghan.

—Good-night, Miss Morkan.

—Good-night, again.

—Good-night, all. Safe home.

—Good-night. Good-night.

The morning was still dark. A dull yellow light brooded over the houses and the river; and the sky seemed to be descending. It was slushy underfoot; and only streaks and patches of snow lay on the roofs, on the parapets of the quay and on the area railings. The lamps were still burning redly in the murky air and, across the river, the palace of the Four Courts stood out menacingly against the heavy sky.

She was walking on before him with Mr Bartell D'Arcy, her shoes in a brown parcel tucked under one arm and her hands holding her skirt up from the slush. She had no longer any grace of attitude but Gabriel's eyes were still bright with happiness. The blood went bounding along his veins; and the thoughts went rioting through his brain, proud, joyful, tender, valorous.

She was walking on before him so lightly and so erect that he longed to run after her noiselessly, catch her by the shoulders and say something foolish and affectionate into her ear. She seemed to him so frail that he longed to defend her against something and then to be alone with her. Moments of their secret life together burst like stars upon his memory. A heliotrope envelope was lying beside his breakfast-cup and he was caressing it with his hand. Birds were twittering in the ivy and the sunny web of the curtain was shimmering along the floor: he could not eat for happiness. They were standing on the crowded platform and he was placing a ticket inside the warm palm of her glove. He was standing with her in the cold, looking in through a grated window at a man making bottles in a roaring furnace. It was very cold. Her face, fragrant in the cold air, was quite close to his; and suddenly she called out to the man at the furnace:

—Is the fire hot, sir?

But the man could not hear her with the noise of the furnace. It was just as well. He might have answered rudely.

A wave of yet more tender joy escaped from his heart and went coursing in warm flood along his arteries. Like the tender fires of stars moments of their life together, that no one knew of or would ever know of, broke upon and illumined his memory. He longed to recall to her those moments, to make her forget the years of their dull existence together and remember only their moments of ecstasy. For the years, he felt, had not quenched his soul or hers. Their children, his writing, her household cares had not quenched all their souls' tender fire. In one letter that he had written to her then he had said: *Why is it that words like these seem to me so dull and cold? Is it because there is no word tender enough to be your name?*

Like distant music these words that he had written years before were borne towards him from the past. He longed to be alone with her. When the others had gone away, when he and she were in their room in the hotel, then they would be alone together. He would call her softly:

—Gretta!

Perhaps she would not hear at once: she would be undressing. Then something in his voice would strike her. She would turn and look at him. . . .

At the corner of Winetavern Street they met a cab. He was glad of its rattling noise as it saved him from conversation. She was looking out of the window and seemed tired. The others spoke only a few words, pointing out some building or street. The horse galloped along wearily under the murky morning sky, dragging his old rattling box after his heels, and Gabriel was again in a cab with her, galloping to catch the boat, galloping to their honeymoon.

As the cab drove across O'Connell Bridge Miss O'Callaghan said:

—They say you never cross O'Connell Bridge without seeing a white horse.

—I see a white man this time, said Gabriel.

—Where? asked Mr Bartell D'Arcy.

Gabriel pointed to the statue, on which lay patches of snow. Then he nodded familiarly to it and waved his hand.

—Good-night, Dan, he said gaily.

When the cab drew up before the hotel Gabriel jumped

out and, in spite of Mr Bartell D'Arcy's protest, paid the driver. He gave the man a shilling over his fare. The man saluted and said:

—A prosperous New Year to you, sir.

—The same to you, said Gabriel cordially.

She leaned for a moment on his arm in getting out of the cab and while standing at the curbstone, bidding the others good-night. She leaned lightly on his arm, as lightly as when she had danced with him a few hours before. He had felt proud and happy then, happy that she was his, proud of her grace and wifely carriage. But now, after the kindling again of so many memories, the first touch of her body, musical and strange and perfumed, sent through him a keen pang of lust. Under cover of her silence he pressed her arm closely to his side; and, as they stood at the hotel door, he felt that they had escaped from their lives and duties, escaped from home and friends and run away together with wild and radiant hearts to a new adventure.

An old man was dozing in a great hooded chair in the hall. He lit a candle in the office and went before them to the stairs. They followed him in silence, their feet falling in soft thuds on the thickly carpeted stairs. She mounted the stairs behind the porter, her head bowed in the ascent, her frail shoulders curved as with a burden, her skirt girt tightly about her. He could have flung his arms about her hips and held her still for his arms were trembling with desire to seize her and only the stress of his nails against the palms of his hands held the wild impulse of his body in check. The porter halted on the stairs to settle his guttering candle. They halted too on the steps below him. In the silence Gabriel could hear the falling of the molten wax into the tray and the thumping of his own heart against his ribs.

The porter led them along a corridor and opened a door. Then he set his unstable candle down on a toilet-table and asked at what hour they were to be called in the morning.

—Eight, said Gabriel.

The porter pointed to the tap of the electric-light and began a muttered apology but Gabriel cut him short.

—We don't want any light. We have light enough from the street. And I say, he added, pointing to the candle, you might remove that handsome article, like a good man.

The porter took up his candle again, but slowly for he was surprised by such a novel idea. Then he mumbled good-night and went out. Gabriel shot the lock to.

A ghostly light from the street lamp lay in a long shaft from one window to the door. Gabriel threw his overcoat and hat on a couch and crossed the room towards the window. He looked down into the street in order that his emotion might calm a little. Then he turned and leaned against a chest of drawers with his back to the light. She had taken off her hat and cloak and was standing before a large swinging mirror, unhooking her waist. Gabriel paused for a few moments, watching her, and then said:

—Gretta!

She turned away from the mirror slowly and walked along the shaft of light towards him. Her face looked so serious and weary that the words would not pass Gabriel's lips. No, it was not the moment yet.

—You looked tired, he said.

—I am a little, she answered.

—You don't feel ill or weak?

—No, tired: that's all.

She went on to the window and stood there, looking out. Gabriel waited again and then, fearing that diffidence was about to conquer him, he said abruptly:

—By the way, Gretta!

—What is it?

—You know that poor fellow Malins? he said quickly.

—Yes. What about him?

—Well, poor fellow, he's a decent sort of chap after all, continued Gabriel in a false voice. He gave me back that sovereign I lent him and I didn't expect it really. It's a pity he wouldn't keep away from that Browne, because he's not a bad fellow at heart.

He was trembling now with annoyance. Why did she seem so abstracted? He did not know how he could begin. Was she annoyed, too, about something? If she would only turn to him or come to him of her own accord! To take her as she was would be brutal. No, he must see some ardour in her eyes first. He longed to be master of her strange mood.

—When did you lend him the pound? she asked, after a pause.

Gabriel strove to restrain himself from breaking out into brutal language about the sottish Malins and his pound. He longed to cry to her from his soul, to crush her body against his, to overmaster her. But he said:

—O, at Christmas, when he opened that little Christmas-card shop in Henry Street.

He was in such a fever of rage and desire that he did not hear her come from the window. She stood before him for an instant, looking at him strangely. Then, suddenly raising herself on tiptoe and resting her hands lightly on his shoulders, she kissed him.

—You are a very generous person, Gabriel, she said.

Gabriel, trembling with delight at her sudden kiss and at the quaintness of her phrase, put his hands on her hair and began smoothing it back, scarcely touching it with his fingers. The washing had made it fine and brilliant. His heart was brimming over with happiness. Just when he was wishing for it she had come to him of her own accord. Perhaps her thoughts had been running with his. Perhaps she had felt the impetuous desire that was in him and then the yielding mood had come upon her. Now that she had fallen to him so easily he wondered why he had been so diffident.

He stood, holding her head between his hands. Then, slipping one arm swiftly about her body and drawing her towards him, he said softly:

—Gretta dear, what are you thinking about?

She did not answer nor yield wholly to his arm. He said again, softly:

—Tell me what it is, Gretta. I think I know what is the matter. Do I know?

She did not answer at once. Then she said in an outburst of tears:

—O, I am thinking about that song, *The Lass of Aughrim.*

She broke loose from him and ran to the bed and, throwing her arms across the bed-rail, hid her face. Gabriel stood stock-still for a moment in astonishment and then followed her. As he passed in the way of the cheval-glass he caught sight of himself in full length, his broad, well-filled shirt-front, the face whose expression always puzzled him when he saw it in a mirror and his glimmering gilt-rimmed eyeglasses. He halted a few paces from her and said:

—What about the song? Why does that make you cry?

She raised her head from her arms and dried her eyes with the back of her hand like a child. A kinder note than he had intended went into his voice.

—Why, Gretta? he asked.

—I am thinking about a person long ago who used to sing that song.

—And who was the person long ago? asked Gabriel, smiling.

—It was a person I used to know in Galway when I was living with my grandmother, she said.

The smile passed away from Gabriel's face. A dull anger

began to gather again at the back of his mind and the dull fires of his lust began to glow angrily in his veins.

—Someone you were in love with? he asked ironically.

—It was a young boy I used to know, she answered, named Michael Furey. He used to sing that song, *The Lass of Aughrim*. He was very delicate.

Gabriel was silent. He did not wish her to think that he was interested in this delicate boy.

—I can see him so plainly, she said after a moment. Such eyes as he had: big dark eyes! And such an expression in them—an expression!

—O then, you were in love with him? said Gabriel.

—I used to go out walking with him, she said, when I was in Galway.

A thought flew across Gabriel's mind.

—Perhaps that was why you wanted to go to Galway with that Ivors girl? he said coldly.

She looked at him and asked in surprise:

—What for?

Her eyes made Gabriel feel awkward. He shrugged his shoulders and said:

—How do I know? To see him perhaps.

She looked away from him along the shaft of light towards the window in silence.

—He is dead, she said at length. He died when he was only seventeen. Isn't it a terrible thing to die so young as that?

—What was he? asked Gabriel, still ironically.

—He was in the gasworks, she said.

Gabriel felt humiliated by the failure of his irony and by the evocation of this figure from the dead, a boy in the gasworks. While he had been full of memories of their secret life together, full of tenderness and joy and desire, she had been comparing him in her mind with another. A shameful consciousness of his own person assailed him. He saw himself as a ludicrous figure, acting as a pennyboy for his aunts, a nervous well-meaning sentimentalist, orating to vulgarians and idealising his own clownish lusts, the pitiable fatuous fellow he had caught a glimpse of in the mirror. Instinctively he turned his back more to the light lest she might see the shame that burned upon his forehead.

He tried to keep up his tone of cold interrogation but his voice when he spoke was humble and indifferent.

—I suppose you were in love with this Michael Furey, Gretta, he said.

—I was great with him at that time, she said.

Her voice was veiled and sad. Gabriel, feeling now how vain it would be to try to lead her whither he had purposed, caressed one of her hands and said, also sadly:

—And what did he die of so young, Gretta? Consumption, was it?

—I think he died for me, she answered.

A vague terror seized Gabriel at this answer as if, at that hour when he had hoped to triumph, some impalpable and vindictive being was coming against him, gathering forces against him in its vague world. But he shook himself free of it with an effort of reason and continued to caress her hand. He did not question her again for he felt that she would tell him of herself. Her hand was warm and moist: it did not respond to his touch but he continued to caress it just as he had caressed her first letter to him that spring morning.

—It was in the winter, she said, about the beginning of the winter when I was going to leave my grandmother's and come up here to the convent. And he was ill at the time in his lodgings in Galway and wouldn't be let out and his people in Oughterard were written to. He was in decline, they said, or something like that. I never knew rightly.

She paused for a moment and sighed.

—Poor fellow, she said. He was very fond of me and he was such a gentle boy. We used to go out together, walking, you know, Gabriel, like the way they do in the country. He was going to study singing only for his health. He had a very good voice, poor Michael Furey.

—Well; and then? asked Gabriel.

—And then when it came to the time for me to leave Galway and come up to the convent he was much worse and I wouldn't be let see him so I wrote a letter saying I was going up to Dublin and would be back in the summer and hoping he would be better then.

She paused for a moment to get her voice under control and then went on:

—Then the night before I left I was in my grandmother's house in Nuns' Island, packing up, and I heard gravel thrown up against the window. The window was so wet I couldn't see so I ran downstairs as I was and slipped out the back into the garden and there was the poor fellow at the end of the garden, shivering.

—And did you not tell him to go back? asked Gabriel.

—I implored of him to go home at once and told him he would get his death in the rain. But he said he did not want to live. I can see his eyes as well as well! He was standing at the end of the wall where there was a tree.

—And did he go home? asked Gabriel.

—Yes, he went home. And when I was only a week in the convent he died and he was buried in Oughterard where his people came from. O, the day I heard that, that he was dead!

She stopped, choking with sobs, and, overcome by emotion, flung herself face downward on the bed, sobbing in the quilt. Gabriel held her hand for a moment longer, irresolutely, and then, shy of intruding on her grief, let it fall gently and walked quietly to the window.

She was fast asleep.

Gabriel, leaning on his elbow, looked for a few moments unresentfully on her tangled hair and half-open mouth, listening to her deep-drawn breath. So she had had that romance in her life: a man had died for her sake. It hardly pained him now to think how poor a part he, her husband, had played in her life. He watched her while she slept as though he and she had never lived together as man and wife. His curious eyes rested long upon her face and on her hair: and, as he thought of what she must have been then, in that time of her first girlish beauty, a strange friendly pity for her entered his soul. He did not like to say even to himself that her face was no longer beautiful but he knew that it was no longer the face for which Michael Furey had braved death.

Perhaps she had not told him all the story. His eyes moved to the chair over which she had thrown some of her clothes. A petticoat string dangled to the floor. One boot stood upright, its limp upper fallen down: the fellow of it lay upon its side. He wondered at his riot of emotions of an hour before. From what had it proceeded? From his aunt's supper, from his own foolish speech, from the wine and dancing, the merrymaking when saying good-night in the hall, the pleasure of the walk along the river in the snow. Poor Aunt Julia! She, too, would soon be a shade with the shade of Patrick Morkan and his horse. He had caught that haggard look upon her face for a moment when she was singing *Arrayed for the Bridal*. Soon, perhaps, he would be sitting in that same drawing-room, dressed in black, his silk hat on his knees. The blinds would be drawn down and Aunt Kate would be sitting beside him, crying and blowing her nose and telling him how Julia had died. He would cast about in his mind for some words that might console her, and would find only lame and useless ones. Yes, yes: that would happen very soon.

The air of the room chilled his shoulders. He stretched himself cautiously along under the sheets and lay down beside his wife. One by one they were all becoming shades. Better pass boldly into that other world, in the full glory of some passion, than fade and wither dismally with age. He thought of how she who lay beside him had locked in her heart for so many years that image of her lover's eyes when he had told her that he did not wish to live.

Generous tears filled Gabriel's eyes. He had never felt like that himself towards any woman but he knew that such a feeling must be love. The tears gathered more thickly in his eyes and in the partial darkness he imagined he saw the form of a young man standing under a dripping tree. Other forms were near. His soul had approached that region where dwell the vast hosts of the dead. He was conscious of, but could not apprehend, their wayward and flickering existence. His own identity was fading out into a grey impalpable world: the solid world itself which these dead had one time reared and lived in was dissolving and dwindling.

A few light taps upon the pane made him turn to the window. It had begun to snow again. He watched sleepily the flakes, silver and dark, falling obliquely against the lamplight. The time had come for him to set out on his journey westward. Yes, the newspapers were right: snow was general all over Ireland. It was falling on every part of the dark central plain, on the treeless hills, falling softly upon the Bog of Allen and, farther westward, softly falling into the dark mutinous Shannon waves. It was falling, too, upon every part of the lonely churchyard on the hill where Michael Furey lay buried. It lay thickly drifted on the crooked crosses and headstones, on the spears of the little gate, on the barren thorns. His soul swooned slowly as he heard the snow falling faintly through the universe and faintly falling, like the descent of their last end, upon all the living and the dead.

A NOTE ON THE TEXT

The text used here is the definitive 1967 Viking Compass text (with pagination unchanged). The principle governing this edition of *Dubliners*, though complicated enough in the execution, can be stated simply. This is the text Joyce would wish to publish at the present time—to the extent that his wishes can be determined. The rationale for determining Joyce's wishes (which is not as mystical a process as it might seem) can be found in my "Observations on the Text of *Dubliners*" in *Studies in Bibliography* (Charlottesville, Va.: University Press of Virginia), Vols. XV and XVII, and in the correspondence of Grant Richards with Joyce in Vol. XVI. In pagination and lineation this text follows the previous Viking Compass editions almost exactly. The ways in which this edition differs from its predecessors are outlined below.

The punctuation and spelling of the first edition (London: Grant Richards, 1914) have been followed—with the exceptions noted below. Joyce read proof on this edition and made over a thousand corrections—mainly removing commas that had been introduced by the printer, but also making some substantive corrections and alterations. This edition was the last to be revised by Joyce, and can properly be used as the basis of any later edition, but it was neither in form nor in substance exactly what Joyce wanted. The reasons for this are very complicated, deriving from the way the book was printed and from the conflicting ideas and habits of author, publisher, and printer.

First of all, the printer's copy for the first edition was not Joyce's manuscript but a partially corrected set of proofs from a version of *Dubliners* set up and printed in Dublin two years earlier for an edition that was not published but destroyed by the Dublin printer. Second, the London publisher, Grant Richards, insisted on using inverted commas to present direct discourse, though Joyce condemned them as an "eyesore" which gave "an impression of unreality." Also, the English printer ignored some "two-hundred" of the corrections Joyce made in reading proof for the first edition, though Joyce himself was unaware of this until four years later. And the publisher ignored a list of twenty-eight corrections Joyce sent him when he discovered that he would not be allowed to correct revised proof. Finally, Joyce did not have any copy of the final version of the destroyed Dublin printing, which contained many changes he had made in the text *after* reading the proofs which were used as the printer's copy for the first edition.

Some of the mischief caused by all this can be undone and has been for this revised edition. Some is beyond repair. In this new text the dash has been used to introduce direct discourse, and italic type has been used for other quotations and for speech reported within direct discourse. Also the twenty-eight additional corrections listed by Joyce have been discovered and introduced here. But the "two-hundred" corrections which the printer ignored have not come to light. Fortunately, a nearly complete copy of the destroyed Dublin printing, incorporating some thirty-seven substantive changes not on the proofs which Joyce sent to Richards, has found its way to the Yale University Library. (A list of these changes is available from the publishers upon request.) These changes, too, have been included in this revised edition, on the assumption that they either numbered among the lost "two-hundred" or would have been made by Joyce had he possessed a copy of the final Dublin version that contained them.

All these matters are presented in greater detail, and the various changes and corrections are listed and discussed, in the "Observations" mentioned above. In establishing the methodology for this edition, the editor has benefited greatly from the advice of Richard Ellmann. The collation of all known manuscripts, proofs, and impressions of *Dubliners* in preparation for this edition could not have been accomplished without the expert assistance of Joan C. Scholes, to whom any expression of gratitude would be an impertinence.

Center for Textual Studies   ROBERT SCHOLES
University of Iowa
October 1968

II

❖❖

Dubliners:
Background

CHRONOLOGY

1882　James Joyce was born in Dublin on February 2, the eldest son of John Stanislaus Joyce, an improvident tax collector, and Mary Jane Joyce.

1884　Birth of Stanislaus Joyce. Of the ten Joyce children who survived infancy, Stanislaus was closest to his brother James.

1888　In September, Joyce entered Clongowes Wood College, a Jesuit boarding school, where he remained (except for holidays) until June 1891.

1891　A crucial year in Joyce's life. Financial difficulties forced John Joyce to withdraw James from Clongowes Wood in June. The death of Parnell on October 6 deeply affected the nine-year-old boy, who wrote a poem, "Et Tu, Healy," denouncing Parnell's "betrayer," Tim Healy; John Joyce was so pleased that he had the poem printed, but no copy has survived. Christmas dinner in the Joyce household was marred by a violent scene, later described in *A Portrait of the Artist*.

1893　In April, Joyce entered another Jesuit school, Belvedere College, where he remained until 1898, making a brilliant academic record.

1898　Joyce began to attend University College, Dublin, a Jesuit institution founded by Cardinal Newman. It was here that his revolt against Catholicism and provincial patriotism took form.

1899　In May, Joyce opposed his fellow students and refused to sign a letter attacking the "heresy" of Yeats's *Countess Cathleen*.

1900　A year of literary activity. In January, Joyce read a paper on "Drama and Life" before the college literary society (see *Stephen Hero*); in April his essay on "Ibsen's New Drama" appeared in the distinguished *Fortnightly Review*.

1901　Late in the year Joyce published "The Day of the Rabblement," an essay attacking the provincialism of the Irish theater (originally designed for a college magazine, it was rejected by the Jesuit adviser).

1 9 0 2   In February, Joyce read a paper on the Irish poet James
Clarence Mangan, claiming that Mangan had been the
victim of narrow nationalism.

Joyce received his degree in October, and finally decided
to study medicine in Paris. He left Dublin in late November, and paused briefly in London to visit Yeats and
investigate possible outlets for his writing.

1 9 0 3   Once in Paris, Joyce soon lost interest in medicine and
began to write reviews for a Dublin newspaper. On April
10 he received a telegram, MOTHER DYING COME HOME
FATHER, and immediately returned to Dublin. His mother
died on August 13.

1 9 0 4   Early in 1904 Joyce began work on his autobiographical
novel with a short piece called "A Portrait of the Artist":
this was later expanded into *Stephen Hero* and then recast
to make *A Portrait of the Artist as a Young Man*.

The situation of the Joyce family had worsened after
Mary Joyce's death, and James gradually withdrew from
the family. In March he took a job as teacher in a Dalkey
school, remaining there until the end of June. On June 10
he met Nora Barnacle, and soon fell in love with her.
Since he was opposed to marriage as an institution, and
could not live with Nora in Dublin, Joyce decided to
make his way in Europe. He and Nora left Dublin on
October 8 and traveled through London and Zurich to
Pola, where Joyce began teaching English at the Berlitz
School.

During the last months of 1904 the first of the
Dubliners stories were published in the *Irish Homestead*:
the early version of "The Sisters" (August 13), "Eveline"
(September 10), and "After the Race" (December 17).
"Clay" (first called "Christmas Eve," later "Hallow Eve")
was begun in November.

1 9 0 5   Joyce moved to Trieste in March, and a son, Giorgio, was
born on July 27. Three months later Joyce's younger
brother Stanislaus joined him in Trieste.

Meanwhile, the writing of *Dubliners* proceeded at a
fast pace. "The Boarding House," "Counterparts," and
"A Painful Case" (originally "A Painful Incident") were
drafted by July, while "Ivy Day in the Committee Room,"
"An Encounter," "A Mother," and "Araby" were completed by the end of September. "Grace" was begun in

October, and on December 3 Joyce submitted the twelve stories already written to the publisher Grant Richards. They made a symmetrical group: three stories of childhood ("The Sisters," "An Encounter," "Araby"), three of adolescence ("The Boarding House," "After the Race," "Eveline"), three of mature life ("Clay," "Counterparts," "A Painful Case"), and a final triad dealing with the public life of Dublin ("Ivy Day," "A Mother," "Grace").

1906 "Two Gallants" was completed in February, and "A Little Cloud" was mailed to Grant Richards in July. *Dubliners* was accepted for publication by Grant Richards in February, but after a long controversy the manuscript was rejected in September. Joyce moved to Rome in July, where he worked in a bank until March of the next year.

1907 "The Dead," which was planned in Rome, was written after Joyce's return to Trieste in March.

In May a London publisher issued *Chamber Music*, a collection of poems.

A daughter, Lucia Anna, was born on July 26.

In September, Joyce began revising *Stephen Hero* and
1908 continued this work into the next year, but after finishing three chapters he temporarily abandoned the manuscript.

1909 On August 1 Joyce traveled to Ireland for a visit. The next month he came back to Trieste, gained financial support, and returned to Dublin to open a cinema. Maunsel and Co., a Dublin publisher, had agreed in April to look at the manuscript of *Dubliners*, and by September the firm had decided to publish the book the next spring.

1910 Joyce returned to Trieste in January, and the cinema venture soon collapsed. He corrected proofs for *Dubliners* in June, but even as the proofs were being corrected Maunsel and Co. began to have second thoughts. The firm objected to certain passages in "Ivy Day," Joyce refused to make changes, and the publication of the stories was delayed.
1911 Negotiations dragged on, and the controversy over *Dubliners* became almost an obsession with Joyce. Finally,
1912 in July 1912, he made his last trip to Dublin, but was unable to arrange for publication. The sheets of *Dubliners* printed for Maunsel and Co. were destroyed, and Joyce left Dublin in great bitterness. On the return journey to Trieste he wrote a savage broadside, *Gas from a Burner*.

1 9 1 3 Late in the year Joyce began to correspond with Ezra Pound; his luck was changing.

1 9 1 4 Joyce's *annus mirabilis*. In January, Grant Richards accepted *Dubliners* for the second time (offering the same contract as in 1906), and the stories were finally published in June. Serial publication of *A Portrait of the Artist as a Young Man* began in the *Egoist* (installments ran from February 1914 to September 1915). In March, Joyce began drafting *Ulysses*, but he soon suspended work on the novel in order to write his play *Exiles*.

1 9 1 5 *Exiles* was completed in the spring.
    In spite of the war, Joyce was allowed to depart in June for neutral Switzerland.

1 9 1 6 *Portrait* was published in book form on December 29.

1 9 1 7 During this year Joyce underwent his first eye operation. By the end of 1917 he had finished drafting the first three episodes of *Ulysses*; the structure of the novel was already taking shape.

1 9 1 8 In March the *Little Review* (New York) began to serialize *Ulysses*. *Exiles* was published on May 25.

1 9 1 9 In October, Joyce returned to Trieste, where he taught English and drove *Ulysses* toward completion.

1 9 2 0 At the insistence of Ezra Pound, Joyce moved to Paris in early July. In October a complaint from the Society for the Suppression of Vice stopped publication of *Ulysses* in the *Little Review*.

1 9 2 1 This year was devoted to completing the last episodes of *Ulysses* and revising the entire work.

1 9 2 2 *Ulysses* was published on February 2, Joyce's fortieth birthday.

1 9 2 3 On March 10 Joyce wrote the first pages of *Finnegans Wake* (known before publication in 1939 as *Work in Progress*). He had been actively planning for this new work through several years.

1 9 2 4 The first published fragment of *Finnegans Wake* appeared in April. During the next fourteen years Joyce was to publish most of *Finnegans Wake* in preliminary versions.

1 9 2 7 – Between April 1927 and November 1929 Joyce published
1 9 2 9   early versions of *Finnegans Wake*, Parts I and III, in the experimental magazine *transition*. During the next ten years several sections of *Work in Progress* were published as books.

1 9 3 1   In May the Joyces traveled to London, and on July 4 James and Nora Joyce were married at a registry office ("for testamentary reasons").

        Joyce's father died on December 29; and a grandson,
1 9 3 2   Stephen Joyce, was born on February 15 of the next year. Both events affected Joyce profoundly: see his poem written at the time, "Ecce Puer."

        In March, Joyce's daughter, Lucia, suffered a nervous breakdown; she never recovered, and the remainder of Joyce's life was darkened by this event.

1 9 3 3   Late in the year an American court ruled that *Ulysses* was not pornographic; this famous decision led to the first authorized American publication of the work in February of the next year (the first English edition was issued in 1936).

1 9 3 4   Most of this year was spent in Switzerland, so that Joyce could be near Lucia (who was confined to an institution near Zurich) and could consult a Zurich doctor who had cared for his failing eyesight since 1930.

1 9 3 5 – During these years Joyce labored slowly to complete
1 9 3 8   *Finnegans Wake*; residence in Paris was broken by frequent trips through France, Switzerland, and Denmark.

1 9 3 9   *Finnegans Wake* was published on May 4, but Joyce received a copy in time for his fifty-seventh birthday.

1 9 4 0   After the fall of France the Joyces managed to reach
1 9 4 1   Zurich; James Joyce died there on January 13, 1941, after an abdominal operation.

... of the Leeret held an inquest on the body of Mrs Emily Sinico of Leoville ... Harrion who was killed ... was killed ... accident at Sydney Parade Station ... yesterday ... on Tuesday last. The evidence ... showed that the deceased lady ... while attempting ... to cross the line was knocked down ... by the buffer of the engine of the 10 ... o'clock slow train from Kingstown ... sustaining severe injuries of the head ... which led to her death ... left side. ... driver of the engine ... platform ... stated that ... had been in the employment ... the train in ... motion and a second or two afterward ... brought it to rest in response to ... cries. The train was going slowly ... P. Kilbride, railway porter stated that ... as the train was about to start he saw ... woman attempting to cross the line. ... he ran towards her and shouted but before she could hear him she was caught by the buffer of the engine and fell to the ground ... You saw the lady fall Witness - Yes.

A page from the first version of "A Painful Case"

Death of a Lady at Sydney Parade
A Painful Case.

Today at Vincent's Hospital the Deputy Coroner (in the absence of Mr L----verett) held an inquest on the body of Mrs Emily Sinico, aged forty-two years, who was killed at Sydney Parade Station yesterday evening. The evidence showed that the deceased lady while attempting to cross the line was knocked down by the engine of the ten o'clock slow train from Kingstown thereby sustaining injuries of the head and right side which led to her death.

James Lennon, driver of the engine, stated that he had been in the employment of the railway company for fifteen years. On hearing the guard's whistle he set the train in motion and a second or two afterwards brought it to rest in response to loud cries. The train was going slowly.

D Dunne, railway porter, stated that as the train was

THE COMPOSITION AND
REVISION OF THE STORIES

We know almost nothing about the earliest stages in the writing of a *Dubliners* story. No really rough draft of a story has survived. In fact, it seems likely that Joyce worked his stories up very thoroughly in his head before setting them down, and then discarded very little of what he had put on paper. We know that it was his habit to write out the stories on sheets of paper with a very large left-hand margin and no margin on the right. His corrections and additions were then made in the left-hand margin. The most heavily revised page in all the extant *Dubliners* manuscripts is a page from the first version of "A Painful Case," reproduced at the beginning of this section. The smooth copy of the page from the second version of this story (also reproduced) is more typical of the extant manuscripts.

Still, the surviving manuscripts can give us many insights into the compositional process behind *Dubliners*. Many of the stories were revised after the manuscripts were complete, and by comparing the final versions with their predecessors we can gain some knowledge of Joyce's artistic methods and intentions. To that end we include in this section a line-for-line reproduction of the first complete manuscript of the first *Dubliners* story, "The Sisters"—which has never appeared in print. A similar version of this story was published by the Dublin agricultural journal *The Irish Homestead* as one of its regular features, *Our Weekly Story*, for the week of August 13, 1904. The manuscript version presented here should enable the student of *Dubliners* to consider the extensive alterations and additions made by Joyce in the final version of the story, which now stands as the introduction to the whole collection. The revisions can be seen as improvements to this one story or as

Portions of this essay are taken from *The Workshop of Daedalus* by Robert Scholes and Richard Kain (Evanston, Ill.: Northwestern University Press, 1964). Reprinted by permission.

adjustments made so that the story could better serve its function as an introduction to the others—or as both of these things. The materials for study and speculation are here.

In this section we also present discussions of Joyce's revision of two other stories. These are of some interest in themselves and may provide suggestions for the investigation of "The Sisters."

REVISIONS OF "EVELINE"

Joyce revised fairly heavily between the *Irish Homestead* version (September 10, 1904) and the first edition. The changes from the *Homestead* text are mainly of two kinds. In revising the narration of Eveline's reverie he sometimes replaced words or phrases not quite appropriate for her with more suitable material, and he sometimes added material for the sake of its naturalistic or symbolic point. Consider the examples below.

Home! She looked round the room, passing in review all its familiar objects. How many times she had dusted it, once a week at least. It was the "best" room, but it seemed to secrete dust everywhere. She had known the room for ten years—more—twelve years, and knew everything in it. Now she was going away. And yet during all those years she had never found out the name of the Australian priest whose yellowing photograph hung on the wall, just above the broken harmonium. He had been a friend of her father's—a school friend. When he showed the photograph to a friend, her father used to pass it with a casual word, "In Australia now—Melbourne." [Homestead version, 1904.]

Home! She looked round the room reviewing all its familiar objects which she had dusted once a week for so many years, wondering where on earth all the dust came from. Perhaps she would never see again those familiar objects from which she had never dreamed of being divided. And yet during all those years she had never found out the name of the priest whose yellowing photograph hung on the wall above the broken harmonium beside the coloured print of the promises made to the Blessed Margaret Mary Alacoque. He had been a school friend of her father's. Whenever he showed the photograph to a visitor her father used to pass it with a casual word:

—He is in Melbourne now.—

[Late Maunsel version, c. 1910.]

Irrelevant matter is pruned away. The word "secrete," which is inappropriate to the thought processes of Eveline, is removed, and the Blessed Margaret Mary Alacoque is inserted. When we learn that this saint paralyzed herself with self-inflicted tortures but was cured miraculously when she vowed to dedicate herself to a holy life, we can see that Joyce is not merely adding to the naturalistic description of the home of Eveline but presenting the reader with a symbolic parallel to her own life of emotional paralysis. In other revisions the speech of the edgy Miss Gavan is sharpened a little and we are given more detail on Eveline's past relationship with her father. Compare the following two passages:

Even now—at her age, she was over nineteen—she sometimes felt herself in danger of her father's violence. Latterly he had begun to threaten her, saying what he would do if it were not for her dead mother's sake.

Even now, though she was over nineteen, she sometimes felt herself in danger of her father's violence. She knew it was that that had given her the palpitations. When they were growing up he had never gone for her, like he used to go for Harry and Ernest, because she was a girl; but latterly he had begun to threaten her and say what he would do to her only for her dead mother's sake.

Here we have not only the interesting addition of the palpitations and the father's past brutality but a significant change in the syntax of the last clause. The formal "if it were not for her dead mother's sake" gives way to the "only for her dead mother's sake" in which we can catch the living rhythm of the father's speech. Though the account is narrated rather than dramatized and the discourse indirect rather than direct, the narrative takes its color from the idiom of the characters rather than from any narrative personality. Through countless little changes of this kind, Joyce carefully eliminated his own personality from *Dubliners*, as he developed a system whereby the events and characters presented in the narrative rather than any assumed narrative persona determine the diction and syntax of the narrative prose. This elimination of the narrator as a personality does away with the need for consistent narrative idiom and paves the way for the experiments of Joyce's later fiction.

REVISIONS OF
"THE BOARDING HOUSE"

This story was extensively rewritten between the 1905 manuscript, which was signed "Stephen Daedalus" and apparently intended for *The Irish Homestead,* and the final version. Several aspects of the rewriting warrant commentary. In one respect the rewriting parallels that of "Eveline" discussed above. In eight significant substantive changes the intent is obviously to make the language more colloquial, more appropriate to the events being narrated than to the more lofty tone of the narrative persona, "Stephen Daedalus." Thus, "obliged to enlist himself" becomes "had to become"; "attacked his wife" becomes "went for his wife"; "started a boarding house" becomes "set up a boarding house"; "an amateur boxer" becomes "handy with the mits"; "she had been specific in her enquiries and Polly had been decided in her answers" becomes "she had been frank in her questions and Polly had been frank in her answers"; plain "Lyons" becomes "Bantam Lyons"; "the loss of his job" becomes "the loss of his sit" (colloquial for *situation*); "had a bit of money put by" becomes "had a bit of stuff put by." In other revisions, Joyce is busy at the usual phrase-sharpening, and in one case he is at some pains to make his irony less heavy-handed. The last sentence, originally reading "She remembered now what she had been waiting for: this was it," becomes "Then she remembered what she had been waiting for."

But the major revision to the early version of this story consists of an insertion some ten lines long. The nature of the insertion throws light on an interesting aspect of Joyce's technique. Joyce is often praised or blamed (depending on the critic's predilections) for the ambivalence or ambiguity of his fiction. When the artist refuses to provide any authoritative commentary, the critics tell us, we are free to believe whatever we want, and to seek for authorial intention is to commit one of the graver critical fallacies. But to this observer it seems that Joyce gives us our heads expecting us to use them. The insertion in question illustrates how we are to proceed. In the original version there was room for some quibbling about the extent to which each of the two principals was seducer or seducee. The added ten lines provide no commentary, but they give us the bit of evidence we need to resolve the problem with considerable certainty.

Then late one night as he was undressing for bed she had tapped at his door, timidly. She wanted to relight her candle at his for hers had been blown out by a gust. It was her bath night. She wore an open combing jacket of printed flannel. Her white instep shone in the opening of her furry slippers and the blood glowed warmly behind her perfumed skin. From her hands and wrists too as she lit and steadied her candle a faint perfume arose.

The Sisters

Three nights in succession I had found
myself in Great Britain Strcct at
that hour, as if by providence. Three
nights I had raised my eyes to that
lighted square of window and speculated.
I seemed to understand that it would
occur at night. But in spite of the
providence which had led my feet
and in spite of the reverent curiosity
of my eyes I had discovered nothing.
Each night the square was lighted
in the same way, faintly and evenly.
It was not the light of candles so
far as I could see. Therefore it had
not ~~yet~~ occurred yet.

On the fourth night at that
hour I was in another part of the
city. It may have been the same
providence that led me there—a
whimsical kind of providence—to
take me at a disadvantage. As I
went home I wondered was that
square of window lighted as before
or did it reveal the ceremonious
candles in the light of which the
Christian must take his last sleep.
I was not ~~surprised, then, when~~ at

supper I found myself a prophet.
Old Cotter and my uncle were talking
at the fire, smoking. Old Cotter was
a retired distiller who owned a batch
of prize setters. He used to be very
interesting when I knew him first,
talking about *faints* and *worms,* but[1]

afterwards he became tedious.
    While I was eating my stirabout
I heard him say to my uncle:
—Without a doubt. The upper storey
(he tapped an unnecessary hand
at his forehead) was gone—
—So they said. I never could see
much of it. I thought he was
sane enough—
—So he was, at times, said old
Cotter—
    I sniffed the *was* apprehensively
and gulped down some stirabout.

Jack

—Is he any better, Uncle ~~John~~?—
—He's dead—
—O . . . . . —
—Died a few hours ago—
—Who told you?—
—Mr Cotter here brought us the
news. He was passing. . . . —
—Yes, I just happened to be passing
and I noticed the windows. . . . You
know. So I just knocked softly—
—Do you think they will bring him
to the chapel? asked my aunt—
—O, no, ma'am. I wouldn't say so—
—Very unlikely, my uncle agreed—

[1] Space breaks indicate where pages ended in the original manuscript.—ED.

So old Cotter had got the better
of me for all my vigilance of
three nights. It is often annoying
the way people will blunder on
what you have elaborately planned
for. I was sure he would die
at night.

The following morning after breakfast
I went down to look at the little
house in Great Britain Street.
It was an unassuming shop
registered under the vague name
of *Drapery*. The drapery consisted
chiefly of children's boots and
umbrellas and on ordinary days
there used to be a notice hanging
in the window which said *Umbrellas
Recovered*. There was no notice
visible now for the shop-blinds
were drawn down and a crape
bouquet was tied to the knocker
of the door with white ribbons.
Three women of the people and
a telegram boy were reading
the card pinned on the crape. I
also went over and read:
      July 2nd, 1890
    The Rev. James Flynn
    (formerly of S. Catherine's
    Church, Meath Street) aged
    Sixty-five Years.
        R.I.P.
Only sixty-five! He looked
much older than that. I often saw
him sitting at the fire in the close

dark room behind the shop, nearly
smothered in his great coat. He
seemed to have almost stupefied
himself with heat and the gesture
of his large trembling hand to
his nostrils had grown automatic.
My aunt, who is what they call
good-hearted, never went into
the shop without bringing him

some High Toast; and he used to
take the packet of snuff from
her hands, gravely inclining his
head for sign of thanks. He used
to sit in that stuffy room for
the greater part of the day from
early morning while Nannie
(who was almost stone deaf)
read out the newspaper to him.
His other sister, Eliza, used to
mind the shop. These two old
women used to look after him,
feed him and clothe him. The
task of clothing him was not
difficult for his ancient priestly
clothes were quite green with
age and his dogskin slippers
were everlasting. When he was
tired of hearing the news he used
to rattle his snuff-box on the
arm of his chair to avoid
shouting at her and then he
used to make believe to read
his prayerbook. Make believe
because whenever Eliza brought

him a cup of soup from the
kitchen she had always to
waken him.

As I stood looking up at the
crape and the card which bore
his name I could not convince
myself that he was dead. He
seemed like one who could have
gone on living for ever if only
he had wanted to; his life was

so methodical and uneventful.
I think he said more to me than
to anyone else. He had an
egoistic contempt for all
women-folk and suffered all
their services to him in polite
silence. Of course neither of
his sisters was very intelligent.
Nannie, for instance, had been
reading out the newspaper
to him every day for years and
could read tolerably well and
yet she always spoke of it
as the *Freeman's General.*
Perhaps he found me more
intelligent and honoured me
with words for that reason.
Nothing, practically nothing,
ever happened to remind him
of his former life (I mean friends
or visitors) but still he could
remember every detail of it
in his own fashion. He had
studied at the college in Rome

pronounce   and he taught me to ~~speak~~
Latin in the Italian way. He
often put me through the
responses of the Mass, smiling
often and pushing huge pinches
of snuff up each nostril
alternately. When he smiled
he used to uncover his big
discoloured teeth and let his
tongue lie on his lower lip.
At first this habit of his used

to make me feel uneasy. Then
I grew used to it.
   That evening my aunt
visited the house of mourning
and took me with her. It was
an oppressive summer evening
of faded gold. Nannie received
us in the hall and, as it was
no use saying anything to
her, my aunt shook hands
with her for all. We followed
the old woman upstairs and
into the dead-room. The room
through the lace end of the
blind was suffused with
dusky golden light amid
which the candles seemed
like pale thin flames. He
had been coffined. Nannie
gave the lead and we three
knelt down at the foot of
the bed. There was no sound
in the room for some minutes

except the sound of Nannie's
mutterings, for she prayed
noisily. The fancy came
to me that the old priest
was smiling as he lay there
in his coffin.

But no. When we rose
and went up to the head
of the bed I saw that he was
not smiling. There he lay

solemn and copious, vested
as for the altar, his large
hands loosely retaining a
cross. His face was very grey
and massive with distended
nostrils and circled with a
scanty white fur. There was
a heavy odour in the room, the
flowers.

We sat downstairs in the
little room behind the shop,
my aunt and I and the two
sisters. We, as visitors, were
given a glass of sherry each.
Nannie sat in a corner and
said nothing but her lips
moved from speaker to
speaker with a painfully
intelligent movement. I
said nothing either, being
too young, but my aunt said
a great deal for she was a
gossip, a harmless one.
—Ah, well, he's gone!—

—To enjoy his eternal reward,
Miss Flynn, I'm sure. He was
a good and holy man—
—He was a good man but . . . . .
you see . . . . he was a disappointed
man. You see . . . . his life was,
you might say, crossed—
—Ah, yes. I know what you mean—

—Not that he was anyway mad,
as you know yourself: but he
was always a little queer. Even
when we were all growing up
together he was queer. One
time he didn't speak hardly
for a month. You know, he
was that kind always—
—Perhaps he read too much,
Miss Flynn—
—O, he read a good deal but
not latterly. It was his
scrupulousness, you see, that
affected his mind. The duties
of the priesthood were too
much for him—
—Did he . . . . peacefully?—
—O, quite peacefully, ma'am. You
couldn't tell when the breath
went out of him. He had a
beautiful death, God be
praised—
—And everything . . . . . . ?—
—Father O'Rourke was in with
him yesterday and gave him
the Last Sacrament—

—He knew then?—
—Yes. He was quite resigned—
    Nannie gave a sleepy nod
and looked ashamed.
—Poor Nannie, said her sister,

    she's worn out. All the work
    we had getting in a woman
    and laying him out! And
    then the coffin and arranging
    about the mass in the chapel.
    God knows we did all we could,
    as poor as we are. We wouldn't
    see him want anything at
    the last—
—Indeed you were both very
    kind to him while he lived—
—Ah, poor James! He was no
    great trouble to us. You wouldn't
    hear him in the house any
    more than now. Still I know
    he's gone and all that I
    won't be bringing him in
    his soup any more nor Nannie
    reading him out the paper
    nor you, ma'am, bringing
    him his snuff! Poor James!—
—O, yes, you'll miss him in a
    day or two more than you
    do now—
    Silence invaded the room
    until memory reawakened
    it, Eliza speaking slowly:
—It was that chalice he broke.
    Of course, it was all right.

I mean it contained nothing.
But still . . . . . They say it was
the boy's fault. But poor

James was so nervous. God be
merciful to him!—
—Yes, Miss Flynn, I heard that
about the chalice. He . . . . his
mind was a bit affected by
that—
—He began to mope by himself,
talking to no-one and wandering
about. Often he couldn't be
found. One night he was wanted
and they looked high up and
low down and couldn't find
him. Then the clerk suggested
the chapel. So they opened the
chapel (it was late at night)
and brought in a light to look
for him . . . . . And there, sure
enough, he was sitting in his
confession-box in the dark, wide
awake, and laughing like—
softly to himself. Then they knew
something was wrong—
—God rest his soul!—

EPIPHANIES AND EPICLETI

Anyone who reads much Joyce criticism will encounter one or both of these two curious Greek words before progressing very far. Joyce's critics use them because Joyce used them, though they do not always use them in the same way he did.

Literally, the word "epiphany" refers to a showing forth, a revelation. In Greek drama it can refer to the climactic moment when a god appears and imposes order on the scene before him. In the Christian religious tradition the Feast of the Epiphany celebrates the revelation of Christ's divinity to the Magi. Joyce used the term in a special but related way. In the theory of art he was working on as a young man, he employed the term "epiphany" to refer to moments in which things or people in the world revealed their true character or their essence. In the second draft of A Portrait of the Artist, called Stephen Hero, he presented the theory in this way:

. . . a trivial incident set him composing some ardent verses which he entitled a "Vilanelle of the Temptress." A young lady was standing on the steps of one of those brown brick houses which seem the very incarnation of Irish paralysis. A young gentleman was leaning on the rusty railings of the area. Stephen as he passed on his quest heard the following fragment of colloquy out of which he received an impression keen enough to afflict his sensitiveness very severely.

The Young Lady—(drawling discreetly) . . . O, yes . . . I was . . . at the . . . cha . . . pel . . .

The Young Gentleman—(inaudibly) . . . I . . . (again inaudibly) . . . I . . .

The Young Lady—(softly) . . . O . . . but you're . . . ve . . . ry . . . wick . . . ed . . .

This triviality made him think of collecting many such moments together in a book of epiphanies. By an epiphany he meant a sudden spiritual manifestation, whether in the vulgarity of speech or of gesture or in a memorable phase of the mind itself. He believed that it was for the man of letters to record these epiphanies with extreme care, seeing that they themselves are the most delicate and evanescent of moments.

Joyce himself actually did collect a "book of epiphanies," with over seventy separate entries. The separate pieces were mainly of two kinds, as the passage from *Stephen Hero* suggests: they recorded "memorable phases" of the young artist's own mind, or instances of "vulgarity of speech or of gesture" in the world around him. In practice this resulted in two quite different *styles* of epiphany: prose poems in which a mental phase of the artist was narrated, and dramatic notations of vulgarity. Here is a typical sample of each kind:

Here are we come together, wayfarers; here are we housed, amid intricate streets, by night and silence closely covered. In amity we rest together, well content, no more remembering the deviousness of the ways that we have come. What moves upon me from the darkness subtle and murmurous as a flood, passionate and fierce with an indecent movement of the loins? What leaps, crying in answer, out of me, as eagle to eagle in mid air, crying to overcome, crying for an iniquitous abandonment?

[Dublin: at the corner of
Connaught St, Phibsborough]

The Little Male Child—(*at the garden gate*). .Na. .o.
The First Young Lady—(*half kneeling, takes his
    hand*)—Well, is Mabie
    your sweetheart?
The Little Male Child—Na. . .o.
The Second Young Lady—(*bending over him, looks
    up*)—Who is your
    sweetheart?

About forty of Joyce's epiphanies have survived. Of these, many were used with little or no change in *Stephen Hero* and *A Portrait*. (Those used in *A Portrait* have been reprinted in the Viking Critical Library edition of that book. The entire collection may be found, with annotations and analyses, in

The Workshop of Daedalus [Evanston, Ill.: Northwestern University Press, 1965].)

In *Stephen Hero* Joyce's young artist worked the notion of epiphany into his esthetic theory to describe the final and climactic moment in the apprehension of the beautiful. He gave this name to the moment when we perceive an object so perfectly that "we recognize that it is *that* thing which it is. Its soul, its whatness leaps to us from the vestment of its appearance." Basing their use of the term on this theory, critics have applied the notion of epiphany to that moment in a *Dubliners* story when some sort of revelation takes place. In "Araby," for example, a trivial dialogue much like the one Stephen overheard in *Stephen Hero*—between "The Young Lady" and "The Young Gentleman"—is overheard by the boy at the bazaar, precipitating his insight into the vanity of his romantic quest. "Epiphany" thus comes to mean a moment of revelation or insight such as usually climaxes a *Dubliners* story. Some characters merely reveal themselves or give themselves away; others achieve insight into their situations. Both Maria's "mistake" in "Clay" and Gabriel's vision in "The Dead" can be referred to as epiphanies.

So far as we know, Joyce himself did not apply the word "epiphany" to *Dubliners,* nor did he use any of the recorded epiphanies in these stories. He did, however, try in them to expose that same paralysis which he felt had been revealed in the banal conversation of "The Young Lady" and "The Young Gentleman." As you will see in the first letter in the next section, he found another related word for the stories. He called them "epicleti."

This word may refer to an invocation to the Holy Ghost (*epiklesis*) still used in the Eastern Church but not in Roman Catholic ritual. In this *epiklesis,* the Holy Ghost is besought to transform the consecrated wafer of bread and the wine into the body and blood of Christ. As Joyce explained to his brother Stanislaus, "there is a certain resemblance between the mystery of the mass and what I am trying to do . . . to give people a kind of intellectual pleasure or spiritual enjoyment by converting the bread of everyday life into something that has a permanent artistic life of its own . . . for their mental, moral, and spiritual uplift."

The word "epicleti" has another related meaning in Greek, which Joyce may have considered. An *epiklesis* can also refer to a reproach or an imputation. And *epikletos* can mean "summoned before a court," or "accused." Thus the epicleti may be considered the accused, summoned up by Joyce to stand trial as specimens of Irish paralysis. The two great priestly powers of transubstantiation and judgment of the sinful were both relished by Joyce in bringing these Dubliners before us in their flesh of words.

THE EVIDENCE
OF THE LETTERS

In this section the editors have brought together materials from Joyce's correspondence which tell the story of *Dubliners*. It is something like a *Dubliners* story, this story of *Dubliners* which Joyce himself called "A Curious History"—it is a tale of paralysis and frustration ending in anguish and anger. At least, that part of it which deals with Joyce's nine-year struggle to get his book published certainly is that sort of tale—worthy of the book itself. But there is more in this correspondence than a record of futility. Here we can find Joyce's own thoughts on the purpose of his book, its style and its plan. We can see the author as a young man of twenty-two or -three, beginning to compare himself to other English and Continental writers of fiction and to measure his work against theirs. We can get a sense of Joyce the man in these letters which should help us to understand the meaning of his work.

The letters that follow are mainly written by Joyce himself, his principal correspondents being his brother Stanislaus and Grant Richards, the London publisher who first accepted *Dubliners* in 1906 but did not publish it until 1914. The central part of this correspondence is the exchange between Joyce and Richards over the alleged obscenity of Joyce's book. The letters of both men are brought together here for the first time, though they have previously been published separately. In his side of this exchange Joyce clearly reveals the wit and the care for his art which are so scrupulously controlled in the stories themselves.

One of these letters, "A Curious History" (see p. 289), was

printed by a number of newspapers to which Joyce sent copies. In 1917, with a preface added by Ezra Pound, it was published as a separate pamphlet by the American publisher of *Dubliners*, B. W. Huebsch. From the first American edition of *Dubliners* in 1916 through his entire career, Joyce had an association with Huebsch far happier than the dealings with English and Irish publishers chronicled in these letters. It was finally through the association of B. W. Huebsch with The Viking Press that *Dubliners* and most of Joyce's other works came to be published by Viking. Joyce's gratitude to his first American publisher was such that he caused to be put into the contract for his last work, *Finnegans Wake*, the following statement:

If at any time during the continuance of this agreement Mr B. W. Huebsch should sever his connection with the said Viking Press and either set up publishing on his own account or acquire interest in another firm of publishers than the Viking Press, then the said Author shall have the option of transferring the benefits of this contract to such new firm.

Fortunately, no such division between Huebsch and Viking came to pass, and the present critical edition continues the association between the name of Joyce and The Viking Press.

(The letters are presented as documents, devoid of annotation and commentary, but the student who refers to the Chronology on pp. 229–33 should have no difficulty in following them. The full texts of Joyce's letters, together with helpful notes and commentary, may be found in the *Letters of James Joyce* [Vol. I ed. Stuart Gilbert, Vols. II and III ed. Richard Ellmann, New York: The Viking Press, 1966], hereafter referred to as *Letters*. All of Richards' side of the correspondence appeared in *Studies in Bibliography*, ed. Fredson Bowers [Charlottesville, Va.: University of Virginia, 1963], Vol. XVI, pp. 139–60.)

From a Letter to Constantine Curran,
August 1904

. . . I am writing a series of epicleti—ten—for a paper. I have written one. I call the series *Dubliners* to betray the soul of that hemiplegia or paralysis which many consider a city. Look out for an edition de luxe of all my limericks instantly. More anon

From Various Letters to
Joyce's Brother Stanislaus in 1905

. . . Your satirical surprise at my proposed 'dedication' of 'Dubliners' to you arises, I imagine from an exaggerated notion you have of my indifference to the encouragement I receive. It is difficult for anyone at my age to be indifferent. I am not likely to die of bashfulness but neither am I prepared to be crucified to attest the perfection of my art. I dislike to hear of any stray heroics on the prowl for me. . . . [*February 28.*]

. . . While I was attending the Greek mass here last Sunday it seemed to me that my story *The Sisters* was rather remarkable. The Greek mass is strange. . . . [*April 4.*]

. . . I send you tomorrow the fifth story of 'Dubliners' that is, 'The Boarding-House'. You are to dispose of it if you can to an English or American paper. I have a copy by me. I have also written the sixth story 'Counterparts' and shall send it to you on Saturday if I have made a copy by then. It is my intention to complete 'Dubliners' by the end of the year and to follow it by a book 'Provincials'. I am uncommonly well pleased with these stories. There is a neat phrase of five words in *The Boarding-House*: find it. . . . [*July 12.*]

. . . Many of the frigidities of *The Boarding-House* and *Counterparts* were written while the sweat streamed down my face on to the handkerchief which protected my collar. . . . Is it possible that, after all, men of letters are no more than entertainers? These discouraging reflections arise perhaps from my surroundings. The stories in *Dubliners* seem to be indisputably well done but, after all, perhaps many people could do them as well. I am not rewarded by any feeling of having overcome difficulties. Maupassant writes very well, of course, but I am afraid that his moral sense is rather obtuse. The Dublin papers will object to my stories as to a caricature of Dublin life. Do you think there is any truth in this? At times the spirit directing my pen seems to me so plainly mischievous that I am almost prepared to let the Dublin critics have their way. All these pros and cons I must for the nonce lock up in my bosom. Of course do not think that I consider contemporary Irish writing anything but ill-written, morally obtuse formless caricature.

The struggle against conventions in which I am at present involved was not entered into by me so much as a protest against these conventions as with the intention of living in conformity with my moral nature. There are some people in Ireland who would call my moral nature oblique, people who think that the whole duty of man consists in paying one's debts; but in this case Irish opinion is certainly only the caricature of the opinion of any European tribunal. To be judged properly I should not be judged by 12 burghers taken at haphazard, judging under the dictation of a hidebound bureaucrat, in accordance with the evidence of policeman but by some jury composed partly of those of my own class and of my own age presided over by a judge who had solemnly forsworn all English legal methods. But why insist on this point? I do so only because my present lamentable circumstances seem to constitute a certain reproach against me. [*July 19*.]

. . . If *Dubliners* is published next spring I hope to be able to help you to get out of your swamp. Do you think it will make money? Nora is writing today to Aunt Josephine. I would be glad of some news of your house generally. Do you think an English publisher will take *Dubliners*? Is it not possible for a few persons of character and culture to make Dublin a capital such as Christiania has become? Is Cosgrave going to become a dispensary doctor by sacerdotal favour? Are you going to become a despised clerk? I hope to be able to prevent this—but what about myself? [*September 1*.]

. . . I am much obliged for your careful criticisms of my stories. Your comparison of them with certain others is somewhat dazzling. The authors you mention have such immense reputations that I am afraid you may be wrong. . . . I hardly think, arguing from the conditions in which they are written, that these stories can be superlatively good. I wish I could talk to you fully on this as on many other subjects. Your remark that *Counterparts* shows a Russian ability in taking the reader for an intracranial journey set me thinking what on earth people mean when they talk of 'Russian.' . . . [*September 18*.]

A *Letter* to *William Heinemann* (*London publisher*), *September 23, 1905*

Dear Sir, I have almost finished a book which I would like to submit to you. It is called 'Dubliners.' It is a collection of twelve short stories. Each story is perhaps of 1800 or 2000 words. The book is not a collection of tourist impressions but an attempt to represent certain aspects of the life of one of the European capitals. I am an Irishman, as you will see by the name. I am anxious that the book should be published as soon as possible and this is the reason why I offer it to you beforehand. I shall be much obliged if you will tell me whether you would like to read it or not and excuse me if my request is an unusual one.

From a Letter to Stanislaus Joyce, September 1905

Dear Stannie Please send me the information I ask you for as follows:

The Sisters: Can a priest be buried in a habit?

Ivy Day in the Committee Room—Are Aungier St and Wicklow in the Royal Exchange Ward? Can a municipal election take place in October?

A *Painful Case*—Are the police at Sydney Parade of the D division? Would the city ambulance be called out to Sydney Parade for an accident? Would an accident at Sydney Parade be treated at Vincent's Hospital?

After the Race—Are the police supplied with provisions by government or by private contracts?

Kindly answer these questions as quickly as possible. I sent my story *The Clay* (which I had slightly rewritten) to *The LITERARY World* but the cursedly stupid ape that conducts that journal neither acknowledged it nor sent it back. This kind of thing is maddening. Am I an imbecile or are these people imbeciles. . . . Will you read some English 'realists' I see mentioned in the papers and see what they are like—Gissing, Arthur Morrison and a man named Keary. I can read very little and am as dumb as a stockfish. But really I think that the two last stories I sent you are very good. Perhaps they will be refused by Heinemann. The order of the stories is as follows. *The Sisters, An Encounter* and another story which are stories of my childhood: *The Boarding-House, After the Race* and *Eveline,* which are stories of adolescence: *The Clay, Counterparts,* and A *Painful Case* which are stories of mature life: *Ivy Day in the Committee Room, A Mother* and the last story of the book which are stories of public life in Dublin. When you remember that Dublin has been a capital for thousands of years, that it is the 'second' city of the British Empire, that it is nearly three times as big as Venice it seems strange that no

artist has given it to the world. I read that silly, wretched book
of Moore's 'The Untilled Field' which the Americans found so
remarkable for its 'craftsmanship.' O, dear me! It is very dull
and flat, indeed: and ill written.

From a Letter from Stanislaus Joyce to James Joyce, October 10, 1905

. . . It seems to me that your book 'Dubliners' is becoming
almost as important as your novel. 'Ivy Day in the Committee
Rooms' is accurate, just, and satisfactory. It is original too. I
don't think that this which forms so great a part of Dublin,
of Irish life has been done before by an artist. To a stranger
your differentiation of character would seem nothing less than
marvellous. And the poem—the 'turn' in this case—is entirely
Irish. Aunt Josephine prefers 'A Painful Case' to any of the
others but slight as that story is I think it is too big for the
form you use. My sense of proportion leads me to prefer 'Ivy
Day in the Committee Rooms' or 'Counterparts.' People will
think 'A Painful Case,' a story of passionate natures. People
who want to be amused by what they read—that large class—
will not find many of them to their taste. 'The Boarding-
House,' perhaps, though the title is more like the title of a
picture. Cosgrave said: 'How delicate he is on the point!' I find
the intellectual serenity and ease with which you draw out these
burgesses a relief after Turgenev's painful and unhappy analysis.
But what is the meaning of writing one half of a story about
'Joe and Leo Dillon' and the other half about a sodomite,
named by me for convenience sake 'the captain of fifty'? To
call it 'An Encounter' will hardly link the two parts together.
However I would not wish for a good deal that this type were
missing in Dubliners. Do you write out of rough copy of these
stories? Like a Shakespeare manuscript there is scarcely ever a
correction in them and yet I can hardly imagine that that

astonishing unravelling of the sodomite's mind was written offhand. The sensation of terror—you were afraid he might catch you by the ankles—is cleverly put in. . . .

From a Letter to Grant Richards, October 15, 1905

. . . The second book which I have ready is called *Dubliners*. It is a collection of twelve short stories. It is possible that you would consider it to be of a commercial nature. I would gladly submit it to you before sending it to Messrs Constable and, if you could promise to publish it soon, I would gladly agree. Unfortunately I am in such circumstances that it is necessary for me to have either of the books published as soon as possible. I do not think that any writer has yet presented Dublin to the world. It has been a capital of Europe for thousands of years, it is supposed to be the second city of the British Empire and it is nearly three times as big as Venice. Moreover, on account of many circumstances which I cannot detail here, the expression 'Dubliner' seems to me to have some meaning and I doubt whether the same can be said for such words as 'Londoner' and 'Parisian' both of which have been used by writers as titles. From time to time I see in publishers' lists announcements of books on Irish subjects, so that I think people might be willing to pay for the special odour of corruption which, I hope, floats over my stories.

A Letter to Grant Richards, February 20, 1906

Dear Mr Grant Richards: I am glad that you are pleased with *Dubliners*. As for the terms you offer me I may say that perhaps it would be best for me to put myself in your hands. I am sure that you will deal with me as generously as you can. As a matter of fact my future work in which you seem to be interested is largely dependent on an improvement of my financial state. I have written nearly a thousand pages of a novel but I have had little leisure, comfort or prospects for continuing it.

I should like to know when you propose to publish the book, in what form and at what price. If you will let me know I can send you the last story I have written—unless perhaps you have as superstitious an objection to the number thirteen as you seem to have with regard to Ireland and short stories in general.

A *Letter from Grant Richards to James Joyce,* *April 23, 1906*

Dear Mr. Joyce,

I am sorry, but I am afraid we cannot publish "The Two Gallants" as it stands; indeed, the printers, to whom it was sent before I read it myself, say that they won't print it. You see that there are still limitations imposed on the English publisher! I am therefore sending it back to you to ask you either to suppress it, or, better, to modify it in such a way as to enable it to pass. Perhaps you can see your way to do this at once.

The same thing has to be done with two passages marked in blue pencil on page 15 of "Counterparts."

Also—you will think I am very troublesome, but I don't want the critics to come down on your book like a cart load of bricks—I want you to give me a word that we ["I" crossed out in ink] can use instead of 'bloody' in the story "Grace."

A *Letter to Grant Richards, April 26, 1906*

Dear Mr Grant Richards: You tell me that the printer to whom you sent my story *Two Gallants* before you read it yourself refuses to print it and therefore you ask me either to suppress it or to modify it in such a way as to enable it to pass. I cannot see my way to do either of these things. I have written my book with considerable care, in spite of a hundred difficulties and in accordance with what I understand to be the classical tradition of my art. You must therefore allow me to say that your printer's opinion of it does not interest me in the least. Moreover, I cannot alter the passages which are marked in blue pencil in the story *Counterparts* nor can I suggest any other word than the word 'bloody' for the story *Grace*.

I intended to send you today the fourteenth and last story of the book, A *Little Cloud* which is now ready. I shall not do so, however, until I hear from you in reply: and I am also retaining the MSS of the two stories which you sent me. If in your next letter you tell me that you can see your way to print my book as I have written it and that you have found a printer who will endanger his immortal soul to that extent I shall then send you the three stories together. If you decide differently you can send me back the other eleven stories and we can consider the matter at an end. Naturally, I should be sorry if our relations ended in such a way. It would be almost a disaster to me but I am afraid the service which you ask me to do for your printer's conscience is not in my power.

A *Letter from Grant Richards to James Joyce,*
May 1, 1906

Dear Mr. Joyce,

Either I must have expressed myself carelessly in my letter to you or you must have misunderstood what I said. I told you what the printer had said not because I cared about his opinion as his opinion, or cared a bit about his scruples, but because if a printer takes that view you can be quite sure that the book-sellers will take it, that the libraries will take it, and that an inconveniently large section of the general public will take it.

You have told me frankly that you look to your future being helped by your literary work. The best way of retarding that result will most certainly be to persist in the publishing of stories which—I speak commercially, not artistically—will get you a name for doing work which most people will regret. You will understand that it is not my view which has to dictate our conduct in this matter. It is both the effect which your persistence would have on the commercial possibilities of the book, and the effect that the publication of that book as it now stands in manuscript would have on our business generally. It would be easier to explain to you why I think you are taking a wrong course when you refuse either to make any alterations or to suppress the stories if I could have the opportunity of talking the matter over with you. I hope, however, that this letter will show you that from the point of view of policy there are two sides to the matter, and that you will see your way to alter the position you have taken up. In any case, please put on one side the idea that you seem to have, that I am at all interested in our printer's conscience.

A Letter to Grant Richards, May 5, 1906

Dear Mr Grant Richards, I am sorry you do not tell me why the printer, who seems to be the barometer of English opinion, refuses to print *Two Gallants* and makes marks in the margin of *Counterparts*. Is it the small gold coin in the former story or the code of honour which the two gallants live by which shocks him? I see nothing which should shock him in either of these things. His idea of gallantry has grown up in him (probably) during the reading of the novels of the elder Dumas and during the performance of romantic plays which presented to him cavaliers and ladies in full dress. But I am sure he is willing to modify his fantastic views. I would strongly recommend to him the chapters wherein Ferrero examines the moral code of the

soldier and (incidentally) of the gallant. But it would be useless for I am sure that in his heart of hearts he is a militarist.

He has marked three passages in *Counterparts*:

'a man with two establishments to keep up, of course he could-
n't. . . .'
'Farrington said he wouldn't mind having the far one and began to
smile at her. . . .'
'She continued to cast bold glances at him and changed the position of her legs often; and when she was going out she brushed
against his chair and said "Pardon!" in a Cockney accent.'

His marking of the first passage makes me think that there is
priestly blood in him: the scent for immoral allusions is certainly very keen here. To me this passage seems as childlike as
the reports of divorce cases in *The Standard*. Or is it possible
that this same printer (or maybe some near relative of his) will
read (nay more, actually collaborate in) that solemn journal
which tells its readers not merely that Mrs So and So misconducted herself with Captain So and So but even how often
she misconducted herself with him! The word 'establishment'
is surely as inoffensive as the word 'misconducted.'

It is easier to understand why he has marked the second
passage, and evident why he has marked the third. But I would
refer him again to that respectable organ the reporters of which
are allowed to speak of such intimate things as even I, a poor
artist, have but dared to suggest. O one-eyed printer! Why has
he descended with his blue pencil, full of the Holy Ghost, upon
these passages and allowed his companions to set up in type
reports of divorce cases, and ragging cases and cases of criminal
assault—reports, moreover, which are to be read by an 'inconveniently large section of the general public.'

There remains his final objection to the word 'bloody.' I
cannot know, of course, from what he derives the word or
whether, in his plain blunt way, he accepts it as it stands. In
the latter case his objection is absurd and in the former case
(if he follows the only derivation I have heard for it) it is

strange that he should object more strongly to a profane use of the Virgin than to a profane use of the name of God. Where is his English Protestantism? I myself can bear witness that I have seen in modern English print such expressions as 'by God' and 'damn.' Some cunning Jesuit must have tempted our stout Protestant from the path of righteousness that he defends the honour of the Virgin with such virgin ardour.

As for my part and share in the book I have already told all I have to tell. My intention was to write a chapter of the moral history of my country and I chose Dublin for the scene because that city seemed to me the centre of paralysis. I have tried to present it to the indifferent public under four of its aspects: childhood, adolescence, maturity and public life. The stories are arranged in this order. I have written it for the most part in a style of scrupulous meanness and with the conviction that he is a very bold man who dares to alter in the presentment, still more to deform, whatever he has seen and heard. I cannot do any more than this. I cannot alter what I have written. All these objections of which the printer is now the mouthpiece arose in my mind when I was writing the book, both as to the themes of the stories and their manner of treatment. Had I listened to them I would not have written the book. I have come to the conclusion that I cannot write without offending people. The printer denounces *Two Gallants* and *Counterparts*. A Dubliner would denounce *Ivy Day in the Committee-Room*. The more subtle inquisitor will denounce *An Encounter*, the enormity of which the printer cannot see because he is, as I said, a plain blunt man. The Irish priest will denounce *The Sisters*. The Irish boarding-house keeper will denounce *The Boarding-House*. Do not let the printer imagine, for goodness' sake, that he is going to have all the barking to himself.

I can see plainly that there are two sides to the matter but unfortunately I can occupy only one of them. I will not fall into the error of suggesting to you which side you should occupy but it seems to me that you credit the printer with too infallible a knowledge of the future. I know very little of the state of English literature at present nor do I know whether it deserves or not the eminence which it occupies as the laughing-stock of Europe. But I suspect that it will follow the other countries of Europe as it did in Chaucer's time. You have opportunities to observe the phenomenon at close range. Do you think that *The Second Mrs Tanqueray* would not have been denounced by a manager of the middle Victorian period, or that a publisher of that period would not have rejected a book by George Moore or Thomas Hardy? And if a change is to take place I do not see why it should not begin now.

You tell me in conclusion that I am endangering my future and your reputation. I have shown you earlier in the letter the frivolity of the printer's objections and I do not see how the publication of *Dubliners* as it now stands in manuscript could possibly be considered an outrage on public morality. I am willing to believe that when you advise me not to persist in the publication of stories such as those you have returned to me you do so with a kind intention towards me: and I am sure you will think me wrong-headed in persisting. But if the art were any other, if I were a painter and my book were a picture you would be less ready to condemn me for wrong-headedness if I refused to alter certain details. These details may now seem to you unimportant but if I took them away *Dubliners* would seem to me like an egg without salt. In fact, I am somewhat curious to know what, if these and similar points have been condemned, has been admired in the book at all.

I see now that my letter is becoming nearly as long as my book. I have touched on every point you raise in order to give you reason for the faith that is in me. I have not, however, said what a disappointment it would be to me if you were unable to share my views. I do not speak so much of a material as of a moral disappointment. But I think I could more easily reconcile myself to such a disappointment than to the thousand little regrets and self-reproaches which would certainly make me their prey afterwards. Believe me, dear Mr Grant Richards, Faithfully yours

From a Letter from Grant Richards to James Joyce, May 10, 1906

Dear Mr. Joyce,
Many thanks for your letter. If I had written your stories I should certainly wish to be able to afford your attitude; but as I stand on the publisher's side, I feel most distinctly that for more than one reason you cannot afford it. You have written a book which, whether it sells or whether it does not, is a very remarkable and striking piece of work; certainly it is what you wanted it to be—a chapter of the moral history of your country. But a book is not written nowadays to any real effect until it is published. You won't get a publisher—a real publisher—to issue it as it stands. I won't say that you won't get somebody to bring it out, but it would be brought out obscurely and in such a way would be certain to do no good to your pocket and would hardly be likely to get into the hands of any but a few people. After all, remember, it is only words and sentences that have to be altered; and it seems to me that the man who cannot convey his meaning by more than one set of words and sentences has not yet realized the possibilities of the English language. That is not your case. . . .

A Letter to Grant Richards, May 13, 1906

Dear Mr Grant Richards, I am sorry that in reply to my letter you have written one of so generalising a character. I do not see how you can expect me to agree with you about the impossibility of publishing the book as it is. Your statement that no publisher could issue such a book seems to me somewhat categorical. You must not imagine that the attitude I have taken

up is in the least heroic. The fact is I cannot see much reason
in your complaints.

You complain of *Two Gallants*, of a passage in *Counterparts*
and of the word 'bloody' in *Grace*. Are these the only things
that prevent you from publishing the book? To begin at the
end: the word 'bloody' occurs in that story twice in the following passage:

—At dinner, you know. Then he has a bloody big bowl of cabbage
before him on the table and a bloody big spoon like a shovel etc . . .

This I could alter, if you insist. I see no reason for doing so
but if this point alone prevented the book from being published
I could put another word instead of 'bloody': But this word
occurs elsewhere in the book, in *Ivy Day in the Committee-
Room*, in *The Boarding-House*, in *Two Gallants*:

—'And one night man, she brought me two bloody fine cigars &c'—
Two Gallants
—'Here's this fellow come to the throne after his bloody owl'
mother keeping him out of it till the man was grey . . . &c'—
Ivy Day in the Committee-Room
—'if any fellow tried that sort of game on with his sister he'd
bloody well put his teeth down his throat, so he would' &c
The Boarding-House

The first passage I could alter. The second passage (with infinite
regret) I could alter by omitting the word simply. But the third
passage I absolutely could not alter. Read *The Boarding-House*
yourself and tell me frankly what you think. The word, the
exact expression I have used, is in my opinion the one expression in the English language which can create on the reader
the effect which I wish to create. Surely you can see this for
yourself? And if the word appears once in the book it may as
well appear three times. Is it not ridiculous that my book cannot
be published because it contains this one word which is neither
indecent nor blasphemous?

The objections raised against *Counterparts* seem to me
equally trivial. Is it possible that at this age of the world in

the country which the ingenuous Latins are fond of calling 'the home of liberty' an allusion to 'two establishments' cannot appear in print or that I cannot write the phrase 'she changed the position of her legs often'? To invoke the name of Areopagitica in this connection would be to render the artist as absurd as the printer.

You say it is a small thing I am asked to do, to efface a word here and there. But do you not see clearly that in a short story above all such effacement may be fatal. You cannot say that the phrases objected to are gratuitous and impossible to print and at the same time approve of the tenor of the book. Granted this latter as legitimate I cannot see how anyone can consider these minute and necessary details illegitimate. I must say that these objections seem to me illogical. Why do you not object to the theme of *An Encounter*, to the passage 'he stood up slowly saying that he had to leave us for a few moments &c ...'? Why do you not object to the theme of *The Boarding-House*? Why do you omit to censure the allusions to the Royal Family, to the Holy Ghost, to the Dublin Police, to the Lord Mayor of Dublin, to the cities of the plain, to the Irish Parliamentary Party &c? As I told you in my last letter I cannot understand what has been admired in the book at all if these passages have been condemned. What would remain of the book if I had to efface everything which might give offence? The title, perhaps?

You must allow me to say that I think you are unduly timid. There is nothing 'impossible' in the book, in my opinion. You will not be prosecuted for publishing it. The worst that will happen, I suppose, is that some critic will allude to me as the 'Irish Zola'! But even such a display of the critical intellect should not be sufficiently terrible to deter you from bringing out the book. I am not, as you may suppose, an extremely business-like person but I confess I am puzzled to know why all these objections were not raised at first. When the contract was signed I thought everything was over: but now I find I must plunge into a correspondence which, I am afraid, tends only to agitate my nerves.

The appeal to my pocket has not much weight with me. Of

course I would gladly see the book in print and of course I would like to make money by it. But, on the other hand, I have very little intention of prostituting whatever talent I may have to the public. (This letter is not for publication). I am not an emissary from a War Office testing a new explosive or an eminent doctor praising a new medicine or a sporting cyclist riding a new make of bicycle or a renowned tenor singing a song by a new composer: and therefore the appeal to my pocket does not touch me as deeply as it otherwise might. You say you will be sorry if the book must pass from your list. I will be extremely sorry. But what can I do? I have thought the matter over and looked over the book again and I think you are making much ado about nothing. Kindly do not misread this as a rebuke to you but put the emphasis on the last word. For, I assure you, not the least unfortunate effect of this tardy correspondence is that it has brought my own writing into disfavour with myself. Act, however, as you think best. I have done my part. Believe me, dear Mr Grant Richards, Faithfully yours

---

A Letter from Grant Richards to James Joyce, May 16, 1906

Dear Mr. Joyce,

I will try to be more categorical. First, though, let me see if I cannot remove a misconception that exists in your mind as to our attitude. My admiration for your book is a thing entirely apart, and necessarily so, from my conviction as to what is wise or not wise for us to publish. Personally I prefer the word 'bloody' in the places in which it occurs to any word you could substitute for it since it is, as you say, the right word; on the other hand a publisher has to be influenced by other considerations. Personally I have no objection to the other stories we have discussed, although I may say that in their present form they would damage their publisher. We are, for various reasons into which I need not go at this distance, peculiarly liable to attack. However, you concede the alteration of the troublesome word in "Grace"; well and good. You concede it in "The Two Gallants"; you concede it in "Ivy Day in the Committee Room"; leave it in "The Boarding House."

In "Counterparts" I have no feeling about the allusion to 'two establishments [']; the other phrase must really come out.

On consideration I should *like* to leave out altogether "The Encounter."

"The Two Gallants" should certainly be omitted. Perhaps you can omit it with an easier mind since originally it did not form part of your book.

The difficulties between us, therefore, narrow themselves down, since you have come some little way to meet me, and I hope now they will disappear entirely. Believe me, dear Mr. Joyce, Sincerely yours,

---

A *Letter to* Grant Richards, *May 20, 1906*

Dear Mr Grant Richards: You say that the difficulties between us have narrowed themselves down. If this be true it is I who have narrowed them. If you will recall your first letter you will see that on your side they have broadened a little. While I have made concessions as to the alteration of a word in three of the stories you are simply allowing me to use it in a story where, not having noticed it until I pointed it out to you, you had not objected to it. Moreover you now say that you wish to leave out altogether the story *An Encounter*. You said nothing of this in your first letter and it was I, again, who pointed out to you the 'enormity' in it. It is true that you concede one of the disputed passages in *Counterparts* but, inasmuch as you say you have no feeling on the subject, I suppose the concession costs you much less than those I have made cost me.

I mention these facts in order that you may see that I have tried to meet your objections. We are agreed now about *Grace, Ivy Day in the Committee-Room* and *The Boarding-House.* There remain only the second passage in *Counterparts* and the story *Two Gallants.* I invite you to read the former story again. The incident described is (in my opinion, if that counts for anything) essential. It occurs at a vital part of the story and, if it is taken out, the effect at the end is (in my opinion) lost. However (you see that it is really I who narrow the difficulties between us) if you can point out to me expressly any word or phrase which I can alter without omitting the incident, much as I dislike to do so, I will try again to meet you.

I have agreed to omit the troublesome word in *Two Gallants.* To omit the story from the book would really be disastrous. It is one of the most important stories in the book. I would rather sacrifice *five* of the other stories (which I could name) than this one. It is the story (after *Ivy Day in the Committee-Room*) which pleases me most. I have shown you that I can concede something to your fears. But you cannot really expect me to mutilate my work!

You state your objection to *An Encounter* (an objection I was imprudent enough to provoke) so mildly that I imagine this will not be one of our difficulties. In all seriousness I would urge the interference of the printer as soon as possible if my book is not to dwindle into a pamphlet, for each bout of letters, as it brings some little concession from my side, brings also some little new demand from yours. And as I have told you all along I am convinced that your fears are exaggerated. Many of the passages and phrases over which we are now disputing escaped you: it was I who showed them to you. And do you think that what escaped you (whose business it is to look for such things in the books you consider) will be surely detected by a public which reads the books for quite another reason?

I regret very much that the interview you suggested earlier in the correspondence is impossible. I believe that in an interview I could much more easily defeat whatever influences you in holding your present position. As for the disastrous effect the book would have if published in its present form it seems to me such a result is more likely to hit me than you. Critics (I think) are fonder of attacking writers than publishers; and, I assure you their attacks on me would in no way hasten my death. Moreover, from the point of view of financial success it seems to me more than probable than [sic] an attack, even a fierce and organised attack, on the book by the press would have the effect of interesting the public in it to much better purpose than the tired chorus of imprimaturs with which the critical body greets the appearance of every book which is not dangerous to faith or morals.

You cannot see anything impossible and unreasonable in my position. I have explained and argued everything at full length and, when argument and explanation were unavailing, I have perforce granted what you asked, and even what you didn't ask, me to grant. The points on which I have not yielded are the points which rivet the book together. If I eliminate them what becomes of the chapter of the moral history of my country? I fight to retain them because I believe that in composing my chapter of moral history in exactly the way I have composed it I have taken the first step towards the spiritual liberation of my country. Reflect for a moment on the history of the literature of Ireland as it stands at present written in the English language before you condemn this genial illusion of mine which, after all, has at least served me in the office of a candlestick during the writing of the book.

A Letter from Grant Richards to James Joyce, June 7, 1906

Dear Mr. Joyce,

An answer to your last letter to me has been delayed owing to my taking a brief Whitsuntide holiday.

Heaven knows that we want to do everything that you want us to do, but for various reasons, which it would take too long to write down, our hands are to some extent tied. If this business were mine it would be a different thing.

But I did notice very clearly "An Encounter" when I first read the manuscript, and we were at that time told by our adviser that we ought to get you to omit it. I was in doubts about it, but came to the conclusion that it was unnecessary to do so. But matter which to a large section of the public will seem questionable is cumulative in its effect, and when I came to read "The Two Gallants" I saw that to publish the book with that story as you had written it would be to draw attention to other things in the book which would otherwise pass. Perhaps you can re-write "The Two Gallants"—although I don't suppose you will. Still, in producing one's first book it is just as well to be guided by somebody's advice, and I don't honestly think that you could have a more competent adviser on the matter than I am. We cannot publish the book as it stands; that I am afraid is clear. We can only publish it with the alterations or omissions that so far I have suggested. If it were I who was publishing the book, admiring it as I do, I might be willing to bear any attack, organized or otherwise. But an attack on this house at the present moment, and on such a subject, would be extremely damaging.

Your letters make me wish to meet you, and they make me wish to have your book as you have written it among my own that I value; but they cannot blind me to the impolicy of the attitude you are taking up. Believe me, dear Mr. Joyce, Sincerely yours,

---

A Letter to Grant Richards, June 10, 1906

Dear Mr Grant Richards, I see by reference to letters that you were sending the book to the printers two months ago. Its transit, however, has been delayed by a copious and futile correspondence which my original reply to your objections certainly did not provoke. This correspondence has been a cause of great and constant worry to me and I now recognise how useless it has been.

I pointed out to you clearly in my last letter that it was I who had made efforts to narrow down the difficulties between us, difficulties which, I think, it would have been much wiser to raise at an earlier stage. I am unable to gather from your letter of this morning whether you hold to your first claims of six weeks ago or whether you agree to the concessions I made in my letter of a fortnight ago. I will ask you to let me know this definitely.

I have nothing further to add to what I have written in defence of my book but I may repeat that, in my opinion, you have allowed yourself to be intimidated by imaginary terrors. You may have difficulties of which I know nothing for I imagine it is not public opinion which deters you. My bag of suggestions is nearly empty but I present you with this last one. Buy two critics. If you could do this with tact you could easily withstand a campaign. Two just and strong men, each armed with seven newspapers—*quis sustinebit?* I speak in parables.

As regards me, I leave this delightful city at the end of next month and go to Rome where I have obtained a position as correspondent in a bank. As the salary (£150 a year) is nearly double my present princely emolument and as the hours of honest labour will be fewer I hope to find time to finish my novel in Rome within a year or, at most, a year and a half. I mention this because in a former letter of yours you were kind enough to inquire about my financial position. Believe me, dear Mr Grant Richards, Faithfully yours

A Letter from Grant Richards to James Joyce, June 14, 1906

Dear Mr. Joyce,

You are under a misapprehension: your book did go to the printers'; they set up a page, which happened to be a page of "The Two Gallants"; they kicked at its nature and it was that that made me read ["it" crossed out] the story, which I had not done previously, and that made me go into the whole question.

I think that if you read the letters that have passed between us you will see exactly what we are willing to put our name to and what we dare not put our name to. It remains, therefore, for you to decide.

Turn specially to the letter of May 16th, which was written in answer to certain concessions on your part. Presumably you are still willing to make those concessions, as detailed in paragraph 1.

In "Counterparts" there is a phrase that must come out if we are to publish the book.

We should like to omit entirely "An Encounter", but if you will give way on the other points we will give way on this.

"The Two Gallants" must be omitted unless you can re-write it in the sense suggested in my letter of June 7th.

Unfortunately as things stand at present you cannot buy one critic of importance, to say nothing of two; sometimes I wish one could! Also, the habit of multiple reviewing has gone out.

I am very happy to hear of your engagement in Rome. In Rome at least you seem to be nearer to London, and more likely to come over; anyhow, I am more likely to be in Rome than I am to go to Trieste. And whatever happens to this book, which is giving you and me the writing of so many letters, I hope you will give us the opportunity of reading the novel. Believe me, dear Mr. Joyce, Sincerely yours,

A *Letter to Grant Richards, June 16, 1906*

Dear Mr Grant Richards, I have turned to your letter of May 16th last and particularly to the first paragraph where I read that in consideration of three omissions conceded by me you allowed me to retain a word originally written in one of the stories. These three concessions I am still disposed to make on certain conditions.

The second paragraph of the same letter contains a withdrawal of one of your objections and a statement that one other phrase in the story under discussion should come out. In that story there are two other phrases marked by somebody's blue pencil: and in reply to your letter I stated that I was disposed to modify the passage but that I could not omit it. You now say that one of the two phrases must come out and I presume you choose this solution in preference to the one proposed by me, namely, a modification of the passage which contains the two phrases objected to. I am still disposed to make either concession that is, either to modify (without omitting) the passage or to allow you to cancel whichever of the phrases you prefer to cancel on certain conditions.

The third paragraph of your letter of 16 May stated that you wished to omit another story of the original book but that you would not insist on this if I gave way on the other points. I replied by making the concessions mentioned above.

In the fourth and fifth paragraphs of the same letter you said that the story *Two Gallants* should certainly be omitted adding that you supposed I could omit it with an easier mind since it did not form part of the original book. I replied to this by pointing out that I had already agreed to make an omission in that story, that it was one of the most important stories in the book in my opinion, that I saw no way in which it could be re-written and that its omission would mean in my opinion a mutilation of the book. I am still disposed to make the omission I agreed to make of the word 'bloody' in that story if you are disposed to include it in the book.

I suppose you are now quite clear as to my present position. The concessions which I made in reference to the original book I made solely with a view to the inclusion of *Two Gallants*, which, if it did not actually form part of the original book, you knew to be in preparation and finally wrote for when the book was going to press. If you cannot possibly include *Two Gallants* with the omission I volunteered to make the motive which would induce me to make the other concessions disappears and I am disposed to allow you to print the book without it as I originally wrote it though, as I have told you, I regard such an omission as an almost mortal mutilation of my work.

The spectre of the printer which I thought I had laid rises again in your letter of 14th instant. This apparition is most distasteful to me and I hope he will not trouble the correspondence again. I do not seek to penetrate the mysteries of his being and existence, for example, how he came by his conscience and culture, how he is permitted in your country to combine the duties of author with his own honourable calling, how he came to be the representative of the public mind, how he happened to alight magically on what he was designed to overlook, and (incidentally) why he began the process of printing my book at the third page of the sixth story, numbered in the manuscript 5A. These for me are mysteries and may remain so. But I cannot permit a printer to write my book for me. In no other civilised country in Europe, I think, is a printer allowed to open his mouth. If there are any objections to be made the publisher can make them when the book is submitted to him: if he withdraws them he pays a printer to print the book and if he cannot withdraw them he decides not to trouble the printer by asking him to print the book. A printer is simply a workman hired by the day or by the job for a certain sum.

I am delighted and surprised to learn that nowadays it is impossible to buy a critic of importance. Evidently since I left the British Isles some extraordinary religious revolution has taken place. I expect to hear shortly that the practices of self-stultification and prostitution have gone out of fashion among authors.

In the last paragraph of your letter you seem to suggest the possibility of our meeting in Rome. I should be glad of such a meeting as correspondence on debated points appears to me most unsatisfactory. However, by dint of exchanging six or seven letters, I hope we have now arrived at a clear understanding of our respective attitudes.

In conclusion I thank you for replying to me so quickly and will be glad if you will answer this with equal promptness. Believe me, dear Mr Grant Richards, Faithfully yours

---

A *Letter from Grant Richards to James Joyce,* *June 19, 1906*

Dear Mr. Joyce,

Your manuscript is presumably the only one with which you are dealing at the present moment; it is one of several dozen with which we are dealing and about which we are corresponding, and although when I started writing to you I remembered perfectly well the different points, some of them now are less clear in my memory. However, I have looked again at that part of the manuscript that we have here and at your letters, and it seems to me that the best course will be for you to make the alterations to the extent that you are willing to make them and in the sense suggested by me, and return the manuscript to me, when, if I understand your concessions aright, the book will no doubt be able to go to the printer. With this object I am sending back to you to-day by registered post the balance of the manuscript.

In "Counterparts" you say you are disposed to modify the passage to which I specially drew attention, but you will not omit it. Of course I do not know how far your modification will go; in any case, I should not care to take the responsibility of cancelling any passage with my own pen.

As to "The Two Gallants," you say that I knew it to be in preparation. But I had no idea of its character. Return it, however, with the omission that you volunteer to make and I will see whether, in the hoped for event of the book going to the printer, it can be included, as I should certainly prefer, knowing your views.

In brief: when I get your stories back I will re-read the whole manuscript and will judge it then afresh. Perhaps, too, with your modifications and read in their proper context, the passages may seem to me less likely to attract undesirable attention.

You speak of the spectre of the printer, which you thought you had laid, rising again in my letter of the 14th. This is unjust. I referred to the printer in answer to a passage in your letter of June 10th, in which you spoke of the transit of the manuscript to his care having been delayed by copious and futile correspondence, in order to show you that the manuscript *had* been to the printer. You speak of his combining the duties of an author with his own honourable calling, and ask how he comes to be the representative of the public mind, and how he happened to alight magically on the particular passages that he did; and proceed to say that the printer is simply a workman hired by the day or by the job for a certain sum. That he should have alighted on that particular passage is a pure coincidence; your other points in this connection will be answered possibly by suggesting that you look inside any book, where you will find a printer's imprint. This im [sic] necessary. If a book is attacked as indecent the printer suffers also from the attack; and if it is sufficiently indecent he also is prosecuted.

There is, I believe, one further story which you design for inclusion in "Dubliners," but which, when this trouble arose, you kept back. Please send that also with the others. I hope there may be no question about that! Believe me, dear Mr. Joyce, Sincerely yours,

A *Letter to Grant Richards, June 23, 1906*

Dear Mr Grant Richards: I have received the manuscript safely. For the next few days I shall be engaged on a translation but during next week I shall read over the whole book and try to do what I can with it. I shall delete the word 'bloody' wherever it occurs except in one passage in *The Boarding-House.* I shall modify the passage in *Counterparts* as best I can. Since you object to it so strongly. These are operations which I dislike from the bottom of my heart and I am only conceding so much to your objections in order that *Two Gallants* may be included. If you cannot see your way to publish it I will have only wasted my time for nothing. As for the fourteenth story *A Little Cloud* I do not expect you will find anything in it to object to. In any case I will send it back with the others, as you direct me.

Some of my suggestions may have seemed to you rather farcical: and I suppose it would be useless for me to suggest that you should find another printer. I would prefer a person who was dumb from his birth, or, if none such can be found, a person who will not 'argue the point.' But let that pass.

Your suggestion that those concerned in the publishing of *Dubliners* may be prosecuted for indecency is in my opinion an extraordinary contribution to the discussion. I know that some amazing imbecilities have been perpetrated in England but I really cannot see how any civilised tribunal could listen for two minutes to such an accusation against my book. I care little or nothing whether what I write is indecent or not but, if I understand the meaning of words, I have written nothing whatever indecent in *Dubliners.*

I send you a Dublin paper by this post. It is the leading satirical paper of the Celtic nations, corresponding to *Punch* or *Pasquino.* I send it to you that you may see how witty the Irish are as all the world knows. The style of the caricaturist will show you how artistic they are: and you will see for yourself that the Irish are the most spiritual race on the face of the earth. Perhaps this may reconcile you to *Dubliners*. It is not my fault that the odour of ashpits and old weeds and offal hangs round my stories. I seriously believe that you will retard the course of civilisation in Ireland by preventing the Irish people from having one good look at themselves in my nicely polished looking-glass.

From Various Letters to Joyce's Brother Stanislaus, October to December 1906

. . . It is impossible for me to write anything in my present circumstances. I wrote some notes for A *Painful Case* but I hardly think the subject is worth treating at much length. The fact is, my imagination is starved at present. I went through my entire book of verses mentally on receipt of Symons' letter and they nearly all seemed to me poor and trivial: some phrases and lines pleased me and no more. A page of A *Little Cloud* gives me more pleasure than all my verses. . . . [*October 18*]

. . . I have read Gissing's *Demos: A Story of English Socialism*. Why are English novels so terribly boring? I think G. has little merit. The socialist in this is first a worker, and then inherits a fortune, jilts his first girl, marries a lydy, becomes a big employer and takes to drink. You know the kind of story. There is a clergyman in it with searching eyes and a deep voice who makes all the socialists wince under his firm gaze. I am going to read another book of his. Then I will try Arthur Morrison and Hardy: and finally Thackeray. Without boasting I think I have little or nothing to learn from English novelists.

I have written to A.J. asking her to send me *By the Stream of Kilmeen* [*sic*] a book of stories by Seamas O'Kelly—you remember him. He was in the degree class with me. I also asked her to try to lay hands on any old editions of Kickham, Griffin, Carleton, H. J. Smyth &c, Banim and to send me a Xmas present made up of tram-tickets, advts, handbills, posters, papers, programmes &c. I would like to have a map of Dublin on my wall. I suppose I am becoming something of a maniac. I am writing to her today to know how you spell Miss McCleod's (?) Reel. I have also added in the story *The Clay* the name of Maria's laundry, the *Dublin by Lamplight Laundry*: it is such a gentle way of putting it. . . . [*November* 6.]

. . . You ask me to explain . . . the meaning of *Dublin by Lamplight Laundry*? That is the name of the laundry at Ballsbridge, of which the story treats. It is run by a society of Protestant spinsters, widows, and childless women—I expect— as a Magdalen's home. The phrase *Dublin by Lamplight* means that Dublin by lamplight is a wicked place full of wicked and lost women whom a kindly committee gathers together for the good work of washing my dirty shirts. I like the phrase because 'it is a gentle way of putting it.' Now I have explained. . . . [*November* 13.]

. . . I was today in the *Biblioteca Vittorio Emanuele*, looking up the account of the Vatican Council of 1870 which declared the infallibility of the Pope. Had not time to finish. Before the final proclamation many of the clerics left Rome as a protest. At the proclamation when the dogma was read out the Pope said 'Is that all right, gents?'. All the gents said 'Placet' but two said 'Non placet'. But the Pope 'You be damned! Kissmearse! I'm infallible!'. The two were, according to one account, the bishops of Capuzzo and Little Rock, according to another account, the bishops of Ajaccio and Little Rock. I looked up MacHale's life. He was bishop of Tuam and of somewhere else in *partibus*. They say nothing of his having voted at the Vatican Council. I shall continue there tomorrow and rewrite that part of the story. *Grace* takes place in 1901 or 2, therefore Kernan at that time 1870 would have been about twenty-five. He would have been born in 1848 and would have been only 6 years of age at time of the proclamation of the Immaculate Conception dogma 1854. I want now an account of the unveiling of Smith

O'Brien's statue to see if MacHale was there. I can get all the dictionaries I want in the Bib. Vitt. Eman. (blast the long name) including a dict of English slang. What a pity I am so handicapped. . . . [*November 13.*]

. . . One of Hardy's stories . . . is about a lawyer on the circuit who seduces a servant, then receives letters from her so beautifully written that he decides to marry her. The letters are written by the servant's mistress who is in love with the lawyer. After the marriage (servant is accompanied to London by mistress) husband says fondly 'Now, dear J.K.–S–&c, will you write a little note to my dear sister, A.B X. etc and send her a piece of the wedding-cake. One of those nice little letters you know so well how to write, love.' Exit of servant wife. She goes out and sits at a table somewhere and, I suppose, writes something like this 'Dear Mrs X—I enclose a piece of wedding-cake.' Enter husband—lawyer, genial. Genially he says 'Well, love, how have you written' and then the whole discovery is found out. Servant-wife blows her nose in the letter and lawyer confronts the mistress. She confesses. Then they talk a page or so of copybook talk (as distinguished from servant's ditto). She weeps but he is stern. Is this as near as T.H. can get to life, I wonder? O my poor fledglings, poor Corley, poor Ignatius Gallaher! [*December 3.*]

A *Letter to Grant Richards, November 23, 1913*

Dear Sir I sent you two years ago a copy of a letter which I sent to the press concerning my book *Dubliners*. Since then the book has had a still more eventful career. It was printed completely and the entire edition of 1000 copies was burned by the publisher. A complete set of printed proofs is in my possession. In view of the very strange history of the book—its acceptance and refusal by two houses, my letter to the present king, his reply, my letter to the press, my negotiations with the second publisher—negotiations which ended in malicious burning of the whole first edition—and furthermore in view of the fact that Dublin, of which the book treats so uncompromisingly, is at present the centre of general interest, I think that perhaps the time has come for my luckless book to appear.

I have written a preface narrating objectively its history and as there are 100 orders ready for it in this city I am prepared, if need be, to contribute towards the expenses of publication—expenses which I presume will be lighter as the book will be set up from printed proofs.

Awaiting your prompt reply I am, dear sir Yours sincerely

Joyce's "Preface" to Dubliners, sent to Grant Richards November 30, 1913

A CURIOUS HISTORY

The following letter, which was the history of a book of stories, was sent by me to the Press of the United Kingdom two years ago. It was published by two newspapers so far as I know: *Sinn Fein* (Dublin) and the *Northern Whig* (Belfast).

To the EDITOR
17 August 1911

Sir May I ask you to publish this letter which throws some light on the present conditions of authorship in England and Ireland?

Nearly six years ago Mr Grant Richards, publisher, of London signed a contract with me for the publication of a book of stories written by me, entitled *Dubliners*. Some ten months later he wrote asking me to omit one of the stories and passages in others which, as he said, his printer refused to set up. I declined to do either and a correspondence began between Mr Grant Richards and myself which lasted more than three months. I went to an international jurist in Rome (where I lived then) and was advised to omit. I declined to do so and the MS was returned to me, the publisher refusing to publish notwithstanding his pledged printed word, the contract remaining in my possession.

Six months afterwards a Mr Hone wrote to me from Marseilles to ask me to submit the MS to Messrs Maunsel, publishers, of Dublin. I did so: and after about a year, in July 1909, Messrs Maunsel signed a contract with me for the publication of the book on or before 1 September 1910. In December 1909 Messrs Maunsel's manager begged me to alter a passage in one of the stories, *Ivy Day in the Committee Room*, wherein some reference was made to Edward VII. I agreed to do so, much against my will, and altered one or two phrases. Messrs Maunsel continually postponed the date of publication and in the end wrote, asking me to omit the passage or to change it radically. I declined to do either, pointing out that Mr Grant Richards of London had raised no objection to the passage when Edward VII was alive and that I could not see why an Irish publisher should raise an objection to it when Edward VII had passed into history. I suggested arbitration or a deletion of the passage with a prefatory note of explanation by me but Messrs Maunsel would agree to neither. As Mr Hone (who had written to me in the first instance) disclaimed all responsibility in the matter and any connection with the firm I took the opinion of a solicitor in Dublin who advised me to omit the passage, informing me that as I had no domicile in the United Kingdom I could not sue Messrs Maunsel for breach of contract unless I paid £100 into court and that, even if I paid £100 into court and sued them, I should have no chance of getting a verdict in my favour from a Dublin jury if the passage in dispute could be taken as offensive in any way to the late king. I wrote then to the present king, George V, enclosing a printed proof of the story with the passage therein marked and begging him to inform me whether in his view the passage (certain allusions made by a person of the story in the idiom of his social class) should be withheld from publication as offensive to the memory of his father. His Majesty's private secretary sent me this reply:

Buckingham Palace

The private secretary is commanded to acknowledge the receipt of Mr James Joyce's letter of the 1 instant and to inform him that it is inconsistent with rule for His Majesty to express his opinion in such cases. The enclosures are returned herewith   11 August 1911

Here is the passage in dispute:

—But look here, John,—said Mr O'Connor.—Why should we welcome the king of England? Didn't Parnell himself . . . ?—
—Parnell,—said Mr Henchy,—is dead. Now, here's the way I look at it. Here's this chap come to the throne after his old mother keeping him out of it till the man was grey. He's a jolly fine decent fellow, if you ask me, and no damn nonsense about him. He just says to himself:—*The old one never went to see these wild Irish. By Christ, I'll go myself and see what they're like.*—And are we going to insult the man when he comes over here on a friendly visit? Eh? Isn't that right, Crofton?—
Mr Crofton nodded his head.
—But after all now,—said Mr Lyons, argumentatively,—King Edward's life, you know, is not the very . . .—
—Let bygones be bygones.—said Mr Henchy—I admire the man personally. He's just an ordinary knockabout like you and me. He's fond of his glass of grog and he's a bit of a rake, perhaps, and he's a good sportsman. Damn it, can't we Irish play fair?—

I wrote this book seven years ago and, as I cannot see in any quarter a chance that my rights will be protected, I hereby give Messrs Maunsel publicly permission to publish this story with what changes or deletions they may please to make and shall hope that what they may publish may resemble that to the writing of which I gave thought and time. Their attitude as an Irish publishing firm may be judged by Irish public opinion. I, as a writer, protest against the systems (legal, social and ceremonious) which have brought me to this pass. Thanking you for your courtesy, I am, Sir, Your obedient servant   JAMES JOYCE

I waited nine months after the publication of this letter. Then I went to Ireland and entered into negotiations with Messrs Maunsel. They asked me to omit from the collection the story 'An Encounter', passages in 'Two Gallants', 'The Boarding House', 'A Painful Case', and to change everywhere through the book the name of restaurants, cake-shops, railway stations, public houses, laundries, bars and other places of business. After having argued against their point of view day after day for six weeks and having laid the matter before two solicitors (who, while they informed me that the publishing firm had made a breach of contract, refused to take up my case or to allow their names to be associated with it in any way.) I consented in despair to all these changes on condition that the book were brought out without delay and the original text were restored in future editions, if such were called for. Then Messrs Maunsel asked me to pay into their bank £1000 as security, or to find two sureties of £500 each. I declined to do either; and they then wrote to me, informing me that they would not publish the book, altered or unaltered, and that if I did not make them an offer to cover their losses on printing it they would sue me to recover the same. I offered to pay sixty per cent of the cost of printing the first edition of one thousand copies if the edition were made over to my order. This offer was accepted, and I arranged with my brother in Dublin to publish and sell the book for me. On the morrow when the draft and agreement were to be signed the publishers informed me that the matter was at an end because the printer refused to hand over the copies. I then went to the printer. His foreman told me that the printer had decided to forego all claim to the money due to him. I asked whether the printer would hand over the complete edition to a London or continental firm or to my brother or to me if he were fully indemnified. He said that the copies would never leave his printing house, and that the type had been broken up and that the entire edition of one thousand copies would be burnt the next day. I left Ireland the next day, bringing with me a printed copy of the book which I had obtained from the publisher.   JAMES JOYCE

From a Letter to Grant Richards, May 7, 1915

Dear Mr Grant Richards I have received your letter of 29 April with statement of sales up to 31 December by which I see that 379 copies of *Dubliners* were sold in the United Kingdom. I was sorry that neither you nor I have gained anything. In your statement I see no mention of the 120 copies which I bought: I believe I owe you some small amount still which I could not remit owing to the outbreak of war. There is no mention also of the stories which the editor of the *Smart Set* appears to have bought. In any case these trifling sums would not change the position which is disastrous for both so far as I can see. . . .

III

$\diamond$

Dubliners:

EDITORS' INTRODUCTION
TO CRITICISM SECTION

Although Joyce's art has received detailed critical attention for well over forty years, most of the significant criticism of *Dubliners* belongs to the past decade. When Brewster Ghiselin's pioneering essay on "The Unity of Joyce's *Dubliners*" appeared in 1956 a substantial body of intelligent commentary had already accumulated around *A Portrait of the Artist, Ulysses,* and *Finnegans Wake,* but the stories of *Dubliners* were still dismissed by most critics as apprentice work, or given a secondary place as skillful but depressing "slices" of Dublin life. Only "The Dead," that obvious masterpiece of symbolic narrative, had received the scrupulous treatment accorded to Joyce's other works (see the early essays by Allen Tate and Kenneth Burke reprinted in this volume). However, the last few years have witnessed a surprising acceleration in the attention given to *Dubliners,* so that we can now speak confidently of "schools" and "tendencies" in criticism of the stories. Some of the best work on Joyce being done today is devoted to the early fiction, and the essays included in this volume testify to the range and vitality of contemporary criticism of *Dubliners.*

This "curious history" of *Dubliners'* reputation was caused in part by the circumstances of publication. If the stories had appeared in 1907—or even in 1910, as once planned—the reviews would have been no more intelligent, but the book might have gained more attention in its own right. Instead, *Dubliners* was published in June 1914, four months after *A Portrait of the Artist* had begun to appear serially in the *Egoist,* and its reception during the next few years was overshadowed by the excited attention given to *Portrait* and the early chapters of *Ulysses.* Even Ezra Pound, Joyce's enthusiastic supporter and unofficial "manager," reviewed *Dubliners* as if it were a minor production by the author of *A Portrait of the Artist* (*The Egoist,* July 1914). Pound praised the "hardness" of Joyce's prose, its freedom from sentimentality, and accurately placed

Joyce in the tradition of the Flaubertian short story, but the review makes it clear that Pound's chief interest lay in *Portrait*, where he was directly responsible for the publication. Many years later, when Joyce's early career could be seen in perspective, the controversy over the publication of *Dubliners* continued to affect the work's critical reception. When Herbert Gorman revealed the full details of Joyce's publishing difficulties in his "official" biography (1939) many readers found this sensational story of the misunderstood artist more interesting than *Dubliners*, and for a number of years Joyce's problems with publisher and printer were more frequently discussed than the stories themselves.

The early notices of *Dubliners*, brief and unsatisfactory though they may be, are of interest because they set a pattern for subsequent critical discussion. Some reviewers made the same objections to the collection's subject-matter that had vexed the many would-be publishers, protesting against the sordid incidents and pessimistic tone; but a more common objection was that the stories lacked "point," that they were mere anecdotes or sketches without a definite structure. At least two reviewers found the longer stories the least satisfactory because Joyce did not sustain a "mood" in them as he did in the shorter pieces. Obviously these critics were reading the stories as impressionistic evocations of a "mood" or atmosphere, and were disappointed when some of the longer tales failed to deliver that "unity of impression" or sustained "single effect" which Poe had called for in his famous review of Hawthorne's *Twice-Told Tales*. Pound was almost alone in seeing the stories not as exercises in a diffuse impressionism, but as examples of a more tough-minded method which imitated "Flaubert's definiteness." Yet although Pound recognized and praised the shadowless quality of Joyce's prose, he gave no indication that he understood Joyce's larger aim, which was to follow Flaubert in making every detail of description and dialogue part of both a "mood" and a highly developed symbolic pattern. Reading the early commentators on *Dubliners*, we find no hint that the stories might share in the symbolic methods that animate *Portrait* and *Ulysses*.

The turning-point in *Dubliners* criticism came when critics who had become skillful at tracing the symbolic motifs in the later works returned to *Dubliners* and found the same patterns adumbrated there. Most of the best essays on *Dubliners* belong to this school of "symbolic" interpretation, and in the present volume the studies by Ghiselin, Tate, and Walzl show how rewarding the approach can be. However, the need today would seem to be for other forms of criticism which will emphasize the non-symbolic dimensions of the stories without sacrificing the achievement of the "symbolic" critics, who were the first to point out those patterns and motifs that give the entire collection, as well as the individual stories, an extraordinary consistency.

Since the recent emphasis on symbolic motifs in *Dubliners* was prompted by our growing understanding of symbolism in *Portrait, Ulysses,* and *Finnegans Wake,* we should not be surprised to find ourselves troubled from time to time by the uneasy feeling that the stories are being "over-read." *Dubliners* is not *Finnegans Wake,* it is not even *Portrait* or *Ulysses,* and when we are forced to draw the limits for a symbolic reading we must be guided by tact, good sense, and a knowledge of Joyce's evolving artistic methods. Between the two versions of "The Sisters" printed in this volume there is an obvious development in symbolic sophistication, and it is fair to say that late stories such as "The Dead" or "A Little Cloud" must be read in slightly different ways from "After the Race" or "Eveline," which were written much earlier. Joyce's artistic development at the time he wrote *Dubliners* must be measured in months, not years.

Perhaps the basic problem is that raised by Robert M. Adams in his study of *Ulysses* entitled *Surface and Symbol*: how do we distinguish between those elements which were parts of Joyce's penchant for realism, products of his fidelity to the actual surface of Dublin life, and those elements which were selected or invented for obviously symbolic purposes? For instance, the bazaar which is the young boy's goal in "Araby" actually came to Dublin in May 1894, billed as "Araby in Dublin: Grand Oriental Fête," but Joyce has clearly worked this fragment of local experience into the larger "Oriental" motif discussed by Brewster Ghiselin in his study of Joyce's symbolism. When so much of local detail and personal experience has been lifted to the level of symbolism, it is tempting to construe all details as hugely symbolic, but our common sense will tell us that many of the places and incidents of *Dubliners* are part of the work's surface, and take their sole authority from the fact that they actually existed. Joyce processed much of his ordinary "reality" into symbol and myth, but in *Dubliners* he did not transform every detail of landscape and history as he did in *Finnegans Wake*. The snow in "The Dead" takes on symbolic overtones, but it has its own commonplace reality; the gold coin in "Two Gallants" may be a symbol of various subtle "betrayals," but it is first and last a fact of economic life. Any symbolic reading of *Dubliners* that compromises the realistic integrity of the stories should fall under immediate suspicion.

A minor controversy over the interpretation of "Clay" provides us with a perfect example of the difficulties that beset a critic of *Dubliners*. In 1953 Marvin Magalaner published a brief symbolic reading of "Clay" in which he claimed that Maria plays a triple role as pathetic employee of the Dublin by Lamplight laundry, as an All Hallows Eve witch, and as a type of the Virgin Mary. The following year Joyce's brother Stanislaus attacked such symbolic readings as "exaggerations" made by supersubtle critics who "can still have the immense satisfaction of knowing that they have dived into deeper depths than the author they are criticizing ever sounded." And Stanislaus continued: "I am in a position to state definitely that my brother had no such subtleties in mind when he wrote the story."[1]

[1] For both sides of the controversy see Marvin Magalaner and Richard M. Kain, *Joyce: The Man, the Work, the Reputation* (New York: Collier Books, 1956), pp. 84–90.

It is easy to sympathize with Stanislaus's position. As the first reader of the stories, and Joyce's confidant during those early years, he was making a plea against the uncontrolled symbolic reading of *Dubliners*. On the other hand, he was clearly wrong in claiming that "Clay" lacks "levels of significance" such as those found in *Ulysses* (in fact, on another occasion Stanislaus took pains to point out that his brother was following a Dantean pattern of "inferno-purgatorio-paradiso" in the structure of "Grace"). Magalaner's interpretation of Maria as witch is obviously *there* in the story. "Clay" was originally called "Hallow Eve," Maria is described as witchlike in appearance ("the tip of her nose nearly met the tip of her chin" when she laughed), and the folklore of Hallowe'en is woven into the tale. But when we turn to the supposed analogy between Maria and the Virgin Mary, Magalaner seems to be reading *Dubliners* as if it were *Ulysses* or *Finnegans Wake*. The similarity of Maria-Mary, and the ambiguous reference to Maria as a "peacemaker," are scarcely enough to support an additional level of symbolism, and Magalaner appears to be aware of this when he confesses that Joyce may not have "sufficiently reinforced the relationship between the witch and the Virgin." This is really an unconscious confession that Joyce has not provided the consistency of symbolism expected by an accomplished reader of his later works. The moral would appear to be that we must use all our tact, and all our knowledge of Joyce's materials and methods, to discriminate between details of "surface" and details with symbolic overtones, or between the overtones and a full-fledged pattern of intricate symbolism. The stories of *Dubliners* gain enormously when we bring to them an understanding of Joyce's mature art, but we must never forget to confront them first on their own terms.

One critical method that has proved to be both illuminating and dangerous is the "autobiographical" reading of the stories. As the details of Joyce's early life and environment have become better known, especially through the publication of the *Letters* and the appearance of Richard Ellmann's monumental biography, it has become evident that the autobiographical strands in *Dubliners* are both intricate and important. In some ways the stories are just as deeply rooted in personal experience as is *A Portrait of the Artist*, and Richard Ellmann's fascinating study of "The Backgrounds of 'The Dead' " shows how much can be done with this kind of information. However, the familiar critical dilemmas which underlie any attempt at an "autobiographical" reading apply just as much to *Dubliners* as to *Portrait*, and when the personal sources have been traced we are still confronted with the irreducible gap between the creator and his work. We know a great deal more now than we did ten years ago about Joyce's intentions and the particular sources of his stories, but the reader can legitimately ask if these facts bring us appreciably closer to an understanding of those interactions of character, place, and incident which compose the stories. Where criticism of *Dubliners* has been deficient is in the general application of those fresh critical methods which, in recent years, have led us to a more precise knowledge of the fictional process. The stories of *Dubliners* have never been satisfactorily "placed" in the tradition of the short story, nor have they been fully related to the major trends in modern fiction. The raw materials of history, biography, and local background are now amply available (it has been one of the editors' aims to provide such material in this volume); what is needed is a criticism that will utilize these materials and then go beyond them to place Joyce's stories in the larger context of the development of modern short fiction.

Another problem in the interpretation of *Dubliners*, one which runs like a *leitmotif* through the essays in this volume, is that of tone and attitude. As in *A Portrait* and *Ulysses*, we must decide whether Joyce's perspective is, on balance, one of ironic dislike or of sympathetic criticism. Although he said that *Dubliners* was composed "for the most part in a style of scrupulous meanness," Joyce's quarrel with his native land was very much a lover's quarrel, and some of the stories—especially "Araby" and "The Dead"—rise above the bitterness and regret that characterize his letters of the time. As all his works testify, Joyce was a sentimental man who used irony as a defense against sentimentality, and even in the cruelest stories of *Dubliners* there are undertones of sympathy and compassion.

Since "The Dead" is in many ways a summary of the entire collection, we should not be surprised to find that its conclusion has been a *crux* for critics. The ending of "The Dead," with its lyric urgency, poses in radical form the general problem of Joyce's attitude toward his subject-matter. Some critics see the final scene as an annihilation of Gabriel Conroy, with his personality absorbed into the snow that symbolizes the general paralysis of Ireland. Others read the conclusion as a moment when Gabriel is gifted with the self-recognition and selfless awareness of all humanity denied to the other characters in *Dubliners*: a moment, in effect, when Joyce renounces his god-like role and merges with his creation. Between these extreme views there lies a wide range of compromised or ambiguous interpretation, and the essays on "The Dead" reprinted in this volume were chosen to reflect this range. Taken together, they form an impressive response to the great story which crowns *Dubliners* and stands as one of the monuments of modern fiction.

FRANK O'CONNOR

Frank O'Connor (pseudonym of Michael O'Donovan), the distinguished Irish critic and short-story writer, lectured at Harvard, Stanford, and Northwestern Universities, and the University of Chicago. He was the author of numerous collections of short stories; several volumes of verse; an autobiography entitled *An Only Child*; and two books of criticism which contain chapters on Joyce, *The Mirror in the Roadway* and *The Lonely Voice: A Study of the Short Story*.

WORK IN PROGRESS

James Joyce is fortunate in having escaped from the necessity of publishing either his collected or selected stories. A good book of stories like a good book of poems is a thing in itself, the summing up of a writer's experience at a given time, and it suffers from being broken up or crowded in with other books. *The Untilled Field, Winesburg, Ohio, England My England, Fishmonger's Fiddle,* and *In Our Time* should be read by themselves, as unities, and preferably in editions that resemble the originals. That is how we have to read *Dubliners,* and its uniqueness is one reason for its continuing reputation.

Joyce has escaped the fate of other storytellers because he gave up writing stories after its publication. Why did he give up? It is typical of the muddle of Joycean criticism in our time that nobody even seems to see the importance of this question, much less tries to answer it. Yet, surely, it is a fairly obvious question. Joyce was a much better storyteller than a poet, but after "Chamber Music" he did not entirely give up lyric poetry, and in fact he improved greatly on his early work. Why did he not write another story after "The Dead"? Is it because he felt that he was not a storyteller or that he believed that he had already done all that could be done with the form? It is as difficult to think of a real storyteller, like Chekhov, who had experienced the thrill of the completed masterpiece, giving up short stories forever as it is to think of Keats giving up lyric poetry. This is a question to which *Dubliners* should suggest an answer, and I am assuming that it does so.

Clearly there is a considerable formal difference between the stories at the beginning of the book and "The Dead" at the end of it, and though they are probably not printed in the strict order of their composition, they illustrate at least four and probably five stages in the development of a storyteller.

The first group of stories are what a magazine editor might legitimately describe as "sketches." The first, "The Sisters," describes two ignorant old sisters of a scholarly priest who has been deprived of his clerical functions because of some sort of nervous breakdown. The point of it still eludes me. There is no doubt about the point of "An Encounter," in which two boys mitching from school meet a sexual "queer." The third describes a small boy who goes late to a fun fair called "Araby" to bring home a present for his favorite girl, the sister of a friend, but arrives just as the fair is closing.

These seem to be all autobiographical fragments from early boyhood and any of them could easily have been included in the autobiographical novel, *A Portrait of the Artist as a Young Man*—that is, if they are not actually fragments from the early draft of this known as *Stephen Hero*. Apart from the very simple Jamesian antithesis in "An Encounter" which, in a more elaborate form, was to become one of Joyce's favorite devices, the stories are interesting mainly for their style. It is a style that originated with Walter Pater but was then modeled very closely on that of Flaubert. It is a highly pictorial style; one intended to exclude the reader from the action and instead to present him with a series of images of the events described, which he may accept or reject but cannot modify to suit his own mood or environment. Understanding, indignation, or compassion, which involve us in the action and make us see it in terms of our own character and experience, are not called for.

One evening I went into the back drawing-room in which the priest had died. It was a dark rainy evening and there was no sound in the house. Through one of the broken panes I heard the rain impinge upon the earth, the fine incessant needles of water playing in the sodden beds. Some distant lamp or lighted window gleamed below me.

Or take this, from the same story:

The high cold empty gloomy rooms liberated me and I went from room to room singing. From the front window I saw my companions playing below in the street. Their cries reached me weakened and indistinct and, leaning my forehead against the cool glass, I looked over at the dark house where she lived.

"Cool" as an adjective for glass and "dark" as an adjective for house would have been perfectly normal in any other writer of the time, but the two used together like this in the one sentence indicate the born stylist. Every word in these passages is right. Even the lack of punctuation in "the high cold empty gloomy rooms," a combination of adjectives that few writers would have allowed themselves, is calculated, and the combination itself is worked out almost experimentally. Because he is so small, the first thing the boy notices is that the rooms are high; then he perceives the cold and associates it with the rooms themselves; then he realizes that they are cold because they are empty, and finally comes the emotive adjective "gloomy" that describes their total impression. But because the impression is total and immediate there is no punctuation.

You may play about as you please with alternatives to this phrase; you will find no combination of adjectives that will produce a similar effect, nor any way of reading the passage that will produce a different one. This is using words as they had not been used before in English, except by Pater—not to describe an experience, but so far as possible to duplicate it. Not even perhaps to duplicate it so much as to replace it by a combination of images—a rhetorician's dream, if you like, but

Joyce was a student of rhetoric. And while the description of the experience in Dickens or Trollope would have been intended to involve the reader in it and make him feel as author and character were supposed to feel, the replacement of the experience by a verbal arrangement is intended to leave him free to feel or not, just as he chooses, so long as he recognizes that the experience itself has been fully rendered. The result is that reading a story like "Araby" is less like one's experience of reading than one's experience of glancing through a beautifully illustrated book.

The stories in *Dubliners* were arranged rather in the way a poet arranges lyrics in a book, to follow a pattern that exists in his own mind, but, as I have said, there is also a clear chronological pattern, and in the middle of the book is a group of stories that must have been written after "The Sisters" and before "The Dead." These are very harsh naturalistic stories about Dublin middle-class life either in the form of mock-heroic comedy or in that of antithesis. In the former are stories like "Two Gallants," which describes with intense gravity the comic anxiety of two wasters as to whether one of them will be able to extract some money from the little servant girl who is his mistress, and "Clay," which describes an old maid who works in a laundry and the succession of utterly minor disasters that threatens to ruin her celebration of Halloween in the home of her married nephew. In the latter group are "Counterparts," in which a drunken Dublin clerk who has been publicly tongue-lashed by his employer takes it out in the flogging of his wretched little boy who has allowed the fire to go out, and "A Little Cloud," in which an unsuccessful poet is confronted by a successful journalist who has had sense enough to clear out of Dublin in time. They are ugly little stories, however you regard them, but in their re-creation of a whole submerged population they prove that Joyce was at the time a genuine storyteller with a unique personal vision.

It is even more important to notice that in these stories there is also a development of the stylistic devices one finds in the early stories. In *A Mirror in the Roadway* I have already analyzed the first paragraph of "Two Gallants," but it is necessary to consider it here as well.

The grey warm evening of August had descended upon the city and a mild warm air, a memory of summer, circulated in the streets. The streets, shuttered for the repose of Sunday, swarmed with a gaily coloured crowd. Like illumined pearls the lamps shone from the summits of their tall poles upon the living texture below which, changing shape and hue unceasingly, sent up into the warm grey evening air an unchanging unceasing murmur.

In this beautiful paragraph we find a remarkable development of the prose style in the earlier stories. Not only are adjectives selected with finicking care ("tall poles"), but some of the words are being deliberately repeated, usually in a slightly different order and sometimes in a slightly different form to avoid giving the reader the effect of mere repetition and yet sustain in his mind the hypnotic effect of repetition. One of the ways in which this is done is by the repetition of a noun at the end of one sentence as the subject of the following sentence—"streets. The streets—" but the key words are "warm," "grey," "unchanging," and "unceasing." The same device is used in another paragraph of the same story, which describes a harpist in Kildare Street.

He plucked at the wires heedlessly, glancing quickly from time to time at the face of each new-comer and from time to time, wearily also, at the sky. His harp too, heedless that her coverings had fallen about her knees, seemed weary alike of the eyes of strangers and of her master's hands. One hand played in the bass the melody of *Silent, O Moyle*, while the other hand careered in the treble after each group of notes. The notes of the air throbbed deep and full.

Here, not only is Joyce insisting that we shall see the scene exactly as he saw it by his use of Flaubert's "proper word," he is insisting that we shall *feel* it as he felt it by a deliberate though carefully concealed juxtaposition of key words like "heedless," "hand," "weary," and "notes." This sort of incantatory writing is something entirely new in English prose, whether or not it is for the benefit of literature. My own impression, for what it is worth, is that in pictorial writing like the first paragraph, it is absolutely justified, but that when—as in the second paragraph—it expands to the expression of mood it is intolerably self-conscious. The personification of the harp as a woman, naked and weary of men's fumbling fingers, reminds me somewhat of the fat beginning to congeal about an otherwise excellent mutton chop. In literature certain dishes are best served cold—and these may be taken to include all material descriptions; others that have to do with passion and mood should come to us piping hot.

The most interesting of these stories are what I assume to be the final group—"Ivy Day in the Committee Room," "Grace," and "The Dead," though the last named might very properly be regarded as belonging to a different type of story again. The first two are in the mock-heroic manner, one dealing with Irish politics after Parnell, the other with Irish Catholicism. In "Ivy Day" a group of canvassers and hangers-on of a local government election are gathered in the cheerless headquarters of the Nationalist candidate, waiting to be paid, or at least hoping for a bottle of stout from the candidate's publichouse. A Parnellite drops in and departs, and Mr. Henchy, the most talkative of the group, suggests that his devotion to Parnell is suspect and that he may even be a British spy. Then the boy arrives with the bottles of stout, the party cheers up, and when Joe Hynes, the Parnellite, returns he is greeted quite warmly—Mr. Henchy even calling him "Joe," a device that we later find, greatly magnified, in *Ulysses*. Three corks, removed by the old-fashioned method of heating the bottles, pop one after another, and Joe recites his reach-me-down lament for the dead Chief. As I have pointed out elsewhere, the three corks represent the three volleys over the hero's grave and the lament is the pinchbeck substitute for a Dead March. This is the mock-heroic at its poker-faced deadliest. In "Two Gallants" the greatest possible demand that the Irish imagination can make on a woman in love is the gift of a pound; in "Ivy Day" the greatest tribute a degenerate nation can pay to a dead leader is the popping of corks from a few bottles of stout, earned by the betrayal of everything for which that leader had stood.

As I have said, there is no difficulty in imagining the first group of stories from *Dubliners* transferred to the pages of *A Portrait of the Artist as a Young Man.* Can one imagine "Ivy Day" transferred to them? In the Christmas Day scene in that book we have the subject of "Ivy Day" but treated with almost hysterical violence; and it is as impossible to imagine transferring "Ivy Day" to that context as it is to imagine *Dubliners* with the Christmas Day scene in place of "Ivy Day in the Committee Room." Already as a storyteller Joyce has reached a parting of the ways; he has excluded certain material from his stories. In doing so, he has made a mistake that is fatal to the storyteller. He has deprived his submerged population of autonomy.

This sounds more difficult than it really is. A storyteller may make his submerged population believe and say outrageous things—that is partly what makes them a submerged population. Gorky's tramps, Chekhov's peasants, Leskov's artisans, believe things that would drive an ordinary schoolchild to hysterics, but this does not mean that they are not intellectually our equals and better. They have skill and wisdom of their own.

This is what the characters in "Grace" do not have. In this story we see the majesty of the Catholic Church as it appears when reflected in the Dublin lower middle classes. According to Joyce's brother, Stanislaus, the story is based on the theme of the *Divine Comedy,* beginning in Hell—the underground lavatory of a publichouse; ascending to Purgatory—the sickbed of a suburban home; and finally to Heaven in Gardiner Street Church. This is likely enough, because Joyce was an intensely literary man, and—in his later work at least—loved to play the well-known literary game of basing his books on underlying myths and theories so that half the reader's fun comes of spotting the allusions—a game which has the incidental advantage that the flattered reader is liable to mistake the author for a literary scholar.

When we first meet him, Mr. Kernan, the commercial

traveler, has fallen down the stairs to the lavatory of a public-house, and lies there unconscious with a portion of his tongue bitten off. The temporal power, in the person of a policeman, appears, ready to lead him to the bridewell, but he is rescued by a Mr. Power, who brings him home instead. Mr. Kernan's friends decide that for the good of his soul he must join them in a retreat, so they gather about his bedside—Mr. Cunningham, Mr. Power, Mr. M'Coy, and Mr. Fogarty. They discuss first the temporal power in the shape of the policeman who had all but arrested Mr. Kernan—a scandalous business, as they agree; and then the spiritual power in terms of all the churchmen they have known or heard of—heard of, one must admit, at some considerable distance, for the whole discussion is on the level of folklore.

Finally, the four men with their penitent friend attend Gardiner Street Church, where they hear a sermon from the eminent Jesuit, Father Purdon. Father Purdon preaches on what he admits is a difficult text—"Wherefore make unto yourselves friends out of the mammon of iniquity so that when you die they may receive you into everlasting dwellings." Father Purdon assumes it to be "a text for business men and professional men," but, whatever it may be, it is quite clear that Father Purdon knows precisely as much about it as Mr. Cunningham does about church history, which is sweet damn all.

—I often heard he [Leo XIII] was one of the most intellectual men in Europe, said Mr Power. I mean apart from his being Pope.
—So he was, said Mr Cunningham, if not *the* most so. His motto, you know, as Pope, was *Lux upon Lux*—*Light upon Light*.
—No, no, said Mr Fogarty eagerly. I think you're wrong there. It was *Lux in Tenebris*, I think—*Light in Darkness*.
—O yes, said Mr M'Coy, *Tenebrae*.
—Allow me, said Mr Cunningham positively, it was *Lux upon Lux*. And Pius IX. his predecessor's motto was *Crux upon Crux*— that is, *Cross upon Cross*—to show the difference between their two pontificates.

Joyce, the ecclesiastical scholar, the all-but-Jesuit, is in a position to sneer at them all. Gorky, Leskov, or Chekhov would not have sneered. Joyce's submerged population is no longer being submerged by circumstances but by Joyce's own irony.

I am sure that Stanislaus Joyce represented truthfully his brother's description of the significance of the story because it is quite clear that Mr. Kernan's fall down the lavatory stairs does represent the Fall of Man. What I am not satisfied of is that Stanislaus was given the full explanation, because it seems to me equally clear that Mr. Cunningham, Mr. M'Coy, Mr. Fogarty, and Mr. Power represent the Four Evangelists, though my mind totters at the thought of trying to find which evangelist each represents and the evangelists' attributes in their names and characters. I do not understand the elaborate antithesis of spiritual and temporal powers, or the discussion of the good and bad types in each, but it seems clear to me that this is the biblical story, told in terms of the Dublin middle classes and reduced to farce by them as the story of the Hero is reduced to farce by them in "Ivy Day in the Committee Room."

"The Dead," Joyce's last story, is entirely different from all the others. It is also immensely more complicated, and it is not always easy to see what any particular episode represents, though it is only too easy to see that it represents something. The scene is the annual dance of the Misses Morkan, old music teachers on Usher's Island, and ostensibly it is no more than a report of what happened at it, except at the end, when Gabriel Conroy and his wife Gretta return to their hotel room. There she breaks down and tells him of a youthful and innocent love affair between herself and a boy of seventeen in Galway, who had caught his death of cold from standing under her bedroom window. But this final scene is irrelevant only in appearance, for in effect it is the real story, and everything that has led up to it has been simply an enormously expanded introduction, a series of themes all of which find their climax in the hotel bedroom.

The setting of the story in a warm, vivacious lighted house in the midst of night and snow is an image of life itself, but every incident, almost every speech, has a crack in it through which we perceive the presence of death all about us, as when Gabriel says that Gretta "takes three *mortal* hours to dress herself," and the aunts say that she must be "perished alive"— an Irishism that ingeniously suggests both life and death. Several times the warmth and gaiety give rise to the idea of love and marriage, but each time it is knocked dead by phrase or incident. At the very opening of the story Gabriel suggests to the servant girl, Lily, that they will soon be attending her wedding, but she retorts savagely that "the men that is now is only all palaver and what they can get out of you," the major theme of the story, for all grace is with the dead: the younger generation have not the generosity of the two old sisters, the younger singers (Caruso, for instance!) cannot sing as well as some long dead English tenor. Gabriel's aunt actually sings "Arrayed for the Bridal," but she is only an old woman who has been dismissed from her position in the local church choir.

Gabriel himself is fired by passion for his wife, but when they return to their hotel bedroom the electric light has failed, and his passion is also extinguished when she tells him the story of her love for a dead boy. Whether it is Gabriel's quarrel with Miss Ivors, who wants him to spend his summer holiday patriotically in the West of Ireland (where his wife and the young man had met), the discussion of Cistercian monks who are supposed to sleep in their coffins, "to remind them of their last end," or the reminiscences of old singers and old relatives, everything pushes Gabriel toward that ultimate dissolution of identity in which real things disappear from about us, and we are as alone as we shall be on our deathbeds.

But it is easy enough to see from "The Dead" why Joyce gave up storytelling. One of his main passions—the elaboration of style and form—had taken control, and the short story is too tightly knit to permit expansion like this. And—what is much more important—it is quite clear from "The Dead" that he had already begun to lose sight of the submerged population that was his original subject. There are little touches of it here and there, as in the sketches of Freddy Malins and his mother —the old lady who finds everything "beautiful"—"beautiful crossing," "beautiful house," "beautiful scenery," "beautiful fish"—but Gabriel does not belong to it, nor does Gretta nor Miss Ivors. They are not characters but personalities, and Joyce would never again be able to deal with characters, people whose identity is determined by their circumstances. His own escape to Trieste, with its enlargement of his own sense of identity, had caused them to fade from his mind or—to put it more precisely—had caused them to reappear in entirely different guises. This is something that is always liable to happen to the provincial storyteller when you put him into a cosmopolitan atmosphere, and we shall see something of the same kind happening to D. H. Lawrence and A. E. Coppard, not always, as I hope my readers will understand, to our loss or theirs.

I have no doubt that if we possessed the manuscript of the short story that Joyce called "Mr. Hunter's Day" and which was written as one of the *Dubliners* group, we should see that process actually at work because it later became *Ulysses*. I assume that it was written in the manner of "Grace" and "Ivy Day in the Committee Room" as a mock-heroic description of a day in the life of a Dublin salesman like Mr. Kernan, with all its petty disasters and triumphs, and would guess that it ended exultantly with an order for twenty pounds' worth of hardware or office equipment. But Mr. Bloom in *Ulysses* is no Mr. Hunter. He is not a member of any submerged population, Irish or Jewish, whose character could be repressed by the loss of a few orders. Mr. Bloom has lost orders before this. He is a man of universal intelligence, capable of meditating quite lucidly, if irregularly, on an enormous variety of subjects. In fact, he is Ulysses, and can achieve anything his great precursor achieved. As for his wayward wife, she is not only Penelope but Earth itself, and her lover, Blazes Boylan, is the Sun, which is forever blazing and boiling—why do Joyce commentators always miss the obvious? But what have those colossi to do with Corley and his pound note and Lenehan and his poor pitiful plate of peas?

And even these, when translated into the pages of *Ulysses* and *Finnegans Wake*, have suffered a sea change. They too have resigned their parts "in the casual comedy." In *Dubliners* Martin Cunningham may talk of "Lux upon Lux" and "Crux upon Crux," but who, reading of him in the Hades episode in *Ulysses*, can imagine that dignified figure committing such childish errors?

However they may delight us in their reincarnations, it is clear that they have nothing to do with the world of the short-storyteller who must make tragedy out of a plate of peas and a bottle of ginger beer or the loss of a parcel of fruitcake intended for a Halloween party. Before such spiritual grandeur as theirs, there is nothing for him to do but bow himself modestly out.

BREWSTER GHISELIN

Brewster Ghiselin is Professor of English at the University of Utah.
He has written articles on contemporary English and American
literature, and has edited a symposium entitled *The Creative Process*.

THE UNITY OF
JOYCE'S DUBLINERS

The idea is not altogether new that the structure of James
Joyce's *Dubliners*, long believed to be loose and episodic, is
really unitary. In 1944, Richard Levin and Charles Shattuck
made it clear that the book is "something more than a collection of discrete sketches." In their essay "First Flight to Ithaca:
A New Reading of Joyce's *Dubliners*," they demonstrated that
like the novel *Ulysses* the stories of *Dubliners* are integrated
by a pattern of correspondence to the *Odyssey* of Homer. To
this first demonstration of a latent structural unity in *Dubliners*
must be added the evidence of its even more full integration
by means of a symbolic structure so highly organized as to suggest the most subtle elaborations of Joyce's method in his
maturity.

So long as *Dubliners* was conceived of only as "a straight
work of Naturalistic fiction," the phrase of Edmund Wilson
characterizing the book in *Axel's Castle*, its unity could appear
to be no more than thematic. The work seemed merely a
group of brilliant individual stories arranged in such a way as
to develop effectively the import which Joyce himself announced, but did not fully reveal, in describing the book as
"a chapter of the moral history of my country" and in suggesting that his interest focused upon Dublin as "the centre of

paralysis." As Harry Levin explained in his introduction to *The Portable Joyce*, "The book is not a systematic canvass like *Ulysses*; nor is it integrated, like the *Portrait*, by one intense point of view; but it comprises, as Joyce explained, a series of chapters in the moral history of his community; and the episodes are arranged in careful progression from childhood to maturity, broadening from private to public scope."

So narrow an understanding of *Dubliners* is no longer acceptable. Recent and steadily increasing appreciation of the fact that there is much symbolism in the book has dispelled the notion that it is radically different in technique from Joyce's later fiction. During the past six or eight years a significant body of critics, among them Caroline Gordon, Allen Tate, and W. Y. Tindall, have published their understanding that the naturalism of *Dubliners* is complicated by systematic use of symbols, which establish relationships between superficially disparate elements in the stories. Discussion of "The Dead," for example, has made it obvious that the immobility of snowy statues in that story is symbolically one with the spiritual condition of Gabriel Conroy turned to the wintry window at the very end of *Dubliners* and with the deathly arrest of paralysis announced on the first page of the book. In the light of this insight other elements of the same pattern, such as the stillness of the girl frozen in fear at the end of the fourth story, virtually declare themselves.

Such images, significantly disposed, give a firm symbolic texture and pattern to the individual stories of *Dubliners* and enhance the integrity of the work as a whole. But no constellation, zodiac, or whole celestial sphere of symbols is enough in itself to establish in the fifteen separate narratives, each one in its realistic aspect a completely independent action, the embracing and inviolable order of full structural unity. That is achieved, however, by means of a single development, essentially of action, organized in complex detail and in a necessary, meaningful sequence throughout the book. Because this structure is defined partly by realistic means, partly by symbols, much of it must remain invisible until the major symbols in which it defines itself are recognized, as too few of them have been, and displayed in their more significant relationships. When the outlines of the symbolic pattern have been grasped, the whole unifying development will be discernible as a sequence of events in a moral drama, an action of the human spirit struggling for survival under peculiar conditions of deprivation, enclosed and disabled by a degenerate environment that provides none of the primary necessities of spiritual life. So understood, *Dubliners* will be seen for what it is, in effect, both a group of short stories and a novel, the separate histories of its protagonists composing one essential history, that of the soul of a people which has confused and weakened its relation to the source of spiritual life and cannot restore it.

In so far as this unifying action is evident in the realistic elements of the book, it appears in the struggle of certain characters to escape the constricting circumstances of existence in Ireland, and especially in Dublin, "the centre of paralysis." As in *A Portrait of the Artist as a Young Man*, an escape is envisaged in traveling eastward from the city, across the seas to the freedom of the open world. In *Dubliners*, none of Joyce's protagonists moves very far on this course, though some aspire to go far. Often their motives are unworthy, their minds are confused. Yet their dreams of escape and the longing of one of them even to "fly away to another country" are suggestive of the intent of Stephen Dedalus in *A Portrait* to "fly by those nets," those constrictions of "nationality, language, religion," which are fully represented in *Dubliners* also. Thus, in both books, ideas of enclosure, of arrest, and of movement in space are associated with action of moral purport and with spiritual aspiration and development.

In *Dubliners*, the meaning of movement is further complicated by the thematic import of that symbolic paralysis which Joyce himself referred to, an arrest imposed from within, not by the "nets" of external circumstance, but by a deficiency of impulse and power. The idea of a moral paralysis is expressed sometimes directly in terms of physical arrest, even in the actual paralysis of the priest Father Flynn, whose condition is emphasized by its appearance at the beginning of the book and is reflected in the behavior of Father Purdon, in the penultimate story "observed to be struggling up into the pulpit" as if he were partially paralyzed. But sheer physical inaction of any kind is a somewhat crude means of indicating moral paralysis. Joyce has used it sparingly. The frustrations and degradations of his moral paralytics are rarely defined in physical stasis alone, and are sometimes concomitant with vigorous action. Their paralysis is more often expressed in a weakening of their impulse and ability to move forcefully, effectually, far, or in the right direction, especially by their frustration in ranging eastward in the direction of release or by their complete lack of orientation, by their failure to pass more than a little way beyond the outskirts of Dublin, or by the restriction of their movement altogether to the city or to some narrow area within it.

The case of the boy in the first story, "The Sisters," is representative. Restive under the surviving influence of his dead mentor Father Flynn, yet lost without him, and resentful of the meager life of the city, he only dreams vaguely and disturbingly of being in a far country in the East, and wakes to wander in the city that still encloses him. At the end of the story he sits among hapless women, all immobile and disconsolate, in the dead priest's own room, in the very house where the priest has died, near the center of the center of paralysis. His physical arrest and his enclosure are expressive, even apart from a knowledge of the rich symbolism which qualifies them in ways too complicated to consider at this stage in discussion. Bereft of spiritual guidance, and deprived of the tension of an interest that has been primary in his life, he sits confused and in isolation, unsustained by the secular world about him, unstirred by anything in the natural world, moved only by a fleeting sense of life still in the coffin in the room overhead, a doubt and a hope like a faint resurgence of faith, instantly dispelled.

It should be no surprise to discover in a book developing the theme of moral paralysis a fundamental structure of movements and stases, a system of significant motions, countermotions, and arrests, involving every story, making one consecutive narrative of the surge and subsidence of life in Dublin. In the development of the tendency to eastward movement among the characters of *Dubliners,* and in its successive modifications, throughout the book, something of such a system is manifest. It may be characterized briefly as an eastward trend, at first vague, quickly becoming dominant, then wavering, weakening, and at last reversed. Traced in rough outline, the pattern is as follows: in a sequence of six stories, an impulse and movement eastward to the outskirts of the city or beyond; in a single story, an impulse to fly away upward out of a confining situation near the center of Dublin; in a sequence of four stories, a gradual replacement of the impulse eastward by an impulse and movement westward; in three stories, a limited activity confined almost wholly within the central area of Dublin; and in the concluding story a movement eastward to the heart of the city, the exact center of arrest, then, in vision only, far westward into death.

Interpreted realistically, without recourse to symbol, this pattern may show at most the frustration of Dubliners unable to escape eastward, out of the seaport and overseas, to a more living world. An orientation so loosely conceived seems quite unsuited to determine a powerful organization of form and meaning. Understood in its symbolic import, however, the eastward motion or the desire for it takes on a much more complicated and precise significance.

Orientation and easting are rich in symbolic meanings of which Joyce was certainly aware. An erudite Catholic, he must have known of the ancient though not invariable custom of building churches with their heads to the east and placing the high altar against the east wall or eastward against a reredos in the depths of the building, so that the celebrant of the mass faced east, and the people entered the church and approached the altar from the west and remained looking in the same direction as the priest. He knew that in doing so they looked toward Eden, the earthly paradise, and he may have felt, like

Gregory of Nyssa, that the force of the sacramental orientation was increased by that fact. Perhaps he did not know that the catechumens of the fourth century turned to the west to renounce Satan and to the east to recite the creed before they stepped into the baptismal font, to receive the sacrament that opens the door of spiritual life. Probably he did know that Christ returning for the Last Judgment was expected to come from the east. And he must have shared that profound human feeling, older than Christianity, which has made the sunrise immemorially and all but universally an emblem of the return of life and has made the east, therefore, an emblem of beginning and a place of rebirth. Many times Joyce must have seen the sun rise out of the Irish Sea, washed and brilliant. He could not have failed to know that washing and regeneration are implicit in the sacrament of baptism, and he may have known that in the earlier ages of Christianity baptism was called Illumination. He could not have failed, and the evidence of his symbolism in *Dubliners* shows that he did not fail, to see how a multitude of intimations of spiritual meaning affected the eastward aspirations and movements of characters in his book, and what opportunity it afforded of giving to the mere motion of his characters the symbolic import of moral action.

In constructing *Dubliners*, Joyce must have responded to the force of something like the whole body of insights of which these are representative. For these insights, with some others closely associated with them, are the chief light by which we shall be enabled to follow the development of what I have called the unifying action of *Dubliners* and, through understanding the structure of the book, to penetrate to its central significance. The unity of *Dubliners* is realized, finally, in terms of religious images and ideas, most of them distinctively Christian.

Among these the most important for the immediate purpose of understanding are the symbols, sacraments, and doctrines of the Catholic Church, especially its version of the ancient sacraments of baptism and the sacrificial meal and its concepts of the soul's powers, its perils, and its destiny. In terms of the religious ideas with which Joyce was most familiar the basic characteristics of his structural scheme are readily definable, and some of them are not definable otherwise. The unifying action may be conceived of, oversimply yet with essential accuracy, as a movement of the human soul, in desire of life, through various conditions of Christian virtue and stages of deadly sin, toward or away from the font and the altar and all the gifts of the two chief sacraments provided for its salvation, toward or away from God. In these ideas all the most essential determinants of the spiritual action which makes of *Dubliners* one consecutive narrative are represented: its motivation, its goal and the means of reaching it, and those empowering or disempowering states of inmost being which define the moral conditions under which the action takes place.

The states of being, of virtue and sin, are doubly important. For in *Dubliners* the primary virtues and sins of Christian tradition function both in their intrinsic character, as moral manifestations and determinants of behavior, and structurally in defining the order of the separate stories and in integrating them in a significant sequence. Thus they are one means of establishing the unity of the book, a simple but not arbitrary or wholly superficial means, supplementing with structural reinforcement and with a deepening of import that more fundamental pattern of motions and arrests already touched upon.

Like the booklong sequence of movements and stases, the various states of the soul in virtue and sin form a pattern of strict design traceable through every story. Each story in *Dubliners* is an action defining amid different circumstances of degradation and difficulty in the environment a frustration or defeat of the soul in a different state of strength or debility. Each state is related to the preceding by conventional associations or by causal connections or by both, and the entire sequence represents the whole course of moral deterioration ending in the death of the soul. Joyce's sense of the incompatibility of salvation with life in Dublin is expressed in a systematic display, one by one in these stories, of the three theological virtues and the four cardinal virtues in suppression, of

the seven deadly sins triumphant, and of the deathly consequence, the spiritual death of all the Irish. Far more than his
announced intention, of dealing with childhood, adolescence,
maturity, and public life, this course of degenerative change in
the states of the soul tends to determine the arrangement of
the stories in a fixed order and, together with the pattern
of motions and arrests, to account for his insistence upon a
specific, inalterable sequence.

Although Joyce's schematic arrangement of virtues and sins in
Dubliners does not conform entirely to the most usual order
in listing them, it does so in the main. In the first three stories,
in which the protagonists are presumably innocent, the theological virtues faith, hope, and love, in the conventional order,
are successively displayed in abeyance and finally in defeat. In
the fourth story, the main character, Eveline, lacking the
strength of faith, hope, and love, wavers in an effort to find a
new life and, failing in the cardinal virtue of fortitude, remains
in Dublin, short of her goal and weakened in her spiritual
powers and defenses against evil. In the fifth through the
eleventh stories the seven deadly sins, pride, covetousness, lust,
envy, anger, gluttony, and sloth, are portrayed successively in
action, usually in association with other sins adjacent in the list.
The seven stories devoted to the sins occupy exactly the central
position in the book. The sequence of their presentation is the
most conventional one, except for the placing of anger before
gluttony, a slight and not unique deviation. Gluttony is strongly
represented, moreover, in the usual position, the fifth place, by
means of the drunkenness of the central character Farrington,
as well as in the sixth. And in the sixth place gluttony is
defined in the attitudes and behavior of others than the main
character, Maria, who is interested in food and much concerned
with it rather than avid of it. Her quiet depression is more
truly expressive of her essential state of soul; and in it another
sin that appears rarely in lists of the seven is apparent, the sin of
tristitia, or gloominess, sometimes substituted for the similar
sin of sloth. Joyce's intent seems to have been to create here a
palimpsest, inscribing three sins in the space afforded for two.

The effect has been to reduce gluttony to secondary importance while giving it full recognition in both of its aspects as over-indulgence in drinking as well as in eating. The sequence of sins completes Joyce's representation of the defeat of the soul in its most inward strength and prepares for its failure in the exercise of rational powers. Alienated wholly from God, it cannot act now even in expression of the natural or cardinal virtues, in the words of Aquinas "the good as defined by reason." In the twelfth through the fourteenth stories, the subversion of the cardinal virtues of justice, temperance, and prudence, and the contradiction of reason, upon which they are based, is displayed in those narratives that Joyce intended to represent "public life" in Ireland. Justice, the social virtue regulating the others, comes first in the group. The placing of prudence or wisdom last instead of first, the commonest position, is perhaps influenced by the sequence of appearance in these stories of those hindrances of the spirit in Ireland the "nets" of "nationality, language, religion." The order, moreover, is climactic. Certainly the culminating subversion of the three virtues is represented in the third story of this group, "Grace," in the sermon of "a man of the world" recommending worldly wisdom for the guidance of "his fellowmen." In the fifteenth and last story of Dubliners, no virtue or sin is given such attention as to suggest its predominance. Perhaps that virtue of magnanimity which Aristotle added to the group of four named by the Greeks is displayed in abeyance in Gabriel Conroy's self-concern, but recovered at last in his final self-abnegation and visionary acceptance of the communion of death. Perhaps merely the consequences of moral degeneration are to be discerned in the final story, the completion of spiritual disintegration, death itself.

The pattern of virtues and sins and the spatial pattern of motions and arrests in Dubliners are of course concomitant, and they express one development. As sin flourishes and virtue withers, the force of the soul diminishes, and it becomes more and more disoriented, until at the last all the force of its impulse toward the vital east is confused and spent and it inclines wholly to the deathly west. All this development is embodied, realistically or symbolically, in the experience of the principal characters as they search for vital satisfaction either in spiritual wholeness or in personal willfulness, apprehending the nature of their goal and their immediate needs truly or falsely, moving effectually toward the means of spiritual enlargement or faltering into meanness and withdrawing into a meager and spurious safety, seeking or avoiding the sacred elements of the font and the altar, those ancient Christian and pre-Christian means of sustaining the life of the spirit through lustration, regeneration, illumination, and communion. The unifying pattern of motions and arrests is manifested, story by story, in the action of the principal figure in each, as he moves in relation to the orient source and to the sacramental resources of spiritual life, expressing in physical behavior his moral condition of virtue or sin and his spiritual need and desire. His activity, outwardly of the body, is inwardly that of the soul, either advancing more or less freely and directly eastward or else confined and halted or wandering disoriented, short of its true goal and its true objects the water of regeneration and the wine and bread of communion, the means of approach to God, and often in revulsion from them, accepting plausible substitutes or nothing whatever.

In *Dubliners* from first to last the substitutes are prominent, the true objects are unavailable. The priest in the first story, "The Sisters," has broken a chalice, is paralyzed, and dies; he cannot offer communion, and an empty chalice lies on his breast in death. The food and drink obtained by the boy whose friend he has been are unconsecrated: wine and crackers are offered to him solemnly, but by secular agents. Again and again throughout *Dubliners* such substitutes for the sacred elements of the altar recur, always in secular guise: "musty biscuits" and "raspberry lemonade," porter and "a caraway seed." Suggestions less overt are no less pointed. The abundant table in "The Dead," loaded with food and with bottled water and liquors, but surrounded by human beings gathered together in imperfect fellowship, emphasizes the hunger of the soul for bread and wine that can nourish it, rather than the body, and assuage its loneliness through restoring it to the communion of love. The symbolism of baptismal water likewise enforces the fact of spiritual privation. In "The Sisters" the secular baptism of a cold bath is recommended by the boy's uncle as the source of his strength. Less certainly symbolic, but suggestive in the context, is the fact that the body of the priest is washed by a woman, a point that Joyce thought important enough to define by explicit statements in two passages. In the house where the priest has lived and died, his sisters keep a shop where umbrellas, devices for rejecting the rain of heaven, are sold and re-covered. The open sea, the great symbol of the font in *Dubliners*, is approached by many of the central characters, longed for, but never embarked upon, never really reached. Canal, river, and estuary are crossed; Kingstown Harbor is attained, but the vessel boarded in the harbor is lying at anchor. When, in fear of drowning, the reluctant protagonist of the fourth story, "Eveline," hangs back refusing to embark on an ocean voyage, she may be understood to have withdrawn as at the brink of the baptismal font, for by her action she has renounced that new life which she had looked forward to attaining through moving eastward out of Dublin Bay on the night sea. The idea of her deprivation is reinforced by her final condition, of insensate terror, the reverse of spiritual refreshment and illumination.

Though the spiritual objects that are imaged in these substitutes represent the gifts of the two chief sacraments of the Church, baptism, the first in necessity, and the Eucharist, the first in dignity, there is no suggestion in *Dubliners* that the soul's needs can be supplied by the Church, in its current condition. The only scene in a church, in the story "Grace," implies exactly the opposite, for the sermon of Father Purdon is frankly designed to serve the purposes of those who "live in the world, and, to a certain extent, for the world." The Church is secularized, and it shares in the general paralysis. Its failure in the lives of Joyce's Dubliners is emphasized by the irony that although the nature of the soul has not altered and the means of its salvation retain their old aspect, its needs must be satisfied in entire dissociation from the Church.

Since those needs cannot be satisfied in Ireland, as Joyce represents it in *Dubliners*, the soul's true satisfaction cannot be exhibited in the experience of those who remain in Ireland. It can only be simulated and suggested, either in their relation to those secular substitutes for spiritual things that intimate the need for baptism and communion or in their turning toward the soul's orient, the symbolic east, variously imaged. Some of Joyce's dissatisfied characters, such as Little Chandler, suppose that they can change their condition by escaping from Ireland eastward across the sea to another life in a different place. Physically their goal must be another country; spiritually it has the aspect of a new life. The association functions symbolically. Throughout *Dubliners*, one of the symbolic images of the spiritual goal is a far country. Like the symbols of water, wine, and bread, the far country images the soul's need for life that cannot be attained in Ireland.

Apparently it is not easily attainable outside of Ireland either. Those Dubliners who have reached England or the Continent, characters such as Gabriel Conroy or Ignatius Gallaher, the journalist whom Little Chandler envies because he has made a life for himself in London, show by their continuing to behave like other Dubliners that to be transported physically overseas is not necessarily to find a new life, or to be changed essentially at all. No doubt their failure to change means that the whole of Europe is secularized, perhaps the whole world. Still more, it emphasizes the subjective nature of the attainment symbolized by arrival in a far country. A new condition of inward life is the goal; not a place, but what the place implies, is the true east of the soul. The far countries reached by the boy in "The Sisters" and sought by the boy in "Araby," perhaps the same boy, are not in the world. In one story he dreams of being in an eastern land which he thinks, not very confidently, is Persia. In the other he goes to a bazaar bearing the "magical name" *Araby*, a word casting "an Eastern enchantment." In both stories the far country is probably the same, that fabulous Arabia which is associated with the Phoenix, symbol of the renewal of life in the resurrection of the sun. To the dreamer it suggests a journey and strange customs, but he cannot conceive its meaning. The meaning is plain, however, to the reader aware of the symbols: the boy has looked inward toward the source of his own life, away from that civilization which surrounds him but does not sustain him. The same import, with further meaning, is apparent in the later story. The response of the boy to the name *Araby* and his journey eastward across the city define his spiritual orientation, as his response to the disappointing reality of the bazaar indicates his rejection of a substitute for the true object of the soul's desire.

The sea too, like the image and idea of a far country, symbolizes the orient goal of life. It may of itself, as water, suggest the baptismal font. And in any case it must tend strongly to do so because of the sacramental import of water established by other water symbolism throughout *Dubliners*. The element itself is highly significant, and the great image of it is the sea, the water of liberating voyage and of change and danger, of death and resurrection. The sheer physical prominence of the sea eastward from Dublin colors the east with the significance of baptismal water. In turn the sea is colored by the significance of the east. The altar, even more immediately than the font, is implied in the concept of orientation.

Perhaps in the symbol of the sea in *Dubliners* the identification of the two chief sacraments should be understood. Their identification would not be altogether arbitrary. For the close relationship and even the essential similarity of the two sacraments is suggested in several ways, apart from their association with the east: by their interdependence in fulfillment of a spiritual purpose; by the invariable mixture of a few drops of water with the wine in the chalice; and above all by the concept of rebirth, in which the font is profoundly associated with the altar, the place where Christ is believed to be reborn at the consecration of the divine sacrifice. That Joyce could make the identification is plain from his having merged font with altar in *Finnegans Wake*, in the conception of the "tubbathaltar" of Saint Kevin Hydrophilos. Going "westfrom" toward a suitable supply of water, and showing his sense of the importance of orientation by genuflecting seven times eastward, Saint Kevin fills up his device of dual function, in "ambrosian eucharistic joy of heart," and sits in it. Though Joyce may not have been ready, so early as in *Dubliners,* to identify font with altar, he has developed a body of symbolism which intimately involves them, and possibly merges them, in the symbol of the orient sea.

In that spatial pattern in which the unity of *Dubliners* is expressed as an action, the orient goal is no one simple thing. It is a rich complex of associated ideas and images, only outwardly a place of places, intrinsically a vital state of being, a condition of grace conferred and sustained, presumably, by all the means of grace. Perhaps the main aspect of the symbolic orient, however, is of the eastward sea, its richest and most constantly represented image. The sea is the image most clearly opposable to that deadly contrary of the symbolic orient in all its import of spiritual life, that deathly state of moral disability, which Joyce conceived to be dominant in Ireland and centered in Dublin. The opposition is basic and clear in *Dubliners* of the eastward sea to the westward land, of ocean water to earth, of movement to fixation, of vital change to passivity in the status quo, of the motion toward new life to the stasis of paralysis in old life ways.

Lesser symbols in *Dubliners* are understandable largely in terms of this opposition, the symbols of water, of color, of music, of clothing, and the various symbols of enclosure. Not even the predominant element of the sea, water itself, always implies the sea or its vital freedom. No doubt in its basic symbolic meaning water is conceivable truly enough in conventional terms as the water of life. But in *Dubliners* it is distinctly this only in a general sense, as it is also the natural water of the globe of earth and sky. For full understanding it must be viewed more exactly in terms of specific symbolism and associations. In the eastern sea, it is the water of the font and the chalice, toward which the soul is oriented. Sluggish in a canal beside which a wastrel walks with his tart, or as the ooze on the lavatory floor where a drunkard lies, at the opening of the story "Grace," it loses virtue. At the end of "Eveline," as the water of voyage which can carry the frightened girl from Ireland to a new life and to fulfilling love, it retains its basic meaning and values as well as those given it by its place in the symbolic complex of the sea.

The colors associated with the sea are established very emphatically in "An Encounter" by the boy narrator's finding to his surprise that none of the foreign sailors has the green eyes that he expected; their eyes are only blue, grey, or "even black." Truly green eyes, "bottle-green," appear to him only when he encounters the demonic gaze of the pervert on the bank in Ringsend near the Dodder. Thus green is dissociated from the sea and associated with degeneracy in Ireland, with crippling spiritual limitations, and with the physical limitation of enclosure in a bottle, an image suggesting water, but not the water of the open sea. The symbols of the bottle and of green are effectively combined later in the book in the symbolic complex of the bottled water on the table in "The Dead," pure water appropriately "white," but precisely marked with "transverse green sashes," the cancelling strokes that declare the contents to be spiritually without virtue. Among the ten colors mentioned in description of the table, and the many more only suggested by the foods and drinks and the dishes and bottles that are described, blue and grey do not appear, black is mentioned once, and brown is markedly predominant. Brown, like green, is associated with the limitations of life in Ireland, but much more emphatically. It recurs many times in the stories. It is mentioned as the tint of Dublin streets and is found in the freckled face and in the eyes of Miss Ivors, in "The Dead," who wears a brooch with "an Irish device and motto" and is militantly Irish. Yellow and red, the colors of fire, are variable in meaning, being associable at one extreme with the vital orient, at another with the punishments of the pit, as at the end of "A Painful Case."

The symbol of music is more clearly related to the east than to the land, but it takes its meaning very largely from the context of association and symbol in which it is represented. In "Eveline," where it is associated with far countries and the sea, an Italian air played on a street organ, the singing of a sailor about a sailor, and the quayside whistle and bell of departure on an ocean voyage, music symbolizes the motion of the soul toward life or the call of life to the soul. As the remembered singing of Michael Furey in "The Dead," it is the call to the past life, to communion with the dead.

Since clothing is an expression of character or of personal preference, or an indication of occupation or other circumstance, its symbolic use is restricted by the requirements of naturalism, the need to conform to objective fact. Its symbolic meaning is given unequivocally only in images associated with it at the free will of the artist. The blackness of Father Flynn's clothing is less certainly symbolic than its green discoloration, but the "suit of greenish-black" worn by the pervert in "An Encounter" is indubitably symbolic in both its hues, since Joyce was free in his choice of both. The "brown-clad" girl worshipped by the boy in "Araby" is a madonna emphatically Irish. Lenehan, in "Two Gallants," is clothed in unmistakable contradictions. His "light waterproof" and "white rubber shoes" express an aversion to water, as W. Y. Tindall has pointed out. It must be noted, however, that he is also wearing a yachting cap, a suggestion of inclination toward the water of the sea. His waterproof, moreover, is "slung over one shoulder in toreador fashion," suggesting the far country of Spain, another symbol of the soul's orient. The symbolism precisely defines his position as a vagrant, a drifter in the city, neither committed to the ways of life in Dublin nor free of them. Generally regarded as a "leech," he seems to be a creature of the pools and streams of the earth, not of the sea. He belongs to the dregs of the established world.

Certain images in *Dubliners*, of closed or circumscribed areas, such as coffin, confession-box, rooms, buildings, the city and its suburbs, become symbolic when they are presented in any way suggesting enclosure, as they frequently are; and by recurrence many of them are early established as conventional symbols. In general they express the restrictions and fixations of life in Ireland. Except for the city itself and its suburbs, the commonest of these symbolic images are the houses of the people of Dublin, which are so well characterized in *Stephen Hero* as "those brown brick houses which seem the very incarnation of Irish paralysis." Such is the home, no doubt, of Little Chandler in the story "A Little Cloud," who supposes himself to be a prisoner simply in the external circumstances of his existence, though really he is afflicted with the prevailing paralysis, the psychic limitation of his commitment to the ways of a society without vitality. Like Eveline of the story that bears her name, who leaves for a while the "little brown houses of her neighborhood," in one of which she lives, Chandler cannot escape the constriction which those houses symbolize. Surely his house too must be of symbolically brown brick, situated somewhere near those houses referred to in *Stephen Hero*, which are in Eccles Street, in the north central part of Dublin, at the very center of paralysis.

EDWARD BRANDABUR

Edward Brandabur teaches at the University of Illinois. He is completing a book on Joyce's early fiction which will include this study of "The Sisters."

"THE SISTERS"

In the first three stories of *Dubliners*, Joyce adumbrates the character of his book as an evaluation of motive. "The Sisters," "An Encounter," "Araby," all portray specific quests by sensitive young Dubliners who stand off from a perverse environment with a degree of disengagement resembling that of Joyce himself. These characters have not yet completely succumbed to the paralysis which afflicts their elders, although they envision the possibility of acquiescence. From the start they figure as judges of Dublin because their standards have not yet dissolved in the acid of Dublin's pious immorality. After these three stories and until "The Dead," the reader's judgment depends on its formation by identification with the adolescents in the first three stories; for the stories intervening between the first three and "The Dead" depict protagonists incapable for the most part of detached self-evaluation, (with the exceptions of Mr. Duffy in "A Painful Case" and Little Chandler in "A Little Cloud," both of whom light up their lives long enough to see the wreckage, but not long enough to escape.) Even Gabriel acquiesces in the annihilating snow that covers Dublin, and we perceive him through the eyes of the first three protagonists.

Upon the death of a paralytic priest who had taught and befriended him, the boy in "The Sisters" discovers that earlier the priest had broken down after having inadvertently dropped a chalice. Through his acquaintance with the priest and through

Printed by permission of the author.

what he discovers about him posthumously the boy achieves a kind of realization—the goal to which the whole work tends. The boy's realization differs from the climax of the story, in fact, stems from it.

The chief irritant is the boy's conflict with the adult world because of his relationship with the priest, disapproved of by Old Cotter, for example, who knows something about the priest of which the boy appears ignorant. In the end the boy's apparent ignorance disappears and his epiphany occurs.

Joyce foreshadows the discovery when, coming downstairs for supper, the boy hears Old Cotter say, "No, I wouldn't say he was exactly . . . but there was something queer . . . something uncanny about him. I'll tell you my opinion." Although angry with Old Cotter, ("tiresome old red-nosed imbecile"), the boy puzzles to "extract meaning from his unfinished sentences." Following this presentation of the problem is an account of the boy's relation with the priest, his initial uneasiness about the priest, and finally his visit to the house where the priest lay in his coffin. Here Eliza provides some explanation of Old Cotter's earlier remarks when she recalls that the old priest had dropped a chalice, and had been discovered later in his confessional, "wide-awake and laughing-like softly to himself."

Structurally, the problem in the story occurs as a question presented about the old priest: the question intensifies through the retelling of the boy's relationship to the priest, and his reactions to this relationship. Finally, it is answered with an account of the priest's breakdown and its immediate cause. The resolution comes with the boy's winning a partial solution to his initial puzzle from those of the adult world who know the priest's secret; in this sense he is a protagonist, although his struggle for an answer is wholly interior, and even deliberately hidden from his adult antagonists: "Old Cotter looked at me for a while. I felt that his little beady black eyes were examining me but I would not satisfy him by looking up from my plate." Furthermore, the boy is aware of his own fear of finding out the truth he seeks: "I wished to go in and look at him, but I had not the courage to knock."

From this simple structure Joyce derives a complicated psychic movement, some of it carefully veiled within his protagonist and, of course, within the warped disposition of the priest. He has also prepared the ground for fourteen other stories and planted seeds of meaning and technique which may be seen in A *Portrait of the Artist as a Young Man,* and which will flower in *Ulysses* and *Finnegans Wake.*

A formulation of the object of the boy's quest, which is the final internal goal of the story, obliges the reader to look with the protagonist at the spiritual condition of the priest, through an evaluation of which the protagonist's epiphany comes about. The boy appears to desire to be a free person in his own right; his compulsive relation with the neurotic priest has enslaved and inhibited him. The priest certainly represents corrupt features of Irish Catholicism, so it goes without saying that Joyce is making a more universal comment on the servile relation of the Dubliners to ecclesiastical authority.[1] But the task here is to determine the boy's quest for a specific benefit and the relation of this quest to his personal involvement with the priest.

The boy appears to want to be free to achieve the fulfilling joy without which one cannot live satisfactorily, and his relationship with the priest is an obstacle. When the priest dies the boy discovers "that neither I nor the day seemed in a mourning mood and I felt even annoyed at discovering in myself a sensation of freedom as if I had been freed from something by his death. I wondered at this. . . ." After reading the funeral notice he feels a "sensation of freedom" which any sensitive youth might prefer instead of an oppressive relationship with a decaying old man. Still the boy in some way wants that relationship. He feels "annoyed" at discovering in himself a sensation of freedom, just as earlier he had been angered at Old Cotter, who disapproved of his relationship with the priest on the grounds that it was "bad for children." Although the reader is obviously expected to shudder at the priest and what

---

[1] For Marvin Magalaner, Joyce illustrates in the dying priest the "decaying Irish Catholic God." *Joyce: The Man, The Work, The Reputation* (New York: Collier Books, 1956), p. 84.

he represents, there is no question of the boy's attraction for what at the same time he abhors—the infectious corruption of a degenerate old man. The first paragraph of the story ends with the well-known statement that *"paralysis . . .* sounded to me like the name of some maleficent and sinful being. It filled me with fear, and yet I longed to be nearer to it and to look upon its deadly work." The boy is drawn to a contemplation of what, infecting him, would inhibit his freedom. One clue to his attraction appears in his phantasm the night after his discovery of the priest's death:

In the dark of my room I imagined that I saw again the heavy grey face of the paralytic. I drew the blankets over my head and tried to think of Christmas. But the grey face still followed me. It murmured; and I understood that it desired to confess something. I felt my soul receding into some *pleasant and vicious* region; and there again I found it waiting for me. [Italics mine.]

Revolted by the perverse face, the boy tries to dispel the image with thoughts of Christmas, which would promise a redemption from compulsions; but this tactic fails, and the boy retreats still further into a region where although the pleasure is not clearly specified it is nonetheless attractively vicious. Here again the grey image waits, and the boy stops where he finds himself cornered by his compulsive, fearful, but still pleasantly corrupt relation with the priest. It is as though the decaying priest were trying to bequeath his own sacerdotal corruption, to which the boy has become so addicted that to be freed from it (even though he tries to retreat) would require too painful a withdrawal. At the end of the phantasm the roles are reversed: the boy is now a confessor, smiling with the vague perversity of his mentor: "[The face] began to confess to me in a murmuring voice and I wondered why it smiled continually and why the lips were so moist with spittle. But then I remembered that it had died of paralysis and I felt that I too was smiling feebly as if to absolve the simoniac of his sin."

The boy's compulsive devotion to a vicious quest forces him to assume the "act" of alienated observer: his stance the necessary corollary to his divided nature. On the one hand he appears however weakly to display the usual adolescent enthusiasm: he walks on the sunny side of the street looking at the theatrical advertisements on a day of mourning: on the way to the wake he notices that "the window-panes of the houses that looked to the west reflected the tawny gold of a great bank of clouds." But his devotion to the old priest forces him to behave towards other adults with a sanctimonious calm which belies his true feelings: when Old Cotter objects to his relation with the priest, the boy crams his mouth with cereal "for fear I might give utterance to . . . anger." And later, at the wake, the boy puts on an air of piety the reverse of his true feelings.

The boy's refusal of the biscuits and his initial refusal of sherry at the wake have been interpreted cleverly, but I think not accurately, as a refusal to partake of the sacraments, as his rejection of the Church.[2] However, in context, the boy actually rejects the secular sacraments of the women who assume an analogously priestly role, because, even though the priest is dead, the boy still savors the wine of the perverse sacraments they had previously celebrated together. He is not so much rejecting the Church, for in context this would be to achieve a joyful freedom: he is rejecting conventional experience, proffered to him by well-meaning old women who cannot provide him with a surrogate for the pleasant and vicious region where in imagination he lives with the old priest. The gesture of refusal is at the same time a gesture of allegiance.

The boy's devotion to a perverse relationship with the priest becomes clearer on investigation of the priest's character and his relation with the boy. Clearly the priest's paralysis, resulting from hemiplegic stroke, images his spiritual condition and, by synecdoche, that of Dublin in general, which Joyce referred to as "hemiplegia."[3] The disease follows an act which the priest interprets as a spiritual transgression. He had dropped and broken a chalice, which mishap "affected his mind" to the extent that shortly afterwards he had been discovered in the con-

[2] Ibid., pp. 85–86.
[3] Letter to Constantine P. Curran, n.d., 1904. *Letters*, Vol. I, p. 55.

fessional-box "wide-awake and laughing-like softly to himself."
The only direct explanation for the priest's behavior is Eliza's
assertion that "poor James was so nervous. . . ." She also says
that "he was too scrupulous always . . . The duties of the
priesthood was too much for him. And then his life was, you
might say, crossed." The apparently inadvertent dropping of
an empty chalice could not itself have accounted for the priest's
breakdown, but no cause beyond this act is directly given in
the story and the only explanation of the act itself is that he
was "nervous." The remote causes of the priest's "nervousness"
are hidden behind Eliza's mysterious assertion that his life had
been "crossed," and the no less enigmatic seconding of the
boy's aunt, "Yes . . . he was a disappointed man. You could
see that." Joyce has left the reader to conjecture from various
hints the priest's unfortunate background, and a substantial
conjecture is needed to explain the priest's mysterious hold on
the protagonist.

One imagines that the priest finds in the boy compensation
for a quest in which he had been mysteriously "disappointed,"
that thing unnamed in which he had been "crossed," frustrated
in some strong desire. Because of this lack of fulfillment "the
duties of the priesthood was too much for him." The boy thinks
early in the story of the word "gnomon" in connection with
"paralysis," with its obvious meaning and "simony" with its
somewhat less obvious meaning in context. Like most of the
Dubliners, the priest is a "gnomon"; he has not fulfilled himself
as a person, which means exactly that he has not achieved
union with that unique benefit which would have precluded
the necessity for speaking of him as "disappointed."[4] His relationship with the boy is a deflected quest for him: a surrogate
for true fulfillment.

The dropping of a chalice represents the penultimate stage
in a breaking of priestly commitment which relieves the priest

[4] A "gnomon" in geometry is a parallelogram with one corner removed:
a figure with something missing. Gerhard Friedrich has pointed out the
importance of "gnomon" as a sign for the general spiritual condition of
Joyce's Dubliners. "The Gnomonic Clue to James Joyce's *Dubliners*,"
Modern Language Notes, LXXII (June 1957), 421–24.

of a species of unfulfilling behavior: his breakdown in the confessional signals the final breaking of commitment. Afterwards a series of "strokes" gradually breaks his commitment to life itself and in his last days he is free to devote himself to the quasi-spiritual liaison with a sensitive boy. This relationship allows his frustrated desires to play out their last chance for fulfillment, only now in a soul-destroying way. The priestly role clearly did not suffice as a surrogate for disappointed expectation. The priest was obliged to slough off a role which was "too much for him" because it did not satisfy his quest. His later relationship with the boy substituted for what the priestly role had failed to satisfy.

There is about this peculiar relationship an odor of perversity because in his role as spiritual father and teacher the priest seduces the boy away from the enthusiasms of childhood into an attachment to the pleasantly vicious sweets of spiritual seduction in which there is apparently an element of erotic perversity, which is never overt. Though he was asked about it, Joyce was not explicit on this point. He wrote Stanislaus: "Roberts I saw again. He asked me very narrowly was there sodomy also in *The Sisters* [as in 'An Encounter'] and what was 'simony' and if the priest was suspended only for the breaking of the chalice."[5] Joyce does not answer the question, even in his letter to Stanislaus. But there is a hint at perversity in the boy's struggle to recall what came in the dream after his absolution of the priest: "I remembered that I had noticed long velvet curtains and a swinging lamp of antique fashion. I felt that I had been very far away, in some land where the customs were strange—in Persia, I thought. . . . But I could not remember the end of the dream." There is also a hint of perversity in the description of the priest smiling: "he used to uncover his big discoloured teeth and let his tongue lie upon his lower lip—a habit which had made me feel uneasy in the beginning of our acquaintance before I knew him well." Finally, the title, "The Sisters," refers not only to Nannie and Eliza, but to an effeminate relationship between the priest and his disciple.

[5] August 20, 1912, *Letters*, Vol. II, pp. 305–306.

There is little evidence that Joyce wants them to be thought of as engaging in overt sexuality; the physical disability of the priest and the social context probably preclude such an affair. More clear is the priest's sadistic posture, the boy's masochism. The priest derives pleasure from a relationship in which he can inflict the double pain of his revolting presence and his Jansenistic doctrine, for both of these exercise on the boy so mysteriously strong an attraction that he feels compelled to look on the loathsome work of physical and spiritual paralysis in spite of (or perhaps because of) his great fear. The boy feels attracted to the priest *because of* the pain he derives from the relationship. The pain stems from his desire to be paralyzed in the way of the priest: especially to be so tied up spiritually that determined action would be hindered by a legal system literally impossible to understand because of its infinitely casuistic character:

Sometimes he had amused himself by putting difficult questions to me, asking me what one should do in certain circumstances or whether such and such sins were mortal or venial or only imperfections. His questions showed me how complex and mysterious were certain institutions of the Church which I had always regarded as the simplest acts.

The boy discovers "the simplest acts" so complex that action is either impossible or fraught with terrible implications. This belief concerning action, linked as it is with the authority of the Church, is a statement of the spiritual paralysis which has destroyed the priest as a human and which, working on the boy, is likely to bring him to the same pass. The priest "had amused himself" in the act of infecting the boy with a paralytic doctrine, for apparently his relationship with the boy was a surrogate by which he could now get pleasure; and the boy falls victim to the pleasure of being seduced into a state of paralyzed passivity, that pleasant and vicious area in his soul.

The priest's heretical doctrine is not amusing. Implicitly Jansenistic, it derives especially from the first of the celebrated "Five Propositions" condemned by Innocent X in 1653. The first reads: "Some of God's commandments are impossible to just men who wish and strive [to keep them], considering the powers they actually have; the grace by which these precepts may become possible is also wanting."[6] The practical meaning of this proposition, and of Jansenism in general, Leon Cristiani explains as follows: "The first feature [of Jansenism] was a merciless doctrinal rigorism which removed all efficacy of human freedom in order to attribute everything to the action of grace. The second feature, not unconnected with the first, was a moral rigorism abounding with requirements of exacting severity."[7] The priest's irresistible hold on the boy is also explained in connection with the Jansenist doctrine of grace: as a priest he is a source of grace, and the second condemned proposition reads: "In the state of fallen nature, no one ever resists interior grace." These uncompromising words describe in theological language the relationship in "The Sisters."[8]

In his natural quest for fulfillment through pleasurable activity, the boy finds his quest converted into pleasure through painful inability to act: the realization and the prospect of the priest's paralysis appeal to the boy more strongly than the prospect of living warmth represented by "the tawny gold of a great bank of clouds," wistfully glimpsed on the way to the wake.

The boy seeks the characteristically human activities of knowledge and friendship; his relationship with the priest corrupts both activities and dehumanizes him. Gradually his quest for knowledge has been frustrated by the priest's corruption of his reason, for the priest's lessons infect his student with a paralyzing skepticism. The priest's disquisitions are neither speculative nor scientific but practical. His questioning and his

[6] *Cum Occasione*, May 31, 1653. Quoted in Leon Cristiani, "Jansenism, or the Third Reform," *Heresies and Heretics* (New York: Hawthorn Books, 1959), p. 108.

[7] Ibid., p. 106.

[8] In *Finnegans Wake*, Joyce describes Shem in relation to two heresies, the Albigensian and the Jansenistic: "swatting his deadbest to think what under the canopies of Jansens Chrest would any decent son of an Albiogenselman who had bin to an university think" (p. 173).

teaching are apparently taken up entirely with moral theology, which pertains to modes of action. But the boy tastes an even more bitter fruit in the corruption of his hunger for the activity of friendship: the paralysis of his capacity for human relationship, about which he has a significant revelation. He dimly realizes that the priest had used him for his own surrogate gains, for his own neurotic pleasure: and furthermore the boy realizes that he had used the priest for surrogate gains. They had used each other as substitute persons for unsatisfactory personal relations in the past. And this is why in his phantasm the boy smiles feebly "as though to absolve the simoniac of his sin."[9] The priest had "sold" his "spiritual gifts," in context his priestly knowledge and his sacramental role, for the perverse gain of hypnotic seduction. The boy "absolves" him because the seduction had filled his own personal need: the feeble smile, like that of the priest, is a smile of mutual understanding, mutual acquiescence, and mutual pleasure in a sado-masochistic system in which both persons get what they need, as is invariably the case in that series of sado-masochistic liaisons throughout *Dubliners*. A moral purpose of Joyce's writing is to free his compatriots (and perhaps himself) from their enslavement to sado-masochism. Thus, he wrote Grant Richards: "I believe that in composing my chapter of moral history in exactly the way I have composed it I have taken the first step towards the spiritual liberation of my country."[10]

The boy's quest for pleasure in a sado-masochistic relationship is a deflection of his search for freedom, for self-fulfillment, for the joy of life. He seeks both the relationship itself and, because he is troubled, he seeks an awareness about the nature of the relationship. Part of this is a wistful awareness of the *joie de vivre* which the surrogate replaces. Joyce expresses the boy's complex desire through a series of images and phantasms, some more obvious than others. The critic must illuminate this

[9] Julian B. Kay discusses the theme of simony in *Dubliners* in "Simony, the Three Simons, and Joycean Myth," *A James Joyce Miscellany*, ed. Marvin Magalaner, (New York: Gotham Book Mart, 1957).

[10] May 20, 1906. *Letters*, Vol. I, pp. 62–63.

image-structure and isolate from it a concept of the protagonist's quest. Joyce's method is to present those images conveying the underlying quest in a juxtaposition which suggests his evaluation. With its repulsive associations, "the heavy grey face of the paralytic" haunts "The Sisters." It is the most fearful and enticing image of quest. In relatively few images can the boy find untroubled satisfaction, and these never enchant him for long. During his bedtime phantasm he tries without success to shun the image of the gargoyle face by thinking of Christmas: his walk on the sunny side of the street looking at "theatrical advertisements," implying a life away from nightmare reality, and his later reflected vision of golden clouds are intermittent images. The images weigh towards the compulsively perverse and against the naturally attractive, which suggests the relative weight of perverse and normal motivation in "The Sisters." The reader's epiphany comes as he assesses the image force in the story. At the end when Eliza comments, "So then, of course, when they saw that, that made them think that there was something gone wrong with him," the reader perceives that the deflected quest is the main thing wrong with Dublin. Along with Joyce, we evaluate Dublin life. Carefully, we peer into Joyce's mirror and "think that there was something gone wrong."

HARRY STONE

Harry Stone has taught at the University of California at Los Angeles,
Northwestern University, and San Fernando Valley State College.
He is a noted authority on Charles Dickens and has published many
articles on that subject.

"ARABY"*AND THE WRITINGS
OF JAMES JOYCE

Love came to us in time gone by
    When one at twilight shyly played
And one in fear was standing nigh—
    For Love at first is all afraid.

We were grave lovers. Love is past
    That had his sweet hours many a one;
Welcome to us now at the last
    The ways that we shall go upon.
        —*Chamber Music*, XXX (written in 1904 or earlier)

And still you hold our longing gaze
With languorous look and lavish limb!
Are you not weary of ardent ways?
Tell no more of enchanted days.
        —*A Portrait of the Artist as a Young Man* (1904–14)

Lust, thou shalt not commix idolatry.
        —*Finnegans Wake* (1922–39)

"We walk through ourselves," says Stephen Dedalus in
Ulysses. Stephen is trying to show how Shakespeare, or for

Reprinted from the *Antioch Review*, Fall 1965, by permission of the
author and the publishers. Copyright © 1965 by the Antioch Press. This
selection comprises sections I–III, VI–VII of the original essay.

that matter how any artist (creator of "Dane or Dubliner"),
forever turns to the themes which agitate him, endlessly body-
ing forth the few crucial events of his life. "Every life is many
days, day after day," says Stephen. "We walk through ourselves, meeting robbers, ghosts, giants, old men, young men,
wives, widows, brothers-in-love. But always meeting ourselves."
Stephen's theory may be an ingenious *jeu d'esprit*—though
Joyce himself was heavily committed to such views. But whether
or not Stephen's words are appropriate to Shakespeare, they
are exactly appropriate to Joyce. In his writings, Joyce was
always meeting himself—in ways which must at times have
been beyond his conscious ordinance—and the pages of
"Araby" are witness to that fact.

For "Araby" preserves a central episode in Joyce's life, an
episode he will endlessly recapitulate. The boy in "Araby,"
like the youthful Joyce himself, must begin to free himself from
the nets and trammels of society. That beginning involves painful farewells and disturbing dislocations. The boy must dream
"no more of enchanted days." He must forgo the shimmering
mirage of childhood, begin to see things as they really are. But
to see things as they really are is only a prelude. Far in the
distance lies his appointed (but as yet unimagined) task: to
encounter the reality of experience and forge the uncreated
conscience of his race. The whole of that struggle, of course, is
set forth in *A Portrait of the Artist as a Young Man*. "Araby"
is the identical struggle at an earlier stage; "Araby" is a portrait
of the artist as a young boy.

II

The autobiographical nexus of "Araby" is not confined to the
struggle raging in the boy's mind, though that conflict—an
epitome of Joyce's first painful effort to see—is central and
controls all else. Many of the details of the story are also rooted
in Joyce's life. The narrator of "Araby"—the narrator is the boy
of the story now grown up—lived, like Joyce, on North Richmond Street. North Richmond Street is blind, with a detached
two-story house at the blind end, and down the street, as the

opening paragraph informs us, the Christian Brothers' school. Like Joyce, the boy attended this school, and again like Joyce he found it dull and stultifying. Furthermore, the boy's surrogate parents, his aunt and uncle, are a version of Joyce's parents: the aunt, with her forbearance and her unexamined piety, is like his mother; the uncle, with his irregular hours, his irresponsibility, his love of recitation, and his drunkenness, is like his father.

The title and the central action of the story are also autobiographical. From May fourteenth to nineteenth, 1894, while the Joyce family was living on North Richmond Street and Joyce was twelve, Araby came to Dublin. Araby was a bazaar, and the program of the bazaar, advertising the fair as a "Grand Oriental Fête," featured the name "Araby" in huge exotic letters, while the design as well as the detail of the program conveyed an ill-assorted blend of pseudo-Eastern romanticism and blatant commercialism. For one shilling, as the program put it, one could visit "Araby in Dublin" and at the same time aid the Jervis Street Hospital.

But the art of "Araby" goes beyond its autobiographical matrix. The autobiographical strands soon entwine themselves about more literary patterns and enter the fiction in dozens of unsuspected ways. For instance, embedded in "Araby" is a story, "Our Lady of the Hills," from a book that Joyce knew well, *The Celtic Twilight* (1893) by William Butler Yeats. "Our Lady of the Hills" tells how a pretty young Protestant girl walking through the mountains near Lough Gill was taken for the Virgin Mary by a group of Irish Catholic children. The children refused to accept her denials of divinity; to them she was "the great Queen of Heaven come to walk upon the mountain and be kind to them." After they had parted and she had walked on for half a mile, one of the children, a boy, jumped down into her path and said that he would believe she were mortal if she had a petticoat under her dress like other ladies. The girl showed the boy her two skirts, and the boy's dream of a saintly epiphany vanished into the mountain air. In his anguish, he cried out angrily, "Dad's a divil, mum's a divil, and I'm a divil, and you are only an ordinary lady." Then he "ran away sobbing."

Probably reverberating in "Araby" also are chords from one of Thomas De Quincey's most famous works, "Levana and Our Ladies of Sorrow." In "Levana," Our Lady of Tears (she bears the additional title "Madonna") speaks about the child who is destined to suffer and to see, a type of the inchoate artist:

"Lo! here is he whom in childhood I dedicated to my altars. This is he that once I made my darling. Him I led astray, him I beguiled, and from heaven I stole away his young heart to mine. Through me did he become idolatrous; and through me it was, by languishing desires, that he worshipped the worm, and prayed to the wormy grave. Holy was the grave to him; lovely was its darkness; saintly its corruption. Him, this young idolater, I have seasoned for thee, dear gentle Sister of Sighs!"

He who is chosen by the Ladies of Sorrow will suffer and be cursed; he will "see the things that ought *not* to be seen, sights that are abominable, and secrets that are unutterable," but he will also be able to read the great truths of the universe, and he will "rise again *before* he dies." In this manner, says Our Lady of Tears, we accomplish the commission we had from God: "to plague [the chosen one's] heart until we had unfolded the capacities of his spirit."

The ideas and images of "Levana" (witness the parody in *Ulysses*) had sunk deep into Joyce's imagination. His imagination had always sought out, always vibrated to, the Levanaesque constellation—a constellation that fuses religion, sexuality, idolatry, darkness, ascension, and art. "Araby," both in its central idea and its characteristic imagery—in the image of Mangan's sister, in the boy's blind idolatry, and in the boy's ultimate insight and dawning ascension—is cognate with "Levana."

Other literary prototypes also contribute to "Araby." In "Araby" as in Joyce's life, Mangan is an important name. In life

Mangan was one of Joyce's favorite Romantic poets, a little-known Irish poet who pretended that many of his poems were translations from the Arabic although he was totally ignorant of that language. Joyce championed him in a paper delivered as a Pateresque twenty-year-old before the Literary and Historical Society of University College, Dublin, and championed him again five years later, in a lecture at the Università Popolare in Trieste, as "the most significant poet of the modern Celtic world, and one of the most inspired singers that ever used the lyric form in any country." In "Araby" Mangan is the boy's friend, but, what is more important, Mangan's sister is the adored girl. In each lecture Joyce discussed Mangan's poetry in words which could serve as an epigraph for the boy's mute, chivalric love for Mangan's sister and for his subsequent disillusionment and self-disdain. In the latter lecture, Joyce described the female persona that Mangan is constantly adoring:

This figure which he adores recalls the spiritual yearnings and the imaginary loves of the Middle Ages, and Mangan has placed his lady in a world full of melody, of lights and perfumes, a world that grows fatally to frame every face that the eyes of a poet have gazed on with love. There is only one chivalrous idea, only one male devotion, that lights up the faces of Vittoria Colonna, Laura, and Beatrice, just as the bitter disillusion and the self-disdain that end the chapter are one and the same.

And one of Joyce's favorite poems by Mangan—a poem whose influence recurs in A Portrait of the Artist as a Young Man, Ulysses, and Finnegans Wake—is "Dark Rosaleen," a love paean to a girl who represents Ireland (Dark Rosaleen is a poetic name for Ireland), physical love, and romantic adoration. In "Araby" Joyce took Mangan's idealized girl as an embodiment of the artist's, especially the Irish artist's, relationship to his beloved, and then, combining the image of the girl with other resonating literary associations, wrote his own story of dawning, worshipful love.

III

It is easy to follow the external events of the story. A young boy becomes fascinated with his boyfriend's sister, begins to dwell on her soft presence, and eventually adores her with an ecstasy of secret love. One day the girl speaks to him—it is one of the few times they have ever exchanged a word—and asks him if he is going to Araby. She herself cannot go, she tells him, for she must participate in a retreat. The boy says if he goes he will bring her a gift. When he finally visits the bazaar he is disillusioned by its tawdriness and by a banal conversation he overhears, and he buys no gift. Instead he feels "driven and derided by vanity" and his eyes burn with "anguish and anger."

"Driven and derided," "anguish and anger"—these reactions seem far too strong. Indeed they seem pretentious when compared to the trivial disillusionment which caused them. And they are pretentious, certainly they are inappropriate, if related only to their immediate external causes. But the boy is reacting to much more than a banal fair and a broken promise. He is reacting to sudden and deeply disturbing insights. These insights are shared by the attentive reader, for by the end of "Araby" the reader has been presented with all that he needs in order to resolve the story's intricate harmony into its component motifs.

Most of those motifs, both personal and public, are sounded at once. The former tenant of the boy's house, a house stale with the smell of mustiness and decay, had been a priest who had died in the back drawing room. In a litter of old papers in a waste room behind the kitchen the boy has found a few damp-stained volumes: *The Abbot,* by Walter Scott, *The Devout Communicant,* and *The Memoirs of Vidocq."* The only additional information Joyce gives us about these books is that the boy liked the last volume best because "its leaves were yellow." The musty books and the boy's response to them are doubly and trebly meaningful. Joyce chose works that would objectify the themes of "Araby," works that would exemplify in the most blatant (yet unexpressed) manner the very confusions, veilings, and failures he was depicting in the priest and the boy. The books and their lurking incongruities help us arraign the priest and understand the boy. That the priest should leave a romance by Scott with a religious title that obscures the fact that it is the secular celebration of a worldly queen, Mary Queen of Scots, a queen enshrined in history as saint and harlot; a book of rules, meditations, anthems, and prayers for Holy Week by a Protestant clergyman named Abednego Seller, a clergyman who had written tracts against "Popish Priests," engaged in published controversy with a Jesuit divine, and was eventually relieved of his office; and a volume of lurid and often sexually suggestive memoirs by a notorious impostor, master of disguise, archcriminal, and police official— all this is a commentary on the priest and the religion he is supposed to represent. At the same time this literary debris objectifies the boy's confusions.

That Scott's unblemished romantic heroine, an idolized Catholic queen by the name of Mary, should also be (though not to Scott) a "harlot queen," a passionate thrice-married woman who was regarded by many of her contemporaries as the "Whore of Babylon," as a murderess who murdered to satisfy her lust— this strange dissonance, muted and obscured by Scott's presentation, is a version of the boy's strikingly similar and equally muted dissonances. That the dead priest's book of devotions is a Protestant manual by a man bearing the significant name Abednego Seller—a name which combines in equal parts ancient religious associations (in particular associations of refusing to worship a golden image and of a faith strong enough to withstand a fiery furnace) with an ironically incongruous modern surname that has to do with selling and commercialism— this juxtaposition, also, is appropriate to the boy: it typifies one of his fundamental confusions.

That Vidocq should escape from a prison hospital disguised in the stolen habit of a nun, a veil over his face; that he should then assist a good-natured curé in celebrating mass, pretending to make the signs and genuflections prescribed for a nun—this is a version of what the boy will do. That *The Memoirs* should also contain the history of a beauty "who seemed to have been created as a model for the divine Madonnas which sprang from the imagination of Raphael," whose eyes "gave expression to all the gentleness of her soul," and who had a "heavenly forehead" and an "ethereal elegance"—but who, from the age of fourteen, had been a debauched prostitute who was ultimately caught by the police because, in the midst of committing a robbery, she and her accomplice became utterly engrossed in fornicating with one another—this, also, is a version, a grotesque extension, of the boy's confusions. The boy does not know, cannot face, what he is. He gazes upon the things that attract or repel him, but they are blurred and veiled by clouds of romantic obfuscation: he likes *The Memoirs of Vidocq* best not because of what it is, a volume of exciting quasi-blasphemous criminal and sexual adventures, but because he finds its outward appearance, its yellowing leaves, romantically appealing. The boy, like the priest, or Vidocq's characters, or disguise-mad Vidocq himself, is, in effect, an impostor—only the boy is unaware of why he feels and acts as he does; the boy is an impostor through self-deception.

Joyce, in accordance with his practice throughout *Dubliners* (and for that matter, in accordance with his method throughout his writings) included these books so that we would make such generalizations about the priest and the boy. This is clear, not merely from his habitual usage in such matters or from the ironic significance of the books themselves, but from the highly directive import of the sentences which immediately follow these details. These sentences tell us that behind the boy's house was a "wild garden" containing a "central apple-tree"—images which strongly suggest a ruined Eden and Eden's forbidden central apple tree, a tree which has to do with man's downfall and his knowledge of good and evil: fundamental themes in "Araby." The last of the sentences is artfully inconclusive. "He had," concludes the narrator, "been a very charitable priest; in his will he had left all his money to institutions and the furniture of his house to his sister." Joyce's ambiguity suggests that the priest's charity may have been as double-edged as other details in the opening paragraphs. Yet the possibility of an incongruity here never occurs to the boy. As usual he fails to examine beneath the veneer of outward appearances; he fails to allow for the possibility of a less public, more cynical interpretation of the priest's charity. If this worldly priest had been so "very charitable" why, at his death, was he able to donate "all his money" to institutions? His charity, so far as we know about it, began at his death.

These and other ambiguously worded ironies had already been sounded by the three opening sentences of "Araby." Joyce begins by telling us that North Richmond Street is blind. That North Richmond Street is a dead end is a simple statement of fact; but that the street is blind, especially since this feature is given significant emphasis in the opening phrases of the story, suggests that blindness plays a role thematically. It suggests, as we later come to understand, that the boy also is blind, that he has reached a dead end in his life. Finally, we are told that the houses of North Richmond Street "conscious of decent lives within them, gazed at one another with brown imperturbable faces." These words, too, are ironic. For the boy will shortly discover that his own consciousness of a decent life within has been a mirage; the imperturbable surface of North Richmond Street (and of the boy's life) will soon be perturbed.

In these opening paragraphs Joyce touches all the themes he will later develop: self-deluding blindness, self-inflating romanticism, decayed religion, mammonism, the coming into man's inheritance, and the gulf between appearance and reality. But these paragraphs do more: they link what could have been the idiosyncratic story of the boy, his problems and distortions, to the problems and distortions of Catholicism and of Ireland as a whole. In other words, the opening paragraphs (and one or two other sections) prevent us from believing that the fault is solely in the boy and not, to some extent at least, in the world that surrounds him, and still more fundamentally, in the nature of man himself. . . .

VI

All women, for Joyce, are Eves: they tempt and they betray. He constantly fashions his women, fictional and real—Mangan's sister, Gretta, Mary Sheehy, Emma, Nora, Molly—into exemplars of this idea. By the same token, men, in their yearning to worship, contrive (perhaps even desire) their own betrayal and insure their own disillusionment. This paradox, which embodies Joyce's personal needs and experiences, is at the center of *Exiles*. It also helps shape *A Portrait, Ulysses,* and *Finnegans Wake*. In the latter work the notion is universalized and multiplied. One of the primal forms of woman in *Finnegans Wake* is woman as temptress. She is portrayed most clearly as Isabel, the daughter of HCE and Anna Livia, and as the Maggies or Magdalenes (who appear in dozens of permutations: maudelenian, Margareena, Marie Maudlin, etc.), the two girls who tempted HCE to his fall in Phoenix Park, and who are often merged with Isabel. This archetypal temptress and goddess, blending and changing in a flux of protean metamorphoses (she is also Issy, Issis, Ishtar, Isolde—as Isolde of Ireland, an embodiment of Ireland) is frequently referred to as "Ysold," "I sold," "Issabil," "eyesoult," and "eyesalt." As her godlike role and legendary names imply, she combines worshipful love and sexual appeal (Isolde), with inevitable commercialism and betrayal (I sold), with bitter grief and disillusionment (eyesalt) —the combination and progression we also find in "Araby."

What Joyce is saying in "Araby" becomes more precise as the details accumulate and fall into patterns. This second evocation of the carefully lit figure of Mangan's sister, now in the guise of the Madonna of the Silver Bracelet, is worth examining once more, this time in the context of what we have just been tracing:

> While she spoke she turned a silver bracelet round and round her wrist. . . . I was alone at the railings. She held one of the spikes, bowing her head towards me. The light from the lamp opposite our door caught the white curve of her neck, lit up her hair that rested

there and, falling, lit up the hand upon the railing. It fell over one side of her dress and caught the white border of a petticoat, just visible as she stood at ease.

This second evocation of Mangan's sister is again filled with strange harmonies. On the one hand the passage calls up Mary Magdalene and the Blessed Virgin Mary (both were present at the crucifixion) and soft overtones of a tender and dolorous *pietà*; one easily extracts and then extrapolates the appropriate images—the patient hand on the cruel spike, the gentle head bowed submissively, the mild neck arched in grief. But a co-equal and coordinate pattern in the scene is the harlotry associations of Mary Magdalene, who, in Catholic liturgy, is specifically associated with exotic Near Eastern imagery, brace-lets, and crossing the city in search of her love—all strong elements in "Araby"; while on the more personal level the name "Mary" is also the name of the girl Joyce regarded as his original "temptress" and "betrayer"—Mary Sheehy; and per-haps, at the same time, this "shady Mary" pattern is connected with the harlotry associations of still another Mary, the "harlot queen," Mary Queen of Scots, the heroine of the dead priest's book, *The Abbot*, who was executed in her petticoat. In any case, the negative pattern incorporated in the shadowy image of Mangan's sister combines hints of commercialism and sensu-ality with connotations of sexuality and betrayal—the turning and turning of the silver bracelet, the head bowing toward the boy, the white curve of the bare neck, the soft hair glowing in the light, the side of the dress accentuated by the dim glow, the white border of the petticoat just visible beneath the dress (one recalls the dream-shattering petticoat of the false Protestant madonna in "Our Lady of the Hills"), and the whole figure standing at ease in the dusk.

The boy now makes his pledge. "If I go," he says, "I will bring you something." The consequences of his pledge are immediately apparent. "What innumerable follies," writes the narrator in the very next sentence, "laid waste my waking and sleeping thoughts after that evening!" The shadowy "image" of Mangan's sister constantly comes between him and everything he undertakes; his schoolmaster, puzzled and then exasperated, hopes that he is "not beginning to idle"—a phrase which again, now punningly, underlines that the boy, like De Quincey's young boy, has indeed begun to worship false idols, that he is well on his way to Araby.

Araby—the very word connotes the nature of the boy's confusion. It is a word redolent of the lush East, of distant lands, Levantine riches, romantic entertainments, mysterious magic, "Grand Oriental Fêtes." The boy immerses himself in this incense-filled dream world. He tells us that "the syllables of the word *Araby* were called to me through the silence in which my soul luxuriated and cast an Eastern enchantment over me." That enchantment, or to put it another way, Near Eastern imagery (usually in conjunction with female opulence or romantic wish fulfillment), always excited Joyce. It reappears strongly in *Ulysses* in a highly intricate counterpoint, which is sometimes serious (Molly's Moorish attributes) and sometimes mocking (Bloom's dream of a Messianic Near Eastern oasis). But the boy in "Araby" always interprets these associations, no matter how disparate or how ambiguous they are, in one way: as correlatives of a baroquely beatific way of living. Yet the real, brick-and-mortar Araby in the boy's life is a bazaar, a market, a place where money and goods are exchanged. The boy is blind to this reality lurking beneath his enchanted dream. To the boy, his lady's silver bracelet is only part of her Eastern finery; his journey to a bazaar to buy her an offering is part of a romantic quest. But from this point on in the story the masquerading pretenses of the boy—and of his church, his land, his rulers, and his love—are rapidly underlined and brought into a conjunction which will pierce his perfervid dream world and put an end to "enchanted days."

The boy has arranged with his aunt and uncle that he will go to the bazaar on Saturday evening, that is, on the evening of the day specially set aside for veneration of the Virgin Mary. Saturday evening arrives but the boy's uncle is late from work and the boy wanders at loose ends through the empty upper reaches of his house. In the "high cold empty gloomy rooms" he begins his second vigil. Off by himself he feels liberated. He goes from room to room singing. Hidden, he watches his companions play and listens to their weakened, indistinct cries. Then he leans his forehead against a cool window pane and looks over at the "dark house" where Mangan's sister lives. "I may have stood there for an hour, seeing nothing but the brown-clad figure cast by my imagination, touched discreetly by the lamplight at the curved neck, at the hand upon the railings and at the border below the dress."

When he goes downstairs again he is brought back from the isolated world of his imagination to the ordinary world of his everyday life. He finds Mrs. Mercer sitting at the fire. "She was an old garrulous woman, a pawnbroker's widow, who collected used stamps for some pious purpose." The sentence is packed with ironic meaning. The old lady's name—Mercer, that is, merchandise, wares, a small-ware dealer—links her to the commercial focus of the story. That her husband was a pawnbroker sharpens this focus, introducing as it does commercialism in its most abhorrent form from the church's point of view—commercialism as usury. But that the church accepts, even lives on, this same commercialism is also made clear: for garrulous old Mrs. Mercer (another embodiment of Ireland) is a pious woman with pious purposes; ironically, she expresses her piety in good works that depend upon empty mechanical acquisitiveness: she collects used stamps. (One recalls, in this connection, the "pious purpose" of the actual Araby bazaar—to collect money for a hospital; and one also recalls that the "Wonderful" or "Perfumed" bazaar in *Ulysses*—the bazaar that allowed Bloom to gaze worshipfully under Gerty's skirts while a choir celebrated the Host and hymned the Virgin Mary—was an attempt to collect money for another "pious purpose," for a hospital named "Mercer's.") Joyce is saying, in effect, that everyday religion and piety in Ireland are based upon self-deluding and mindless materialism. When Mrs. Mercer's unexamined commercial religion is remembered in conjunction with the boy's and then the dead priest's (one recalls that the priest's book of heretical devotions was by a man named "Seller")—we get some idea of how insidiously mammonistic is Ireland's religious bankruptcy.

The boy will soon have some insight into this and other bankruptcies, but at the moment he is taut with frustrated anticipation. "I am afraid," says his aunt, when his uncle still fails to appear, "you may put off your bazaar for this night of Our Lord"—counterpointing "bazaar" and "Our Lord," money and religion. Then, at nine o'clock, the uncle finally returns, tipsy and talking to himself. He has forgotten the bazaar, and he tries to put the boy off, but the aunt insists that he give the boy money for the bazaar, and he finally agrees, after the boy tells him twice that he is going to Araby. The word "Araby" sets the uncle's mind working. He asks the boy if he knows *The Arab's Farewell to His Steed*, and as the boy leaves the room, the uncle is about to recite the opening lines of the poem to his wife. Those lines never appear in the story, but they are fraught with thematic significance:

My beautiful, my beautiful! that standeth meekly by,
With thy proudly-arched and glossy neck, and dark and fiery eye!
Fret not to roam the desert now with all thy wingèd speed;
I may not mount on thee again!—thou'rt sold, my Arab steed!

The notion of betrayal, of something loved and beautiful being sold for money, of something cherished and depended upon being lost forever, is central to what has already happened in "Araby" and what is about to take place. But the poem goes on with even greater cogency:

The stranger hath thy bridle-rein, thy master hath his gold;—
Fleet-limbed and beautiful, farewell!—thou'rt sold, my steed, thou'rt sold!

This cogency—turning the bridle reins over to a foreign master for money, saying farewell to a beautiful part of the past—has another and even more startling appropriateness. For the poem is by Caroline Norton, a great beauty and a member of a famous Irish family (her grandfather was Richard Brinsley

Sheridan), who was sued for divorce by her husband, the Hon. George Chapple Norton, on the grounds that she had committed adultery with Lord Melbourne, then Home Secretary but at the time of the suit in 1836 Prime Minister of Great Britain. As Home Secretary, Lord Melbourne had been the minister responsible for Ireland, and in 1833, while still Home Secretary, he had supported the Coercion Bill, a bill of great severity aimed at Irish nationalists. The trial which ensued— one of the most notorious in the nineteenth century—was used by Dickens in the breach-of-promise suit in *Pickwick*, by Thackeray in the Lord Steyne-Becky Sharp relationship in *Vanity Fair*, and by Meredith in some of the climactic scenes of *Diana of the Crossways*. The jury found for the defendants, but chiefly on grounds other than Caroline Norton's constancy. The defendants won after conclusive testimony was introduced showing that Norton had been the chief advocate of his wife's liaison with Lord Melbourne, that he had initiated and perpetuated the liaison as a means of advancing himself, and that he had brought suit only after he had suffered reverses in that advancement.

That an Irish woman as beautiful as Caroline Norton should have been sold by her husband for English preferments; that she should have been sold to the man who, in effect, was the English ruler of Ireland; that she, in turn, should have been party to such a sale; that this very woman, writing desperately for money, should compose a sentimental poem celebrating the traitorous sale of a beautiful and supposedly loved creature; and that this poem should later be cherished by the Irish (the uncle's recitation is in character, the poem was a popular recitation piece, it appears in almost every anthology of Irish poetry) —all this is patently and ironically appropriate to what Joyce is saying.

So also is the next scene in "Araby." This boy leaves his house on the way to Araby with a florin, a piece of silver money, clutched tightly in his hand. That Joyce, out of all the coins and combinations of coins available to him, chose to have the boy clutch a florin is doubly meaningful. The original florin, the prototype of all future coins bearing that name, was a gold coin, famed for its purity, minted in Florence in 1252. It received its name, "florin," that is, "flower," because, like many of its progeny, it bore a lily, the flower of Florence and of the Virgin Mary, on one side. On the other side it bore the figure of Saint John the Baptist in religious regalia, a man who gave his life rather than betray his religion. The florin the boy clutches, however, is a silver coin minted by the English with a head of Queen Victoria on one side and the Queen's coat of arms (including the conquered harp of Ireland) on the other. Owing to the fact that the customary "Dei Gratia, F.D." ("by the grace of God, defender of the faith") was omitted from the coin when originally issued in 1847, it became infamous as the "Godless and Graceless Florin" and aroused such a popular outcry that it had to be called in before the year was out. As a result, the Master of the Mint, a Roman Catholic, was dismissed, and a few years later a new but almost identical florin was issued with the usual motto. The malodorous genesis of the English coin, its association with a Catholic scapegoat, and the restitution of a motto which, from an Irish Catholic point of view, made the coin as idolatrous and offensive as the Godless version—all this is ideally suited to Joyce's purpose.

For the duped boy is now acting out his betrayal in the most emblematic way. We recall the intricate liturgy of his self-delusion. Despising the market place, he had summoned and protected the image of Mangan's sister as a holy chalice antithetical to all such worldly commerce; mistaking his impulses, he had transformed his sexual desires into prayers and praises for the Virgin, into worshipful Catholic devotions. That the boy who immersed himself in such ceremonious self-deception should be hastening to buy at a bazaar (where, incidentally, he will meet his English masters) and that he should be clutching an English florin, an alien and notorious silver coin sans Virgin's lily and sans Catholic saint but bearing instead symbols of his and Ireland's servitude and betrayal, is, of course, supremely ironic.

That irony continues and expands in what follows. It is Saturday night. The boy tells us that "the sight of streets thronged with buyers and glaring with gas recalled to me the purpose of my journey." The flaring streets "thronged with buyers" and the clutched silver coin call to the reader's mind a purpose far different from that which the boy thinks he is pursuing. The sights, the words, the Saturday evening, the silver florin, also recall that the last time the boy went into the flaring streets shopping through throngs of buyers on a Saturday night, he had said, speaking particularly of those buyers, "I imagined that I bore my chalice safely through a throng of foes." They recall also that Saturday is the day most particularly devoted to veneration of the Blessed Virgin Mary. We now see clearly what the boy bears through a throng of foes, what his chalice is: it is not the image of a mild spiritual madonna, it is money, the alien florin of betrayal—betrayal of his religion, his nation, his dream of supernal love; he, like his country, has betrayed himself for the symbolic piece of alien silver he clutches in his hand as he hurries on to Araby. We also begin to get a better notion of who the shadowy madonna is that he worships with such febrile spirituality. We recall that he is rushing head-long to a bazaar to buy his lady a token (he, too, is one of the throng of buyers), and then we recall how his madonna—could she be a false, sensual, materialistic madonna, a projection of his own complicated self-betrayal?—"turned a silver bracelet round and round her wrist."

The boy at last arrives at the large building which displays "the magical name" of *Araby*. In his haste to get into the closing bazaar, he passes through a shilling rather than a six-penny entrance, handing the gatekeeper his silver coin as he goes through the turnstile. The interior of the building is like a church. The great central hall, circled at half its height by a gallery, contains dark stalls, dim lights, and curtained, jar-flanked sanctuaries. Joyce wants us to regard this temple of commerce as a place of worship. "I recognised a silence," says the boy as he stands in the middle of the hall, "like that which pervades a church after a service." The service is, of course, the worship of mammon, and Joyce, by his use of religious imagery here and throughout the story, lets us see both that the money-changers are in the temple (if one looks at the bazaar as a correlative of the church), and that the really devout worship which goes on in Ireland now, goes on in the market place: the streets thronged with buyers, the shrill litanies of shopboys, the silver-braceleted madonnas, the churchlike bazaars. Even he who imagined that he bore his chalice safely through a throng of foes finds himself in the temple of the money-changers ready to buy. Shocked, and with growing awareness, the boy begins to realize where he is and what he is doing. In the half-dark hall, as the bazaar closes and the remaining lights begin to go out, he watches as two men work before a curtain lit overhead by a series of colored lamps upon which a commercial inscription is emblazoned. The two men "were counting money on a salver. I listened to the fall of the coins." The boy also has fallen. We recall the "wild garden" with its "central apple-tree," that the words "falling" and "fell" are crucial to the description of Mangan's sister during her epiphany before the boy, and that the word "fall" again recurs—again in connection with money—when the boy, in his penultimate action, an action reminiscent of how Judas let the silver of betrayal fall upon the ground after his contrition, allows "two pennies to fall against the sixpence" in his pocket as he finally turns to leave the bazaar. But right now the fallen boy is witnessing the counting of the collection before the sanctuary of this church of mammon (the curtain, the salver, the lamps, the inscription all suggest simultaneously the sanctuary of a Catholic church); he is listening to the music of this service of mammon, the clink of falling coins. The boy is so stupefied that he can remember only "with difficulty why [he] had come."

His shock and his disillusionment are not yet over. He sees a young saleslady standing at the door of one of the dark stalls. The reader, like the boy, instantly feels that he has viewed this scene before: the girl standing in the doorway, the dim lighting, the churchlike atmosphere. Then, suddenly, the reader realizes that the scene enforces a crucial juxtaposition; the waiting salesgirl is a parody of the boy's obsessive image of female felicity, she is a counterpart (an everyday, commercial counterpart) of Mangan's tenebrous sister. The boy looks steadily at this vulgar avatar of his longings; and then his other vision—his vision of a comely waiting presence, of a heavenly dolorous lady —dissolves and finally evaporates. The boy, at last, glimpses reality unadorned; he no longer deceives himself with his usual romanticizing. For the moment, at least, he truly sees. There before him stands a dull, drab, vacuous salesgirl; she is no mild Irish madonna, no pensive *pietà*, no mutely beckoning angel. He listens as she talks and laughs with two young gentlemen; the three of them have English accents:

> —O, I never said such a thing!
> —O, but you did!
> —O, but I didn't!
> —Didn't she say that?
> —Yes, I heard her.
> —O, there's a . . . fib!

This snippet of banal conversation is Joyce's, the boy's, and now the reader's epiphany—the word "epiphany" used here in Joyce's special literary sense of "a sudden spiritual manifestation, whether in the vulgarity of speech or of gesture or in a memorable phase of the mind itself"—and the conversation the boy overhears bears an unmistakable resemblance to a well-defined type of epiphany which Joyce recorded (bald exchanges of fatuous, almost incoherent conversation), several examples of which have survived. But what we have here is the epiphany surrounded by all that is needed to give it significance; the private *quidditas* has been transformed into a public showing forth; the artist, the priest of the eternal imagination, has transmuted (to paraphrase another of Joyce's religious metaphors) the daily bread of experience into the radiant body of everliving art.

For what the boy now sees, and what we now know he sees, is that his worshiped madonna is only a girl, like the ordinary girl who stands before him, that his interest in his madonna is akin to the gentlemen's interest in the young lady before

them, and that their pedestrian conversation about fibbing—
the very word is a euphemism for "lying"—is only a banal
version of his own intricate euphemisms, his own gorgeous
lying to himself. Like the Catholic boy in Yeats' "Our Lady of
the Hills," who sobs in anguish because his vision of a palpable
madonna must give way to the reality of an ordinary Protestant
girl, the boy in "Araby" can now also cry out angrily, "I'm a
divil, and you are only an ordinary lady."

That this ordinary lady is an English lady is another shatter-
ing part of the boy's painful epiphany. The English accents are
the accents of the ruling race, the foreign conquerors—Joyce
makes much of this notion in *A Portrait* and more in *Ulysses*—
and now the boy begins to understand that England, this
nation which rules over him, is quintessentially vulgar, the servant par excellence of mammon. England is one with Ireland
and Ireland's church, and the boy is one with all of these. He
has felt the first stirrings of desire and converted them into
masquerading religiosity; he has wanted to go shopping at a
bazaar and has told himself that he is making an enchanted
journey to fetch a chivalric token; he has been exposed to the
debased vulgarities of *The Memoirs of Vidocq* and has admitted
only that he liked its yellow pages. Yet he is no worse than the
rest of Ireland—its dead priests (part of a dying church), its
Mrs. Mercers, its faithless drunken surrogate fathers—and for
that matter, no worse than Ireland's rulers. Ireland and Ireland's
church, once appropriately imaged as a romantic lady or a sor-
rowful madonna, has now become cuckquean and harlot—she is
sold and sells for silver.

Joyce returned to this theme again and again, often with
startling repetitions of details and symbols. In *Ulysses*, for
example, Ireland appears personified not as a young girl, but
as an old milkwoman. She enters and leaves *Ulysses* in a page
or two, yet within that cramped space, and despite the vast difference, on the realistic level, between the role she must play
in *Ulysses* and the roles of those who appear in "Araby," Joyce
manages to associate her with many of the idiosyncratic features that characterize Ireland and Ireland's betrayal in "Araby."

In *Ulysses* the old milkwoman is depicted as "an immortal serving her conqueror [Haines, the Englishman] and her gay betrayer [Mulligan, the Irishman], their common cuckquean." Mulligan sings a song about her "hising up her petticoats"; she tells him she is ashamed she must speak in foreign accents; she is depicted "slipping the ring of the milkcan on her forearm" (the silver bracelet again); and she is paid by Mulligan with a silver florin.

VII

Other elements in "Araby" are also connected to patterns that transcend the immediate action. The two most crucial events in the story, the two vigils, harmonize with specific occasions in the Roman Catholic liturgy. The first vigil—the one in which Mangan's sister appears after the boy's invocation, "O love! O love!"—suggests the Vigil of the Epiphany. The most striking passage in that Vigil tells how "in those childish days of ours we toiled away at the schoolroom tasks which the world gave us, till the appointed time came"—a passage which is exactly appropriate to how the boy, after his first visitation or epiphany (that is, after Mangan's sister has appeared to him and directed him to Araby—just as in the original Epiphany an angel appeared to Joseph directing him to go from Egypt to Israel) feels about the schoolroom tasks ("child's play, ugly monotonous child's play") while he waits for the time of his journey to Araby. But the "appointed time" spoken of in the Vigil is the time of the journey to Israel and of the coming of the spirit of Jesus, not of a trip to Araby; it is the time when the spirit of Jesus cries out to a child, "Abba, Father," and he becomes no longer a child, a slave, but a son of God, entitled to "the son's right of inheritance." For the boy in "Araby" that cry and that inheritance turn out to be far different from what he believed them to be—he comes into a majority, but it is the disillusioning majority of the flesh, of all the sons of Adam, not of the spirit; he makes his journey, but it is a journey to Egypt, to Araby, to the market place, not back to the Holy Land.

These reverberating liturgical harmonies are continued in the boy's second vigil—the one he keeps during his long evening wait, and then during his journey to and sojourn in Araby. The connections here are with Holy Week (especially the Passion) and with Holy Saturday (the night before Easter Sunday). In "Araby" the trip to the bazaar takes place on a Saturday night; the boy's aunt refers to the Saturday night in question as "this night of Our Lord," an expression which can be applied to any Saturday (or Sabbath) night, but which calls up most particularly the pre-eminent Saturday "night of Our Lord," that is, Holy Saturday. The service appointed for this occasion is the Mass of Holy Saturday. This Mass, owing to its great beauty, and especially to the rich symbolism of the Tenebrae, haunted Joyce. (The whole of Book IV of *Finnegans Wake*, for example, takes place in the instant between Holy Saturday and Easter Sunday.) The Mass of Holy Saturday was the only Mass Joyce regularly tried to witness later in life, always leaving, however, before communion. Central to this Mass is the imagery of light and darkness, the extinguishing of the old lights and then the rekindling of new lights from new fire. On the other hand, prominent in the Passion is the notion of betrayal: Peter's lying threefold denial of Jesus, and Judas' selling of Jesus for thirty pieces of silver. The idea of profound betrayal, then the adumbration of awakening and rising, all combined with imagery of light and dark, and the whole counterpointed with liturgical overtones, informs the conclusion of "Araby."

The boy, for instance, comes to Araby with silver in his hand (with the idolatrous successor to the Godless Florin, it will be remembered); and he watches as the money of betrayal (his and his nation's) falls clinking on the salver. Like Peter's lying threefold denial of Jesus, the banal conversation about lying that the boy overhears also involves a threefold denial (the girl denies three times that she said what she is accused of saying). The foreign English accents continue the parallel, for Peter, like the English, is a foreigner, and his denials involve his accent. "Even thy speech betrays thee," he is told. When Peter recognized his betrayal (at the crowing of the cock) he "wept bitterly"; when the boy recognized his (at the call that the light was out) his "eyes burned with anguish and anger." In the service for Holy Saturday the lights are extinguished and then relit; in the service the boy witnesses there is no re-kindling, the boy merely gazes "up into the darkness." And yet, of course, here too a new light is lit; for though an old faith is extinguished, we witness a dawning.

These liturgical and religious parallels and disparities (one could list other much more subterranean ones: the story of Abednego is told *in extenso* in the Holy Saturday Mass, and Abednego Seller's heretical *Devout Communicant* is a manual for Holy Week), these parallels lie unobtrusively in the back-ground. They are not meant to be strictly or allegorically interpreted; they are meant to suggest, to hint, perhaps to con-dition. Unconsciously they tinge our associations and responses; they also harmonize with the more explicit motifs of the story.

The boy standing in front of the young lady's shadowy booth, listening to her bantering inanities, perceives all these signifi-cances only dimly. He is shocked, hurt, angered; but he intui-tively feels, and will later understand, what the reader already comprehends. Yet even in his dim awareness he is ready to make one decision. While still at the "dark entrance" of the young lady's stall, he tells her he is no longer interested in "her wares." He lets the two pennies fall against the sixpence in his pocket; he has come to buy, but he has not bought. Someone calls that the light is out. The light is indeed out. Like De Quincey's young boy, the boy in "Araby" has been ex-cluded from light, has worshiped the "lovely darkness" of the grave; he has (in the words of *Chamber Music*, XXX) been a "grave lover." But again like De Quincey's young boy, at last he has seen. He has risen again *before* he has died; he has begun to unfold "the capacities of his spirit." As *Chamber Music*, XXX, has it, he welcomes now "the ways that [he] shall go upon." For the boy has caught a glimpse of himself as he really is—a huddled, warring, confused paradox of romantic dreams, mistaken adorations, and mute fleshly cravings—and one por-tion of his life, his innocent, self-deluding childhood, is now

behind him. In his pride and arrogance, and, yes, in his purity
and innocence too, he had imagined that he bore his chalice
safely through a throng of foes; instead, he had rushed head-
long toward that which he thought he most despised. In a land
of betrayers, he had betrayed himself. But now he understands
some of this; and now, raising his eyes up into the blackness,
but totally blind no more—the Christlike fusion here of ascent,
of sight, and of agony is all-important—he can say, "Gazing up
into the darkness I saw myself as a creature driven and derided
by vanity; and my eyes burned with anguish and anger."

A. WALTON LITZ

A. Walton Litz, who has taught at Columbia and Princeton, is the author of two books on Joyce: *The Art of James Joyce* and *James Joyce*. Among his other publications are *Jane Austen: A Study of Her Artistic Development* and *Modern American Fiction: Essays in Criticism*.

"TWO GALLANTS"

"Two Gallants" was a late addition to *Dubliners*. When Joyce conceived and wrote the story, during the winter of 1905–1906, he had already submitted to the publisher Grant Richards a collection of twelve stories with a symmetrical design. As he explained to his brother Stanislaus, the first part of the collection was devoted to "stories of [his] childhood" ("The Sisters" —"An Encounter"—"Araby"); the second to "stories of adolescence" ("Eveline"—"After the Race"—"The Boarding House"); the third to "stories of mature life" ("Counterparts" —"Clay"—"A Painful Case"); while the last three tales ("Ivy Day in the Committee Room"—"A Mother"—"Grace") were "stories of public life in Dublin."[1] On February 22, 1906, Joyce sent "Two Gallants" to Grant Richards, with instructions that it "be inserted between *After the Race* and *The Boarding-House*,"[2] and in this position the new story greatly strengthened the second "aspect" of *Dubliners*, which would otherwise have

Reprinted from *James Joyce's* Dubliners: *Critical Essays*, edited by Clive Hart. © 1969 by Faber and Faber Ltd.

[1] *Letters of James Joyce*, Vol. II, p. 111 (September 1905). Although the arrangement of the stories within the four sections, as outlined in this letter, differs slightly from the final arrangement, Joyce's correspondence of early 1906 shows that the manuscript submitted to Grant Richards contained the stories in their final order. "A Little Cloud" and "The Dead" were added after "Two Gallants."

[2] Ibid., p. 130.

been the weakest part of the collection. The thirty-year-old Lenehan of "Two Gallants," poised between the younger Jimmy of "After the Race" and the rapidly aging Doran of "The Boarding House," completes Joyce's gallery of frustrated "adolescents"; as he wanders back and forth through the city he acts out the plight of young Dublin. "Two Gallants" provides an essential transition from the tawdry romanticism of "After the Race" to the claustrophobic reality of the later stories. The opening paragraph, with its twilight Dublin of "gaily coloured" crowds illuminated by pearl-white lamps, sustains the atmosphere of false glamour established in "After the Race"; but by the end of the story the lamplight has become an agent of harsh realism, revealing the greed and dishonesty which characterize life in "The Boarding House."

"Two Gallants" precipitated Joyce's long and frustrating quarrel with his publisher, since the printer refused to set up the story and thereby alerted Grant Richards to the "controversial" nature of the entire work. In the early stages of his negotiations with Joyce, when a compromise settlement still seemed possible, Grant Richards suggested that "Two Gallants" could be omitted without too much damage to the collection, "since originally it did not form part of your book."[3] Joyce's response to this suggestion leaves no doubt as to his admiration for the story, or its importance in the general design of *Dubliners*:

I have agreed to omit the troublesome word [bloody] in *Two Gallants*. To omit the story from the book would really be disastrous. It is one of the most important stories in the book. I would rather sacrifice *five* of the other stories (which I could name) than this one. It is the story (after *Ivy Day in the Committee-Room*) which pleases me most. I have shown you that I can concede something to your fears. But you cannot really expect me to mutilate my work![4]

[3] Robert Scholes, "Grant Richards to James Joyce," *Studies in Bibliography*, XVI, ed. Fredson Bowers (Charlottesville, Va.: University Press of Virginia, 1963), 147 (May 16, 1906).
[4] *Letters*, Vol. I, p. 62 (May 20, 1906).

Most readers of *Dubliners* would agree with Joyce's judgment. In contrast to the rather thin and stilted "After the Race," written nearly two years before, "Two Gallants" shows Joyce in full command of those techniques which made *Dubliners* a turning point in the development of English fiction. In "Two Gallants" we find that combination of scrupulously detailed realism and complex symbolism which is the hallmark of Joyce's achievement in the major stories of *Dubliners* and in *A Portrait of the Artist*.

"Two Gallants" is a cold-blooded assault upon the conditions of Irish society. Although in a moment of nostalgia for the attractions of Dublin life Joyce could say that *"Two Gallants*—with the Sunday crowds and the harp in Kildare Street and Lenehan—is an Irish landscape," he knew full well that he had described that landscape in the "style of scrupulous meanness" which was his special barrier against sentiment and regret.[5] Like most of the stories which deal with Dubliners of Joyce's own generation, "Two Gallants" goes beyond a dispassionate rendering of Irish "paralysis" and treats the theme of active betrayal. Joyce had left Dublin in 1904 feeling that he had been "betrayed" by many of his contemporaries, and his self-imposed exile in Pola and Trieste only intensified this feeling. When he came to write "Two Gallants" his sense of personal betrayal was at its height; only a short time before he had given full vent to his bitterness in a letter to his brother Stanislaus.

For the love of the Lord Christ change my curse-o'-God state of affairs. Give me for Christ' sake a pen and an ink-bottle and some peace of mind and then, by the crucified Jaysus, if I don't sharpen that little pen and dip it into fermented ink and write tiny little sentences about the people who betrayed me send me to hell. After all, there are many ways of betraying people.[6]

[5] Ibid., Vol. II, p. 166 (letter to Stanislaus Joyce, September 25, 1906). The phrase "style of scrupulous meanness" was used in a letter to Grant Richards, May 5, 1906 (ibid., p. 134).
[6] Ibid., p. 110 (September 1905).

This is the mood in which Joyce wrote his tale of Corley, "base betrayer," and the "disciple" Lenehan, and it is a tribute to his art that such personal rancor could be transmuted into analytic irony.

The fundamental irony of "Two Gallants" is suggested by the title. Corley, with his military bearing, and Lenehan, with his jaunty yachting cap and raincoat "slung over one shoulder in toreador fashion," are shabby replicas of the gallants of romantic fiction, and their exploitation of the young slavey is an ironic reversal of the conventional pattern of "gallant" behavior. But Joyce's irony cuts two ways, and the story strongly implies that the parasitic attitudes of Corley and Lenehan were always a part of the traditional code of gallantry. Stanislaus Joyce believed that "Two Gallants" was "inspired by a reference in Guglielmo Ferrero's *Europa Giovane* to the relations between Porthos and the wife of a tradesman in *The Three Musketeers*,"[7] presumably a reference to that episode in which Porthos uses his status as a "gallant" to obtain money from the procurator's wife (the wife, dazzled by Porthos' glamour, steals her husband's money in order to provide him with the trappings of a gallant). I have not been able to locate this particular passage in Ferrero's study, but Ferrero's scathing analysis of the essential hypocrisy of the "militaristic" mind must have struck a responsive chord in Joyce's imagination. Corley is persistently described in "militaristic" terms: the "son of an inspector of police" who had "inherited his father's frame and gait," he "always stared straight before him as if he were on parade," and "was often to be seen walking with policemen in plain clothes, talking earnestly." That Joyce considered this

[7] Richard Ellmann, *James Joyce* (New York: Oxford University Press, 1959), p. 228 fn. In his *L'Europa giovane* (1898) Ferrero surveyed the differences between the "Germanic" and "Latin" temperaments, devoting a long section to the various codes of sexual and romantic love. Joyce may have been drawn to Ferrero's work during 1905 and 1906 by his rather vague interest in socialist theory. Writing to Stanislaus on February 11, 1907, Joyce commented in passing that Ferrero gave him the idea for "Two Gallants" (*Letters*, Vol. II, p. 212).

alliance of "gallantry" and "militarism" central to his story may be seen in his shrewd comments on the prudish reactions of the English printer:

Dear Mr Grant Richards, I am sorry you do not tell me why the printer, who seems to be the barometer of English opinion, refuses to print *Two Gallants* and makes marks in the margin of *Counterparts*. Is it the small gold coin in the former story or the code of honour which the two gallants live by which shocks him? I see nothing which should shock him in either of these things. His idea of gallantry has grown up in him (probably) during the reading of the novels of the elder Dumas and during the performancc of romantic plays which presented to him cavaliers and ladies in full dress. But I am sure he is willing to modify his fantastic views. I would strongly recommend to him the chapters wherein Ferrero examines the moral code of the soldier and (incidentally) of the gallant. But it would be useless for I am sure that in his heart of hearts he is a militarist.[8]

The bracketing of Dumas and Ferrero in this letter would seem to confirm Stanislaus Joyce's account of the story's origin. In a very real sense, "Two Gallants" is an attack upon the stock responses and illusions of romantic fiction.

But if Joyce's aim, when he began to write "Two Gallants," was to expose the hypocrisy of a debased code of gallantry, he soon moved beyond this theme and wove into his story the leading motifs of *Dubliners*: political frustration, economic degradation, and spiritual paralysis. Next to "The Dead," "Two Gallants" is Joyce's most successful synthesis of the major themes of *Dubliners*, and—as we might expect from its place in the process of composition—it is resonant with echoes from the other stories. By the time Joyce came to write "Two Gallants," "A Little Cloud," and "The Dead," he had developed a prose style in which every detail of description contributes both to a local effect and to some larger artistic pattern. Thus the place-names along Lenehan's route, which are supplied with such frequency and precision that his progress can be easily traced on a map of Dublin, contribute a sense of local

[8] *Letters*, Vol. II, pp. 132–33 (May 5, 1906).

reality while at the same time emphasizing his lack of "direction" (like the warm summer air of the opening sentence, Lenehan "circulates" in the streets). Similarly, the information that Corley "aspirated the first letter of his name after the manner of Florentines" is both a detail of characterization and a suggestion that the relationship between Corley and the slavey is an ironic inversion of the truly "gallant" relationship between Dante and Beatrice. In reading "Two Gallants" we must be alive to every nuance of description and dialogue.

Most critics of "Two Gallants" agree that the harp in Kildare Street is the central emblem of the story, a point of intersection for the major symbolic motifs.[9]

They walked along Nassau Street and then turned into Kildare Street. Not far from the porch of the club a harpist stood in the roadway, playing to a little ring of listeners. He plucked at the wires heedlessly, glancing quickly from time to time at the face of each new-comer and from time to time, wearily also, at the sky. His harp, too, heedless that her coverings had fallen about her knees, seemed weary alike of the eyes of strangers and of her master's hands. One hand played in the bass the melody of *Silent, O Moyle*, while the other hand careered in the treble after each group of notes. The notes of the air throbbed deep and full.

The music of the harpist has no apparent effect on Corley, who moves toward his assignation with a solid tread that has "something of the conqueror" in it. But the melody haunts the more sensitive Lenehan, and once he is left alone the music breaks through to remind him of his loneliness.

His gaiety seemed to forsake him, and, as he came by the railings of the Duke's Lawn, he allowed his hand to run along them. The air which the harpist had played began to control his movements.

[9] See William T. Noon, *Joyce and Aquinas* (New Haven: Yale University Press, 1957), pp. 83–84; W. Y. Tindall, *A Reader's Guide to James Joyce* (New York: Farrar, Straus & Giroux, 1959), pp. 24–25; and especially Robert Boyle, " 'Two Gallants' and 'Ivy Day in the Committee Room,' " *James Joyce Quarterly*, I (Fall 1963), 3–6. Boyle convincingly demonstrates that the harp, and the verses of Moore's "Silent, O Moyle," are crucial elements in Joyce's symbolic structure.

His softly padded feet played the melody while his fingers swept a scale of variations idly along the railings after each group of notes.

Like the "Distant Music" which Gabriel Conroy hears in "The Dead," the sound of the harp works on Lenehan's subconscious and forces him to act out his own dumb existence. Under his "idle" hands the harp of passion and patriotism remains mute.

The significance of the harp, however, is not limited to its impact on Lenehan. The harp is a traditional symbol of Ireland's glorious past, and in his personification of the harp Joyce suggests Ireland's modern degradation: "heedless that her coverings had fallen about her knees, [she] seemed weary alike of the eyes of strangers and of her master's hands." The melody played on the harp is that of Thomas Moore's "The Song of Fionnuala," and the unsung words are a gloss on Joyce's story:

> Silent, O Moyle! be the roar of thy water,
> > Break not, ye breezes, your chain of repose,
> While, murmuring mournfully, Lir's lonely daughter
> > Tells to the night-star her tale of woes.
> When shall the swan, her death-note singing,
> > Sleep with wings in darkness furled?
> When will heaven, its sweet bell ringing,
> > Call my spirit from this stormy world?
>
> Sadly, O Moyle, to thy winter-wave weeping,
> > Fate bids me languish long ages away;
> Yet still in her darkness doth Erin lie sleeping,
> > Still doth the pure light its dawning delay.
> When will that day-star, mildly springing,
> > Warm our isle with peace and love?
> When will heaven, its sweet bell ringing,
> > Call my spirit to the fields above?

In his *Irish Melodies* Moore provided a note on the song's legendary background: "Fionnuala, the daughter of Lir, was by some supernatural power transformed into a swan, and condemned to wander, for many hundred years, over certain lakes and rivers in Ireland, till the coming of Christianity; when the

first sound of the mass bell was to be the signal of her release."[10]
Lir was the sea in Irish legend, and the plight of "Lir's lonely
daughter"—the plight of Ireland—may be linked to that of
the servant girl, whose "blue dress" and "white sailor hat"
remind us of the sea. Like the harp, the servant girl must submit to the "eyes of strangers" and obey "her master's hands."
We should also have in mind a tradition recounted in the
opening stanza of another of Moore's *Irish Melodies*, "The
Origin of the Harp":

> 'Tis believ'd that this Harp, which I wake now for thee,
> Was a Siren of old, who sung under the sea,
> And who often, at eve, thro' the bright waters rov'd,
> To meet on the green shore a youth whom she lov'd.

The sordid circumstances of the slavey's affair with Corley are
placed in tragic perspective by the romantic and patriotic
legends associated with the Irish harp.

Clearly the young slavey and the harp in Kildare Street
represent Ireland's contemporary subjugation, her lack of political independence and national pride. But these symbolic values
would have little impact on our imaginations if the human
situation were not so powerfully presented. The servant girl,
with her "frank rude health" and "unabashed blue eyes," stands
in ironic contrast to Lenehan. His "servility" has been a matter
of choice, hers was thrust upon her by economic necessity. In
her we see the peasant virtues—which Joyce, like Yeats, admired—corrupted by the pressures of Dublin life. She thinks of
Corley as a "gallant" belonging to another social class, one who

[10] Joyce was well acquainted with the legend. When his son, Giorgio,
was singing in New York in 1934 and 1935, Joyce gave him advice on a
repertoire, and one of his letters included a note on "Silent, O Moyle":
"Moyle is that part of the Irish Sea which is now called St George's
Channel. The three daughters of Lir (the Celtic Neptune and the original
of Shakespeare's King Lear) were changed into swans and must fly over
those leaden waters for centuries until the sound of the first Christian bell
in Ireland breaks the spell" [*Letters*, Vol. III, p. 341]. The song was
clearly one of Joyce's favorites. In February of 1935 he wrote to Giorgio:
"*Silent, O Moyle*. Of course I know it, IT. You must have heard me sing
it often. . . . It goes very well with a harp accompaniment" [ibid., p. 348].

could have "girls off the South Circular," and Corley plays upon this social advantage in his exploitation of her. On one level the story is clearly susceptible to a Marxist interpretation, and it is this grounding in social and economic reality which makes Joyce's elaborate symbolic performances possible. The sovereign which Corley holds up for Lenehan's admiration at the end of the story is, of course, a complex symbol, but it is first and most importantly a gold coin. Just as in "The Boarding House" Joyce never allows the theological connotations of the word "reparation" to dominate its economic meaning, so in "Two Gallants" Joyce keeps our attention fixed on the shabby social and economic circumstances of Dublin life.

Another important motif in "Two Gallants" is that of religious "betrayal." As Florence L. Walzl has pointed out, the story abounds in religious and liturgical references.[11] Lenehan's thrice-repeated "That takes the biscuit!" is not only a characteristic speech-pattern (he uses the same phrase in *Ulysses*) but a reference to the Sacred Host. His lonely meal may be an ironic inversion of the Last Supper, and at the end of the story he is presented to us as Corley's "disciple." The mass bell of Moore's song never rings. The colors of the slavey's dress are those of the Virgin. These references, and many less obvious ones explored by Miss Walzl, cannot be denied. Just as the futile pilgrimage of the little boy in "Araby" is given religious significance through a series of liturgical references, so the betrayal of the slavey takes on religious overtones. Communion among men has been broken in Dublin; what should have been a Love Feast has become a solitary and furtive meal. In their daily betrayals of themselves and others the citizens of Dublin are acknowledging their spiritual paralysis.

It is these carefully developed symbolic motifs which give "Two Gallants" that "unity of effect" we demand of a great short story. By deliberately withholding from the reader until his last paragraph the true purpose of Corley's mission, Joyce ran the danger of constructing a suspense story which would

[11] Florence L. Walzl, "Symbolism in Joyce's 'Two Gallants,' " *James Joyce Quarterly*, II (Winter 1965), 73–81.

depend, in the manner of Maupassant or even O. Henry, upon a "trick" ending. Certainly most readers of "Two Gallants" are shocked, upon first reading, by the revelation of the "small gold coin." But after this initial surprise has been assimilated the reader realizes that the dénouement was inevitable, that the entire story tends toward this shocking conclusion. The gold coin—probably stolen, like the cigars, from the servant girl's employer—is a final symbol of debased "gallantry," but it is also a fitting climax to the related motifs of Ireland's political, economic, and spiritual degradation. It is a true epiphany, a showing forth of hidden reality, and like all of Joyce's epiphanies it is wholly dependent upon its context.

The symbolic motifs in "Two Gallants" which we have been discussing may appear to be obvious and even mechanical, but within the living form of the story they are unobtrusive. Much more obvious upon first reading are Joyce's careful modulations of mood and atmosphere. The story opens with a description of the Sunday streets which matches the jaunty mood of the two gallants.

The grey warm evening of August had descended upon the city and a mild warm air, a memory of summer, circulated in the streets. The streets, shuttered for the repose of Sunday, swarmed with a gaily coloured crowd. Like illumined pearls the lamps shone from the summits of their tall poles upon the living texture below which, changing shape and hue unceasingly, sent up into the warm grey evening air an unchanging unceasing murmur.

Soon, however, the appearance of a "large faint moon circled with a double halo" brings the thought of rain to Lenehan, and perhaps of something more: "He watched earnestly the passing of the grey web of twilight across its face." As the twilight fades into darkness, and the moon is obscured by rain-clouds, Lenehan's thoughts darken. After Corley has departed with the girl his mind turns in upon itself.

He was tired of knocking about, of pulling the devil by the tail, of shifts and intrigues. He would be thirty-one in November. Would he never get a good job? Would he never have a home of his own?

He thought how pleasant it would be to have a warm fire to sit by and a good dinner to sit down to. He had walked the streets long enough with friends and with girls. He knew what those friends were worth: he knew the girls too. Experience had embittered his heart against the world. But all hope had not left him. He felt better after having eaten than he had felt before, less weary of his life, less vanquished in spirit. He might yet be able to settle down in some snug corner and live happily if he could only come across some good simple-minded girl with a little of the ready.

But Lenehan cannot escape from the aimless life of the streets, which is all we see of Dublin in this story; and by the time ten o'clock arrives his earlier jauntiness has given way to anxiety and suspicion. The romantic moon of illusion has vanished. Perhaps, he thinks, Corley will betray him as he has betrayed the girl. As the first drops of rain begin to fall Lenehan witnesses Corley's return, but by now he feels that his own sense of failure must be assuaged through Corley's success. The old tone of camaraderie is gone, and a "note of menace" enters his voice as he demands an answer: "Did you try her?"

These parallels between Lenehan's moods and the changing tones of Joyce's "Irish landscape" should remind us that "Two Gallants" is, above all else, Lenehan's story. We see Corley only from the outside; we know what he says and does, and how he looks, but not how he feels. It is this external presentation which makes Corley such a menacing and inhuman figure, the true embodiment of a perverted code of gallantry. In the case of Lenehan, however, we are given a record of his inner life, and our sympathy is inevitably elicited by the pathetic aspects of his existence. As he whiles away the time during Corley's absence, we begin to share his prurient interest in Corley's affair, until at the end of the story we are as anxious as Lenehan to know the truth: "Did it come off? . . . Did you try her?" And when the "small gold coin" is revealed, we are likely to feel—to the extent of our interest in Corley's mission —that we too have been his "disciples." In "Two Gallants" Joyce shows as little pity for his readers as he does for his characters.

ROBERT SCHOLES

Professor of English at the University of Iowa, Robert Scholes has also taught at the University of Virginia. He is the author of *The Cornell Joyce Collection: A Catalogue*; co-editor with Richard Kain of *The Workshop of Daedalus*; and co-author with Robert Kellogg of *The Nature of Narrative*. His latest publication is *The Fabulators*, a study of recent experimental fiction.

"COUNTERPARTS" AND THE METHOD OF *DUBLINERS*

"Counterparts" offers us, in its title and in its plan, a major clue to the whole structure of *Dubliners*—to the almost musical fabric of themes and variations on the people of Dublin which Joyce has so carefully arranged for us. The title of this story suggests both the harmonious balance of counterpointed musical parts and the anonymous interchangeability of cogs in a great machine. In the story itself, Mr. Alleyne bullies the shiftless Farrington, and Farrington bullies the hapless Tom. The Farringtons—father and son—are counterparts as unlovely victims. But Farrington and Mr. Alleyne are counterparts as abusers of authority. And beyond this story, the brutal Farrington's return to his wifeless home and whining son is the counterpart of Little Chandler's encounter with *his* tiny son in the previous story, "A Little Cloud." Similarly, Gallaher in that story is related to Weathers in "Counterparts," representing an alien London world which challenges and in some sense defeats Dublin as the Englishman Routh defeats Jimmy Doyle at cards in "After the Race." From story to story we can trace strand after strand of such linkages. The "gallant" Corley with his slavey's coin in his palm is connected by a thread of counterpointed irony to Lily, the caretaker's bitter daughter (in "The

Reprinted from *James Joyce's* Dubliners: *Critical Essays*, edited by Clive Hart. © 1969 by Faber and Faber Ltd.

Dead"), with Gabriel Conroy's clumsily bestowed but well-intended coin clutched in her hands. Gabriel cannot, of course, compensate Lily for a world full of Corleys and Lenehans, and that is part of the irony, but the connection of the coins enriches our perspective on these events and other similar ones with many shades of thought and feeling beyond simple irony. Connections like these, multiplied many times over, are the principal means by which Joyce has blended his separate stories into an imposing portrait of a city and a whole race of people. Not just details, but details alive with echoes and resonances, make these Dubliners vibrate with significance for us.

Farrington himself, waiting for a tram with twopence in his pocket after his evening of frustration, reminds us of the boy in "Araby," with eightpence in *his* pocket and a fourpenny train ride home ahead of him: both are "driven and derided" by similar but separate vanities, even as they are frustrated financially. The finances of "Counterparts"—so carefully accounted for—remind us of the astonishing role petty cash plays in so many of these stories. The pettiness of Dublin life as Joyce presents it here is in part a response to the pressures of financial distress on a pretentious gentility. The "gallant" Lenehan, "glancing warily up and down the street" lest he should be seen entering a cheap eating house and thereby lose another iota of his remnant of status, is a typical figure in this shabby-genteel society. Even in the upper reaches of Joyce's resolutely middle-class spectrum, Mrs. Kearney ("A Mother") grimly struggles for the extra shilling that makes a pound a guinea; and Gabriel Conroy, casting about for a safe subject to cover his sexual embarrassment, mentions to Gretta the surprising return of a pound he had lent Freddy Malins. The question "And how does he knock it out?" which Mr. O'Connor asks Mr. Henchy in "Ivy Day," referring to the disreputable Father Keon, is a great question for many of these Dubliners. M'Coy's stratagem (in "Grace"), of borrowing (and presumably pawning or selling) valises, echoes the "gallant" Lenehan's adroit manner in sponging. And Weathers's trick of ordering costly Irish and Apollinaris at Farrington's expense makes Farrington think of him as a "sponge," soaking up the precious six shillings he has obtained by pawning his watch. In story after story, we find ourselves counting shillings and pence. Farrington, insisting on six shillings for his watch instead of the five offered him ("a crown"), is typical of many of these Dubliners in that he has much more trouble "knocking it out" than modern citizens of affluent societies and welfare states can readily appreciate.

The financial stagnation which contributes to the musty odor Joyce felt he had achieved in *Dubliners* has *its* counterpart in the city's spiritual paralysis. The paralyzed priest of "The Sisters" is a counterpart to the Blessed Margaret Mary Alacoque —the paralytic saint who presides over Eveline Hill's failure of nerve and loss of faith in her beloved at the North Wall. In "Counterparts" Farrington's wife seeks "at the chapel" a consolation which is the counterpart of that Farrington seeks in the pub (where a waiter is called a curate); and little Tom Farrington vainly calls on Mary the Intercessor to save him from the wrath of a father who is definitely not in heaven. Maria, the virgin of "Clay," appears on the page following Tom's invocation, but she is a Peacemaker who cannot even reconcile her own brothers; and—though a virgin—she is not blessed but victimized by her celibacy: flustered by an inebriated "colonel-looking gentleman," she loses her plumcake; and confronted with the marriage verse of "I dreamt that I dwelt" she makes a revealing Freudian slip by omitting it. But nobody tells her about "her mistake." Maria's spinsterhood, the counterpart of Mr. Duffy's purposeful but destructive chastity in "A Painful Case," is ironically related to the bad marriage forced upon Bob Doran in "The Boarding House"—partly through economic and religious pressure. (Its badness is confirmed by his reappearance in *Ulysses* as a hopeless drunkard.) It also reminds us of the other marriages we see, including that of the Farringtons: well-matched counterparts in that she "bullied her husband when he was sober and was bullied by him when he was drunk." A puritanical religion of senseless rigidity insists upon a destructive chastity or impossible marriages for these Dubliners, and it often combines neatly with powerful financial pressures to add to their worldly torments. These two motifs blend into a symphony of simony in "Grace," where Father Purdon encourages commerce between Christ and Mammon, reducing the spiritual life to the bland mathematics of book-keeping.

In a letter to his wife, Joyce once explained that he, like other Irish writers, was trying to "create a conscience" for his race. This phrase, which he also gave to his character Stephen Dedalus at the end of A *Portrait*, has much to do with these stories. Why, we must ask, should people need to have a conscience created for them—especially a people so conspicuously religious as the Irish? Joyce felt—and his letters support the evidence of the works themselves—that it was precisely their religious orthodoxy, combined with other sorts of "belatedness," that made the Irish so conscienceless. They had turned over the moral responsibility for their lives to their confessors and religious leaders. Thus their ability to react sensitively to moral problems, to make ethical discriminations—to use their consciences—had atrophied. In *Dubliners* he offered his countrymen his own counterpart to St. Ignatius's *Spiritual Exercises*. The evaluation of motive and responsibility in these stories— the histories of "painful" cases for the most part—must inevitably lead the reader beyond any easy orthodoxy. These case histories encourage us to exercise our spirits, develop our consciences: to accept the view that morality is a matter of individual responses to particular situations rather than an automatic invocation of religious or ethical rules of thumb. And though Joyce's own race—the Irish—were first in his mind, he was certainly addressing all of us. Nothing is easier than to slip into the habit of invoking formulae instead of making judgments. New orthodoxies always arise to replace the old. All the rebellious prophets tend to become saints in time—as the history of Freudian ethical thought shows so clearly. But Joyce's cases always bring us back to individuality. In entering the world of *Dubliners* we all acknowledge our Irishness. As Martin Cunningham so complacently puts it, "we're a nice collection of scoundrels, one and all." But what *we* must see—precisely what Mr. Cunningham does not—is that it is our moral complacency that *makes* us scoundrels. Because the spiritual life is an art and not a science, because it is rich and subtle beyond all orthodox formulae, only art can begin to do it justice.

Joyce's art has the necessary delicacy. Not only does he develop a formidable structure of interconnections, making of his cases a unified portrait of a city; he also presents each of these cases with an exquisite control of tone. Inviting us to consider and evaluate, he guides our responses without coercing them; he allows us freedom of response but suggests an order in which some responses are more valuable than others. These stories do justice to the complexity of moral evaluation without denying its possibility. Even Farrington, as crude and simple as any character in the book, is presented with a patient attention to detail that makes him worthy of our interest and prevents us from dismissing his brutality as too banal to require any consideration from us. Joyce's care in such matters is well worth our investigation, for by studying the texture of his work we can begin to appreciate the extent to which his range and power as a writer derive from a delicacy of feeling which manifests itself through his special linguistic gifts. In all his work, Joyce has shown an amazing ability at the fundamental task of poetic or imaginative writing, putting the right words in the right order to do his subject the most justice. And even in a story like "Counterparts"—a simple episode in the life of a crude man—we can, if we look carefully, discover the sources of Joyce's literary strength.

We can, for example, note such a simple thing as the way the narrator of this tale refers to the central character. In the office scenes we learn Farrington's name through its use by Mr. Alleyne. But to the narrator—and hence to us—he is just "the man": "The man muttered"—"The man entered"—"The man stared"—"The man recognized"—"The man drank"—"The man went"—"The man glanced"—"The man returned"—

"The man listened"—"The man got up"—"The man answered"—"The man glanced." So many simple declarative sentences beginning with "The man." Why? What is their effect? The effect—which is worked for us without our being especially aware of how it is managed—is to give us a keen sense of the dull routine of Farrington's existence: of the extent to which he is in his work merely a replaceable cog in a mechanical operation—that sort of counterpart. Calling him "the man" emphasizes both his dullness and his plain brutal masculinity. And the repetitious sentence pattern drums into our heads the dull round of the man's workaday existence which has certainly helped to brutalize him; just as in the larger pattern of the story the man's bullying of his son shows us the brutalizing process at work upon the coming generation.

After work Farrington becomes more human. He is still sometimes called "the man" but he is mainly "he" (as he occasionally was before). In the pawn shop he is reduced to his contractual status—"the consignor held out for six shillings"— but finally, in the pub, he is given by the narrator for the first time the dignity of being referred to as "Farrington." When Nosey Flynn stands "Farrington a half-one," Farrington has achieved—temporarily—a human individuality which persists until O'Halloran's closing "one little smahan more" concludes the evening's festivities. After that we hear his name no more. He is, when we next see him, waiting for his tram, not even "the" man but "a" man: "A very sullen-faced man stood . . ." And in the closing scene we have—as the narrator refers to them—not Farrington and Tom but "the man" and "the little boy," as father and son are reduced by Joyce's distancing conclusion to the general outlines of bully and victim.

In this small matter we can see how Joyce's selection of words and sentence-patterns has conveyed to us the whole rhythm of Farrington's life in the course of presenting a few episodes from it. By such subtle means Joyce makes us aware of the quality of Dublin life in all these stories. It is an important part of his method that he guide us rather than coerce us in such matters. In the early story "Araby" the boy hears his uncle come home: "I heard him talking to himself and heard the hallstand rocking when it had received the weight of his overcoat. I could interpret these signs." The uncle has been drinking, but we are not told so directly. Like the boy himself we must "interpret these signs." This is Joyce's way in story after story. We must interpret for ourselves, but the signs are meaningful, making some interpretations better than others. In the work of interpretation, sifting and weighing details, listening carefully for the various tones of irony and pathos, we develop and refine our consciences.

That this *is* indeed Joyce's way is borne out by some interesting revisions he made in "Counterparts" between its first completion in July 1905 and the time it appeared in print. Here are the earlier and later versions of a passage from the pub scene:

1.

Farrington said he wouldn't mind having the far one and began to smile at her but when Weathers offered to introduce her he said "No," he was only chaffing because he knew he had not money enough. She continued to cast bold glances at him and changed the position of her legs often and when she was going out she brushed against his chair and said "Pardon!" in a Cockney accent.

2.

Farrington's eyes wandered at every moment in the direction of one of the young women. There was something striking in her appearance. An immense scarf of peacock-blue muslin was wound round her hat and knotted in a great bow under her chin; and she wore bright yellow gloves, reaching to the elbow. Farrington gazed admiringly at the plump arm which she moved very often and with much grace; and when, after a little time, she answered his gaze he admired still more her large dark brown eyes. The oblique staring expression in them fascinated him. She glanced at him once or twice and, when the party was leaving the room, she brushed against his chair and said *O, pardon!* in a London accent. He watched her leave the room in the hope that she would look back at him, but he was disappointed.

The revisions were undertaken in part because a potential publisher felt that there might be objections to the sexual frankness of the passage (though it seems tame enough now). But in undertaking them Joyce must have agreed that the passage was too outspoken—not that it was too frank but that it told the reader too much and did not allow him to infer enough. The narrator of the first version conveys all too clearly his disdain for the "bold" glances and "Cockney accent" of the woman. In the second version we are closer to Farrington's point of view. We register the impression on him of her graceful arms and fascinating eyes, the alien allure of a "London accent." By putting us into closer and more sympathetic touch with Farrington's point of view here, Joyce makes it harder for us to take a merely disdainful attitude toward Farrington. We have enough information to make up our minds about the behavior of all concerned. We can form our own impression of the "striking" blue and yellow outfit worn by the woman, and we can make the easy inference from London to Cockney. But we must do it ourselves, and we must do it with full awareness of how real and exotic is the appeal of this creature for Farrington. We can see Joyce growing as a writer and a man in this revision, broadening his range of sympathy and refining his control of irony, moving toward the richness of vision which makes his later work such a rewarding challenge for the thoughtful reader. Joyce invites us to judge Farrington, but he insists that we first understand him and feel his situation—that we see the connections between him and his counterparts in all the other stories who feel the appeal of an exotic feminine otherness, including Gabriel Conroy, whose situation is so rooted in Joyce's own biography, and the boy in "Araby," who is so clearly a counterpart of the young Stephen Dedalus.

Joyce's way, then, as illustrated in this story, is to give us much food for interpretation and put the work of interpretation squarely upon us. He gives us the maximum of conscience-creating labor by inviting us to participate with him in the creative process. To become the ideal reader of *Dubliners* each of us must accept this complicity. Between the mind of the reader and the mind of the artist these stories can flower fully and achieve their richest shape. The opportunity—and the challenge—offered us is that of becoming, in our own small way, Joyce's counterparts.

RICHARD ELLMANN

Richard Ellmann, Professor of English at Yale University, has taught at Harvard and Northwestern Universities. He has edited Joyce's letters, and his authoritative biography, *James Joyce*, won the 1959 National Book Award for nonfiction. He has also edited *My Brother's Keeper*, by Stanislaus Joyce, and is the co-editor with Ellsworth Mason of *The Critical Writings of James Joyce*. His other books include *The Identity of Yeats* and *Yeats: The Man and the Masks*. He is currently at work on a study of Oscar Wilde.

THE BACKGROUNDS
OF "THE DEAD"

The silent cock shall crow at last. The west shall shake the east awake. Walk while ye have the night for morn, lightbreakfastbringer. . . .

—Finnegans Wake, p. 473

The stay in Rome had seemed purposeless, but during it Joyce became aware of the change in his attitude toward Ireland and so toward the world. He embodied his new perceptions in "The Dead." The story, which was the culmination of a long waiting history, began to take shape in Rome, but was not set down until he left the city. The pressure of hints, sudden insights, and old memories rose in his mind until, like King Midas's barber, he was compelled to speech.

Although the story dealt mainly with three generations of his family in Dublin, it drew also upon an incident in Galway in 1903. There Michael ("Sonny") Bodkin courted Nora Barnacle; but he contracted tuberculosis and had to be confined to bed. Shortly afterwards Nora resolved to go to Dublin, and Bodkin stole out of his sickroom, in spite of the rainy weather, to sing to her under an apple tree and bid her good-by. In Dublin Nora soon learned that Bodkin was dead, and when she met Joyce she was first attracted to him, as she told a sister, because he resembled Sonny Bodkin.[1]

Joyce's habit of ferreting out details had made him conduct minute interrogations of Nora even before their departure from Dublin. He was disconcerted by the fact that young men before him had interested her. He did not much like to know that her heart was still moved, even in pity, by the recollection of the boy who had loved her. The notion of being in some sense in rivalry with a dead man buried in the little cemetery at Oughterard was one that came easily, and gallingly, to a man of Joyce's jealous disposition. It was one source of his complaint to his Aunt Josephine Murray that Nora persisted in regarding him as quite similar to other men she had known.[2]

A few months after expressing this annoyance, while Joyce and Nora Barnacle were living in Trieste in 1905, Joyce received another impulsion toward "The Dead." In a letter Stanislaus happened to mention attending a concert of Plunket Greene, the Irish baritone, which included one of Thomas Moore's *Irish Melodies* called "O, Ye Dead!"[3] The song, a dialogue of living and dead, was eerie enough, but what impressed Stanislaus was that Greene rendered the second stanza, in which the dead answer the living, as if they were whimpering for the bodied existence they could no longer enjoy:

> It is true, it is true, we are shadows cold and wan;
> And the fair and the brave whom we loved on earth are gone;
> But still thus ev'n in death,
> So sweet the living breath
> Of the fields and the flow'rs in our youth we wandered o'er,
> That ere, condemn'd, we go
> To freeze, 'mid Hecla's snow,
> We would taste it awhile, and think we live once more!

[1] Letter to me from Mrs. Kathleen Barnacle Griffin.
[2] See p. 222 of this biography.
[3] S. Joyce, "The Background to 'Dubliners,' " *Listener*, LI (March 25, 1954), 526–7.

James was interested and asked Stanislaus to send the words, which he learned to sing himself. His feelings about his wife's dead lover found a dramatic counterpart in the jealousy of the dead for the living· in Moore's song: it would seem that the living and the dead are jealous of each other. Another aspect of the rivalry is suggested in *Ulysses*, where Stephen cries out to his mother's ghost, whose "glazing eyes, staring out of death, to shake and bend my soul, . . . to strike me down," he cannot put out of mind: "No, mother. Let me be and let me live."[4] That the dead do not stay buried is, in fact, a theme of Joyce from the beginning to the end of his work; Finnegan is not the only corpse to be resurrected.

In Rome the obtrusiveness of the dead affected what he thought of Dublin, the equally Catholic city he had abandoned, a city as prehensile of its ruins, visible and invisible. His head was filled with a sense of the too successful encroachment of the dead upon the living city; there was a disrupting parallel in the way that Dublin, buried behind him, was haunting his thoughts. In *Ulysses* the theme was to be reconstituted, in more horrid form, in the mind of Stephen, who sees corpses rising from their graves like vampires to deprive the living of joy. The bridebed, the childbed, and the bed of death are bound together, and death "comes, pale vampire, through storm his eyes, his bat sails bloodying the sea, mouth to her mouth's kiss."[5] We can be at the same time in death as well as in life.[6]

By February 11, 1907, after six months in Rome, Joyce knew in general what story he must write. Some of his difficulty in beginning it was due, as he said himself, to the riot in Dublin over *The Playboy of the Western World*. Synge had followed the advice of Yeats that Joyce had rejected, to find his inspiration in the Irish folk, and had gone to the Aran Islands. This old issue finds small echoes in the story. The nationalistic Miss

---

[4] *Ulysses* (New York: Vintage Books, 1961), p. 10.

[5] Ibid., p. 48.

[6] The converse of this theme appears in *Ulysses* (p. 115), when Bloom, walking in Glasnevin, thinks, "They are not going to get me this innings. Warm beds: warm fullblooded life."

Ivors tries to persuade Gabriel to go to Aran (where Synge's *Riders to the Sea* is set), and when he refuses twits him for his lack of patriotic feeling. Though Gabriel thinks of defending the autonomy of art and its indifference to politics, he knows such a defense would be pretentious, and only musters up the remark that he is sick of his own country. But the issue is far from settled for him.

"The Dead" begins with a party and ends with a corpse, so entwining "funferal" and "funeral" as in the wake of Finnegan. That he began with a party was due, at least in part, to Joyce's feeling that the rest of the stories in *Dubliners* had not completed his picture of the city. In a letter of September 25, 1906, he had written his brother from Rome to say that some elements of Dublin had been left out of his stories: "I have not reproduced its ingenuous insularity and its hospitality, the latter 'virtue' so far as I can see does not exist elsewhere in Europe." He allowed a little of this warmth to enter "The Dead." In his speech at the Christmas party Gabriel Conroy explicitly commends Ireland for this very virtue of hospitality, though his expression of the idea is distinctly after-dinner: "I feel more strongly with every recurring year that our country has no tradition which does it so much honour and which it should guard so jealously as that of its hospitality. It is a tradition that is unique as far as my experience goes (and I have visited not a few places abroad) among the modern nations." This was Joyce's oblique way, in language that mocked his own, of beginning the task of making amends.

The selection of details for "The Dead" shows Joyce making those choices which, while masterly, suggest the preoccupations that mastered him. Once he had determined to represent an Irish party, the choice of the Misses Morkans' as its location was easy enough. He had already reserved for *Stephen Hero* a Christmas party at his own house, a party which was also to be clouded by a discussion of a dead man. The other festive occasions of his childhood were associated with his hospitable great-aunts Mrs. Callanan and Mrs. Lyons, and Mrs. Callanan's daughter Mary Ellen, at their house at 15 Usher's Island, which was also known as the "Misses Flynn school."[7] There every year the Joyces who were old enough would go, and John Joyce carved the goose and made the speech. Stanislaus Joyce says that the speech of Gabriel Conroy in "The Dead" is a good imitation of his father's oratorical style.[8]

In Joyce's story Mrs. Callanan and Mrs. Lyons, the Misses Flynn, become the spinster ladies, the Misses Morkan, and Mary Ellen Callanan becomes Mary Jane. Most of the other party guests were also reconstituted from Joyce's recollections. Mrs. Lyons had a son Freddy, who kept a Christmas card shop in Grafton Street.[9] Joyce introduces him as Freddy Malins, and situates his shop in the less fashionable Henry Street, perhaps to make him need that sovereign Gabriel lent him. Another relative of Joyce's mother, a first cousin, married a Protestant named Mervyn Archdale Browne, who combined the profession of music teacher with that of agent for a burglary insurance company. Joyce keeps him in "The Dead" under his own name. Bartell d'Arcy, the hoarse singer in the story, was based upon Barton M'Guckin, the leading tenor in the Carl Rosa Opera Company. There were other tenors, such as John McCormack, whom Joyce might have used, but he needed one who was unsuccessful and uneasy about himself; and his father's often-told anecdote about M'Guckin's lack of confidence furnished him with just such a singer as he intended Bartell d'Arcy to be.

The making of his hero, Gabriel Conroy, was more complicated. The root situation, of jealousy for his wife's dead lover, was of course Joyce's. The man who is murdered, D. H. Lawrence has one of his characters say, desires to be murdered;[10] some temperaments demand the feeling that their friends and sweethearts will deceive them. Joyce's conversation often returned to the word "betrayal,"[11] and the entangled innocents

[7] Interview with Mrs. May Joyce Monaghan, 1953.
[8] He excepts the quotation from Browning, but even this was quite within the scope of the man who could quote Vergil when lending money to his son. (See p. 316 of this biography.)
[9] Interview with Mrs. Monaghan.
[10] Birkin in *Women in Love*.
[11] Information from Professor Joseph Prescott.

whom he uses for his heroes are all aspects of his conception of himself. Though Gabriel is less impressive than Joyce's other heroes, Stephen, Bloom, Richard Rowan, or Earwicker, he belongs to their distinguished, put-upon company.

There are several specific points at which Joyce attributes his own experiences to Gabriel. The letter which Gabriel remembers having written to Gretta Conroy early in their courtship is one of these; from it Gabriel quotes to himself the sentiment, "Why is it that words like these seem to me so dull and cold? Is it because there is no word tender enough to be your name?" These sentences are taken almost directly from a letter Joyce wrote to Nora in 1904.[12] It was also Joyce, of course, who wrote book reviews, just as Gabriel Conroy does, for the *Daily Express*. Since the *Daily Express* was pro-English, he had probably been teased for writing for it during his frequent visits to the house of David Sheehy, M.P. One of the Sheehy daughters, Kathleen, may well have been the model for Miss Ivors, for she wore that austere bodice and sported the same patriotic pin.[13] In Gretta's old sweetheart, in Gabriel's letter, in the book reviews and the discussion of them, as well as in the physical image of Gabriel with hair parted in the middle and rimmed glasses, Joyce drew directly upon his own life.

His father was also deeply involved in the story. Stanislaus Joyce recalls that when the Joyce children were too young to bring along to the Misses Flynns' party, their father and mother sometimes left them with a governess and stayed at a Dublin hotel overnight instead of returning to their house in Bray.[14] Gabriel and Gretta do this too. Gabriel's quarrels with his mother also suggest John Joyce's quarrels with his mother, who never accepted her son's marriage to a woman of lower station.[15] But John Joyce's personality was not like Gabriel's; he had no doubts of himself, in the midst of many failures he was full of self-esteem. He had the same unshakable confidence as

[12] At Cornell.
[13] Interview with Mrs. Mary Sheehy Kettle, 1953.
[14] *My Brother's Keeper* (New York: The Viking Press, 1958), p. 38.
[15] See p. 17 of this biography.

his son James. For Gabriel's personality there is among Joyce's friends another model.[16] This was Constantine Curran, sometimes nicknamed "Cautious Con." He is a more distinguished man than Joyce allows, but Joyce was building upon, and no doubt distorting, his memories of Curran as a very young man. That he has Curran partly in mind is suggested by the fact that he calls Gabriel's brother by Curran's first name Constantine, and makes Gabriel's brother, like Curran's, a priest.[17] Curran has the same high color and nervous, disquieted manner as Gabriel, and like Gabriel he has traveled to the Continent and has cultivated cosmopolitan interests. Curran, like Conroy, married a woman who was not a Dubliner, though she came from only as far west as Limerick. In other respects he is quite different. Gabriel was made mostly out of Curran, Joyce's father, and Joyce himself. Probably Joyce knew there was a publican on Howth named Gabriel Conroy; or, as Gerhard Friedrich has proposed,[18] he may have borrowed the name from the title of a Bret Harte novel. But the character, if not the name, was of his own compounding.[19]

Joyce now had his people, his party, and something of its development. In the festive setting, upon which the snow keeps offering a different perspective until, as W. Y. Tindall suggests,[20] the snow itself changes, he develops Gabriel's private tremors, his sense of inadequacy, his uncomfortable insistence on his small pretensions. From the beginning he is vulnerable; his well-meant and even generous overtures are regularly checked. The servant girl punctures his blithe assumption that everyone is happily in love and on the way to the altar. He is

[16] Interview with S. Joyce, 1953.

[17] Suggested to me by Professor Vivian Mercier.

[18] Gerhard Friedrich, "Bret Harte as a Source for James Joyce's 'The Dead,'" *Philological Quarterly*, XXXIII (October 1954), 442–44.

[19] The name of Conroy's wife Gretta was borrowed from another friend, Gretta (actually Margaret) Cousins, the wife of James H. Cousins. Since Joyce mentioned in a letter (to Stanislaus Joyce, February 1907) at the same time that he was meditating "The Dead," the danger of becoming "a patient Cousins," this family was evidently on his mind.

[20] W. Y. Tindall, *The Literary Symbol* (New York: Columbia University Press, 1955), p. 227.

not sure enough of himself to put out of his head the slurs he has received long ago; so in spite of his uxorious attitude towards Gretta he is a little ashamed of her having come from the west of Ireland. He cannot bear to think of his dead mother's remark that Gretta was "country cute," and when Miss Ivors says of Gretta, "She's from Connacht, isn't she?" Gabriel answers shortly, "Her people are." He has rescued her from that bog. Miss Ivors's suggestion, a true Gaelic Leaguer's, that he spend his holiday in the Irish-speaking Aran Islands (in the west) upsets him; it is the element in his wife's past that he wishes to forget. During most of the story, the west of Ireland is connected in Gabriel's mind with a dark and rather painful primitivism, an aspect of his country which he has steadily abjured by going off to the Continent. The west is savagery; to the east and south lie people who drink wine and wear galoshes.

Gabriel has been made uneasy about this attitude, but he clings to it defiantly until the ending. Unknown to him, it is being challenged by the song, "The Lass of Aughrim." Aughrim is a little village in the west not far from Galway. The song has a special relevance; in it a woman who has been seduced and abandoned by Lord Gregory comes with her baby in the rain to beg for admission to his house. It brings together the peasant mother and the civilized seducer, but Gabriel does not listen to the words; he only watches his wife listening. Joyce had heard this ballad from Nora; perhaps he considered also using Tom Moore's "O, Ye Dead" in the story, but if so he must have seen that "The Lass of Aughrim" would connect more subtly with the west and with Michael Furey's visit in the rain to Gretta. But the notion of using a song at all may well have come to him as the result of the excitement generated in him by Moore's song.

And now Gabriel and Gretta go to the Hotel Gresham, Gabriel fired by his living wife and Gretta drained by the memory of her dead lover. He learns for the first time of the young man in Galway, whose name Joyce has deftly altered from Sonny or Michael Bodkin to Michael Furey. The new name implies, like the contrast of the militant Michael and the amiable Gabriel, that violent passion is in her Galway past, not in her Dublin present. Gabriel tries to cut Michael Furey down. "What was he?" he asks, confident that his own profession of language teacher (which of course he shared with Joyce) is superior; but she replies, "He was in the gasworks," as if this profession was as good as any other. Then Gabriel tries again, "And what did he die of so young, Gretta? Consumption, was it?" He hopes to register the usual expressions of pity, but Gretta silences and terrifies him by her answer, "I think he died for me."[21] Since Joyce has already made clear that Michael Furey was tubercular, this answer of Gretta has a fine ambiguity. It asserts the egoism of passion, and unconsciously defies Gabriel's reasonable question.

Now Gabriel begins to succumb to his wife's dead lover, and becomes a pilgrim to emotional intensities outside of his own experience. From a biographical point of view, these final pages compose one of Joyce's several tributes to his wife's artless integrity. Nora Barnacle, in spite of her defects of education, was independent, unself-conscious, instinctively right. Gabriel acknowledges the same coherence in his own wife, and he recognizes in the west of Ireland, in Michael Furey, a passion he has himself always lacked. "Better pass boldly into that other world, in the full glory of some passion, than fade and wither dismally with age," Joyce makes Gabriel think. Then comes that strange sentence in the final paragraph: "The time had come for him to set out on his journey westward." The cliché runs that journeys westward are towards death, but the west has taken on a special meaning in the story. Gretta Conroy's west is the place where life had been lived simply and passionately. The context and phrasing of the sentence sug-

[21] Adaline Glasheen has discovered here an echo of Yeats's nationalistic play, *Cathleen ni Houlihan* (1902), where the old woman who symbolizes Ireland sings a song of "yellow-haired Donough that was hanged in Galway." When she is asked, "What was it brought him to his death?" she replies, "He died for love of me; many a man has died for love of me." I am indebted to Mrs. Glasheen for pointing this out to me.

gest that Gabriel is on the edge of sleep, and half-consciously accepts what he has hitherto scorned, the possibility of an actual trip to Connaught. What the sentence affirms, at last, on the level of feeling, is the west, the primitive, untutored, impulsive country from which Gabriel had felt himself alienated before; in the story, the west is paradoxically linked also with the past and the dead. It is like Aunt Julia Morkan who, though ignorant, old, grey-skinned, and stupefied, seizes in her song at the party "the excitement of swift and secure flight."

The tone of the sentence, "The time had come for him to set out on his journey westward," is somewhat resigned. It suggests a concession, a relinquishment, and Gabriel is conceding and relinquishing a good deal—his sense of the importance of civilized thinking, of Continental tastes, of all those tepid but nice distinctions on which he has prided himself. The bubble of his self-possession is pricked; he no longer possesses himself, and not to possess oneself is in a way a kind of death. It is a self-abandonment not unlike Furey's, and through Gabriel's mind runs the imagery of Calvary. He imagines the snow on the cemetery at Oughterard, lying "thickly drifted on the crooked crosses and headstones, on the spears of the little gate, on the barren thorns." He thinks of Michael Furey who, Gretta has said, died for her, and envies him his sacrifice for another kind of love than Christ's. To some extent Gabriel too is dying for her, in giving up what he has most valued in himself, all that holds him apart from the simpler people at the party. He feels close to Gretta through sympathy if not through love; now they are both past youth, beauty, and passion; he feels close also to her dead lover, another lamb burnt on her altar, though she too is burnt now; he feels no resentment, only pity. In his own sacrifice of himself he is conscious of a melancholy unity between the living and the dead.

Gabriel, who has been sick of his own country, finds himself drawn inevitably into a silent tribute to it of much more consequence than his spoken tribute to the party. He has had illusions of the rightness of a way of life that should be outside of Ireland; but through this experience with his wife he grants a kind of bondage, of acceptance, even of admiration to a part of the country and a way of life that are most Irish. Ireland is shown to be stronger, more intense than he. At the end of A *Portrait of the Artist*, too, Stephen Dedalus, who has been so resolutely opposed to nationalism, makes a similar concession when he interprets his departure from Ireland as an attempt to forge a conscience for his race.

Joyce did not invent the incidents that conclude his story, the second honeymoon of Gabriel and Gretta which ends so badly. His method of composition was very like T. S. Eliot's, the imaginative absorption of stray material. The method did not please Joyce very much because he considered it not imaginative enough, but it was the only way he could work. He borrowed the ending for "The Dead" from another book. In that book a bridal couple receive, on their wedding night, a message that a young woman whom the husband jilted has just committed suicide. The news holds them apart, she asks him not to kiss her, and both are tormented by remorse. The wife, her marriage unconsummated, falls off at last to sleep, and her husband goes to the window and looks out at "the melancholy greyness of the dawn." For the first time he recognizes, with the force of a revelation, that his life is a failure, and that his wife lacks the passion of the girl who has killed herself. He resolves that, since he is not worthy of any more momentous career, he will try at least to make her happy. Here surely is the situation that Joyce so adroitly recomposed. The dead lover who comes between the lovers, the sense of the husband's failure, the acceptance of mediocrity, the resolve to be at all events sympathetic, all come from the other book. But Joyce transforms them. For example, he allows Gretta to kiss her husband, but without desire, and rarefies the situation by having it arise not from a suicide but from a memory of young love. The book Joyce was borrowing from was one that nobody reads any more, George Moore's *Vain Fortune*; but Joyce read it,[22] and in his

[22] He evidently refreshed his memory of it when writing "The Dead," for his copy of *Vain Fortune*, now at Yale, bears the date "March 1907."

youthful essay, "The Day of the Rabblement," overpraised it as "fine, original work."[23]

Moore said nothing about snow, however. No one can know how Joyce conceived the joining of Gabriel's final experience with the snow. But his fondness for a background of this kind is also illustrated by his use of the fireplace in "Ivy Day," of the streetlamps in "Two Gallants," and of the river in *Finnegans Wake*. It does not seem that the snow can be death, as so many have said, for it falls on living and dead alike, and for death to fall on the dead is a simple redundancy of which Joyce would not have been guilty. For snow to be "general all over Ireland" is of course unusual in that country. The fine description: "It was falling on every part of the dark central plain, on the treeless hills, falling softly upon the Bog of Allen and, farther westward, softly falling into the dark mutinous Shannon waves," is probably borrowed by Joyce from a famous simile in the twelfth book of the *Iliad*, which Thoreau translates:[24] "The snowflakes fall thick and fast on a winter's day. The winds are lulled, and the snow falls incessant, covering the tops of the mountains, and the hills, and the plains where the lotus-tree grows, and the cultivated fields, and they are falling by the inlets and shores of the foaming sea, but are silently dissolved by the waves." But Homer was simply describing the thickness of the arrows in the battle of the Greeks and Trojans; and while Joyce seems to copy his topographical details, he uses the image here chiefly for a similar sense of crowding and quiet pressure. Where Homer speaks of the waves silently dissolving the snow, Joyce adds the final detail of "the mutinous Shannon waves" which suggests the "Furey" quality of the west. The snow that falls upon Gabriel, Gretta, and Michael Furey, upon the Misses Morkan, upon the dead singers and the living, is mutuality, a sense of their connection with each other, a sense that none has his being alone. The partygoers prefer dead

[23] *The Critical Writings of James Joyce*, ed. Ellsworth Mason and Richard Ellmann (New York: Viking, 1959), p. 71.
[24] Professor Walter B. Rideout kindly called my attention to the similarity of these passages.

singers to living ones, the wife prefers a dead lover to a live lover.

The snow does not stand alone in the story. It is part of the complex imagery that includes heat and cold air, fire, and rain, as well as snow. The relations of these are not simple. During the party the living people, their festivities, and all human society seem contrasted with the cold outside, as in the warmth of Gabriel's hand on the cold pane. But this warmth is felt by Gabriel as stuffy and confining, and the cold outside is repeatedly connected with what is fragrant and fresh. The cold, in this sense of piercing intensity, culminates in the picture of Michael Furey in the rain and darkness of the Galway night.

Another warmth is involved in "The Dead." In Gabriel's memory of his own love for Gretta, he recalls incidents in his love's history as stars, burning with pure and distant intensity, and recalls moments of his passion for her as having the fire of stars. The irony of this image is that the sharp and beautiful experience was, though he has not known it until this night, incomplete. There is a telling metaphor: he remembers a moment of happiness, standing with Gretta in the cold, looking in through a window at a man making bottles in a roaring furnace, and suddenly calling out to the man, "Is the fire hot?" The question sums up his naïve deprivation; if the man at the furnace had heard the question, his answer, thinks Gabriel, might have been rude; so the revelation on this night is rude to Gabriel's whole being. On this night he acknowledges that love must be a feeling which he has never fully had.

Gabriel is not utterly deprived. Throughout the story there is affection for this man who, without the sharpest, most passionate perceptions, is yet generous and considerate. The intense and the moderate can meet; intensity bursts out and declines, and the moderated can admire and pity it, and share the fate that moves both types of mankind towards age and death. The furthest point of love of which Gabriel is capable is past. Furey's passion is past because of his sudden death. Gretta is perhaps the most pitiful, in that knowing Furey's passion, and being of his kind, she does not die but lives to wane in Gabriel's way; on this night she too is fatigued, not beautiful, her clothes lie crumpled beside her. The snow seems to share in this decline; viewed from inside at the party, it is desirable, unattainable, just as at his first knowledge of Michael Furey, Gabriel envies him. At the end as the partygoers walk to the cab the snow is slushy and in patches, and then, seen from the window of the hotel room, it belongs to all men, it is general, mutual. Under its canopy, all human beings, whatever their degrees of intensity, fall into union. The mutuality is that all men feel and lose feeling, all interact, all warrant the sympathy that Gabriel now extends to Furey, to Gretta, to himself, even to old Aunt Julia.

In its lyrical, melancholy acceptance of all that life and death offer, "The Dead" is a linchpin in Joyce's work. There is that basic situation of cuckoldry, real or putative, which is to be found throughout. There is the special Joycean collation of specific detail raised to rhythmical intensity. The final purport of the story, the mutual dependency of living and dead, is something that he meditated a good deal from his early youth. He had expressed it first in his essay on Mangan in 1902, when he spoke already of the union in the great memory of death along with life;[25] even then he had begun to learn like Gabriel that we are all Romes, our new edifices reared beside, and even joined with, ancient monuments. In *Dubliners* he developed this idea. The interrelationship of dead and living is the theme of the first story in *Dubliners* as well as of the last; it is also the theme of "A Painful Case," but an even closer parallel to "The Dead" is the story, "Ivy Day in the Committee Room." This was in one sense an answer to his university friends who mocked his remark that death is the most beautiful form of life by saying that absence is the highest form of presence. Joyce did not think either idea absurd. What binds "Ivy Day" to "The Dead" is that in both stories the central agitation derives from a character who never appears, who is dead, absent. Joyce wrote Stanislaus that Anatole France had given him the idea for both

[25] *The Critical Writings*, p. 83.

stories.[26] There may be other sources in France's works, but a possible one is "The Procurator of Judaea." In it Pontius Pilate reminisces with a friend about the days when he was procurator in Judaea, and describes the events of his time with Roman reason, calm, and elegance. Never once does he, or his friend, mention the person we expect him to discuss, the founder of Christianity, until at the end the friend asks if Pontius Pilate happens to remember someone of the name of Jesus, from Nazareth, and the veteran administrator replies, "Jesus? Jesus of Nazareth? I cannot call him to mind." The story is overshadowed by the person whom Pilate does not recall; without him the story would not exist. Joyce uses a similar method in "Ivy Day" with Parnell and in "The Dead" with Michael Furey.

In *Ulysses* the climactic episode, *Circe*, whirls to a sepulchral close in the same juxtaposition of living and dead, the ghost of his mother confronting Stephen, and the ghost of his son confronting Bloom. But Joyce's greatest triumph in asserting the intimacy of living and dead was to be the close of *Finnegans Wake*. Here Anna Livia Plurabelle, the river of life, flows toward the sea, which is death; the fresh water passes into the salt, a bitter ending. Yet it is also a return to her father, the sea, that produces the cloud which makes the river, and her father is also her husband, to whom she gives herself as a bride to her groom. Anna Livia is going back to her father, as Gabriel journeys westward in feeling to the roots of his fatherland; like him, she is sad and weary. To him the Shannon waves are dark and mutinous, and to her the sea is cold and mad. In *Finnegans Wake* Anna Livia's union is not only with love but with death; like Gabriel she seems to swoon away.

That Joyce at the age of twenty-five and -six should have written this story ought not to seem odd. Young writers reach their greatest eloquence in dwelling upon the horrors of middle age and what follows it. But beyond this proclivity which he shared with others, Joyce had a special reason for writing the story of "The Dead" in 1906 and 1907. In his own mind he had thoroughly justified his flight from Ireland, but he had not

[26] Letter to S. Joyce, February 11, 1907.

decided the question of where he would fly *to*. In Trieste and Rome he had learned what he had unlearned in Dublin, to be a Dubliner. As he had written his brother from Rome with some astonishment, he felt humiliated when anyone attacked his "impoverished country."[27] "The Dead" is his first song of exile.

[27] Letter to S. Joyce, September 25, 1906.

ALLEN TATE

Allen Tate, the distinguished Southern poet and man of letters, was founder and editor of *The Fugitive* (1922–25). He has taught at many American colleges and universities, including Princeton and Vanderbilt Universities, University of the South, and University of Minnesota. He has published numerous books of verse, and among his collections of critical essays are *Reactionary Essays on Poetry and Ideas, Reason in Madness*, and *The Man of Letters in the Modern World*. He held the Chair of Poetry of the Library of Congress in 1943 and 1944, and in 1956 he was awarded the Bollingen Prize in Poetry.

"THE DEAD"

In "The Dead" James Joyce brings to the highest pitch of perfection in English the naturalism of Flaubert; it may be questioned whether his great predecessor and master was able so completely to lift the objective detail of his material up to the symbolic level, as Joyce does in this great story. If the art of naturalism consists mainly in making *active* those elements which had hitherto in fiction remained *inert*, that is, description and expository summary, the further push given the method by Joyce consists in manipulating what at first sight seems to be mere physical detail into dramatic symbolism. As Gabriel Conroy, the "hero" of "The Dead," enters the house of his aunts, he flicks snow from his galoshes with his scarf; by the time the story ends the snow has filled all the visible earth, and stands as the symbol of the revelation of Gabriel's inner life.

Joyce's method is that of the roving narrator; that is to say, the author suppresses himself but does not allow the hero to tell his own story, for the reason that "psychic distance" is

Reprinted with the permission of Charles Scribner's Sons from *The House of Fiction*, pp. 279–82, by Caroline Gordon and Allen Tate. Copyright 1950, Charles Scribner's Sons. This essay originally appeared in the *Sewanee Review*, Winter 1950.

necessary to the end in view. This end is the *sudden* revelation to Gabriel of his egoistic relation to his wife and, through that revelation, of his inadequate response to his entire experience. Thus Joyce must establish his central intelligence through Gabriel's eyes, but a little above and outside him at the same time, so that we shall know him at a given moment only through what he sees and feels in terms of that moment.

The story opens with the maid, Lily, who all day has been helping her mistresses, the Misses Morkan, Gabriel's aunts, prepare for their annual party. Here, as in the opening paragraph of Joyce's other masterpiece in *Dubliners*, "Araby," we open with a neutral or suspended point of view; just as Crane begins "The Open Boat" with: "None of them knew the color of the sky." Lily is "planted" because, when Gabriel arrives, he must enter the scene dramatically, and not merely be *reported* as entering; if his eye is to *see* the story, the eye must be established actively, and it is so established in the little incident with Lily. If he is to see the action for us, he must come authoritatively out of the scene, not throw himself at us. After he flicks the snow, he sounds his special note; it is a false note indicating his inadequate response to people and even his lack of respect for them. He refers patronizingly to Lily's personal life; when she cries out in protest, he makes it worse by offering her money. From that moment we know Gabriel Conroy, but we have not been *told* what he is: we have had him rendered.

In fact, from the beginning to the end of the story we are never told anything; we are shown everything. We are not told, for example, that the *milieu* of the story is the provincial, middle-class, "cultivated" society of Dublin at the turn of the century; we are not told that Gabriel represents its emotional sterility (as contrasted with the "peasant" richness of his wife Gretta), its complacency, its devotion to genteel culture, its sentimental evasion of "reality." All this we see dramatized; it is all made active. Nothing is given us from the externally omniscient point of view. At the moment Gabriel enters the house the eye shifts from Lily to Gabriel. It is necessary, of course, at this first appearance that *we* should see him: there is a brief description; but it is not Joyce's description: we see him as Lily sees him—or might see him if she had Joyce's superior command of the whole situation. This, in fact, is the method of "The Dead." From this point on we are never far from Gabriel's physical sight; we are constantly looking through his physical eyes at values and insights of which he is incapable. The significance of the *milieu*, the complacency of Gabriel's feeling for his wife, her romantic image of her lover Michael Furey, what Miss Ivors means in that particular society, would have been put before us, in the pre-James era in English fiction, as exposition and commentary through the direct intercession of the author; and it would have remained inert.

Take Miss Ivors: she is a flat character, she disappears the moment Joyce is through with her, when she has served his purpose. She is there to elicit from Gabriel a certain quality, his relation to his culture at the intellectual and social level; but she is not in herself a *necessary* character. It is to this sort of character, whose mechanical use must be given the look of reality, that James applied the term *ficelle*. She makes it possible for Joyce to charge with imaginative activity an important phase of Gabriel's life which he would otherwise have been compelled to give us as mere information. Note also that this particular *ficelle* is a woman: she stands for the rich and complex life of the Irish people out of which Gabriel's wife has come, and we are thus given a subtle dramatic presentation of a spiritual limitation which focuses symbolically, at the end of the story, upon his relation to his wife.

The examples of naturalistic detail which operate also at the symbolic level will sufficiently indicate to the reader the close texture of "The Dead." We should say, conversely, that the symbolism itself derives its validity from its being, in the first place, a visible and experienced moment in the consciousness of a character.

Take the incident when Gabriel looks into the mirror. It serves two purposes. First, we need to *see* Gabriel again and more closely than we saw him when he entered the house; we know him better morally and we must see him more clearly physically. At the same time, he looks into the mirror because he is not, and has never been, concerned with an objective situation; he is wrapped in himself. The mirror is an old and worn symbol of Narcissism, but here it is effective because its first impact is through the action; it is not laid on the action from the outside.

As the party breaks up, we see Gabriel downstairs; upstairs Mr. Bartell D'Arcy is singing (hoarsely and against his will) "The Lass of Aughrim." Gabriel looks up the stairs:

A woman was standing near the top of the first flight, in the shadow also. He could not see her face but he could see the terracotta and salmonpink panels of her skirt which the shadow made appear black and white. It was his wife. . . . Gabriel was surprised at her stillness. . . .

She is listening to the song. As she stands, one hand on the banister, listening, Gabriel has an access of romantic feeling. "*Distant Music* he would call the picture if he were a painter." At this moment Gabriel's whole situation in life begins to be reversed, and because he will not until the end be aware of the significance of the reversal, its impact upon the reader from here on is an irony of increasing power. As he feels drawn to his wife, he sees her romantically, with unconscious irony, as "Distant Music," little suspecting how distant she is. He sees only the "lower" part of her figure; the "upper" is involved with the song, the meaning of which, for her, we do not yet know. The concealment of the "upper" and the visibility, to Gabriel, of the "lower," constitute a symbol, dramatically and naturalistically *active*, of Gabriel's relation to his wife: he has never acknowledged her spirit, her identity as a person; he knows only her body. And at the end, when he tries to possess her physically, she reveals with crushing force her full being, her own separate life, in the story of Michael Furey, whose image has been brought back to her by the singing of Mr. Bartell D'Arcy.

The image of Michael provides our third example. The incident is one of great technical difficulty, for no preparation, in its own terms, was possible. How, we might ask ourselves, was Joyce to convey to us (and to Gabriel) the reality of Gretta's boy lover? Could he let Gretta say that a boy named Michael Furey was in love with her, that he died young, that she had never forgotten him because, it seemed to her, he must have died for love of her? This would be mere statement, mere reporting. Let us see how Joyce does it.

—Someone you were in love with? he asked ironically.
—It was a young boy I used to know, she answered, named Michael Furey. He used to sing that song, *The Lass of Aughrim.* He was very delicate.

Having established in the immediate dramatic context, in relation to Gabriel, her emotion for Michael, who had created for her a complete and inviolable moment, she is able to proceed to details which are living details because they have been acted upon by her memory: his big, dark eyes; his job at the gasworks; his death at seventeen. But these are not enough to create space around him, not enough to present his image.

. . . I heard gravel thrown up against the window. The window was so wet I couldn't see so I ran downstairs as I was and slipped out the back into the garden and there was the poor fellow at the end of the garden, shivering.

Up to this passage, we have been *told* about Michael; we now begin to *see* him. And we see him in the following passage:

I implored of him to go home at once and told him he would get his death in the rain. But he said he did not want to live. I can see his eyes as well as well! He was standing at the end of the wall where there was a tree.

Without the wall and the tree to give him space he would not exist; these details cut him loose from Gretta's story and present him in the round.

The overall symbol, the snow, which we first see as a scenic detail on the toe of Gabriel's galoshes, gradually expands until at the end it gathers up the entire action. The snow is the story. It is not necessary to separate its development from the dramatic structure or to point out in detail how at every moment, including the splendid climax, it reaches us through the eye as a naturalistic feature of the background. Its symbolic operation is of greater importance. At the beginning, the snow is the cold and even hostile force of nature, humanly indifferent, enclosing the warm conviviality of the Misses Morkan's party. But just as the human action in which Gabriel is involved develops in the pattern of the plot of Reversal, his situation at the end being the opposite of its beginning, so the snow reverses its meaning, in a kind of rhetorical dialectic: from naturalistic *coldness* it develops into a symbol of warmth, of expanded consciousness; it stands for Gabriel's escape from his own ego into the larger world of humanity, including "all the living and the dead."

KENNETH BURKE

Kenneth Burke, the well-known critic and man of letters, has lectured widely at American colleges and universities. He was a Fellow of the Institute for Advanced Study in 1948 and 1949. His books of criticism and philosophical inquiry include *Counter-Statement*, *Permanence and Change*, *The Philosophy of Literary Form*, *A Grammar of Motives*, *A Rhetoric of Motives*, and *Language as Symbolic Action*.

"STAGES" IN "THE DEAD"

Joyce's story, "The Dead" (in *Dubliners*), seems particularly to profit by a close attention to "stages."

In the first of its three parts, the keynote is expectancy, which is amplified by many appropriate details: talk of preparations, arrivals, introductions, apprehensions, while fittingly the section ends on an unfinished story. All these details are in terms of everyday sociality, to do with the warming-up of the party, stressing an avid engrossment in such an order of motives, as though they were the very essence of reality. There are a few superficial references to the theme of death (the passing mention of two dead relatives who are never mentioned again, and Gabriel's remark that he had been delayed because it had taken his wife "three mortal hours" to dress). And there is one enigmatic detail, though at this stage of the story it looks wholly realistic: the reference to the snow on Gabriel's galoshes and overcoat as he enters, bringing in a "cold fragrant air from out-of-doors."

The second stage, dealing with the party at its height, could be analysed almost as a catalogue of superficial socialities, each in its way slightly false or misfit. The mood was set incipiently

From *Perspectives by Incongruity* by Kenneth Burke, edited by Stanley E. Hyman and Barbara Karmiller. Copyright © 1954 by Kenneth Burke. Reprinted with permission from the author and Indiana University Press.

in the first part, when Gabriel offers the servant a tip. He had known her before she became a servant, hence his act (involving sociality of a sort) is not quite right. In the second stage, there is a welter of such intangible infelicities, as with the fact that Mary Jane's singing received the most vigorous applause from "four young men in the doorway who had gone away to the refreshment-room at the beginning of the piece but had come back when the piano had stopped." This section is a thesaurus of what we might call "halfway" socialities, such as Miss Ivors' "propagandism" for the Irish movement (in leaving early, she cries, *"Beannacht libh"*), Freddy's drunken amiability, Gabriel's dutiful conversation with Freddy's mother, the parlor talk about music, the conviviality through common participation in the materials of the feast, Gabriel's slightly hollow after-dinner speech that was noisily acclaimed, Gabriel's distant relationship to two of the women who are giving the party, the few words with his wife indicating familiarity without intimacy, the somewhat gingerly treatment of the one Protestant among Catholics.

Such is the theme amplified, with apparent realistic engrossment, in this section. There are also a few explicit but glancing references to death. One threatens to be serious, when some of the Catholics try to tell the Protestant why certain monks sleep in their coffins; but "as the subject had grown lugubrious it was buried in a silence of the table," etc. And twice there is the enigmatic antithesis, the theme of the snow in the night, still wholly realistic in guise: "Gabriel's warm trembling fingers tapped the cold pane of the window. How cool it must be outside! How pleasant it would be to walk out alone, first along by the river and then through the park! The snow would be lying on the branches of the trees and forming a bright cap on the top of the Wellington Monument." In the other passage, there is likewise a reference to the "gleaming cap of snow" that Gabriel associated with the Monument. (One never knows how exacting to be, when comparing such passages; yet, as regards these references to the "cap" of snow, looking back we note that, when Gabriel first entered, the light

fringe of snow lay "like a cape" on his shoulders. Cap—cape.
Where secret identifications are taking form, since we are in
time to learn that this snow stands for some essence beyond
the appearances of halfway sociality, might not the signatures
mark their secret relationship thus punwise?)

In any case, the third section deals with events following the
party. The cycle of realistic expectations and eventualities is
drawing to a close. The party breaks up. We are now free
to penetrate the implications of the antithetical moment.
("How much more pleasant it would be there than at the
supper-table!" Gabriel had thought, in one of those two outlaw
flashes when he had imagined the snow outside in the night.)

The first two sections were best described, we think, by a
block-like method. Thus, for the first, we simply noted how
the theme of expectancy could be stated in variation; and for
the second, we broke the analysis into a list of variations on the
theme of halfway sociality. For the point we were trying to
make, it didn't matter in what order we listed these details.
But the third section concerns initiation into a mystery. It is
to take us beyond the realm of realism, as so conceived, into
the realm of *ideality*. Hence, there is a strict succession of
stages, in the development towards a more exacting kind of
vision. Each stage is the way-in to the next, as the narrow-
visioned expectations of the party had been the way-in to the
disclosures following the party.

The party is over. Where will we go? Is there not a symbolism emerging in the realism, when Gabriel tells the anecdote
of the old horse that went round and round the monument?
Next, the topic becomes that of every-whichway (we are still
undecided), as the cabman is given conflicting directions by
different members of the party. "The confusion grew greater
and the cabman was directed differently by Freddy Malins
and Mr Browne, each of whom had his head out through a
window of the cab. The difficulty was to know where to drop
Mr Browne along the route and Aunt Kate, Aunt Julia and
Mary Jane helped the discussion from the doorstep with cross-
directions and contradictions and abundance of laughter."

Finally, "the horse was whipped up and the cab rattled off along the quay amid a chorus of laughter and adieus." We are en route, so far as realistic topics are concerned. But Gabriel and his wife have not yet left. And the development from now on is to concern them. Tableau: A man is singing; Gabriel's wife, Gretta, is listening attentively, standing on the staircase, "near the top of the first flight"; Gabriel, below, is looking up admiringly. And "he asked himself what is a woman standing on the stairs in the shadow, listening to distant music, a symbol of."

Previously we mentioned the form of the *Theaetetus*: how, every time Socrates had brought things to an apparently satisfactory close, each such landing-place was found to be but the occasion for a new flight, a new search, that first seemed like an arrival, then opened up a new disclosure in turn. We believe that the remainder of this story possesses "dialectical form" in much that same sense. You might even call it the narrative equivalent of a Platonic dialogue. For from now on, Gabriel goes through a series of disclosures. Each time, he thinks he is really close to the essence; then another consideration emerges, that requires him to move on again. Let's be as bluntly schematic as possible. It is not our job to regive the quality of the story; for that, one should go to the story itself. The stages, schematized, are these:

(1) As against the familiar but not intimate relations we have already seen, between Gabriel and his wife, here is a new motive; Gabriel sees "grace and mystery in her attitude as if she were a symbol of something." And later, just before she asks the name of the song, at the sight of her flushed cheeks and shining eyes "a sudden tide of joy went leaping out of his heart."

(2) They had arranged to spend the night in a nearby hotel. Hence, passages to suggest that he is recovering some of the emotions he had felt at the time of their honeymoon. ("Their children, his writing, her household cares had not quenched all their souls' tender fire," a reflection growing out of realistic reference to a literal fire.)

(3) Crossing a bridge, amid talk of the snow on the statue, while "Gabriel was again in a cab with her, galloping to catch the boat, galloping to their honeymoon."

(4) Building up the sense of Gabriel's possessiveness ("happy that she was his, proud of her grace and wifely carriage . . . a keen pang of lust . . . a new adventure," etc.).

(5) But, after the porter has assigned them to their room and left, the moment does not seem right. Gabriel's irritation.

(6) She kisses him, calls him "a generous person." His self-satisfaction. "Now that she had fallen to him so easily he wondered why he had been so diffident."

(7) Then the disclosures begin. He finds that he has mis-gauged everything. She has been thinking of that song. (Gabriel sees himself in the mirror.)

(8) At first taken aback, he next recovers his gentleness, then makes further inquiries. Angry, he learns that the song reminds her of a boy, Michael Furey, who used to sing the song. His jealousy. (Thus, up to now, each step nearer to her had been but the preparation for a more accurate sense of their separation.)

(9) On further inquiry, he learns of the boy's frail love for her. "I think he died for me," Gretta said, whereat "A vague terror seized Gabriel at this answer as if, at that hour when he had hoped to triumph, some impalpable and vindictive being was coming against him, gathering forces against him in its vague world."[1] He died for her? Died that something might live? It is an arresting possibility.

[1] One observer, analyzing the *Portrait*, noted that among the body-spirit equations were grease and gas, grease being to body as gas is to spirit. Hence, on learning that Michael Furey "was in the gasworks," we assume that his spirituality is thus signalized roundabout, too. But we don't quite know what to make of the possible relation between "Gretta" and "great" in these lines:

    —I suppose you were in love with this Michael Furey, Gretta, he said.
    —I was great with him at that time, she said.

Probably nothing should be made of it. But we do believe that such correlations should be noted tentatively. For we would ask ourselves how methodic a terminology is. Correspondences should be noted. But they should be left at loose ends, except when there are good reasons for tying such ends together.

(10) After telling of this adolescent attachment, she cries herself to sleep.

So, we have narrowed things down, from all the party, to Gabriel and Gretta, and now to Gabriel alone. The next two pages or so involve a silent discipline, while he brings himself to relinquish his last claims upon her, as specifically *his.* The world of *conditions* is now to be transcended. Gretta had called him "generous," in a passage that Gabriel had misgauged. Now we learn that "generous tears filled Gabriel's eyes." The transcending of conditions, the ideal abandoning of property, is stated in Joyce's own words, thus: "His own identity was fading out into a grey impalpable world: the solid world itself which these dead had one time reared and lived in was dissolving and dwindling." For "his soul had approached that region where dwell the vast hosts of the dead."

Understandably, for if the world of conditions is the world of the living, then the transcending of conditions will, by the logic of such terms, equal the world of the dead. (Or, Kantwise, we contemplate the divine; for if God transcends nature, and nature is the world of conditions, then God is the unconditioned.)

Psychologically, there are other likely interpretations here. Gabriel, finally, loves his wife, not even in terms of his honeymoon (with its strong connotations of ownership), but through the medium of an adolescent, dead at seventeen. With this dead boy he identifies himself. Perhaps because here likewise was a kind of unconditionedness, in the Gidean sense, that all was still largely in the realm of unfulfilled possibilities, inclinations or dispositions not yet rigidified into channels? There is even the chance that, in his final yielding, his identification with the dead boy, he is meeting again his own past adolescent self, with all its range of susceptibilities, surviving now only like a shade in his memory.

In any case, once we have been brought to this stage of "generosity," where Gabriel can at last arrive at the order of ideal sociality, seeing all living things in terms of it, we return to the topic of snow, which becomes the *mythic image,* in the world of conditions, standing for the transcendence above the conditioned.

It was falling on every part of the dark central plain, on the treeless hills, falling softly upon the Bog of Allen and, farther westward, softly falling into the dark mutinous Shannon waves. It was falling, too, upon every part of the lonely churchyard on the hill where Michael Furey lay buried. It lay thickly drifted on the crooked crosses and headstones, on the spears of the little gate, on the barren thorns. His soul swooned slowly as he heard the snow falling faintly through the universe and faintly falling, like the descent of their last end, upon all the living and the dead.

"Upon all the living and the dead." That is, upon the two as merged. That is, upon the world of conditions as seen through the spirit of conditions transcended, of ideal sociality beyond material divisiveness.

C. C. LOOMIS, JR.

Chauncey C. Loomis, Jr., has taught at the University of Vermont and at Dartmouth College, where he is now an Associate Professor.

STRUCTURE AND SYMPATHY IN JOYCE'S "THE DEAD"

James Joyce's "The Dead" culminates in Gabriel Conroy's timeless moment of almost supreme vision. The fragments of his life's experience, of the epitomizing experiences of one evening in particular, are fused together into a whole: "self-bounded and self-contained upon the immeasurable background of space and time."[1] Initiated by a moment of deep, if localized, sympathy, his vision and his sympathy expand together to include not only himself, Gretta, and his aunts, but all Ireland, and, with the words "all the living and the dead," all humanity.

Gabriel's epiphany manifests Joyce's fundamental belief that true, objective perception will lead to true, objective sympathy; such perception and such sympathy, however, ultimately defy intellectual analysis. Joyce carefully avoids abstract definition of Gabriel's vision by embodying it within the story's central symbol: the snow, which becomes paradoxically warm in the moment of vision, through which Gabriel at long last feels the deeply unifying bond of common mortality.

Gabriel's experience is intellectual only at that level on which intellect and emotional intuition blend, and the full power of the story can be apprehended by the reader only if he sympa-

Reprinted by permission of the Modern Language Association from *PMLA*, March 1960.

[1] James Joyce, *A Portrait of the Artist as a Young Man* (New York: Modern Library, 1928), p. 249. See also Irene Hendry, "Joyce's Epiphanies" in *Critiques and Essays on Modern Fiction*, ed. John W. Aldridge (New York: Ronald Press, 1952), p. 129.

thetically shares the experience with Gabriel. As understanding of himself, then of his world, then of humanity floods Gabriel, so understanding of Gabriel, his world, and humanity in terms of the story floods the reader. The understanding in both cases is largely emotional and intuitive; intellectual analysis of the snow symbol, however successful, leaves a large surplus of emotion unexplained.

Therefore, Joyce had to generate increasing reader-sympathy as he approached the vision, but this sympathy could not be generated by complete reader-identification with Gabriel. If the reader identifies himself unreservedly with Gabriel in the first ninety per cent of the story, he will lose that critical insight into him which is necessary for full apprehension of his vision. It is, after all, Gabriel's vision, and there is no little irony in this fact. The vision is in sharp contrast with his previous view of the world: in fact, it literally opens a new world to him. If the reader identifies himself uncritically with Gabriel at any point in the story, he is liable to miss those very shortcomings which make the vision meaningful. Yet, in the actual moments of vision, the reader must share Gabriel's view; in a real sense, he must identify himself with Gabriel: "feel with" him.

Joyce, therefore, had to create sympathy without encouraging the reader to a blind, uncritical identification. One aspect of his solution to this problem is a monument to his genius. In the main body of the story, while he is constantly dropping meaningful, often semi-symbolic details which deepen the gulf between the reader and Gabriel, he is also generating what can best be called "aesthetic sympathy"; by the very structure of the story, he increasingly pulls the reader into the story.

"The Dead" can be divided, not arbitrarily, into five sections: the *musicale*, the dinner, the farewells and the drive to the hotel, the scene between Gabriel and Gretta in their room, and, finally, the vision itself. A few of these sections are separated by a time lapse, a few flow smoothly into one another; in all cases, however, the reader is aware of a slight "shifting of gears" between sections.

These sections become shorter as the story progresses. The

effect of this constant shortening of scenes, together with a constant speeding up in the narrative line, is an almost constant increase of pace. Within each of the sections, Joyce carefully builds up to a climax, then slackens the pace slightly at the beginning of the next section as he begins to build up to a new climax. The pace in the sections is progressively more rapid, however, partially because of the cumulative effect of the narrative. As the story progresses, more things happen in less time.

The effect of increasing pace is complemented and strengthened by another structural aspect of the story. As the pace increases, the focus narrows. The constantly narrowing focus and the constantly increasing pace complement one another and act to pull the reader into the story. He is caught up in a whirlpool movement, ever-narrowing, ever-faster.

There is much activity in the first part of "The Dead," but the activity is diffuse and the effect is not of great pace. We are given a slightly confused, over-all picture of activity: dancing, drinking, singing, chatter. Characters are introduced one after another: Lily, Gabriel, Gretta, the Misses Morkan, Mary Jane, Mr. Browne, Freddy Malins and his mother, Miss Ivors, and so on. Our scope is broad and general. Increasingly, Gabriel becomes our mode of consciousness, but he himself cannot assimilate all the activity. He retreats, isolates himself within his deep but insecure egotism. Rationalizing that "their grade of culture differed from his," he bides his time until dinner, when he knows he will be the center of all eyes.

In this first section, it is interesting to note how Joyce gives us Gabriel's point of view without compromising his own fundamental objectivity; even though we see largely through Gabriel's "delicate and restless" eyes, we nevertheless become increasingly aware of his character, of his defensive feelings of intellectual and social superiority in particular. His eyes are offended by the glittering, waxed floors, his ears by the "indelicate clattering" of the dancers, his intellect by all those present, particularly Miss Ivors, who "has a crow to pluck" with him, and constitutes a threat to his shaky feelings of superiority. His attitude can best be summed up by his reflection, ironic and revealing in view of the toast to come, that his aunts are "only two ignorant old women." Such comments are introduced quietly, but they serve to keep the reader from identifying himself too wholeheartedly with Gabriel. We feel with him to a degree even in these early sections of the story, but our sympathy is seriously reserved and qualified.[2]

In the second section, our focus narrows to the dinner table, and to a few characters at it; the others are blurred in the background. Tension about Gabriel's toast has been built up in the first section; now the pace increases as this particular tension is relieved. The toast, hypocritical and condescending, makes us further aware of Gabriel's isolation from those around him.

The pace in this scene is considerably more rapid than in the first. It builds up to the climax, the toast, in a few brief pages; then there is a slackening with the applause and singing.

There is a time-lapse between the conclusion of the toast and the next section; Joyce seems to shift to a higher range. From this point to the moment of vision, the pace increases and the focus narrows almost geometrically.

The shouts and laughter of the departure signal the end of the party, but are counter-balanced by the fine, almost silent tableau of Gabriel watching Gretta on the staircase. Our focus is beginning to narrow down to these two main characters. Gretta has been deliberately held in the background until this moment; now she emerges.

The repeated goodnights and the noisy trip through silent, snow-blanketed Dublin are given increased pace through Gabriel's increasing lust; the pace becomes the pace of "the blood bounding along his veins" and the "thoughts rioting through his brain." The fires of this lust begin to thaw the almost life-deep frost of his self-consciousness. The superiority and self-delusion are still dominant: there is much irony in his

---

[2] For an enlightening discussion of the problem of reader-identification and "extraordinary perspective" in 19th- and 20th-century literature, see R. W. Langbaum, *The Poetry of Experience* (New York: Random House, 1957).

remembering "their moments of ecstasy," for his lust is far from ecstatic love. It is, however, the first step toward the moment of objective vision.

We are now approaching the still center of the increasingly rapid, increasingly narrow whirlpool. The scene in the hotel room between Gabriel and Gretta takes up only a few brief minutes, but in these minutes much happens. Gabriel "discovers" Gretta: suddenly she becomes more than a mere appendage to his ego. He discovers himself, in a mirror. His lust turns to anger, then his anger to humility. Gretta, caught up in her memories of the "boy in the gasworks," Michael Furey, is not even aware of his presence. "A shameful consciousness of his own person assailed him. He saw himself as a ludicrous figure, acting as a pennyboy for his aunts, a nervous well-meaning sentimentalist, orating to vulgarians and idealising his own clownish lusts, the pitiable fatuous fellow he had caught a glimpse of in the mirror."

The peak of intensity is reached with Gretta's "O, the day I heard that, that he was dead." She collapses on the bed, sobbing, and Gabriel, quietly, shyly, retires to the window. At this moment, Joyce creates another time-lapse to lead into the vision itself.

Until this moment, the pace has increased and the focus has narrowed almost constantly. Now Joyce does something remarkable and effective: he reverses the process. In doing so, he makes the structure of the story not only useful as a means of generating an "aesthetic sympathy" (perhaps "empathy" with its impersonal connotations would be a more accurate word), but also makes it reinforce the ultimate emotional-intellectual meaning of the vision itself.[3]

[3] William T. Noon, S.J., in *Joyce and Aquinas* (New Haven: Yale University Press, 1957), pp. 84–85, places Gabriel's epiphany at "the moment when the full impact of Gretta's disclosure of her secret strikes him": before the snow image of the closing paragraphs. Father Noon separates Gabriel's moment of vision from the reader's, and seems to state that the snow image is for the reader's enlightenment, not Gabriel's. I agree with Father Noon that the reader cannot possibly apprehend the depth of

Pace simply ceases to exist in the vision, and, of course, this is fitting. We are in an essentially timeless world at this point; true, the vision involves time and mortality, but it is timeless time and eternal mortality, man's endless fate as man. The snow "falling faintly through the universe" measures absolute, not relative time. The impact of this sudden cessation of pace on the reader is great; in fact, it parallels the impact on Gabriel himself. With this sudden structural change, we share Gabriel's vision; we do not merely analyze it.

Gabriel's vision begins with Gretta; it is narrow in focus. The whole story has led us down to this narrow focus. Now, as he does with pace, Joyce reverses the process. As the vision progresses toward the ultimate image of the snow falling through the universe, the focus broadens, from Gretta, to his aunts, to himself, to Ireland, to "the universe." Time and space are telescoped in the final words of the story: The snow falls on "all the living and the dead."

"The Dead" follows a logical pattern; we move from the general to the particular, then to a final universal. We see Gabriel's world generally; then we focus down to the particular, and from the combination of the general and particular we are given a universal symbol in the vision itself.

The logic of "The Dead," however, is not the logic of mere intellect; it is the logic which exists on a plane where intellectual perception and emotional intuition, form and content, blend.

Gabriel's sudden sympathy with Gretta until Joyce gives him the closing image, but I do not believe that Gabriel's own vision is complete until this final image; the epiphany begins with his sympathy for Gretta, but is not complete, because not universal, until he "heard the snow falling faintly through the universe."

FLORENCE L. WALZL

Florence L. Walzl, Professor of English at the University of Wisconsin (Milwaukee), is an outstanding authority on *Dubliners*. She has published articles on Joyce in *College English*, *The James Joyce Quarterly*, and other journals.

GABRIEL AND MICHAEL:
THE CONCLUSION OF "THE DEAD"[1]

Dubliners as a collection and "The Dead" as a narrative both culminate in the great epiphany of Gabriel Conroy, the cosmic vision of a cemetery with snow falling on all the living and the dead. As an illumination, it follows Gabriel's meeting with the spirit of Michael Furey and seems to evolve from it. Though commentators generally agree on the structural design of *Dubliners* and the plot pattern of "The Dead," they have not agreed on the interpretation of this conclusion, or even of the principal symbol, the snow, which to some represents life, to others death, and to still others life or death depending on the context of the passage. Such lack of agreement at the crux of a work seems surprising. The purpose of this study is to suggest that the ambiguity of this conclusion was deliberate on Joyce's part and that it arose from the history and development of *Dubliners* as a collection.

The context in which "The Dead" is read affects interpretations of the story. For the reader who approaches "The Dead" by way of the preceding fourteen stories of frustration, inaction

Reprinted from the *James Joyce Quarterly*, Fall 1966, by permission of the author and the publishers. Copyright, 1966, by the University of Tulsa. Reprinted by permission of the University of Tulsa and the editor of the *James Joyce Quarterly*, Thomas F. Staley.

[1] Portions of this paper were given in a somewhat different form at the College and University Conference of the Wisconsin Council of Teachers of English, October 24, 1964, and published in the report of the conference, *Wisconsin Studies in English*, Number 2, under the title "Ambiguity in the Structural Symbols of Gabriel's Vision in Joyce's 'The Dead.'"

and moral paralysis, this story is likely to seem a completion of these motifs, and Gabriel's epiphany a recognition that he is a dead member of a dead society. But when "The Dead" is read as a short story unrelated to *Dubliners*, the effect is different: the story seems one of spiritual development and the final vision a redemption.

A survey of the critiques of "The Dead" shows significant differences in interpretation.[2] Explications which discuss the story and its final vision primarily as the conclusion of the book as a whole, such as those of Hugh Kenner and Brewster Ghiselin, tend to interpret the snow vision as Gabriel's self-identification with the dead.[3] However, structural analyses of

[2] See Kenneth Burke, "Three Definitions," *Kenyon Review*, XIII (Spring 1951), 186–92; David Daiches, *The Novel and the Modern World* (Chicago: University of Chicago Press, 1939), pp. 91–100; Richard Ellmann, *James Joyce* (New York: Oxford University Press, 1959), pp. 252–63; Brewster Ghiselin, "The Unity of Joyce's 'Dubliners,'" *Accent* (Spring 1956) 76–78, and (Summer 1956) 207–12; Julian B. Kaye, "The Wings of Daedalus: Two Stories in 'Dubliners,'" *Modern Fiction Studies* IV (Spring 1958), 37–41; Hugh Kenner, *Dublin's Joyce* (Bloomington, Ind.: University of Indiana Press, 1956), pp. 62–68; Richard Levin and Charles Shattuck, "First Flight to Ithaca: A New Reading of Joyce's 'Dubliners,'" in *James Joyce: Two Decades of Criticism*, ed. Seon Givens (New York: Vanguard Press, 1948), pp. 87–92; C. C. Loomis, Jr., "Structure and Sympathy in Joyce's 'The Dead,'" *PMLA*, LXXV (March 1960), 149–51; Marvin Magalaner and Richard M. Kain, *Joyce: The Man, the Work, the Reputation* (New York: Collier Books, 1956), pp. 92–98; Virginia Moseley, "'Two Sights for Ever a Picture' in Joyce's 'The Dead,'" *College English*, XXVI (March 1965), 426–33; Frank O'Connor, "Joyce and Dissociated Metaphor," in *The Mirror in the Roadway: A Study of the Modern Novel* (New York: Alfred A. Knopf, 1956), pp. 299–301; Brendan P. O Hehir, "Structural Symbol in Joyce's 'The Dead,'" *Twentieth Century Literature*, III (April 1957), 3–13; Allen Tate, "Three Commentaries," *Sewanee Review*, LVIII (Winter 1950), 10–15; and William York Tindall, *The Literary Symbol* (New York: Columbia University Press, 1955), pp. 224–28 and *A Reader's Guide to James Joyce* (New York: Farrar, Straus & Giroux, 1959), pp. 42–49.

[3] Kenner states that "The Dead" is the final "definition of living death" toward which the "entire book is oriented" and Gabriel's "proper medium" is death (pp. 62 and 67); Ghiselin states that "Gabriel's enlargement and liberation in his final vision is not a restoration to life" (p. 210). See also the views of Kaye that "the epiphany of 'The Dead' is a revelation of death" (p. 41), and of O'Connor that the snow is "death's symbol" (p. 299).

the story *per se*, such as those of Kenneth Burke, David Daiches, Allen Tate, and others, generally agree that the story is one of maturation and that the snow vision is a rebirth experience.[4] Though studies of the symbolism vary greatly, a number, among them the critiques of Ellmann, Magalaner and Kain, and Tindall, note ambivalence in the symbols, or "different perspectives" in the imagery.[5] All commentators agree on the essential significance of the snow vision both for *Dubliners* and "The Dead."

When Joyce left Ireland in 1904, he took with him the manuscripts of a number of the *Dubliners* stories, and by 1906 he had completed a work that consisted of fourteen stories. It did not include "The Dead," which was not written until 1907. It was this version that Joyce described as "a chapter of the moral history" of Ireland and as having its setting in Dublin because that city seemed to him the "centre of paralysis."[6] There is no question that this work represents Joyce's view of Ireland at the time he left his native land—as a moribund country that destroyed or paralyzed its children because of its provinciality and conformism.

A number of studies have demonstrated *Dubliners* to have an organized inner structure.[7] The stories are placed in four chron-

---

[4] Burke regards the snow as a "mythic image" of "transcendence" above the "world of conditions," of "ideal sociality" (pp. 191–192); Daiches calls the snow vision a "symbol of Gabriel's new sense of identity with the world, of the breakdown of the circle of his egotism" (p. 99); Tate states the snow "reverses its meaning," becoming a "symbol of warmth" which represents the hero's escape from his own ego into the larger world of humanity" (p. 15). See also the analyses of Loomis and O Hehir.

[5] Ellmann, pp. 256–262. See also Magalaner and Kain, pp. 95–98; and Tindall, *The Literary Symbol*, pp. 224–228 and *Guide*, pp. 45–48.

[6] From a letter to Grant Richards, May 5, 1906. *Letters*, Vol. II, p. 134.

[7] See James R. Baker, "Ibsen, Joyce, and the Living-Dead: A Study of 'Dubliners,'" in *A James Joyce Miscellancy*, Third Series, ed. Marvin Magalaner (Carbondale, Ill.: University of Southern Illinois Press, 1962), pp. 19–32; Ghiselin, pp. 75–88 and 196–213; William Powell Jones, *James Joyce and the Common Reader* (Norman, Okla.: University of Oklahoma Press, 1955), pp. 9–23; Kenner, pp. 53–68; Robert S. Ryf, *A New Approach to Joyce: The Portrait of the Artist as a Guidebook*

ological groups, which Joyce described as an order of "child-hood, adolescence, maturity and public life"; and all develop a dominant paralysis symbolism.[8] The 1906 version was highly symmetrical, consisting of an opening triad of stories of indi-vidual children ("The Sisters," "An Encounter," and "Araby"), a quartet of stories dealing with youthful men and women ("Eveline," "After the Race," "Two Gallants," and "The Board-ing House"), another quartet picturing mature characters ("A Little Cloud," "Counterparts," "Clay," and "A Painful Case"), and a final triad dealing with public groups in public situa-tions ("Ivy Day in the Committee Room," "A Mother," and "Grace"). The first and final triads obviously balance individ-uals and groups, and all the stories in the middle quartets are arranged in pairs contrasting sex, age, and social type or status. Also, the characterizations have a patterning that is unusual in short story collections. Though the protagonist of each story is a different character, all—children or adults—are variants of a basic type, a central everyman figure. Since each main char-acter is older in the first eleven tales, a life cycle is presented. This chronological structure is matched to a thematic one of hemiplegia. The result is a progression in which children are depicted as disillusioned, youths as frustrated or trapped, men and women as passive and non-productive, and social groups as completely static. The central image of the book is a creeping paralysis that ends in a dead society.

Analyses of the individual stories have shown that the paraly-sis motif tends to be developed by a number of related images, all variations on a basic death-life symbolism. They are stasis versus action, darkness versus light, cold versus warmth, and blindness versus perception. Prior to discussion of the handling of these images in "The Dead," their use in the 1906 *Dubliners* needs brief analysis. As a general pattern in the early version, they present a clear death symbolism.

(Berkeley, Cal.: University of California Press, 1962), pp. 59–76; Tindall, *Guide*, pp. 3–8; and Florence L. Walzl, "Pattern of Paralysis in Joyce's *Dubliners*," *College English*, XX (January 1961), 221–228.

[8] From a letter to Grant Richards, May 5, 1906. *Letters*, Vol. II, p. 134.

Inaction or arrest imagery is the most obvious variant of the paralysis motif. Joyce devises plots in which characters are immobilized by weakness or circumstance, symbolizes the resulting psychological situations by imagery of traps and cages, and employs settings with constricted spaces, such as confessionals, cells, cabins, narrow rooms, and little houses—all suggestive of graves or vaults (*e.g.*, "Eveline," "A Little Cloud," or "Clay"). In addition, Ghiselin has pointed out a variation of this stasis-action imagery in the directional symbolism in *Dubliners*:[9] movement eastward generally representing youthful attempts to escape life in Dublin ("An Encounter," "Araby," and "Eveline"); circular movement or essential immobility at the center of the city, the frustration of more mature characters ("Two Gallants," "The Boarding House," "A Little Cloud," and "Counterparts"); and movements westward a drift toward death of the elderly ("Clay" and "A Painful Case"). The stories of public life in the 1906 version all depict groups of people sitting inertly in public places. It should be noted that in this pattern of movement, Joyce is using traditional imagery that associates life with dawn and the east and death with twilight and the west.

Darkness and cold are also used either separately or in combination throughout *Dubliners* for death suggestions in contrast to light-warmth-life imagery. The opening pages set the tone with the repetitions of the words *night, darkened*, and *paralysis*, and in the succeeding stories images of shadow, mist, dimness, dust, gloom, and night appear as scenic details and symbols. Changes from light to darkness and warmth to cold (or the reverse) sometimes parallel the action of the plot (*e.g.*, "An Encounter," "Araby," "Two Gallants," and "A Painful Case"). Twilight and night scenes have symbolic significance in most of the stories, and in the latter part of the book darkness and chill imagery is cumulative.

Blindness and sight imagery is also evident as a pattern. First, the tales, examined in succession, show a steady decline in the perceptivity of the characters as to the reality of their situations.

[9] Ghiselin, pp. 77–79.

The youths are painfully aware of their disappointments; the more mature suffer but lack insight; characters in the final stories seem totally insensitive. As a result the epiphanies of these final stories are usually manifestations for the reader rather than the character. In addition, throughout *Dubliners* Joyce uses frequent eye imagery, a practice consistent with his view of the epiphany as an enlightenment. At the climactic moment of revelation, lack of insight on the part of the character may be indicated by eyes that are dim, blinded, or unseeing (*e.g.*, "Eveline," "After the Race," or "Clay"). By contrast a sudden view, a flash of light or color, may bring enlightenment (*e.g.*, "A Painful Case").

These imagistic patterns are in general consistent throughout the 1906 version of *Dubliners*. Though the same images appear in "The Dead," they are treated differently in that story.

The end of the 1906 version was carefully planned to round out the beginning. "The Sisters" opens *Dubliners* with a story of defective religion and a picture of a priest dying of paralysis, a figure symbolic of clerically dominated Ireland, according to Joyce's brother.[10] "Grace" ends this version with an ironic story of faith and a picture of a corrupt priest preaching a materialistic sermon to a group of morally insensible Dubliners. Both congregation and cleric exemplify Joyce's judgment that Ireland is spiritually dead.

Dubliners did not appear in the 1906 version. A series of disagreements over revisions of the stories delayed publication. When the book was finally published in 1914, a new story, "The Dead," provided the conclusion.

"The Dead" is markedly different from the earlier stories in several important respects. It is not only a longer, more fully developed narrative, but it presents a more kindly view of Ireland. Exile had modified Joyce's views of his native land.[11] He had found Italian cities like Pola and Trieste provincial in their own way, and Rome had seemed to him as much a city

[10] See Stanislaus Joyce, "James Joyce: A Memoir," trans. Felix Giovanelli, *Hudson Review*, II (1949–1950), 502.

[11] See Ellmann, pp. 252–263.

of the dead as Dublin. He complained that Rome lived as if by exhibiting its "grandmother's corpse."[12] He now felt that his picture of Ireland had been "unnecessarily harsh," and that he had not shown Ireland's "ingenuous insularity" and unique "hospitality."[13] "The Dead" reflects these modified views, but the changes presented Joyce a problem. For in adding "The Dead" to *Dubliners*, he was not merely appending another narrative to an ordinary collection of short stories: he was adding to a highly structured book already complete, a different kind of story with a different kind of conclusion.

As a narrative, "The Dead" has a plot of oscillation and reversal which mirrors the psychological changes in the chief character. The protagonist is Gabriel Conroy, a Dublin schoolteacher, who, with his wife, Gretta, attends a Christmas party given by his two old aunts, the Miss Morkans. During the evening a series of small events makes him alternate between emotions of confidence and inferiority. His self-esteem is undermined by the remarks of a bitter maid, Lily, by the criticisms of a fellow teacher, Molly Ivors, and by the doubts he secretly feels. On the other hand, his ego is bolstered by his aunts' dependence on him, his presiding at the carving, and his making the after-dinner speech. The attention, the festivities, and the prospect of an unaccustomed night at a hotel arouse in Gabriel romantic emotions and memories of his wife that have long lain dormant. When later at the hotel he approaches her amorously, he finds that she too is remembering a past love, but it is a different love from his. It is for a boy of her youth, Michael Furey, now dead. The sudden realization that for his wife the memory of a long dead lover has greater reality than does the physical presence of her living husband precipitates a crisis of self-evaluation in Gabriel. For the first time he gains an insight into his own identity and that of his society. In imagination he has a confrontation with his long dead rival, and from this

[12] From a letter to Stanislaus Joyce, September 25, 1906. *Letters*, Vol. II, p. 165.
[13] From a letter to Stanislaus Joyce, September 25, 1906. *Letters*, Vol. II, p. 166.

meeting evolves the snow vision which ends the story and the book.

Obviously "The Dead" is a story of insight and realization, and it seems to reverse the pattern of increasing insensibility that *Dubliners* otherwise traces.

Nonetheless, in a number of ways, "The Dead" was clearly designed to provide an appropriate conclusion for *Dubliners*. Commentators have tended to apply the terms *coda* and thematic *reprise* to it.[14] Structurally it fits neatly into the tales of public life depicting groups of provincial and conformist people. Its characters tend to recall earlier figures. Its atmosphere, despite the holiday scene, becomes one of funereal gloom as the conversation is devoted increasingly to the past, to people dead and gone, and discussions of death, monks, and coffins. There are constant intimations that the group will soon reconvene for a wake in these same rooms. In its own way, it rounds out the book as "Grace" had the 1906 version. Its setting, a gathering at the home of two ancient sisters, seems a scenic repetition of "The Sisters," and Gabriel's final vision of a cemetery in the night is a fitting close for a book that began as a deathwatch outside the house of a dying man.

Despite these thematic repetitions, Joyce's problem in integrating "The Dead" into *Dubliners* was not easily solved. For "The Dead" is a story of maturation, tracing the spiritual development of a man from insularity and egotism to humanitarianism and love. No earlier character in *Dubliners* undergoes a comparable change or has such an enlightenment. It cannot be fit with easy logic into the dominant paralysis pattern of *Dubliners*. I suggest that Joyce made his accommodation by two means: first, use of ambiguous or ambivalent images that mirror the oscillation in Gabriel's character, and second, by means of a conclusion in which a series of key images, all employed earlier in both the story and the book as a whole, operate to reflect one set of meanings from *Dubliners* as a total entity

---

[14] See Gerhard Friedrich, "The Perspective of Joyce's *Dubliners*," *College English*, XXVI (March 1965), 421–426; and Ryf, p. 73.

and a slightly different set from "The Dead" as an individual story.

Gabriel's final epiphany, comprising his ghostly meeting with Michael Furey and his vision of the snow, is the chief means by which Joyce effects this resolution. Every image in it is a symbol, and since each symbol is multi-faceted in reflecting earlier ambiguities, the epiphany allows for either a life or death interpretation. Paradoxical images of arrest and movement, darkness and light, cold and warmth, blindness and sight, are used in this conclusion to recall both the central paralysis-death theme of *Dubliners* as a collection and the rebirth-life theme of "The Dead" as a narrative.

The ambiguity of this ending succeeds because Joyce had already described ambivalent attitudes on the part of the hero, largely by means of these same symbols, used in shifting, paradoxical ways. To illustrate: at first view "The Dead" seems to employ the patterns of arrest and motion used earlier in *Dubliners*. For instance constricted motion is definitely associated with the frustrated Gabriel. The most obvious instance is the family anecdote that he dramatizes, of the treadmill horse that on a Sunday drive in Dublin insisted on going round and round and round King William's statue. Though Gabriel does not realize it, he is acting out symbolically the vicious circle of his own daily round in Dublin. Also, the directional symbolism seems that of the earlier tales: the east is the direction of Gabriel's holiday escapes to freedom on the continent, the center of Dublin is made the scene of his revelation, and the west is associated with his final vision of the graveyard. However, it soon becomes evident that Joyce is developing, side by side with this east-west symbolic pattern, another one that is its opposite in certain ways. In this system the east suggests the old, traditional, and effete; the west, the new, primitive, and vital. These symbols are largely developed through the characters. The story develops a contrast between the cultivated, urban East Coast society and people from the wilder Gaelic west of Ireland. The Dubliners are shown as a dull, elderly

group. As exemplified at the party, the upper-middle-class
Dubliner seems commonplace and his culture mediocre. The
conversation is stereotyped, the famed Irish hospitality consists
chiefly of eating and drinking, and the arts seem provincial.
The one writer present produces critical rather than creative
work; the pianist's playing is pretentious sound without substance. The "Three Graces of the Dublin musical world" are
a spinster and two ancient ladies who Gabriel privately and
hypocritically admits are "only two ignorant old women."[15]
In contrast, the westerners are more simple, direct and passionate. For example, several of the strongest characters are
associated with the west, among them Gabriel's argumentative
colleague, Miss Ivors, who urges him to visit the west to learn
Gaelic and see the real Ireland; his attractive wife, Gretta, who
has come from Connacht and is "country cute"; and above all,
Gabriel's ghostly rival, Michael Furey, who is strongly identified
with the west country. The character contrast between east and
west is made explicit in the opposition between Gabriel's
mother and his wife, the two principal women in his life. His
dead mother is identified as a chief representative of the cultivated Dublin milieu. The "brains carrier" of the family, she
saw that her sons were educated for the proper professions. She
exists in the story as a photograph in which she holds a book.
She opposed Gabriel's marriage to a girl from the west country.
In contrast, his wife, Gretta, seems representative of a more
natural west. She is always associated with color and perfume,
music and stars, and her reactions always seem direct and
ingenuous. It should be noted that in this second pattern of
east-west symbolism Joyce is developing traditional symbolism,
also. From the Ulysses myth to the American mystique of the
West, the east has represented the old and tried, and the west
the new and unknown. Westward movement in this association
tends to symbolize man's utopian possibilities and connote
search and adventure. Thus, in "The Dead" Joyce deliberately
builds an ambivalent symbolism of motion and direction that

[15] James Joyce, *Dubliners*, Compass Edition (New York: The Viking
Press, 1967), p. 192.

in some contexts equates the east with dawn and life and the west with sunset and death, but in other contexts associates the east with the old and sterile and the west with the new and vital.

The darkness-cold and light-warmth images are also developed paradoxically in shifting patterns of meaning.[16] Several episodes will illustrate this. When Gabriel first comes out of the dark and cold into the light and warmth of the Morkan house, his marked insulation against the cold and snow by means of heavy clothes and galoshes suggests a conventional symbolism which associates heat with life. But ironically the lights within seem to illuminate a society that is stuffy and dead rather than warm and alive, and Gabriel soon longs for the cold fresh air and the great darkness outside, which now seem to represent the vitality of nature and perhaps also the living culture of Europe beyond the seas. Later as the characters prepare to leave the party, there is a shift back in the symbolism. The "cold fragrant air" is no longer emphasized, but seemingly casual remarks about the cold and night build up a death-journey symbolism. The departing guests remark about the sharp wind, the bitter cold, the snow which is "general all over Ireland," and the fact that "everybody has colds." Mary Jane shivers as she tells the leave-takers that she "wouldn't like to face . . . [their] journey home." The repetitive farewells of "Good-night," "Good-night, again," "Good-night, all. Safe home," "Good-night. Good-night" (the word is repeated ten times) hint of a "last journey." These suggestions are imagistic preparations for the scene in the hotel bedroom where the death imagery is unmistakable. The box-like room, the removal of a candle, the darkness, the chill, and the bed on which Gretta lies, all build the impression of a vault where the dead rest frozen on their biers. There is no question that the symbols have shifted back and forth in these episodes.

These shifting images of darkness-cold and light-warmth are supported by marked ambiguity in the handling of the snow imagery. The snow mirrors the very paradox Joyce is develop-

[16] Ellmann, pp. 260–261.

ing. For snow exposed to heat turns into water, but exposed to cold solidifies into ice. (Water is an archetypal life symbol, and ice a traditional death symbol.) In "The Dead" the snow symbol unites all the other images.

The coldness and warmth imagery developed in connection with Gabriel is extraordinarily complex. Every commentator on "The Dead" has remarked how the snow is associated with Gabriel from his first appearance to his final vision. Throughout the story a complicated interplay of attraction and repulsion is evident in his attitudes. Though he boasts of the galoshes that insulate him from the snow, he also longs for physical contact with it. Though he is moved by the sight of the snow on the roofs, he is irritated by the slush under foot. Though he thinks of statues and monuments covered with snow during the evening, he never sees the relevance of these pictures to himself. (It is the reader that notes the likeness to the opening description of Gabriel.) His final epiphany involves a vision in which snow is both falling and melting. The inherent flexibility of snow as a symbol allows Joyce to shift symbolic suggestions rapidly in these contexts. The warmth imagery will be discussed in connection with the angel symbolism.

The imagery of blindness and sight combines ambivalence and ambiguity. It is used initially to indicate Gabriel's lack of insight and his unconscious avoidance of reality, but it later is employed to describe the gradual enlargement of perspective that leads to his final cosmic vision. Images of eyes, eyesight, glasses, mirrors and windows appear in the story in varied and paradoxical meanings. Of all these images, the mirror is most significant and like the snow it tends to shift its meaning with the context of the passage. For the mirror in "The Dead" represents successively illusion, human reality, and intuitive vision.

The first use of reflection imagery is Narcissistic, and here Joyce is working in a rich literary tradition that extends from Ovid through Shakespeare's Richard II and Milton's Eve to modern psychological fiction. The story opens with a protagonist preoccupied by his own image. How he appears to other people engrosses Gabriel, to the point that his sense of his own identity becomes the view of him reflected from his aunts, the guests at the party, and even the maid, Lily. His concern for a flattering self-image is shown imagistically by eyesight-glasses references. Gabriel's eyes are described as "screened" by his "scintillat[ing]" or "glimmering" glasses. His "delicate and restless eyes" are dazzled by the "glitter" from the polished floor and bright chandelier. In short, his view of the world is distorted by the reflections from his environment, and Gabriel is unable to see reality as it is. Since his eyes are easily irritated, he goes several times to the windows to look out on the darkness, actions suggesting his psychological uncertainty. This Narcissistic imagery culminates with his first direct look into a mirror. Joyce has both Gretta and Gabriel look into a large cheval-glass shortly after they reach the hotel. What Gretta sees is not immediately revealed, for she turns away "serious and weary." Gabriel looks in the mirror and what he sees is an illusion—a "broad, well-filled shirt-front, the face whose expression always puzzled him . . . , and his glimmering gilt-rimmed eye-glasses." His blind egotism masks the truth from him, for actually this image is the pompous front he has been at the party. The mirror has reflected a flattering distortion for him. But the same mirror will later reflect reality. After Gabriel learns the truth that he has not been the only love in his wife's life and that his sense of possession of Gretta has been only an illusion, he again looks in the mirror and this time he does see reality in an extended view that includes himself and his society. This time he sees "a ludicrous figure, acting as a pennyboy for his aunts, a nervous well-meaning sentimentalist, orating to vulgarians and idealising his own clownish lusts." This is the figure he has really cut that evening. Moreover, he now identifies himself with the social group that he has secretly despised and yet feared all evening long: he is a "pitiable fatuous fellow" in a society of "vulgarians."[17] Finally, at the end of *Dubliners*

[17] See the letter to Grant Richards in *Letters*, Vol. I, p. 64, in which Joyce alludes to *Dubliners* as a "nicely polished looking-glass" in which the Irish people could get "one good look at themselves."

the mirror seems to shift significance again and becomes a reflection of intuitive or visionary truth. After Gabriel has realized the nature of his limitations and acknowledged that as a man he has never really lived, he turns humbly to the window where he had earlier imagined his rival standing. The physical scene of falling snow dwindles and dissolves for him, and the cosmic snow vision replaces it. In this scene the mirror has become a reflecting window, and ultimate reality is shown in an image of a cemetery in the snow. The symbolism seems highly Dantean in its concept of the glass as a reflection of transcendent reality and in its presentation of that reality through a symbolic image. In the final canto of the *Paradiso* Dante, after perceiving an image, achieved a direct view of Being. Whether or not Gabriel does at the end of "The Dead" is one of the cruxes of *Dubliners*.

The climax of *Dubliners* is the imaginary conformation of Gabriel and Michael from which the snow vision evolves. At this point both characters become larger than life, and it is clear that both are mythic figures and archetypes. At the first level they are characters in a story, rivals in a love triangle, the only unusual aspect of which is that one of the rivals has long been dead. At another level, they are archetypes. At a still different level their opposition is represented by their angel names and the legendary associations with each.

At the narrative level, the Gabriel-Michael opposition is illustrated in the scene at the Gresham Hotel. This episode marks a final phase of Gabriel Conroy's development as a character, for in it Gabriel moves from blindness and conceit to self-knowledge and sympathy for others. His enlightenment is effected by Gretta's telling him the story of Michael Furey, the frail boy who, because he loved her more than life, left his sick bed on a night of rain and cold to come to see her. Gabriel's sudden realization that he has never experienced a love like this brings with it the discovery that he has never lived to the full depth of being. Hence to his wife he is less real than Michael Furey, this shade of her youth. Joyce creates a polarity in the reader's mind between the lover and the husband. Both are shown as seeking the woman's love in the night, the dead lover standing in the falling rain, happy in his moment of love; the living husband, frustrated and unhappy in the dark, vault-like hotel room watching the snow fall. Ironically the ghost seems alive, the man dead. Here the Michael-Gabriel contrast opposes life-in-death to death-in-life.

As an archetype, Gabriel is the central everyman figure of *Dubliners* in its final configuration. In numerous ways he brings together in his character and life all the earlier protagonists. In his sensitivity and insecurity he recalls the little boys of "The Sisters," "An Encounter," or "Araby," whose quests for answers end in disappointment. He seems a projection of the youths like Eveline Hill, Jimmy Doyle, and Lenehan, who lack the energy to undertake vital careers and the courage to leave Ireland. He is not betrayed like Doran of "The Boarding House," but he has himself betrayed his own best possibilities. Like Little Chandler and Farrington he is caught in a dull round of domesticity and uncreative work. He is like Maria of "Clay" in that he has never experienced the full meaning of love, and he is clearly on his way to becoming a prim, fuss-budgety Mr. Duffy. When he recognizes himself as a "fatuous fellow," he has pronounced his own identification with all the "sentimentalists," "vulgarians," pennyboys, pretentious fools, and ineffectual Dubliners of "Ivy Day," "A Mother," and "Grace." In short, Gabriel Conroy is The Dubliner. And he is Man.

Michael Furey also is more than a character and an angel namesake. This should not be surprising, since in a number of earlier *Dubliners* stories, great names of myth and legend, heroes and God figures, are invoked as ironic contrasts. (Such examples as the Christ-Judas references in "Two Gallants," the Mary contrast of "Clay," and the Parnell and disciple figures of "Ivy Day" come readily to mind.) A phrase in Gretta's description of him identifies him. Speaking of Michael's end, she says, "I think he died for me." The phrase echoes the words of the Poor Old Woman who is Ireland in disguise in Yeats's *Cathleen ni Houlihan*. Speaking of her patriot-lover, "yellow-haired Donough that was hanged in Galway," she says, "He died for love of me."[18] Michael represents Ireland—an older traditional Ireland of the Gaelic west, of Galway and the Aran Islands, an Ireland that Gabriel is unwilling to visit or to view as important. Michael is a fatherland figure. But he is more. The phrase "he died for me" and the picture of him standing under a tree identifies him as Christ.[19] He is a symbol of sacrificial love in both configurations. To love a cause or a person more than life is the action of the hero and the God, and Michael is so identified. Gabriel the Dubliner has been incapable of such sacrifice. At this point, a question seems pertinent: who is the betrayer and who the betrayed? *Dubliners* as a whole work suggests that Ireland betrays its children. "The Dead" in this symbolic identification seems to imply that the Dubliner betrays Ireland. This is only one of the ambiguities that "The Dead" offers.

The central ambiguity of "The Dead" is the conclusion, and it is developed in large part by the Archangel Gabriel and Michael contrasts. Several polarities between Michael and Gabriel as angels' namesakes appear.[20] The first involves a dif-

[18] William Butler Yeats, *Collected Plays* (New York: The Macmillan Co., 1953), p. 54. Adaline Glasheen noted this echo: see Ellmann, p. 258.

[19] Ellmann, p. 259.

[20] "Gabriel," and "Michael," *The Catholic Encyclopedia*, 1911, VI, 330, and X, 275–277; "Gabriel," and "Michael," *The Jewish Encyclopedia*, 1910, V, 540–543, and VIII, 535–538; and Louis Ginzberg, *The Legends of the Jews*, trans. Henrietta Szold (Philadelphia, 1909), 7 vols. See also Gerhard Friedrich, "Bret Harte as a Source for James Joyce's 'The Dead,'" *PQ*, XXXIII (October 1954), 442–444; and George Knox, "Michael Furey: Symbol-Name in Joyce's 'The Dead,'" *The Western Humanities Review*, XIII (Spring 1959), 221–222. Ginzberg states that "the rivalry of these two angels (Michael and Gabriel) is met with in Jewish legends throughout the centuries" (V, 4); and notes that the identification of them with the elements differs in various Jewish authorities. "Michael is . . . said to consist of fire, the heavenly element; Gabriel of snow, the primordial substance of which the earth was made. According to others, Michael is of snow, and Gabriel of fire" (V, 70). Joyce used the traditions of angelology as they best suited his purpose in "The Dead." His identification of his angels with directions does not fit the usual tradition, which associated Michael with the east, Raphael with the west, Gabriel with the north and Uriel with the south.

ference in rank between these angels. In the angelic hierarchies, Michael as an archangel has precedence over Gabriel as an angel, a relationship which is probably exemplified in the ascendancy of Michael over Gabriel in Gretta's consciousness. The second polarity involves the elements in nature which these two angels represent. In both Jewish and Christian occult tradition the four chief angels, Michael, Gabriel, Raphael, and Uriel, are correspondent with the four elements, seasons, directions, and winds. Michael represents symbolically the element water, is called "the prince of snow," and is associated with silver. Gabriel represents fire, is called "the prince of fire," and associated with gold.[21] These suggestions all appear in "The Dead." A third polarity involves a contrast in New Testament tradition: Michael is primarily the angel of the Last Judgment and Gabriel of the Annunciation. All these motifs join in clusters of shifting symbols in the final section of "The Dead," especially the scene at the Gresham Hotel, which introduces the snow epiphany.

This episode presents a paradoxical contrast between the "living" ghost, Michael, and the "dead" man of flesh, Gabriel. This paradox affects certain images, deriving from the angelic traditions, that are applied to Michael and Gabriel. Michael, named for the angel of water and snow, is always associated with cold, sometimes in combination with rain, sometimes with snow. His memory is first evoked by Gretta when she hears the song, "The Lass of Aughrim," with its picture of a loved one deserted and standing in the cold. Then in her story of Michael, she describes how, when he came to say good-by to her, he stood shivering in the streaming rain under a tree outside her window. Finally, through a series of imaginative suggestions, Joyce creates in Gabriel's (and the reader's) imagination the illusion that throughout the whole scene in the hotel room, the ghost of Michael is standing outside the window in the snow under the gas lamp looking in. These suggestions come to an eerie climax when the "few light taps" of snow upon the window pane recreated the sound of the gravel Michael had

[21] *The Jewish Encyclopedia*, VIII, 538.

thrown long ago to attract Gretta's attention. Now they call Gabriel to a different rendezvous, the vision of the graveyard where Michael lies buried under the drifting snow.

While the linking of Michael to cold is consistent throughout these scenes, there is an interesting shift from rain to snow imagery. In Gretta's memories Michael is always evoked in rain, but in Gabriel's evocation he is usually associated with snow. The rain and water symbolism suggests that to Gretta, Michael brought an experience of life and love. The snow symbolism suggests that to Gabriel he now brings an experience of death.

The heat and fire imagery associated with Gabriel is partly explained by Gabriel's representation as the angel of fire. Metaphors of fire describe his feelings for Gretta, but paradoxically because they are applied both to his lust and his love. His present emotions "glow angrily" and are termed "the dull fires of . . . lust." The pure, intense love of his youth is depicted as the soul's "tender fire" and likened to the "fire of stars." In thus making a distinction between a love that is life-giving and good and one that is destructive and evil, Joyce is developing a life-death contrast. In using fire in such opposite meanings Joyce probably took Dante as model.[22] In the *Purgatorio*, where the punishments image the sins, the lustful are purged in fire, but in the *Paradiso* fire as light is the image for God's love. In fact, Joyce's very phraseology, the "fire of stars," suggests Dante's pictures of the planetary heavens as rings of light and of the angelic choirs as circles of fire. In use of this imagery Gabriel seems rightly named for the angel of fire.

Ambiguities extend also to the roles Michael and Gabriel play as namesakes of great angels. St. Michael is the warrior angel of the Last Judgment, depicted in art holding scales and associated with the settling of accounts. One of his chief offices

[22] See Moseley on the flame imagery, pp. 431–433. This study points out numerous Dante motives in "The Dead" and calls attention to the passage in which Dante states that "Holy Church represents Gabriel/ and Michael with human faces/ and the other (Raphael) by whom Tobit was healed" since because of human limitations man can learn "only from sense impressions," *Paradiso*, IV, 37–48 (trans. H. R. Huse).

is to bring men's souls to judgment. And this is precisely the role Michael Furey plays in "The Dead." Though he exists only as a memory in Gretta's mind, he brings Gabriel to a judgment of himself. No ambiguity lies in the fact of this judgment; the ambiguity lies in the nature of the judgment. In this context a second office of the archangel Michael is pertinent: his duty to rescue the souls of the faithful at the hour of death. Since the verdict in Gabriel's case is not in the form of a statement, but a vision, it is not clear which of these functions Michael performs. Does he bring Gabriel, as his final verdict, a knowledge that he is one of the dead? Or does he bring him an illumination that rescues him at the brink of spiritual death? Joyce leaves the role of Michael ambiguous.

In contrast to the stern role of the archangel Michael, Gabriel is a messenger angel associated with God's beneficence. In the Old Testament he is the angel sent to Daniel to interpret two great visions of salvation, one of them a Messianic prophecy. His words to Daniel, "Understand, O son of man, for in the time of the end the vision shall be fulfilled" (*Daniel* 8.17), may have relevance to "The Dead." In the New Testament he is the angel of the Annunciation to the Virgin Mary and to Elizabeth. The vision of Zacharias has particular significance: to a man who was old and sterile and whose wife was barren, the angel Gabriel brought promise of new life. Does this name symbolism suggest birth and renewal for Gabriel? Or is it ironic in connection with this frustrated man? Joyce is not explicit.

All these complex motifs reach culmination in Gabriel's vision. This epiphany is the final stage of a development that has carried Gabriel from a selfish preoccupation with self to sympathy with Gretta, pity for his relatives, and love for all men. His illumination takes place when he realizes he is part of common humanity and shares its mutable state of being. At this moment of enlightenment he loses even the sense of his own identity, and his soul approaches "that region where dwell the vast hosts of the dead." As he watches the snow fall, he reflects that the "time had come for him to set out on his journey westward." Because of the earlier ambiguities, Joyce has made it possible for this strange statement to be either a life or a death suggestion. It is the keynote symbol of the vision, and its significance is all-important, since the meaning of the rest of the vision depends on the interpretation of this image. If it is read as a death symbol, all successive images take a like coloration. If it is read as a life symbol, the succeeding images all suggest rebirth. It signals the opening of one of the most remarkable ambiguities in literature, a conclusion that offers almost opposite meanings, each of which can be logically argued.

For the reader who has come to this conclusion by way of the fourteen preceding stories of disillusioned children, frustrated youths, sterile adults and paralyzed social groups in *Dubliners*, the cosmic vision of "The Dead" seems the last stage in a moribund process. The final fate of the *Dubliners* everyman is a death in life, and Gabriel Conroy's illumination is that he is dead. In this interpretation the vision is a final statement of the death themes of the book. The snow that covers all Ireland images the deadly inertia of the nation. The lonely churchyard where Michael Furey lies buried pictures the end of individual hope and love. The crooked crosses on which the snow drifts represent the defective and spiritually dead Irish Church. The spears and barren thorns suggest the futility of Christ's sacrifice for a people so insensible. To the hero it is an irrevocable last judgment. Such an interpretation is a powerful and symbolically logical conclusion for *Dubliners*.

This is not the conclusion that the reader who knows only "The Dead" draws. Interpreting the journey westward as a start toward a new life of greater reality, he sees a succession of rebirth images. The snow, though it is general over Ireland, is quickly swallowed in the Shannon waves—its static iciness melting in the great waters of life. The melting snow is seen as subtly paralleling the change in the hero, whose cold conceit has disappeared with his warming humanitarianism. The snow melting is thus a baptismal symbol, and as such offers renewed life not only to Gabriel, but also all the dead who lie here.

The lonely churchyard where Michael Furey is buried serves only as a reminder that the grave has already yielded up its dead. For Michael lives vibrantly in the memory of a vibrant act. The recollections of Christ's passion in the spears and thorns are reminders that sacrifice of self is the condition of revival. The judgment that Michael brings is a salvation, and Gabriel's swoon is a symbolic death from which he will rise revivified. Gabriel is rightly named: he is a figure of annunciation and new life.

Joyce thus resolved the problem in logic which arose from his changed viewpoints by composing a conclusion for "The Dead" and *Dubliners* that employed a pattern of ambivalent symbols and a great final ambiguity.

Topics for Discussion and Papers

❖❖❖❖❖❖❖❖❖❖❖❖❖❖❖❖❖❖❖❖❖❖❖❖❖❖❖❖❖❖❖❖❖❖❖❖❖❖

TOPICS FOR GENERAL DISCUSSION

1. Joyce once said that it was his intention "to write a chapter of the moral history of [his] country," using Dublin for the scene because that city seemed to be the "centre of paralysis." Beginning with the paralyzed priest in "The Sisters," trace the theme of paralysis (social, spiritual, and economic) as it appears in several stories.

2. Another leading motif in the stories is that identified by Brewster Ghiselin as the "Oriental motif," a longing for escape expressed through fantasies of flight to some Eastern and exotic refuge. Trace this motif as it appears in at least two stories.

3. When the earliest stories of *Dubliners* were published in the *Irish Homestead* Joyce used the pseudonym "Stephen Daedalus," and he later spoke of the first three stories of the collection as being "stories of my childhood." Readers of *A Portrait of the Artist as a Young Man* will be interested in comparing the young Stephen Dedalus with the small boy of "The Sisters," "An Encounter," and "Araby."

4. As the stories of *Dubliners* move from the narrow but intense experiences of childhood into the wider areas of adult and public life, Joyce alters his narrative methods to suit the changes in point-of-view. Compare the point-of-view in one of the first three stories with the point-of-view in a later story.

5. The satirist, or the writer who aspires to social criticism, must

445

measure the realities of the present against some ideal of moral and social behavior. At the same time, the Joycean aesthetic would seem to preclude direct judgments on the part of the author. How does Joyce manage to convey his moral judgments without resorting to direct authorial commentary? Choose one class of social relationships (such as that between husband and wife) and show how Joyce makes his indirect judgments.

6. Joyce often said that one of his purposes in *Dubliners* was to present his native city to the world in all its variety, and with a total lack of sentimentality. The result is that almost every social type or professional class is represented in the stories. Choosing one social type or professional class (e.g., mothers, servants, priests, *artistes*, newspapermen, businessmen, loafers), show how Joyce has used these particular characters in portraying the life of the city.

7. As pointed out in the editors' Introduction to the selection of critical essays, this volume contains examples of both the "naturalistic" and the "symbolic" approaches to *Dubliners*. Choose a story not considered in one of the essays and write a paper on it, utilizing both of these approaches.

8. Using the early drafts of "The Sisters" and "A Painful Case," show how Joyce's revisions were aimed at achieving the general stylistic ideals evident in *Dubliners*.

9. No critical study, no matter how subtle and elaborate it may be, can hope to do justice to the complexities of a work of art. Choose one of the critical essays reprinted in this collection and discuss its strengths and limitations, using your own reading of *Dubliners* as an "ideal" response.

10. Joyce once thought of writing a story for *Dubliners* based on the wanderings of Ulysses, and he had other stories in mind which remained titles only: "The Last Supper," "The Street," "Vengeance," "At Bay." Using one of the shorter stories as a model, write your own addition to *Dubliners*. This "sixteenth" story could be a parody of Joyce's method, or a sequel to one of his stories, or an original story using either Joyce's characters or characters of your own invention.

11. Using the letters reprinted in this collection, discuss either Joyce as a critic of his own writing or Joyce's evolving sense of *Dubliners* as a unified work.

TOPICS ON INDIVIDUAL STORIES

"The Sisters"

12. Why is the story called "The Sisters"?
13. What has been the young boy's relationship with Father Flynn? How has this relationship been changed by the circumstances surrounding the priest's death?
14. In what ways do Joyce's revisions of "The Sisters" indicate his growing awareness of the story's function as a prelude to the entire collection?

"An Encounter"

15. How does the last paragraph of the story illuminate the relationship between the two boys? In what ways has this relationship been affected by their "encounter" with the stranger?
16. Does Joyce sustain our sense of adolescent adventure throughout the story? What is the function of the "Tom Sawyer" element in "An Encounter"?

"Araby"

17. How does Joyce give some general significance to the sense of personal desolation felt by the boy at the end of the story?

18. "I imagined that I bore my chalice safely through a throng of foes." What aspects of the story are brought to a focus by this complex image?

"Eveline"

19. How have the three preceding stories prepared us for an understanding of the forces that "paralyze" Eveline?
20. On page 40 Joyce has carefully indicated a break in the narrative which is also a break in the time-scheme. What other changes (such as changes in language and tone) do you find in the short final section, and how do these changes reinforce the conclusion to the story?

"After the Race"

21. What is Jimmy's true relationship with the other young men? How do the various nationalities interact in the story?

"Two Gallants"

22. Discuss the implications of the harp in Kildare Street and the playing of "Silent, O Moyle."
23. In what ways does "Two Gallants" modify the notions of glamour and gallantry found in "After the Race"?
24. What does Joyce achieve by presenting Corley's "betrayal" of the servant girl solely through the eyes of Lenehan?

"The Boarding House"

25. How is "The Boarding House" related, both thematically and structurally, to "Eveline"?

26. Compare the treatments of erotic and economic realities in "Two Gallants" and "The Boarding House."

"A Little Cloud"

27. Compare the last paragraph of "A Little Cloud" with the last paragraph of "Araby." How do the tears of childhood differ from those of adult life?
28. How does Gallaher act as a catalyst for Little Chandler's feelings?
29. What is the significance of Little Chandler's "artistic" aspirations?

"Counterparts"

30. How do the different styles of speech reflect the conflicting forces in "Counterparts"?
31. "Two Gallants" is a tale of the Dublin streets, "Counterparts" is a story of the city's offices and pubs and houses. How do the different atmospheres and settings affect our reading of these two stories?

"Clay"

32. In the process of composition Joyce changed the name of this story from "Hallow Eve" to "The Clay" to "Clay." Would these different titles lead to somewhat different readings of the story?
33. Compare the structural and symbolic uses of Byron's poem in "A Little Cloud" with the uses of "I dreamt that I dwelt in marble halls" in "Clay."
34. On page 101 Maria admires herself in the mirror. How does this scene contribute to our sense of her personality?

"A Painful Case"

35. As with many of the characters in *Dubliners*, Joyce tells us a good deal about Mr. Duffy's reading and literary tastes. How does this knowledge contribute to the story's themes?

36. In the course of the story's composition Joyce took particular pains with the phrasing of the newspaper report. Why did he choose this particular method for conveying the details of Mrs. Sinico's death?

"Ivy Day in the Committee Room"

37. In contrast to some of the earlier stories, "Ivy Day in the Committee Room" is developed almost entirely through dialogue. What does Joyce achieve by this method of presentation? How does it affect our responses to characters and situations?

38. Joyce intended this story to sum up his view of Irish politics in the years after Parnell's death. How does the remembered presence of Charles Stewart Parnell sharpen our understanding of what takes place in the committee room?

39. To what extent does the dramatic function of Mr. Hynes's poem on "The Death of Parnell" depend upon our evaluation of its poetic merit?

"A Mother"

40. Joyce once said that he wrote *Dubliners* in "a style of scrupulous meanness." Does this phrase accurately describe the style of "A Mother"?

41. Consider "A Mother" as a story of "public life in Dublin." How are the public and private aspects of the story related to each other?

"Grace"

42. At one point in the writing of *Dubliners* Joyce thought of "Grace" as the concluding story. In what ways is it an appropriate conclusion to the stories that precede it?
43. As indicated in the headnote to "Grace," Stanislaus Joyce believed that his brother organized the story by following a three-part Dantean pattern of "inferno-purgatorio-paradiso." How does this knowledge of Joyce's possible intention contribute to our understanding of the story?
44. Compare the thematic and structural functions of Father Purdon's sermon with those of Mr. Hynes's poem at the end of "Ivy Day in the Committee Room." To what extent are both performances treated satirically?
45. Using the notes to the story as a base, discuss the function of theological information (and *misinformation*) in "Grace."
46. Compare Mrs. Kernan's attitudes toward religion (see pp. 155–58) with those of the wives in "Counterparts" and "A Little Cloud."

"The Dead"

47. In his essay reprinted in this collection Frank O'Connor makes the claim that "The Dead" is radically different from the other stories in *Dubliners*. Do you agree?
48. "The Dead" was planned and written well after the other stories in *Dubliners* had been completed and submitted for publication. To what extent does it develop and draw together the leading themes and symbolic motifs of the entire collection?
49. Through a detailed analysis of imagery and rhythm, distinguish between the prose styles of the first and last paragraphs of "The Dead." What other distinct prose styles can you isolate in the story, and how do they contribute to our sense of a developing pattern?
50. Richard Ellmann has discussed in great detail the autobiographical elements in "The Dead" (see his essay reprinted in

this collection). How legitimate is it to read the story as a form of autobiography?

51. Using the essays by Richard Ellmann and Florence Walzl as a starting-point, discuss the various ways in which outside information may contribute to a reading of "The Dead."

52. "The Dead" progresses by means of clearly defined scenes or episodes which mark the stages in Gabriel's developing self-awareness. Choose a single episode or scene and discuss its contribution to this process.

53. Interpretations of the conclusion to "The Dead" have tended to be either "positive" or "negative": the snow which is general all over Ireland is seen either as an agent of expanding consciousness and awareness for Gabriel, or as a symbol of total paralysis affecting both Gabriel and Ireland. What proportions of sympathy and criticism do you find in the last paragraphs of the story?

Selected Bibliography

❖❖❖

I. WORKS BY JAMES JOYCE

This section lists in chronological order the first editions of Joyce's most important works. For a comprehensive study of his publications see John J. Slocum and Herbert Cahoon, *A Bibliography of James Joyce* (New Haven: Yale University Press, 1953).

"Ibsen's New Drama." *Fortnightly Review*, LXVII (April 1900), 575–90.

"The Day of the Rabblement." In F. J. C. Skeffington and James A. Joyce, *Two Essays*. Dublin: Gerrard Bros., 1901.

The Holy Office. Pola: Privately printed, 1905.

[In addition to the three items listed above, a number of early essays and reviews have survived; for the texts of these early pieces see *The Critical Writings of James Joyce*, ed. Ellsworth Mason and Richard Ellmann (New York: The Viking Press, 1959).]

Chamber Music. London: Elkin Mathews, 1907.

Gas from a Burner. [Trieste]: Privately printed, 1912.

Dubliners. London: Grant Richards Ltd., 1914.

A Portrait of the Artist as a Young Man. New York: B. W. Huebsch, 1916.

Exiles. London: Grant Richards Ltd., 1918.

Ulysses. Paris: Shakespeare and Co., 1922. Versions of episodes 1–14 appeared serially in *The Little Review*, 1918–1920.

Pomes Penyeach. Paris: Shakespeare and Co., 1927.

Anna Livia Plurabelle [*Finnegans Wake* 196–216]. New York: Crosby Gaige, 1928.

Tales Told of Shem and Shaun [FW 152–59, 282–304, 414–19]. Paris: The Black Sun Press, 1929.

Haveth Childers Everywhere [FW 532–54]. Paris: Henry Babou and Jack Kahane; New York: The Fountain Press, 1930.

The Mime of Mick Nick and the Maggies [FW 219–59]. The Hague: The Servire Press, 1934.

Collected Poems. New York: The Black Sun Press, 1936.

Storiella As She Is Syung [FW 260–75, 304–308]. London: Corvinus Press, 1937.

Finnegans Wake. London: Faber & Faber, 1939. In addition to the book publications listed above, fragments of Joyce's *Work in Progress* appeared in several periodicals between 1924 and 1938.

Stephen Hero, ed. Theodore Spencer. New York: New Directions, 1944. A new edition was issued in 1963, including additional manuscript pages edited by John J. Slocum and Herbert Cahoon.

Letters of James Joyce, Vol. I, ed. Stuart Gilbert. New York: The Viking Press, 1957 (revised 1966).

Letters of James Joyce, Vols. II and III, ed. Richard Ellmann. New York: The Viking Press, 1966.

The Critical Writings of James Joyce, ed. Ellsworth Mason and Richard Ellmann. New York: The Viking Press, 1959. Includes the early essays and reviews, the Paris and Pola notebooks, later political articles, and the broadsides (*The Holy Office* and *Gas from a Burner*).

The Workshop of Daedalus, ed. Robert Scholes and Richard M. Kain. Evanston, Ill.: Northwestern University Press, 1965. Contains important manuscript materials, including all the extant epiphanies and the 1904 autobiographical fragment, "A Portrait of the Artist."

II. IMPORTANT BIOGRAPHICAL SOURCES

Budgen, Frank. *James Joyce and the Making of "Ulysses."* London, 1934; new edn., Bloomington, Ind.: University of Indiana Press, 1960. An invaluable account of Joyce's attitudes at the time when *Ulysses* was nearing completion (1918–1921). Budgen was an intimate friend during the Zurich period.

Colum, Mary and Padraic. *Our Friend James Joyce.* New York: Dolphin Books, 1958. Reminiscences by two lifelong friends.

Curran, C. P. *James Joyce Remembered.* New York and London: Oxford University Press, 1968. Recollections by a fellow student at University College who knew Joyce intimately in the years 1900–1904.

Ellmann, Richard. *James Joyce.* New York: Oxford University Press, 1959. The standard biography, an exhaustive and intelligent synthesis of published and unpublished sources. The treatment of Joyce's early life is particularly illuminating.

Joyce, Stanislaus. *My Brother's Keeper.* New York: The Viking Press, 1958.

————. *The Dublin Diary of Stanislaus Joyce,* ed. George H. Healey. Ithaca, N.Y.: Cornell University Press, 1962. Joyce as seen by his brilliant and exasperating brother. Taken together these two works cover the first twenty-three years of Joyce's life.

Sullivan, Kevin. *Joyce among the Jesuits.* New York: Columbia University Press, 1958. This account of Joyce's education at Clongowes Wood, Belvedere, and University College illuminates the complex relationship between Stephen Dedalus and his creator. By defining Joyce's actual attitude toward the Jesuits, Sullivan has helped us to understand the ways in which Joyce transformed autobiographical materials.

III. GENERAL CRITICISM

This section is limited to a listing of significant general studies. Inevitably, much useful criticism has been omitted, and the student who seeks further information should consult one of the following checklists:

Beebe, Maurice, and Litz, Walton. "Criticism of James Joyce: A Selected Checklist with an Index to Studies of Separate Works." *Modern Fiction Studies*, IV (1958), 71–99.

Deming, Robert. A *Bibliography of James Joyce Studies*. Lawrence, Kan.: University Press of Kansas, 1964.

Adams, Robert M. *James Joyce: Common Sense and Beyond*. New York: Random House, 1966. A general survey, especially good on *Dubliners*.

Givens, Seon, ed. *James Joyce: Two Decades of Criticism*. New York: Vanguard Press, 1948, 1963. A collection of important essays from the 1923–1948 period.

Goldberg, S. L. *James Joyce*. New York: Evergreen Books, 1962. A brief but suggestive survey of Joyce's total achievement.

Goldman, Arnold. *The Joyce Paradox*. Evanston, Ill.: Northwestern University Press, 1966. An attempt to mediate between the extremes of Joyce criticism.

Kenner, Hugh. *Dublin's Joyce*. Bloomington, Ind.: Indiana University Press, 1956. An extended analysis of all the works: crotchety but full of brilliant insights.

Levin, Harry. *James Joyce: A Critical Introduction*. Norfolk, 1941; revised edn., New York: New Directions, 1960. Still one of the best introductions to Joyce's art. Levin emphasizes Joyce's place in the European literary tradition.

Litz, A. Walton. *James Joyce*. New York: Twayne Publishers, 1966. A guide to the major works which emphasizes the continuity of Joyce's artistic development.

Magalaner, Marvin, and Kain, Richard. *Joyce: The Man, the Work, the Reputation*. New York: Collier Books, 1956. A panoramic study which examines Joyce's life, presents interpretations of the individual works, and charts the progress of Joyce's reputation.

Particularly useful for its summaries of critical trends and opinions. Annotated bibliography.

Morse, J. Mitchell. *The Sympathetic Alien.* New York: New York University Press, 1959. A series of essays on Joyce and Catholicism.

Noon, William. *Joyce and Aquinas.* New Haven: Yale University Press, 1957. The religious aspects of Joyce's art examined from a Catholic viewpoint.

Tindall, William York. *James Joyce: His Way of Interpreting the Modern World.* New York: Charles Scribner's Sons, 1950. A broad study which stresses the symbolic unity of Joyce's work.

_____. *A Reader's Guide to James Joyce.* New York: Farrar, Straus & Giroux, 1959. Close analyses of each work, designed for the general reader.

Wilson, Edmund. "James Joyce," in *Axel's Castle: A Study in the Imaginative Literature of 1870–1930.* New York: Charles Scribner's Sons, 1931. A pioneering study of Joyce's place in modern literature; Wilson's opinions profoundly influenced the course of subsequent criticism.

IV. DUBLINERS

A. *General Studies* (the student should also consult the comprehensive studies listed in Part III).

Baker, James R. "Ibsen, Joyce, and the Living-Dead: A Study of *Dubliners*," in *A James Joyce Miscellany*, 3rd series, ed. Marvin Magalaner. Carbondale, Ill.: Southern Illinois University Press, 1962, pp. 19–32.

Carrier, Warren. "*Dubliners*: Joyce's Dantean Vision." *Renascence*, XVII (1965). 211–15.

Daiches, David. *The Novel and the Modern World*. Chicago: University of Chicago Press, 1939, pp. 80–100.

Ellmann, Richard. *James Joyce*. New York: Oxford University Press, 1959, pp. 252–63 and *passim*.

Friedrich, Gerhard. "The Perspective of Joyce's *Dubliners*." *College English*, XXVI (1965), 421–26.

Ghiselin, Brewster. "The Unity of Joyce's *Dubliners*." *Accent*, XVI (1956), 75–88 and 196–213.

Gifford, Don. *Notes for Joyce*. New York: E. P. Dutton & Co., 1967.

Levin, Richard, and Shattuck, Charles. "First Flight to Ithaca," in *James Joyce: Two Decades of Criticism*, ed. Seon Givens. New York: Vanguard Press, 1948, 1963, pp. 47–94.

Magalaner, Marvin. *Time of Apprenticeship: The Fiction of Young James Joyce*. New York: Abelard-Schuman, 1959.

O'Connor, Frank. *The Mirror in the Roadway*. New York: Alfred A. Knopf, 1956, pp. 295–312.

_____. *The Lonely Voice*. New York: Alfred A. Knopf, 1963, pp. 113–27.

Scholes, Robert. "Some Observations on the Text of *Dubliners*: 'The Dead'." *Studies in Bibliography*. Charlottesville, Va.: University Press of Virginia, XV (1962), 191–205.

_____. "Further Observations on the Text of *Dubliners*." *Studies in Bibliography*. Charlottesville, Va.: University Press of Virginia, XVII (1964), 107–22.

Walzl, Florence L. "Pattern of Paralysis in Joyce's *Dubliners*." *College English*, XXII (1961), 221–28. Reply by Gerhard Friedrich, 519–20.

B. *Studies of Individual Stories* (the *James Joyce Quarterly* is abbreviated as *JJQ*).

"The Sisters"
Benstock, Bernard. " 'The Sisters' and the Critics." *JJQ*, IV (1966), 32–35.
Connolly, Thomas E. "Joyce's 'The Sisters': A Pennyworth of Snuff." *College English*, XXVII (1965), 189–95.
Senn, Fritz. " 'He Was Too Scrupulous Always': Joyce's 'The Sisters.' " *JJQ*, II (1965), 66–72.
Spielberg, Peter. " 'The Sisters': No Christ at Bethany." *JJQ*, III (1966), 192–95.
"An Encounter"
Feshbach, Sidney. "Death in 'An Encounter.' " *JJQ*, II (1965), 82–89.
Kaye, Julian B. "The Wings of Daedalus: Two Stories in *Dubliners*." *Modern Fiction Studies*, IV (1958), 31–41.
"Araby"
ap Roberts, R. P. " 'Araby' and the Palimpsest of Criticism; or, Through a Glass Eye Darkly." *Antioch Review*, XXVI (1966–1967), 469–89.
Lyons, John O. "James Joyce and Chaucer's Prioress." *English Language Notes* (University of Colorado), II (1964), 127–32.
Stein, William B. "Joyce's 'Araby': Paradise Lost." *Perspective*, XII (1962), 215–22.
Stone, Harry. " 'Araby' and the Writings of James Joyce." *Antioch Review*, XXV (1965), 375–410.
"Eveline"
Stein, William B. "The Effects of Eden in Joyce's 'Eveline.' " *Renascence*, XV (1963), 124–26.
"Two Gallants"
Boyle, Robert. " 'Two Gallants' and 'Ivy Day in the Committee Room.' " *JJQ*, I (1963), 3–9.
Walzl, Florence L. "Symbolism in Joyce's 'Two Gallants.' " *JJQ*, II (1965), 73–81.
"The Boarding House"
Rosenberg, Bruce A. "The Crucifixion in 'The Boarding House.' " *Studies in Short Fiction* (Newberry, S.C.), V (1967), 44–53.

"A Little Cloud"

Brodbar, Harold. "A Religious Allegory: Joyce's 'A Little Cloud.'" *Midwest Quarterly*, II (1961), 221–27.

Ruoff, James. "'A Little Cloud': Joyce's Portrait of the Would-be Artist." *Research Studies of the State College of Washington*, XXV (1957), 256–71.

Short, Clarice. "Joyce's 'A Little Cloud.'" *Modern Language Notes*, LXXII (1957), 275–78.

"Counterparts"

Hagopian, John V. "The Epiphany in Joyce's 'Counterparts.'" *Studies in Short Fiction* (Newberry, S.C.), I (1964), 272–76.

Stein, William B. "'Counterparts': A Swine Song." *JJQ*, I (1963), 30–32.

"Clay"

Carpenter, Richard, and Leary, Daniel. "The Witch Maria." *James Joyce Review*, III (1959), 3–7.

Connolly, Thomas E. "Marriage Divination in Joyce's 'Clay.'" *Studies in Short Fiction* (Newberry, S.C.), III (1966), 293–99.

Noon, William T. "Joyce's 'Clay': An Interpretation." *College English*, XVII (1955), 93–95.

Staley, Thomas F. "Moral Responsibility in Joyce's 'Clay.'" *Renascence*, XVIII (1966), 125–28.

"A Painful Case"

Corrington, J. W. "Isolation as Motif in 'A Painful Case.'" *JJQ*, III (1966), 182–91.

Magalaner, Marvin. "Joyce, Nietzsche, and Hauptmann in James Joyce's 'A Painful Case.'" *PMLA*, LXVIII (1953), 95–102.

Wright, Charles D. "Melancholy Duffy and Sanguine Sinico: Humors in 'A Painful Case.'" *JJQ*, III (1966), 171–81.

"Ivy Day in the Committee Room"

Blotner, Joseph L. "'Ivy Day in the Committee Room': Death without Resurrection." *Perspective*, IX (1957), 210–17.

Boyle, Robert. "'Two Gallants' and 'Ivy Day in the Committee Room.'" *JJQ*, I (1963), 3–9.

"A Mother"

O'Neill, Michael J. "Joyce's Use of Memory in 'A Mother.'" *Modern Language Notes*, LXXIV (1959), 226–30.

"Grace"

Baker, Joseph E. "The Trinity in Joyce's 'Grace.'" *JJQ*, II (1965), 299–303.

Jackson, Robert S. "A Parabolic Reading of James Joyce's 'Grace.'" *Modern Language Notes*, LXXVI (1961), 719–24.

Newman, F. X. "The Land of Ooze: Joyce's 'Grace' and *The*

Book of Job." *Studies in Short Fiction* (Newberry, S.C.), IV (1966), 70–79.

Niemeyer, Carl. " 'Grace' and Joyce's Method of Parody." *College English*, XXVII (1965), 196–201.

"The Dead"

Bierman, Robert. "Structural Elements in 'The Dead.' " *JJQ*, IV (1966), 42–45.

Blum, Morgan. "The Shifting Point of View: Joyce's 'The Dead' and Gordon's 'Old Red.' " *Critique*, I (1956), 45–66.

Cox, Roger L. "Johnny the Horse in Joyce's 'The Dead.' " *JJQ*, IV (1966), 36–41.

Damon, Phillip. "A Symphasis of Antipaties in 'The Dead.' " *Modern Language Notes*, LXXIV (1959), 111–14.

Ellmann, Richard. "The Backgrounds of 'The Dead,' " in *James Joyce*. New York: Oxford University Press, 1959, pp. 252–63.

Friedrich, Gerhard. "Bret Harte as a Source for James Joyce's 'The Dead.' " *Philological Quarterly*, XXXIII (1954), 442–44.

Kaye, Julian B. "The Wings of Daedalus: Two Stories in *Dubliners*." *Modern Fiction Studies*, IV (1958), 31–41.

Kelleher, John V. "Irish History and Mythology in James Joyce's 'The Dead.' " *Review of Politics* (Notre Dame), XXVII (1965), 414–33.

Loomis, C. C., Jr. "Structure and Sympathy in Joyce's 'The Dead.' " *PMLA*, LXXV (1960), 149–51.

Ludwig, Jack B. "James Joyce's *Dubliners*," in *Stories British and American*, ed. Jack B. Ludwig and W. R. Poirier. Boston: Houghton Mifflin Co., 1953, pp. 384–91.

Moseley, Virginia. " 'Two Sights for Ever a Picture' in Joyce's 'The Dead.' " *College English*, XXVI (1965), 426–33.

O Hehir, Brendan P. "Structural Symbol in Joyce's 'The Dead.' " *Twentieth Century Literature*, III (1957), 3–13.

Scheuerle, William H. " 'Gabriel Hounds' and Joyce's 'The Dead.' " *Studies in Short Fiction* (Newberry, S.C.), II (1965), 369–71.

Schmidt, Hugo. "Hauptmann's *Michael Kramer* and Joyce's 'The Dead.' " *PMLA*, LXXX (1965), 141–42.

Smith, Thomas F. "Color and Light in 'The Dead.' " *JJQ*, II (1965), 304–309.

Tate, Allen. "Three Commentaries: Poe, James, and Joyce." *Sewanee Review*, LVIII (1950), 10–15. Reprinted in Caroline Gordon and Allen Tate, *The House of Fiction*. New York: Charles Scribner's Sons, 1950, pp. 279–82.

Walzl, Florence L. "Gabriel and Michael: The Conclusion of 'The Dead.' " *JJQ*, IV (1966), 17–31.

David Daiches - The Novel & the Modern World (Chicago, U. of C. Press, 1939) 91-100

Notes to the Stories

The aim of these notes is to explain those important literary allusions, religious usages, topical references, slang terms, and Irishisms which are likely to baffle the present-day reader of *Dubliners*. Although the stories do not have the density of reference and allusion found in Joyce's later works, they do pose a number of problems in symbolic interpretation. In these notes we have tried to avoid explicit interpretations, preferring to provide the raw materials from which such interpretations may be constructed.

Joyce wrote *Dubliners* with a loving care for the geographical and social details of his native city. Although some of the place-names are fictitious, most of the local references are scrupulously exact; they are part of a "realism" which existed as much for Joyce's benefit as for ours. These references often suggest the social nuances of Dublin life, or they may indicate the "tone" of a particular place or area. Although we have not attempted to gloss all the names of streets, pubs, churches, public buildings, and newspapers, we have supplied information where the significance of these references appears to extend beyond a sense of local "realism."

Most of the sources referred to in these notes are listed in the Bibliography. For other extensive annotations of *Dubliners* the student should consult Marvin Magalaner, *Time of Apprenticeship: The Fiction of Young James Joyce* (New York: Abelard-Schuman, 1959), pp. 147–71, and Don Gifford, *Notes for Joyce* (New York: E. P. Dutton, 1967—available in Dutton Paperback).

The editors are grateful to Mr. William Stowe and the Reverend Austin MacCurtain, S.J., for their help with some of the more specialized annotations.

"THE SISTERS"

The first of the *Dubliners* stories to be written, "The Sisters" was published in a Dublin weekly, *The Irish Homestead*, on August 13, 1904. This early version, which was conceived as a self-sufficient tale, was later radically revised when Joyce turned it into the "program piece" for the entire collection. The original text of "The Sisters" is reprinted on pp. 243–52.

9.6 "two candles must be set at the head of a corpse"—an Irish custom, not part of prescribed religious ritual.

9.11 "*gnomon* in the Euclid"—in geometry, a gnomon is that part of a parallelogram which remains when a similar parallelogram is taken away from one of its corners. In schoolboy jargon "the Euclid" would refer to any geometry text based on the *Elements* of Euclid, a Greek mathematician of the 3rd century B.C.

9.12 "*simony* in the Catechism"—simony is worldly traffic in spiritual things, such as the medieval practice of buying or selling ecclesiastical preferments. The term derives from the Biblical account of Simon Magus, a Samaritan "magician" who was impressed by the spiritual power of the Apostles and offered a sum of money for the secret (Acts 8: 18–19). In the Roman Catholic Catechism simony is listed as one of the sins against the First Commandment.

9.17 "stirabout"—porridge made by stirring oatmeal into hot milk or water.

10.5 "faints and worms"—technical terms from the distillery. "Faints" is the impure spirit which appears first and last in the process of distillation; the "worm" is the coiled tube connected with the head of the still in which the vapor is condensed.

11.2 "box his corner"—hold his own in any fight.

11.2 "Rosicrucian"—in its strict sense, the term refers to a member of the mystical order of Father Christian Rosenkreuz, a legendary figure who was reputed to have found the secret wisdom of the East while on a pilgrimage in the 15th century. By extension, the term became a slang description of anyone given to dreamy or unworldly behavior. The study of Rosicrucian-ism and other esoteric systems was popular with Dublin intellectuals at the turn of the century.

11.30 "simoniac"—one who practices simony (see note on 9.12).

12.9 "R.I.P."—*Requiescat in Pace*, "Rest in Peace."

12.15 "High Toast"—a brand of snuff.

13.2 "the Irish college in Rome"—an Irish-sponsored foundation in Rome for the training of Irish priests. The implication is that Father Flynn had a promising youth.

13.13 "the Eucharist"—the sacrament of the Lord's Supper or Holy Communion.

13.13 "the secrecy of the confessional"—the confessional is the cabinet or stall in which the Roman Catholic priest hears the confessions of penitents. The priest is bound to secrecy, and any violation of "the seal of the confessional" can lead to excommunication.

14.28 "chalice"—the cup used to hold the wine in the celebration of the Eucharist.

15.20 "anointed him and prepared him and all"—the Roman Catholic sacrament of Extreme Unction, administered in cases of mortal illness. The sick in danger of death are anointed by the priest for the sake of body and soul.

16.12 *"Freeman's General"*—the *Freeman's Journal*, a Dublin newspaper. Eliza is given to malapropisms: see her confusion of "rheumatic" and "pneumatic," 17.8.

16.33 "breviary"—the book containing the "Divine Office" for each day, which those holding major orders in the Roman Catholic Church are bound to recite.

17.5 "Irishtown"—a Dublin slum.

17.8 "rheumatic"—malapropism for "pneumatic."

17.28 "the boy's fault"—that is, the fault of the young acolyte who attends the priest at the altar and carries the candles.

"AN ENCOUNTER"

Ninth in the order of composition, "An Encounter" was completed sometime before September 18, 1905. When the English printer refused to set up two other stories, "Two Gallants" and "Counterparts," Joyce remarked that a "more subtle inquisitor will denounce *An Encounter*, the enormity of which the printer cannot see because he is, as I said, a plain blunt man" (*Letters*, II, 134). Joyce's younger brother Stanislaus has given this account of the story's origin: "In 'An Encounter,' my brother describes a day's miching which he and I planned and carried out while we were living in North Richmond Street, and our encounter with an elderly pederast. For us he was just a 'juggins.' Neither of us could have any notion at the time what kind of 'juggins' he was, but something funny in his speech and behaviour put us on our guard at once. We thought he might be an escaped madman. As he looked about fifty and had a military air, I nicknamed him 'the captain of fifty' from a phrase I had seen somewhere in a Biblical quotation" (*My Brother's Keeper* [New York: The Viking Press, 1958], p. 62).

19.2   *"The Union Jack, Pluck* and *The Halfpenny Marvel"*—magazines containing popular adventure stories for boys. *The Halfpenny Marvel* first appeared in 1893, followed in 1894 by *The Union Jack* and in 1895 by *Pluck.* These magazines had a "healthy" tone, and were designed to counter the influence of the "penny dreadfuls."

19.16   "—Ya! yaka, yaka, yaka!"—imitation of an Indian chant.

20.25   "college"—probably Belvedere College, a Jesuit school for boys. Joyce attended the school after leaving Clongowes Wood College, and Stephen Dedalus follows the same pattern in *A Portrait of the Artist.*

20.29   "National School boys"—the government-sponsored National Schools were feared by Catholic educators, since they pursued an English and nonsectarian theory of education. They were also considered to be socially inferior.

21.11   "miching"—truancy.

21.16 "the Pigeon House"—a fort located on a breakwater in Dublin bay, now used as a public power plant.

21.32 "pipeclayed"—cleaned with a fine white clay.

22.8 "catapult"—a sling-shot.

22.15 "funk it"—to lose one's nerve.

22.18 "a bob"—a shilling.

22.18 "a tanner"—a sixpence, half a shilling.

22.20 "Vitriol Works"—an actual landmark, The Dublin Vitriol Works Co.

22.26 "*Swaddlers!*"—an Irish nickname for Protestants.

22.29 "the Smoothing Iron"—probably the slang name for a local landmark.

23.11 "it would be right skit"—it would be good fun.

23.26 "green eyes"—to see green in an eye is to detect gullibility or inexperience. Throughout "An Encounter" Joyce exploits the various connotations of the color green: see "those green stems on which girls tell fortunes" (24.19), "a suit of greenish-black" (24.23), and "a pair of bottle-green eyes" (27.17).

24.8 "the Dodder"—a local river, tributary of the Liffey.

24.19 "those green stems on which girls tell fortunes"—evidently a version of "he-loves-me-he-loves-me-not."

24.24 "jerry hat"—a round felt hat.

25.7 "the poetry of Thomas Moore or the Works of Sir Walter Scott and Lord Lytton"—Thomas Moore (1779–1852), Irish poet and songwriter; Sir Walter Scott (1771–1832), Scottish poet and novelist; Edward George Earle Lytton Bulwer-Lytton (1803–1873), British novelist and dramatist. All three writers were famous for their romantic themes and situations.

25.16 "some of Lord Lytton's works which boys couldn't read"—although Bulwer-Lytton's novels were constructed with a didactic purpose, their freedom in subject matter led many nineteenth-century critics to question their sincerity and morality. Scandal associated with Bulwer-Lytton's private life also contributed to the "undesirable" reputation of some of his works.

25.23 "totties"—derived from "Hotten*tot*," the term has vulgar overtones and was often used to describe a high-class prostitute.

26.27 "a queer old josser"—a "juggins," a simpleton: in Pidgin English the term "joss" means a "god" or an "idol." See Stanislaus Joyce's account of the origin of "An Encounter," quoted in the headnote to this section.

"ARABY"

The eleventh story to be written, "Araby" was finished in October 1905.

29.1 "North Richmond Street"—the Joyce family lived at 17 North Richmond Street from 1894 to 1896, while James was a student at Belvedere College.

29.1 "blind"—closed at one end.

29.2 "the Christian Brothers' School"—a day school operated by the Irish Christian Brothers, a lay order proud of its conservatism. The Joyce children attended this school for a short time in 1893, but in later years James never referred to this break in his Jesuit education. Evidently James and his father felt that the schooling of the Christian Brothers (which was "principally but not exclusively for the sons of the poor and of the working class") was inferior to that of the Jesuits, both socially and intellectually. In *A Portrait of the Artist* Mr. Dedalus remarks: "Christian Brothers be damned! . . . Is it with Paddy Stink and Mickey Mud? No, let him stick to the jesuits. . . . Those are the fellows that can get you a position" (Viking Compass edition, p. 71).

29.12 "*The Abbot,* by Walter Scott"—a prose romance concerning Mary Queen of Scots, published in 1820.

29.12 "*The Devout Communicant*"—*The Devout Communicant: or Pious Meditations and Aspirations for the Three Days Before and Three Days After Receiving the Holy Eucharist* (1813), a straightforward religious tract written by a Franciscan friar, Pacificus Baker.

29.13 "*The Memoirs of Vidocq*"—François Eugène Vidocq (1775–1857), a French detective, was imprisoned early in life and spent some time in the company of criminals, making a study of their methods. In 1809 he offered his services to the Paris police, and subsequently became chief of detectives. He retired in 1827, but in 1832 he returned to the police service and sought to re-establish his reputation by arranging and then "discovering" a theft. He was dismissed from the service, and after an abortive career as a private detective he died in great poverty. It is doubtful if Vidocq had a hand in writing the *Memoirs*.

For further information on these books and their relevance to "Araby," see Harry Stone, " 'Araby' and the Writings of James Joyce," p. 344 of this collection.

30.9 "the rough tribes from the cottages"—children from the poorer houses.

31.7 "a *come-all-you*"—any popular song beginning "Come all you Irishmen . . ."

31.8 "O'Donovan Rossa"—Jeremiah O'Donovan (1831–1915), known as "Dynamite Rossa," an Irish nationalist who was imprisoned in 1865 for his revolutionary activities. He was banished to the United States in 1870, but returned to Ireland in the early 1890s and remained there until 1900.

31.10 "chalice"—see note on "The Sisters," 14.28.

31.32 "*Araby*"—a bazaar held in Dublin on May 14–19, 1894. Described as a "Grand Oriental Fête," the bazaar probably took its name from the popular song "I'll Sing Thee Songs of Araby":

> I'll sing thee songs of Araby,
> And tales of far Cashmere,
> Wild tales to cheat thee of a sigh,
> Or charm thee to a tear;
> And dreams of delight shall on thee break,
> And rainbow visions rise,
> And all my soul shall strive to wake
> Sweet wonder in thine eyes.

32.3 "a retreat"—a period of withdrawal from the world devoted to prayer and meditation.

32.21 "Freemason affair"—the Masonic Order was thought to be an enemy of the Catholic Church. The boy's aunt evidently associates the exotic bazaar with the secret rites of Freemasonry.

34.9 "*The Arab's Farewell to his Steed*"—a sentimental poem by Caroline Norton (1808–1877), also called "The Arab's Farewell to His Horse." The speaker imagines his desolation after selling his favorite steed, and in the last stanza he awakes from the "fevered dream" and flings back "their gold." The following are the first and last stanzas of one version of the poem:

> My beautiful! my beautiful!
> That standest meekly by
> With thy proudly arched and glossy neck,
> And dark and fiery eye;

Fret not to roam the desert now,
  With all thy winged speed—
I may not mount on thee again—
  Thou'rt sold, my Arab steed!
Fret not with that impatient hoof—
  Snuff not the breezy wind—
The further that thou fliest now,
  So far am I behind;
The stranger hath thy bridle rein—
  Thy master hath *his* gold—
Fleet-limbed and beautiful! farewell!—
  Thou'rt sold, my steed—thou'rt sold!

. . . .

When last I saw thee drink!—away!
  The fevered dream is o'er—
I could not live a day, and *know*
  That we should meet no more!
They tempted me, my beautiful!
  For hunger's power is strong—
They tempted me, my beautiful!
  But I have loved too long.
Who said that I had given thee up?—
  Who said that thou wert sold?
'Tis false,—'tis false, my Arab steed!
  I fling them back their gold!
Thus, *thus*, I leap upon thy back,
  And scour the distant plains;
Away! who overtakes us now,
  Shall claim *thee* for his pains.

34.12 "florin"—a two-shilling piece.
34.34 *"Café Chantant"*—a café providing musical entertainment.
35.8–13 This brief exchange resembles the dramatic epiphanies
  recorded by Joyce (see p. 253 of this collection).

"EVELINE"

Second in the order of composition, "Eveline" was first published in *The Irish Homestead* (September 10, 1904).

36.9 "a man from Belfast"—an outsider, a Protestant from the north of Ireland.

36.17 "to keep *nix*"—to serve as a lookout.

37.13 "the promises made to Blessed Margaret Mary Alacoque"—Born in 1647 at Janots, in Burgundy (France), Saint Margaret-Mary Alacoque made a vow of chastity at the age of four, although she later admitted that at this age she did not understand what either a vow or chastity was. At the age of eight her father died and she was sent to a convent school, where her piety so impressed the nuns that she was allowed to make her first Communion one year later. From ages eleven to fifteen she suffered from rheumatism and paralysis. She also inflicted bizarre punishments upon herself, once carving the name "Jesus" on her breast with a penknife.

On December 27, 1673, her devotion and mortifications were rewarded by the first of her great revelations; it was as though the Lord took her heart and put it within His own, returning it burning with divine love into her breast. For eighteen months the Lord continued to appear to her, directing that she establish certain acts of reparation, but when she carried the matter to her superior she was severely rebuffed. She fell gravely ill, but the Lord fulfilled His promise of an understanding director and sent the Blessed Claude de la Colombière to the convent, who immediately recognized the genuineness of Saint Margaret-Mary's experiences. Finally, in November 1677, the young nun obeyed the Lord's command and knelt before her sisters, telling them in the name of Christ that she was appointed to be the victim of their failings.

After a subsequent life of great trials and sickness, Saint Margaret-Mary died in October 1690. She was beatified in 1864 and canonized by Pope Benedict XV in 1920. Saint Margaret-Mary was instrumental in establishing the Devotion to the Sacred

Heart of Jesus. (For further details see *Butler's Lives of the Saints.*)

39.3 *"The Bohemian Girl"*—an opera with music by the Irish composer Michael William Balfe, libretto by Alfred Bunn, first produced in 1843. The scene is laid in Austria, and the romantic plot—based on a tale by Cervantes—involves kidnaping and hidden identities. Arline, the Bohemian girl, is stolen by gypsies at the age of six and lives with them for twelve years, tended by Thaddeus, an exiled Polish nobleman who has fallen deeply in love with her. Although Arline does not know the secret of her high birth she is vaguely aware that she is not of the gypsy race, and she tells Thaddeus of her dreamlike memories in the famous song "I Dreamt that I Dwelt in Marble Halls." Thaddeus, not wishing to lose Arline, does not reveal her origins, but she is ultimately recognized by her father the count and restored to him. She remains true to her lover, and Thaddeus finally claims her hand by proving himself to be of noble birth.

39.6 "the lass that loves a sailor"—a song by Charles Dibdin (1745–1814), English dramatist and songwriter.

> The moon on the ocean was dimmed by a ripple,
> Affording a chequered delight,
> The gay jolly tars passed the word for the tipple
> And the toast, for 'twas Saturday night.
> Some sweetheart or wife, he loved as his life,
> Each drank, and wished he could hail her,
> But the standing toast that pleased the most,
> Was the wind that blows, the ship that goes,
> And the lass that loves a sailor.
> . . . .
> Some drank our Queen, and some our land—
> Our glorious land of freedom!
> Some, that our tars might never stand,
> For heroes brave to lead 'em!
> That beauty in distress might find,
> Such friends as ne'er would fail her,
> But the standing toast that pleased the most,
> Was the wind that blows, the ship that goes,
> And the lass that loves a sailor.

39.11 "the Allan Line"—a steamship line serving England and North America.

39.30 "the Hill of Howth"—located nine miles northeast of Dublin, the hill dominates Dublin Bay.

40.8 "sixpence"—an exorbitant tip.

40.16 "—Derevaun Seraun! Derevaun Seraun!"—although it appears to be Gaelic, this mysterious exclamation has never been satisfactorily explained. Joyce may have intended it as delirious gibberish.

"AFTER THE RACE"

Third in the order of composition, "After the Race" was first published in *The Irish Homestead* (December 17, 1904). Early in April 1903 Joyce, who was then in Paris, interviewed the French racing-car driver Henri Fournier, and he obviously had this experience in mind when writing "After the Race" (Joyce's "Interview with the French Champion" was published in the *Irish Times*, April 7, 1903: for the text see Ellsworth Mason and Richard Ellmann, eds., *The Critical Writings of James Joyce*, [New York: The Viking Press, 1959], pp. 106–108). As *Dubliners* took shape Joyce became increasingly dissatisfied with the form of this early story: in August 1906 he told his brother Stanislaus that he would like to "rewrite" it, and in November 1906 he referred to "After the Race" and "A Painful Case" as "the two worst stories" (*Letters*, II, 151, 189).

43.15 "an advanced Nationalist"—an enthusiastic supporter of Parnell and Home Rule for Ireland.

43.19 "police contracts"—contracts to provision the jails, usually at a set amount per head. These contracts could be immensely lucrative.

43.23 "Dublin University"—i.e., Trinity College, the ancient and prestigious university which was predominantly Protestant and maintained close ties with the English universities. The alternative titles of "Trinity College" and "Dublin University" are explained by the fact that the university consists of only one college, that of "the Holy and Undivided Trinity."

45.15 "the Bank"—the Bank of Ireland, located at the intersection of Dame and Grafton streets in the center of Dublin.

47.17 *"Cadet Roussel"*—a French drinking song with topical (and often improvised) verses, first made popular in 1792. The refrain runs: "Ah! ah! mais vraiment, *Cadet Rousselle est bon enfant*."

47.19 "—Ho! Ho! Hohé, *vraiment!*"—a variation on the refrain of "Cadet Rousselle."

48.15 *"The Belle of Newport"*—Newport, Rhode Island, was a rendezvous for fashionable yachtsmen.

"TWO GALLANTS"

"Two Gallants" was written in the winter of 1905–1906, after Joyce had submitted to his publisher a symmetrical collection of twelve stories. In this original grouping, as Joyce explained to his brother Stanislaus (*Letters*, II, 111), the first section was devoted to "stories of [his] childhood" ("The Sisters"—"An Encounter"—"Araby"); the second to "stories of adolescence" ("Eveline"—"After the Race"—"The Boarding House"); the third to "stories of mature life" ("Counterparts"—"Clay"—"A Painful Case"); while the last three tales ("Ivy Day in the Committee Room"—"A Mother"—"Grace") were "stories of public life in Dublin." "Two Gallants" was inserted between "After the Race" and "The Boarding House" as an additional story of adolescent life. In May of 1906 Joyce remarked to his publisher: "It is one of the most important stories in the book. I would rather sacrifice *five* of the other stories (which I could name) than this one. It is the story (after *Ivy Day in the Committee-Room*) which pleases me most" (*Letters*, I, 62).

"Two Gallants" is a tale of the Dublin streets—Joyce once referred to it as an "Irish landscape" (*Letters*, II, 166)—and the geography of the story is rendered with scrupulous realism. Lenehan's route through Dublin can be traced on a map, where he describes an aimless circle (like the "mild warm air" which "circulates" in the story's opening sentence).

50.10 "That takes the biscuit!"—equivalent to "That takes the cake!" Evidently this was a characteristic phrase of Lenehan's real-life prototype, since Lenehan uses it again when he appears in *Ulysses*.

50.27 "racing tissues"—tip sheets or racing forms.

50.31 "tart"—a woman of loose morals, a prostitute.

50.33 "slavey"—a maid-of-all-work; the most menial of domestic servants.

51.11 "Pim's"—a large Quaker dry-goods store in Dublin. The implication is that Corley was employed in a reputable establishment.

51.11 "hairy"—cautious.

52.2   "aspirated the first letter of his name after the manner of Florentines"—that is, he pronounced his name as if it were spelled "Horley." This affectation may suggest an ironic contrast between Corley's "gallantry" toward the servant girl and Dante's "gallantry" toward Beatrice.

52.17 "a gay Lothario"—a lady-killer or libertine. The phrase is applied to Lothario, the seducer in Nicholas Rowe's play *The Fair Penitent* (1703).

53.8   "on the turf"—become a prostitute.

54.7   "the club"—the Kildare Street Club, an exclusive Anglo-Irish social club.

54.11 "harp"—a traditional emblem of Ireland's glorious past.

54.14 *"Silent, O Moyle"*—the melody played on the harp is that of "The Song of Fionnuala" in Thomas Moore's *Irish Melodies*.

> Silent, O Moyle! be the roar of thy water,
>   Break not, ye breezes, your chain of repose,
> While, murmuring mournfully, Lir's lonely daughter
>   Tells to the night-star her tale of woes.
> When shall the swan, her death-note singing,
>   Sleep with wings in darkness furled?
> When will heaven, its sweet bell ringing,
>   Call my spirit from this stormy world?
>
> Sadly, O Moyle, to thy winter-wave weeping,
>   Fate bids me languish long ages away;
> Yet still in her darkness doth Erin lie sleeping,
>   Still doth the pure light its dawning delay.
> When will that day-star, mildly springing,
>   Warm our isle with peace and love?
> When will heaven, its sweet bell ringing,
>   Call my spirit to the fields above?

In his *Irish Melodies* Moore provides this note on the song: "Fionnuala, the daughter of Lir [the sea in Irish legend], was by some supernatural power transformed into a swan, and condemned to wander, for many hundred years, over certain lakes and rivers in Ireland, till the coming of Christianity; when the first sound of the mass bell was to be the signal of her release." Joyce was well acquainted with this legend. When his son, Giorgio, was singing in New York in 1934 and 1935 Joyce sent him this note on "Silent, O Moyle": "Moyle is that part of the Irish Sea which is now called St George's Channel. The three daughters of Lir (the Celtic Neptune and the original of Shakespeare's King Lear) were changed into swans and must fly over those leaden waters for centuries until the sound of the first Christian bell in Ireland breaks the spell" (*Letters*, III, 341). The song was clearly one of Joyce's favorites. In February of 1935 he wrote to Giorgio: "*Silent, O Moyle*. Of course I know it, IT. You must have heard me sing it often. . . . It goes very well with a harp accompaniment" (*Letters*, III, 348).

57.11 "curates"—bartenders in Dublin slang. The term properly refers to ecclesiastics who have charge of a body of laymen. Unlike the owner of the public house, the "curate" would not be expected to mingle socially with the customers.

58.12 "a little of the ready"—ready cash.

60.30 "a small gold coin"—presumably a sovereign, a twenty-shilling gold piece. This was a considerable sum; in "Eveline" the heroine's weekly income is seven shillings.

"THE BOARDING HOUSE"

Fifth in the order of composition, "The Boarding House" is dated in manuscript July 1, 1905. In a letter to his brother Stanislaus, July 19, 1905, Joyce referred to the "frigidities" of "The Boarding House" and "Counterparts" (*Letters*, II, 98).

61.7   "take the pledge"—swear to give up drinking.

61.15   "a sheriff's man"—a process-server.

62.10   *"The Madam"*—a term often used for the proprietress of a house of prostitution.

62.25   "vamped"—improvised.

63.2   "corn-factor's office"—a cornfactor is a dealer in corn or grain.

64.23   "short twelve"—the noon mass, shortest of the day.

64.32   "reparation"—used both in the economic sense (compensation for an unjust loss) and the theological sense (the amends man must make for the insults given to God by sin; especially, the duty to repay God for the reparation of man's loss made through the suffering of Jesus Christ).

65.15   "sit"—situation, employment.

65.17   "screw"—wages.

65.17   "a bit of stuff"—money.

65.20   "the pier-glass"—a full-length mirror, usually attached to the wall.

66.11   *"Reynolds's Newspaper"*—founded in 1850, *Reynolds Weekly Newspaper* was "a fourpenny record of social and political scandals." Radical in politics, it was "a formidable spokesman of the most irreconcilable portions of the community."

68.6   *"Bass"*—a brand of ale.

68.9   "the return-room"—a room for the filling or exchanging of bottles.

"A LITTLE CLOUD"

Written in the first half of 1906, "A Little Cloud" was fourteenth in the order of composition. Joyce was fond of the story, and in October 1906 he declared that "a page of *A Little Cloud* gives me more pleasure than all my verses" (*Letters*, II, 182). The title is drawn from 1 Kings 18:44. Ahab and the people of Israel had turned against Jehovah, worshiping their strange gods, and Elijah had prophesied that there should be no dew or rain except according to his word. At last after two years Elijah confronted Ahab, defeated the prophets of Baal, and the people returned to the Lord. The long drought was broken, and as a first sign of the coming rains Elijah's servant reported that "there ariseth a little cloud out of the sea, like a man's hand."

70.1 "the North Wall"—the quay used by passenger ships departing from Dublin.

70.2 "Gallaher"—Ignatius Gallaher's career is discussed in the "Aeolus" episode of *Ulysses*. Joyce based his character on the well-known Dublin figure Fred Gallaher, who worked for both Irish and English newspapers (see Richard Ellmann, *James Joyce*, pp. 46–47n.).

71.1 "the King's Inns"—a residence for lawyers, similar to London's Inns of Court.

72.11 "like alarmed Atalantas"—Atalanta, the beautiful huntress of Greek mythology, was noted for her grace and agility.

73.3 "Half time"—slow down, reduce the tempo.

74.4 "the Celtic school"—a term applied to those Irish poets of the 1890s and later, such as W. B. Yeats and AE, who drew their subjects from Irish legend and sought to revitalize the Irish past. Their poems were marked by a dreamlike quality and were often melancholy in tone. The notices imagined by Little Chandler (74.7–9) could well have come from contemporary reviews of "the Celtic school."

74.30 "Lithia"—a bottled mineral water.

75.7 "orange tie"—Orangemen (named after William of Orange) were the defenders of Anglo-Irish Protestantism. The color implies that Gallaher owes his allegiance to England.

75.32   "a good sit"—a good position or situation.

75.33   "the Land Commission"—an important bureaucratic organization which "managed the transfer of farm lands from landlords to tenants. Until the land reforms of the late nineteenth
century Ireland had been dominated by a few great landowners
who had almost feudal power over their tenants. The Land
Purchase Bills, 1891, 1896, and 1903, provided for the tenants'
purchase of their farms from the landlords through the backing
of British credit. The amounts of money involved (together with
bonuses paid after 1903 to encourage landlords to sell) made the
Commission a notorious porkbarrel" (Don Gifford, *Notes for
Joyce* [New York: E. P. Dutton & Co., 1967], p. 50).

77.21   "*cocottes*"—French for prostitutes.

78.10   "a rum world"—a strange or queer world.

80.3   "*parole d'honneur*"—word of honor.

80.8   "a.p."—appointment.

80.11   "*deoc an doruis*"—Gaelic for a farewell drink. Literally,
"the drink of the door."

83.20   "on the hire system"—on the installment plan.

83.31–34   "*Hushed are the winds* . . ."—the first stanza of Byron's
poem "On the Death of a Young Lady." This poem, which
opens *Hours of Idleness*, stands first in most editions of Byron's
poetry.

84.12–13   "*Within this narrow cell* . . ."—Little Chandler breaks
off in the middle of the second stanza. The remainder of the
poem follows:

> Within this narrow cell reclines her clay,
>   That clay, where once such animation beam'd;
> The King of Terrors seized her as his prey,
>   Not worth nor beauty have her life redeem'd.
> Oh! could that King of Terrors pity feel,
>   Or Heaven reverse the dread decrees of fate,
> Not here the mourner would his grief reveal,
>   Not here the muse her virtues would relate.
> But wherefore weep? Her matchless spirit soars
>   Beyond where splendid shines the orb of day;
> And weeping angels lead her to those bowers
>   Where endless pleasures virtue's deeds repay.
> And shall presumptuous mortals Heaven arraign,
>   And, madly, godlike Providence accuse?
> Ah! no, far fly from me attempts so vain;—
>   I'll ne'er submission to my God refuse.

Yet is remembrance of those virtues dear,
  Yet fresh the memory of that beauteous face;
Still they call forth my warm affection's tear,
  Still in my heart retain their wonted place.

85.17 "Lambabaun!"—"lamb-child."
85.18 "lamb of the world!"—in Scripture and liturgy Christ is often referred to as the Lamb of God.

"COUNTERPARTS"

The sixth in the order of composition, "Counterparts" was written almost simultaneously with "The Boarding House" and finished by July 12, 1905. Joyce's attitude toward Farrington was not entirely unsympathetic. In November 1906 he wrote to his brother Stanislaus: "I am no friend of tyranny, as you know, but if many husbands are brutal the atmosphere in which they live (vide Counterparts) is brutal and few wives and homes can satisfy the desire for happiness" (*Letters*, II, 192).

86.2   "the tube"—a speaking tube for interoffice communication.

86.2   "North of Ireland accent"—the conflict in "Counterparts" reflects the tension between the Protestant, English-oriented North of Ireland and the Catholic South, as well as the tension between England and Ireland.

88.30   "the dark snug of O'Neill's shop"—a small room in the public house kept by Patrick O'Neill in Henry Street. Throughout "Counterparts" Joyce uses the actual names of Dublin pubs.

88.34   "a g. p."—a glass of porter, i.e., a glass of dark brown beer.

89.1   "curate"—bartender. See "Two Gallants," 57.11.

89.2   "caraway seed"—to sweeten the breath.

91.13   "manikin"—used contemptuously of a little man.

92.33   "dart"—a plan or scheme.

93.3   "A *crown!*"—five shillings.

93.28   "the liberal shepherds in the eclogues"—in *Hamlet* IV.vii the Queen refers to "liberal [i.e., gross or free-spoken] shepherds." Joyce may be alluding to Virgil's *Eclogues* in this particular passage, but it is more likely that he has in mind the bumptious humor of some Renaissance pastorals.

94.3   "*my nabs*"—variant of "nob" or "nibs": a gentleman or person of note.

94.14   "the Ballast Office"—administrative headquarters of Dublin harbor.

94.20   "the Tivoli"—a Dublin theater.

94.22   "a small Irish and Apollinaris"—a short drink of Irish whisky with Apollinaris water (a sparkling mineral water).

95.3   "small hot specials"—hot toddies, whisky mixed with hot water and sugar.

96.25 "gab"—beak, snout.

96.28 "Pony up"—pay up.

96.29 "smahan"—a sip.

97.26 "the chapel"—the phrase "at the chapel" refers to attendance at evening devotions.

98.23 *Hail Mary*—the Angelic Salutation (cf. Luke 1:58). A devotional recitation which begins "Hail Mary, full of grace, the Lord is with thee."

"CLAY"

The fourth story in the order of composition, "Clay" seems to have cost Joyce more pains than most. In November of 1904 he began a story, "Christmas Eve," which he abandoned half finished, apparently because the idea for another, "Hallow Eve," had superseded it. (The manuscript of "Christmas Eve" was published in *The James Joyce Miscellany, Third Series,* [Carbondale, Ill.: Southern Illinois University Press], 1962.) "Hallow Eve" was completed and sent to Stanislaus Joyce in January 1905 for possible publication in *The Irish Homestead.* James Joyce may have done some revision on the story at this point. It was much in his mind and mentioned frequently in his correspondence during the next few months. By September 1905 the title had been changed to "The Clay." In November of 1906 Joyce was working on the story again, adding the name of the laundry where Maria is employed.

99.6 "barmbracks"—speckled cakes or buns containing currants, usually sold only at Hallowe'en (see note on 101.9).

99.16 "peace-maker"—see Matthew 5:9. "Blessed are the peace-makers: for they shall be called the children of God."

99.17 "Board ladies"—members of the governing board of the *Dublin by Lamplight* laundry. See note on 100.23.

100.1 "the dummy"—the deafmute.

100.8 "A *Present from Belfast*"—Belfast, a large city on the northeast coast of Ireland, was a stronghold of Protestantism.

100.11 "Whit-Monday"—Whit Sunday is the seventh Sunday after Easter, observed in commemoration of the day of Pentecost. The following Monday is a traditional holiday.

100.23 "*Dublin by Lamplight* laundry"—in November 1906 Joyce wrote to his brother Stanislaus: "The meaning of *Dublin by Lamplight Laundry*? That is the name of the laundry at Ballsbridge, of which the story treats. It is run by a society of Protestant spinsters, widows, and childless women—I expect—as a Magdalen's home. The phrase *Dublin by Lamplight* means that Dublin by lamplight is a wicked place full of wicked and lost women whom a kindly committee gathers together for the good work of washing my dirty shirts. I like the phrase because 'it is a gentle way of putting it' " (*Letters*, II, 192).

100.31   "the tracts on the walls"—Protestant religious tracts.

101.9   "to get the ring"—like an English Christmas pudding, the All Hallow Eve cake contains a ring. Whoever gets the ring is supposed to be the first to be married.

101.10   "Hallow Eves"—All Hallow Eve (Hallowe'en) is October 31, the eve of All Saints' Day. It is traditionally a time of superstition and horseplay. In the Old Celtic calendar the year began on November 1, so that the last evening of October was the night of all the witches, which the Church transformed into the Eve of All Saints. "Hallow Eve" was Joyce's intermediate title for the story.

101.17   "porter"—dark brown beer.

101.25   "a mass morning"—Maria would attend mass on All Saints' Day.

102.28   "—Two-and-four"—two shillings and fourpence, a considerable sum for Maria.

103.13   "a drop taken"—too much to drink.

105.1   "saucers"—part of a game of divination. The saucers contain various things (prayer-book, ring, water, clay) which are supposed to suggest a person's fate.

105.13   "a soft wet substance"—the clay.

106.2   "*I Dreamt that I Dwelt*"—the famous song from Act II of Michael William Balfe's *The Bohemian Girl*. See note on "Eveline," 39.3.

106.12   "her mistake"—Maria sings the first verse twice, omitting the more poignant second verse. The second verse reads:

> I dreamt that suitors besought my hand,
>   That knights upon bended knee,
> And with vows no maiden heart could withstand,
>   That they pledged their faith to me.
> And I dreamt that one of this noble host
>   Came forth my hand to claim;
> Yet I also dreamt, which charmed me most,
>   That you lov'd me still the same.

106.14   "poor old Balfe"—Michael William Balfe (1808–1870), the Dublin-born composer of the song.

"A PAINFUL CASE"

The seventh story in the order of composition, "A Painful Case" (originally entitled "A Painful Incident") was first written in July 1905. Joyce seems never to have been satisfied with the story, and there are several references in the letters to possible changes or revisions. See the facsimiles on pp. 234–35 for examples of the revisions.

Stanislaus Joyce claimed that "A Painful Case" was based on his own brief and abortive relationship with an older woman, whom he first sighted at a concert. "Out of this unpromising material, which he found in my diary, my brother made the story of 'A Painful Case,' which he wrote much later in Trieste when the turbid life of Dublin was beginning to settle and clarify in his mind. He gave the woman in it, Emily Sinico, a Triestine name. Giuseppe Sinico was the composer of the 'Inno di San Giusto,' the patron saint of Trieste. Mr. Duffy is the type of the male celibate, as Maria in 'Clay' is of the female celibate, but he is also intended to be a portrait of what my brother imagined I should become in middle age. The portraiture has 'the grim Dutch touch' he spoke of. He has used many characteristics of mine in composing Mr. Duffy, such as intolerance of drunkenness, hostility to socialism, and the habit of noting short sentences on a sheaf of loose pages pinned together. The title Jim suggested for this distillation of tabloid wisdom was *Bile Beans* [see 108.9]. Two of them are included in the story: 'Every bond is a bond to sorrow,' and 'Love between man and man is impossible because there must not be sexual intercourse, and friendship between a man and a woman is impossible because there must be sexual intercourse,' both of which, for some vague reason, were added after the chance encounter [between Stanislaus and the older woman] at the concert. Jim had also lent Mr. Duffy some traits of his own, the interest in Nietzsche and the translation of *Michael Kramer*, in order to raise his intellectual standard" (*My Brother's Keeper* [New York: The Viking Press, 1958], pp. 159–60).

107.1 "Chapelizod"—a western suburb of Dublin, associated

by legend with the tragic love story of Tristan and Isolde. Chapelizod is the home of the Earwicker family in *Finnegans Wake*.

107 108.1 "the *Maynooth Catechism*"—the standard catechism for Ireland, ordered by the National Synod of Maynooth. Saint Patrick's College, the chief seminary in Ireland, is located at Maynooth, a few miles from Dublin.

108.4 "Hauptmann's *Michael Kramer*"—Gerhart Hauptmann, the German dramatist and novelist (1862–1946), published his play *Michael Kramer* in 1900. Joyce admired the play and translated it during the summer of 1901. The similarities between Mr. Duffy and Hauptmann's hero are striking. Both Duffy and Kramer are isolated figures, holding themselves aloof from the public. Both feel that the artist must be a "true hermit." And both are incapable of love: Kramer cannot communicate with his son (who finally commits suicide), just as Duffy cannot communicate with Mrs. Sinico. For further details on the parallels between the two works, see Marvin Magalaner, *Time of Apprenticeship: The Fiction of Young James Joyce* (New York: Abelard-Schuman, 1959), pp. 40–45.

108.9 "*Bile Beans*"—a patent medicine, pills to alleviate a bilious condition.

108.16 "saturnine"—sluggish, cold, and gloomy in temperament: originally, born under the influence of the watery planet Saturn.

109.18 "the Rotunda"—a theater and concert hall.

110.33 "Irish Socialist Party"—a small and ineffectual movement at the turn of the century.

112.15 "Nietzsche: *Thus Spake Zarathustra* and *The Gay Science*"—these two works, first published in the early 1880s, embody Friedrich Nietzsche's "master morality," which opposed Christian principles and celebrated the "superman" who is independent of conventional social and political values. Their presence on Mr. Duffy's shelves marks him as a conscious "radical" and free-thinker. The Nietzschean "superman" has no need for society or the love of women; he respects only the self-sufficient and the powerful.

In criticizing Mr. Duffy's Nietzschean attitudes Joyce was indulging in a measure of self-criticism. He had discovered and read Nietzsche during his own youthful rebellion, and a postcard of July 1904 is mockingly signed "James Overman" (Nietzsche's *Übermensch*, or superman—see *Letters*, I, 56).

113.9 "the buff *Mail*"—"a Tory newspaper which 'opposed every national movement'" (Magalaner, *Time of Apprenticeship*, p. 161). Presumably the cover sheet was light yellow in color.

113.18 *"Secreto"*—Latin, "in secret": a "Secret Prayer" is said silently by the priest celebrating Mass immediately before the Preface.

115.7 "a league"—a temperance organization opposed to the sale and use of spirits.

116.19 "the *Herald*"—*The Evening Herald*, a Dublin newspaper.

"IVY DAY IN THE COMMITTEE ROOM"

Eighth in the order of composition, this story was completed in all essentials by August 29, 1905. In May 1906, before he had written "The Dead," Joyce spoke of "Ivy Day in the Committee Room" as the story that had pleased him most (*Letters*, I, 62). Of all the stories in *Dubliners*, "Ivy Day" is most dependent upon a knowledge of Irish politics at the turn of the century. The shade of Charles Stewart Parnell presides over the entire tale.

Charles Stewart Parnell (1846–1891), although born into a Protestant family of English origin, was to be hailed as the "Uncrowned King of Ireland." He was elected to Parliament in 1875, and two years later he became the leader of those among the Home Rule movement who were convinced that "obstructionism," rather than compromise, was the best tactic to use against the English. When the general election of 1880 returned Gladstone and the Liberals to power, Parnell took over leadership of the Irish party in Parliament; he adopted a deliberate policy of refusing alliances with either English party, thereby holding the balance of power. In 1882 the English chief secretary for Ireland and his aide were assassinated in Phoenix Park, and subsequently attempts were made to implicate Parnell in the assassination; but by 1889 these attempts had failed and Parnell was firmly established as a national hero.

However, at the moment of Parnell's greatest triumph a scandal broke which was to bring about his tragic fall. He was accused of adultery in the divorce suit of Captain William O'Shea, one of his political followers (Mrs. O'Shea had been Parnell's mistress for some time). At first it appeared that Parnell might weather even this scandal, but a coalition of political enemies and fanatical Catholics ousted him from the leadership of the Irish Parliamentary Party, and the rural population of Ireland turned against their former hero with savage hatred. Even Parnell's lieutenant Tim Healy, who had vowed never to abandon his leader, went over to the opposition. After a year of campaigning against his enemies Parnell died on October 6, 1891.

Joyce's father reacted bitterly to the "betrayal" of Parnell, and the nine-year-old James was so affected that he wrote a poem called "Et Tu, Healy." His delighted father had the poem printed and distributed copies to his friends. None of these has survived, but we know from Joyce's brother Stanislaus that at the end of the poem "the dead Chief is likened to an eagle, looking down on the grovelling mass of Irish politicians from

> His quaint-perched aerie on the crags of Time
> Where the rude din of this . . . century
> Can trouble him no more."

The young Joyce's sympathetic identification with Parnell had a profound effect on his developing personality. The arrogance and pride of the hero, the fear of betrayal, and the hypocrisy of the rabble, these were to become leading themes in Joyce's life and art (see the famous Christmas dinner scene in Chapter I of *A Portrait of the Artist*). The fall of Parnell was Joyce's first intimation that Ireland could be "the old sow that eats her farrow." As he matured, the pattern of Parnell's life seemed a foreshadowing of his own career. In the bitter broadside "Gas from a Burner" (1912), which was occasioned by his frustrations in finding a publisher for *Dubliners*, Joyce linked his own fate with Parnell's:

> But I owe a duty to Ireland:
> I hold her honour in my hand,
> This lovely land that always sent
> Her writers and artists to banishment
> And in a spirit of Irish fun
> Betrayed her own leaders, one by one.
> 'Twas Irish humour, wet and dry,
> Flung quicklime into Parnell's eye. . . .

And in the same year as "Gas from a Burner" Joyce wrote an article for a Trieste newspaper called "The Shade of Parnell," which ends with this bitter passage:

> The ghost of the 'uncrowned king' will weigh on the hearts of those who remember him . . . but it will not be a vindictive ghost. The melancholy which invaded his mind was perhaps the profound conviction that, in his hour of need, one of the disciples who dipped his hand in the same bowl with him would betray him. That he fought to the very end with this desolate certainty in mind is his greatest claim to nobility.
>
> In his final desperate appeal to his countrymen, he begged them not to throw him as a sop to the English wolves howling

around them. It redounds to their honour that they did not fail this appeal. They did not throw him to the English wolves; they tore him to pieces themselves. [*The Critical Writings of James Joyce*, ed. Ellsworth Mason and Richard Ellmann (New York: The Viking Press, 1959), pp. 228, 243]

After the death of Parnell it became a custom for his followers to wear a sprig of ivy on October 6, in memory of their dead leader.

119.10   "MUNICIPAL ELECTIONS/ROYAL EXCHANGE WARD" —the Royal Exchange Ward is an actual political ward near the center of Dublin. Those in the Committee Room have been canvassing voters for the coming municipal elections.

119.12   "P.L.G."—Poor Law Guardian, an elected administrator of the Poor Law Act in charge of the local relief rolls.

119.23   "a leaf of dark glossy ivy"—in memory of Parnell.

119.29   "the Christian Brothers"—see note on "Araby," 29.2.

120.4   "cocks him up"—gives him false and inflated ideas.

120.20   "Freemasons' meeting"—see note on "Araby," 32.21.

121.14   "tinker"—tinkers had a reputation for being shiftless and unreliable.

121.19   "the Corporation"—the political organization governing the city.

121.21   "shoneens"—used contemptuously of would-be gentlemen, imitators of English fashions.

121.21   "with a handle to his name"—with a title.

121.25   "hunker-sliding"—laziness.

121.34   "a German monarch"—Edward VII, King of England (1901–1910), related through his parents to the German royal family.

122.2   "an address of welcome to Edward Rex"—Edward VII visited Ireland in July 1903, "and though the Dublin corporation refused to vote a loyal address the reception was generally cordial."

122.6   "the Nationalist ticket"—Irish Parliamentary Party, which opposed English rule.

122.10   "spondulics"—money.

122.18   "—Musha"—an Irish exclamation of surprise.

122.30   "serve"—canvass.

123.26   "the houses"—pubs or alehouses.

123.27   "moya!"—an ironic exclamation.

123.34   "stump up"—pay up.

124.17   "—'Usha"—musha (see note on 122.18).

124.24   "Do you twig?"—do you understand?

124.25 "decent skin"—good chap.

125.5 "hillsiders and fenians"—the Fenians were members of an organization formed to assist revolutionary movements and overthrow the English government in Ireland. They took their name from the body of warriors said to be the defenders of Ireland in the time of the legendary king Finn MacCool. The name "Hillside men" was applied to the Fenians.

125.8 "in the pay of the Castle"—in the pay of the English rulers, who used the Castle as their headquarters.

125.11 "Castle hacks"—see note on 125.8.

125.12 "there's a certain little nobleman with a cock-eye"— Queen Victoria and King Edward VII bestowed so many knighthoods on Dublin politicians and professional men that one wit referred to turn-of-the-century Dublin as "The City of Dreadful Knights."

125.16 "Major Sirr"—Henry Charles Sirr (1764–1841), born in Dublin Castle, succeeded his father as chief of the Dublin police. He worked with the English in suppressing the rebellion of 1798, and became in the popular mind the type of the Irish turncoat.

126.6 "Father Keon, speaking in a discreet indulgent velvety voice"—in the first draft of "Ivy Day" this sentence continued: "which is not often found except with the confessor or the sodomite."

126.9 "the *Black Eagle*"—a public house.

126.33 "how does he knock it out?"—how does he make ends meet?

127.11 "goster"—noisy and boastful gossip.

127.16 "Yerra"—a mild oath, "O God well!"

127.16 "hop-o'-my-thumb"—used contemptuously of a little man.

127.28 "Mansion House"—residence of the Lord Mayor of Dublin.

127.29 "vermin"—pun on ermine. The ceremonial robes of the Lord Mayor were trimmed with ermine.

128.2 "*And how do you like your new master*"—a new Lord Mayor was elected each year by the Corporation.

128.10 "*Wisha!*"—exclamation of surprise.

129.6 "tinpot"—cheap, ineffectual.

130.13 "Did the cow calve?"—is there something to celebrate?

131.4–6 "the Conservatives . . . the Nationalist candidate"— presumably the English-oriented Conservatives, a minority party, had to choose between a moderate Nationalist candidate and a more radical candidate of the United Irish League.

131.17 "toff"—someone who behaves handsomely, a "regular gentleman."

131.23 *"Poor Law Guardian"*—see 119.12.

132.2 "Didn't Parnell himself . . ."—when the Prince of Wales (later Edward VII) visited Ireland in 1885 Parnell opposed an official reception.

132.8 *"The old one never went to see these wild Irish"*—in fact Queen Victoria made a state visit to Ireland in 1900.

132.13 "King Edward's life, you know, is not the very . . ."—Edward's private life while he was Prince of Wales was marked by gossip and scandal.

132.26 "a fit man to lead us?"—in the second manuscript draft Joyce inserted the following sentence (never printed) in the margin: "Do you think he was a man I'd like the lady who is now Mrs Lyons to know?"

133.15 "the Chief"—a common title for Parnell.

134.7 "Our Uncrowned King"—the title given to Parnell by his aide Tim Healy, who later "betrayed" him.

"A MOTHER"

Tenth in the order of composition, "A Mother" was finished by late September 1905.

136.1   "the *Eire Abu* Society"—a patriotic society, whose Gaelic motto means "Ireland to Victory!"

137.10   "he went to the altar every first Friday"—devotion to the Sacred Heart was especially strong in Dublin, and its principal exercise was the receiving of the Eucharist on the first Friday of every month. According to one of the promises made to Saint Margaret-Mary Alacoque (see 37.13), anyone who received the Eucharist on nine consecutive first Fridays would not face death unprepared.

137.21   "the Academy"—the Royal Academy of Music.

137.24   "Skerries . . . Howth . . . Greystones"—holiday resorts near Dublin.

137.25   "the Irish Revival"—the renewed interest in Irish legend and the Irish language associated with Nationalist politics in the 1890s. See note on "the Celtic school," 74.4.

137.26   "to take advantage of her daughter's name"—Kathleen-ni-Houlihan, the traditional personification of Ireland, was celebrated by the writers of the Irish Revival. She is usually represented as a poor old woman who is in reality a queen. Yeats's *Countess Cathleen* and *Cathleen ni Houlihan* popularized the name.

137.30   "pro-cathedral"—a church used as a substitute for a cathedral. The traditional cathedrals of Saint Patrick and Christ Church were used by the Church of Ireland (Protestant).

137.33   "Nationalist"—the Nationalist party sought Home Rule for Ireland.

138.6   "the language movement"—the study and rehabilitation of Gaelic was one aspect of the patriotic Irish Revival.

138.10   "the Antient Concert Rooms"—a hall which could be leased for the presentation of music or drama. Some of the early plays of the Irish literary revival were presented here, including Yeats's *Countess Cathleen*, and the Feis Ceoil in which Joyce competed was held here (see note on 142.32).

138.15 "eight guineas"—eight pounds, eight shillings.

138.32 "Brown Thomas's"—a shop noted for Irish lace and Irish linen.

139.1 "two-shilling tickets"—probably the best in the house.

140.19 "the house was filled with paper"—many in the audience had free passes.

142.23 "the part of the king in the opera of *Maritana* at the Queen's Theatre"—*Maritana* (music by William Vincent Wallace, libretto by Edward Fitzball) was first presented in Dublin in 1846. By Joyce's time this sentimental opera was already somewhat dated, although it was still popular "in the provinces."

142.32 "the Feis Ceoil"—an annual music festival begun in 1897. It was held in the Antient Concert Rooms in 1904 and Joyce competed, failing to win only because he refused to participate in the sight-reading test. He received the bronze medal for third place. Joyce's attitude toward the Feis Ceoil was edged with contempt at its parochial nature.

144.27 "*Freeman* man"—reporter for the *Freeman's Journal*, a morning newspaper.

144.27 "Mr O'Madden Burke"—reappears in *Ulysses* as a newspaperman.

144.30 "the Mansion House"—residence of the Lord Mayor of Dublin.

146.22 "Mrs Pat Campbell"—a popular British actress.

147.10 "*Killarney*"—a sentimental ballad by the Irish composer Michael William Balfe, with the refrain: "Beauty's home, Killarney, / Ever fair Killarney."

"GRACE"

The twelfth in order of composition, this story was called "the last" by Joyce, since it completed the original plan of twelve stories in four groups of three. He began it in October 1905 and finished it sometime before the twelve stories (all but "Two Gallants," "A Little Cloud," and "The Dead") were sent to the publisher Grant Richards in December of that year. But during his stay in Rome in 1906 he did additional research in the Biblioteca Vittorio Emmanuele for the theological parts of the story (see *Letters*, II, 192–93). In his detailed account of the backgrounds to the story (*My Brother's Keeper* [New York: The Viking Press, 1958], pp. 225–228), Stanislaus Joyce reports that his brother planned "Grace" with the pattern of Dante's *Divine Comedy* in mind: "Mr. Kernan's fall down the steps of the lavatory is his descent into hell, the sickroom is purgatory, and the Church in which he and his friends listen to the sermon is paradise at last."

150.9   "curates"—bartenders. See note on "Two Gallants," 57.11.

153.5   "an outsider"—a two-wheeled horse-drawn vehicle which carries four persons, two on each side seated back-to-back.

153.17   "the Ballast Office"—administrative headquarters of Dublin harbor.

154.5   "the great Blackwhite"—presumably a famous local salesman.

154.9   "E.C."—mailing district for the commercial section of London.

154.17   "Royal Irish Constabulary Office"—a prestigious position.

156.6   "Star of the Sea Church in Sandymount"—an actual church on the seacoast near Dublin. As protector of Mariners the Virgin is called the Star of the Sea.

158.5   "the Sacred Heart"—although private worship of Christ's heart is of great antiquity in the Church, the specific worship of the Sacred Heart resulted from the revelations to Saint Margaret-Mary Alacoque (see note on "Eveline," 37.13). Devotion to the Sacred Heart has as its object that Heart which is the natural symbol of Christ's love, and finds its chief liturgical expressions in the feast of the Sacred Heart and in public representations of the Heart by statues and pictures.

158.8 "the banshee"—a supernatural being supposed by the peasantry to wail beneath the windows of a house where someone has died.

158.22 "for *The Irish Times* and for *The Freeman's Journal*"— both papers were noted for their conservative editorial policies.

159.24 "*bona-fide* travellers"—on Sundays the public houses were allowed to serve drinks to "legitimate" travellers but not to local customers.

160.32 "bostoons"—variant of "bosthoon": a "weak reed," an awkward or spiritless fellow.

160.33 "Castle official"—the Castle was headquarters for the British officials and their Irish associates.

161.10 "omadhauns"—an Irish term of abuse: a fool.

161.20 "yahoos"—a name invented by Swift in *Gulliver's Travels* to describe a bestial type of human being.

162.17 "M'Auley's"—a public house.

162.34 "make a retreat"—to withdraw from the world for a period of prayer and meditation.

163.2 "wash the pot"—wipe the slate clean.

163.15 "a four-handed reel"—a lively dance.

163.27 "General of the Jesuits"—the Society of Jesus, an order established in 1540 by Saint Ignatius of Loyola, is organized along military lines. The head or "General" of the Order is responsible only to the Pope.

164.4 "—That's a fact, said Mr Cunningham. That's history"— Mr. Cunningham's history is not entirely accurate. Although the Jesuit Order may never have been "reformed," it was frequently subject to attacks and suppressions, and the character of the Order changed over the centuries.

The long theological discussion which follows Mr. Cunningham's remarks on the Jesuits (pp. 164–71) is a mixture of legend, half-truths, oversimplifications, and downright mistakes. For an illuminating discussion of the uses Joyce makes of this "popular" theology, see Robert M. Adams, *Surface and Symbol* (New York: Oxford University Press, 1962), pp. 177–81.

164.27 "Father Purdon"—Purdon Street was located in Dublin's notorious red-light district.

165.6 "—Father Tom Burke"—Thomas Nicholas Burke (1830–1882), the son of a Galway baker, studied in Rome and became a Dominican friar. He had a great reputation as an orator, and on a speaking tour of the United States in 1872 he collected 100,000 pounds sterling for American charities. He was a staunch defender of the Irish cause, and in his *Ireland's Case Stated* (1873) he gave a point-by-point refutation of the case made by the historian J. A. Froude in support of English occupation.

165.19 "pit"—the rear part of the main floor in a theater.

165.24 *"The Prisoner of the Vatican"*—Pope Leo XIII deplored the Italian seizure of the Pope's temporal powers in 1870, and considered himself a prisoner in the Vatican as long as Rome was ruled by the Italian government. His predecessor Pius IX was also known as "The Prisoner of the Vatican."

165.27 "Orangeman"—technically a member of a Protestant political society founded in 1795, but used in general to describe anyone who was pro-English and Protestant.

167.5 "Pope Leo XIII."—Gioacchino Pecci (1810–1903), Pope from 1878 to 1903, a learned and literary pontiff whose political and theological attitudes were basically conservative.

167.10 "His motto . . . was *Lux upon Lux*"—the Popes do not adopt official mottoes. However, in "The Prophecy of the Popes," a work attributed to Saint Malachy of Armagh (1094–1148), the 111 successors to Pope Celestine II (elected 1143) are designated by short prophetic epithets. Leo XIII is given the motto *Lumen in coelo* (Light in the Sky), while Pius IX is designated as *Crux de cruce* (Cross from a Cross). The "Prophecy" of Saint Malachy is now thought to be a sixteenth-century forgery, contrived to support the election of a particular cardinal to the papal chair. Mr. Cunningham's versions of these papal mottoes are revealing distortions.

167.18 "Pius IX."—Giovanni Maria Mastai-Ferretti (1792–1878), Pope from 1846 to 1878, began his reign as a reformer but was soon embittered by the political restrictions imposed after 1848. Henceforth he was hostile to every form of political liberalism or national sentiment. The most important events of Pius IX's pontificate were his proclamation of the dogma of the Immaculate Conception of the Virgin Mary (1854) and the Vatican Council's proclamation of the infallibility of the Pope (1870).

167.30 "penny-a-week school"—a National School. See note on "An Encounter," 20.29.

167.32 "with a sod of turf under his oxter"—with a block of peat (fuel for the fire) under his arm.

168.5 "Pope Leo's poems"—Leo XIII did, in fact, write a Latin poem on the invention of the photograph, but as Robert M. Adams has pointed out the poem is "no marvel either of Latin versification or of scientific insight" (*Surface and Symbol*. pp. 178–79).

The Art of Photography (A.D. 1867)

Drawn by the sun's bright pencil,
How well, O glistening stencil,
You express the brow's fine grace,
Eyes' sparkle, and beauty of face.
O marvelous might of mind,
New prodigy! A design
Beyond the contrival
Of Apelles, Nature's rival.
(Trans. Robert M. Adams)

168.14   "*Great minds are very near to madness*"—John Dryden, *Absalom and Achitophel*, I, 163: "Great Wits are sure to Madness near allied." Dryden was adapting an ancient commonplace, quoted by Seneca in his *Moral Essays:* "There is no great genius without some touch of madness."

168.21   "up to the knocker"—up to snuff.

168.27   "*ex cathedra*"—when the Pope speaks *ex cathedra* (from his office) the doctrine of papal infallibility applies (see note on 167.18).

168.33   "the infallibility of the Pope"—see notes on 167.18 and 168.27.

169.16   "a German cardinal"—Johann Döllinger (1799–1890), not a cardinal but a German theologian, who was excommunicated for his opposition to the doctrine of papal infallibility. Döllinger was not a member of the Vatican Council of 1869–1870.

169.21   "John MacHale"—John MacHale (1791–1881), archbishop of Tuam, was first drawn to the cause of Irish nationalism by the uprising of 1798. In 1820 he began a series of letters that appeared in various newspapers, appealing for Catholic emancipation and seeking relief from the famine. He traveled to Rome in 1831 and won the friendship of Pope Gregory XVI. An enthusiastic advocate of Irish culture and the Irish language, he supported the Irish tenants and the Irish Land League. At the Vatican Council of 1870 he opposed papal primacy and papal infallibility, but when the Council had made its decision he accepted without difficulty (see note on 169.24).

169.24   "I thought it was some Italian or American"—Mr. Fogarty is more nearly correct than Mr. Cunningham. On July 18, 1870, at the fourth public session of the Vatican Council, the dogma of papal infallibility was accepted by all but two members of the council. The two dissenters were Bishops Riccio of Italy and Fitzgerald of Arkansas; they cast ballots of *non placet*, but as soon as the balloting was over they submitted to the dogma. John MacHale appears to have been conveniently absent from this session, and the dramatic scene recounted by Mr. Cunningham (169.28–34) never took place.

169.34   *"Credo!"*—"I believe."

170.17   "Sir John Gray's statue"—Sir John Gray (1816–1875), owner of the *Freeman's Journal*, was a Protestant patriot who supported Home Rule for Ireland. His statue stands on O'Connell Street in Dublin.

170.17   "Edmund Dwyer Gray"—son of Sir John Gray, he was noted for his indecisiveness.

170.25   *"taped"*—classified, figured out.

171.12   "—Get behind me, Satan!"—the reply of Jesus to the flattery of Peter, "Get thee behind me, Satan" (Matthew 16:23).

171.16   "—All we have to do . . . is to stand up with lighted candles in our hands and renew our baptismal vows"—a conscious reaffirmation of the vows made by the godparents on behalf of the child at the time of Infant Baptism. The ceremony customarily took place on the last evening of a retreat.

172.12   "the distant speck of red light"—the sanctuary light suspended near the altar which indicates the presence of the Blessed Sacrament.

172.20   "a quincunx"—five objects outlining the four corners and the center of a square. The quincunx is a pattern associated with the Cross and the five wounds of Christ.

172.26   "registration agent"—person in charge of voter registration.

173.22–25   *"For the children of this world . . ."*— from the parable of the unjust steward, Luke 16:8–9. Father Purdon's interpretation of this text should be compared with the original.

"THE DEAD"

Joyce began to plan "The Dead" during his stay in Rome (July 1906–March 1907), but he did not begin to write the story until he had returned to Trieste in the spring of 1907. For details of the story's composition and biographical dimensions, see Richard Ellmann, "The Backgrounds of 'The Dead,'" pp. 388–403 of this collection.

176.8 "had the organ in Haddington Road"—was hired to play the organ in a church on Haddington Road.

176.9 "the Academy"—see note on "A Mother," 137.21.

176.11 "Antient Concert Rooms"—see note on "A Mother," 138.10.

176.15 "Adam and Eve's"—a Dublin church, prominent in Joyce's *Finnegans Wake*.

176.26 "Gabriel"—in the Bible, the heavenly messenger who announced the birth of John the Baptist to Zacharias and that of the Messiah to the Virgin Mary. The name in Hebrew means "man of God." Along with Michael, Gabriel is one of the four great archangels. See Florence L. Walzl, "Gabriel and Michael: The Conclusion of 'The Dead,'" pp. 423–43 of this collection.

176.27 "screwed"—drunk.

179.11 "the Melodies"—Thomas Moore's *Irish Melodies* (published 1807–1834), the most popular collection of Irish songs.

180.18 "stirabout"—see note on "The Sisters," 9.17.

180.26 "—Goloshes!"—rubber galoshes were introduced in the mid-nineteenth century.

181.12 "Christy Minstrels"—the famous nineteenth-century minstrel show organized by Edwin T. Christy.

181.17 "the Gresham"—a fashionable Dublin hotel.

183.31 "—Quadrilles!"—a square dance of French origin.

186.16 "the balcony scene in *Romeo and Juliet*"—Act II, scene ii.

186.17 "the two murdered princes in the Tower"—the young sons of Edward IV, allegedly murdered in the Tower of London in 1483 by order of their uncle, Richard III.

187.1 "the Royal University"—established in 1882 after the model of English universities, the Royal University of Ireland was simply an examining body, no residence in any college or attendance at lectures being obligatory.

187.23 "an Irish device"—Miss Ivors is an enthusiastic supporter of the Irish Revival (see note on "A Mother," 137.25).

187.34 *"The Daily Express"*—"a Conservative paper, opposed to the national struggle" (Marvin Magalaner, *Time of Apprenticeship* [New York: Abelard-Schuman, 1959], p. 169).

188.4 "a West Briton"—a derogatory term for an "Anglicized" Irishman.

188.27 "the University question"—although religious tests were abolished in 1873, Dublin's ancient and prestigious university, Trinity College (founded 1591), remained overwhelmingly Protestant. The "University question" concerned efforts to provide equal educational opportunities for Roman Catholic students. The Royal University (see 187.1) and University College (the Jesuit-directed institution which Joyce attended) represented different attempts to alleviate this problem.

188.33 "Aran Isles"—islands off the West coast of Ireland where the natives still spoke Gaelic and preserved their traditional ways. Supporters of the Irish Revival looked to the Aran Isles for inspiration, and John Millington Synge (who first visited the Isles in 1898) drew much of his subject-matter from them.

189.2 "Kathleen Kearney"—character in "A Mother."

189.4 "Connacht"—an area along the West coast of Ireland.

190.13 "lancers"—a form of the quadrille (183.31).

192.5 "the park"—Phoenix Park, a large park on the western edge of Dublin.

192.6 "the Wellington Monument"—a monument to the Duke of Wellington, who was born in Ireland (Arthur Wellesley, 1769–1852) but became an English hero. Located at the eastern end of Phoenix Park.

193.2 "—*Arrayed for the Bridal*"—a song by George Linley, set to music from Bellini's opera *I Puritani*.

Array'd for the bridal, in beauty behold her,
A white wreath entwineth a forehead more fair;
I envy the zephyrs that softly enfold her, enfold her,
And play with the locks of her beautiful hair.
May life to her prove full of sunshine and love, full of love, yes! yes! yes!
Who would not love her
Sweet star of the morning! shining so bright,
Earth's circle adorning, fair creature of light,
Fair creature of light.

(Magalaner, *Time of Apprenticeship*, p. 170)

194.21 "for the pope to turn out the women out of the choirs . . . and put little whipper-snappers of boys over their heads"—Pope Pius X declared in his *Motu Proprio*, November 22, 1903: ". . . singers in churches have a real liturgical office, and . . . therefore women, as being incapable of exercising such office, cannot be admitted to form part of the choir or of the musical chapel. Whenever, then, it is desired to employ the acute voices of sopranos and contraltos, these parts must be taken by boys, according to the most ancient usage of the church" (Don Gifford, *Notes for Joyce* [New York: E. P. Dutton & Co., 1967], p. 78).

196.3 "—*Beannacht libh*"—"farewell," a Gaelic benediction.

198.23 "the Gaiety"—a Dublin theater.

199.2 "*Mignon*"—an opera by Ambroise Thomas, based on Goethe's *Wilhelm Meister*. First produced in Paris in 1866.

199.3 "Georgina Burns"—unidentified.

199.5 "Tietjens, Ilma de Murzka, Campanini, the great Trebelli, Giuglini, Ravelli, Aramburo"—a gallery of famous nineteenth-century singers. Therese Tietjens (1831–1877), a great prima donna, was especially known for the role of Lucrezia Borgia. Ilma de Murska (1836–1889) was a dramatic soprano. Italo Campanini (1846–1896) was a tenor famous for the role of Gennaro in *Lucrezia Borgia*. Zelia Trebelli (1838–1892) was a prima donna also noted for her performance in *Lucrezia*. Antonio Giuglini and Antonio Aramburo were both tenors. Ravelli remains unidentified.

199.8 "the old Royal"—destroyed by fire in 1880.

199.10 "*Let Me Like a Soldier Fall*"—from the opera *Maritana* (see note on "A Mother," 142.23).

199.15 "*Dinorah*"—the original Italian title of the French opera *Le Pardon de Poermel* (1859), music by Giacomo Meyerbeer. Its Dublin début was in 1869.

199.15 "*Lucrezia Borgia*"—Italian opera based on Victor Hugo's *Lucrèce Borgia*, music by Gaetano Donizetti. First Dublin production, 1852.

199.22 "Caruso"—Enrico Caruso (1874–1921), the internationally famous tenor.

199.32 "Parkinson"—evidently a fictitious name.

200.25 "Mount Melleray"—location of a Trappist monastery in the south of Ireland.

201.4 "slept in their coffins"—a spurious "rule of the order" suggested by the strictness of the Trappist regime.

202.12 "Fifteen Acres"—part of Phoenix Park (see note on 192.5).

203.33 "the world will not willingly let die"—a paraphrase of

Milton's statement of hopes for his career as a poet, this tag was recorded by Joyce in his Pola Notebook (a notebook used in 1904 during his first months of residence on the Continent). See Robert Scholes and Richard M. Kain, eds., *The Workshop of Daedalus* (Evanston, Ill.: Northwestern University Press, 1965), p. 90.

204.16 "the Three Graces"—the daughters of Zeus and Eurynome, companions to the Muses, the Three Graces embodied beauty and grace.

204.26 "the part that Paris played on another occasion"—judging the beauty of three goddesses, Hera, Athena, and Aphrodite.

206.11 "laid on"—provided from outside.

208.7 "King Billy's statue"—a statue of William of Orange, King William III, who defeated the forces of Irish Catholicism at the Battle of the Boyne (1690). A symbol of British domination.

210.24 "O, *the rain falls on my heavy locks* . . ."—part of the refrain from "The Lass of Aughrim," a ballad which exists in many versions in Scotland and Ireland. It tells of a young lass who is seduced and abandoned. When her lover returns she attempts to see him, standing in the rain with her babe in her arms, but he subjects her to a series of questions without letting her in.

In his *James Joyce Remembered* (New York: Oxford University Press, 1968, pp. 41–42), C. P. Curran—Joyce's fellow student at University College—recalls that Joyce's sisters "laughingly spoke of a sad ballad, 'The Lass of Aughrim,' which, they said, Joyce was perpetually singing at home. He purported to know thirty-five verses of it but they could recall only a few lines:

> The rain falls on my heavy hair
> And the dew wets my skin,
> If you be the Lord Gregory
> Open and let me in.

A dialogue proceeds with the man's

> What was my last gift to you?

and the girl's reply:

> My babe lies cold in my arms,
> Lord Gregory, let me in.

The version quoted by Curran resembles that recorded as Child Ballad 76. H., two stanzas of which follow:

> "Oh Gregory, don't you remember
> One night on the hill,
> When we swapped rings off each other's hands,
> Sorely against my will?
> Mine was of the beaten gold,
> Yours was but black tin."
> The dew wets my yellow locks,
> The rain wets my skin,
> The babe's cold in my arms,
> Oh Gregory, let me in!

> "Oh if you be the lass of Aughrim,
> As I suppose you not to be,
> Come tell me the last token
> Between you and me."
> The dew wets, etc.

212.10   *"The Lass of Aughrim"*—see note on 210.24.

213.2   "the palace of the Four Courts"—the Irish law courts, seen across the river Liffey.

214.31   "the statue"—of Daniel O'Connell (1775–1847), the Irish patriot for whom the bridge is named. O'Connell was leader of the struggle for Catholic emancipation in the early years of the nineteenth century.

219.5   "Michael"—Saint Michael the archangel is usually represented with a sword, standing over the dragon he must fight (see Revelation 12:7–9). At the hour of death he conducts the souls to God. See Florence L. Walzl, "Gabriel and Michael: The Conclusion of 'The Dead,'" pp. 423–43 of this collection.

219.30   "the gasworks"—plant for the manufacture of coal-gas.

220.2   "pennyboy"—errand boy.

220.32   "Oughterard"—a village near Galway, in the West of Ireland.

222.28   *"Arrayed for the Bridal"*—see note on 193.2.

223.29   "Bog of Allen"—a few miles southwest of Dublin.

223.31   "Shannon waves"—the estuary of the river Shannon, on the southwest coast of Ireland.